MAIDEN VOYAGE

BY

ROGER   HARVEY

www.newgeneration-publishing.com

 New Generation Publishing

ISBN 978-1-78719-357-4

Typeset in Garamond. Cover design by Heather MacPherson at Raspberry Creative Type, Edinburgh; visit raspberrycreativetype.com.

MAIDEN VOYAGE

The biggest ship ... the greatest love ...

the most dangerous secret

Tyneside, 1904. Elegant Edwardian houses ring to sounds of celebration; but in the brutal clang of the shipyards, work begins on what will be the largest and fastest liner yet to cross the Atlantic. While engineers and artists forge an exciting new century, young women like scheming Philippa and warm-hearted Maisie seize opportunities for freedom and romance, and a secret door in *Mauretania's* exquisite panelling conceals a plan that could change the course of history and alter the balance of power as Europe marches towards revolution and war. Then the gigantic ship sails for New York…and into the passionate climax of this sweeping saga of power and politics, luxury and lust.

AUTHOR'S NOTE

This book should be read as a work of fiction. Even a novel set in real places with its story based upon real occurrences cannot pretend to be a reliable record of actual events. However, creators of fiction take inspiration from many sources, not least from fact. I have built this story around the construction and maiden voyage of *Mauretania* and some elements of my family history during the early years of the Twentieth Century; but time has been compressed, fictional characters introduced, and situations invented for dramatic purposes. Where real events and persons do occur in the story I have striven to represent them as accurately as possible. I am indebted to the excellent books *Mauretania, Pride of the Tyne* by Ken Smith (Newcastle Libraries and Information Service, 1997) and *The Only Way to Cross* by John Maxtone-Grahame (Macmillan, New York, 1972) and to selected issues of *The Shipbuilder* magazine for factual information about the great transatlantic liner, but any distortions of history, by error or design, are entirely my own. *Maiden Voyage* was begun many years before I married Sheila Young, but it would not have been completed as it now stands without the love and support of my wife. I thank her for her diligent proof-reading, her good sense, and her inventive encouragement on a long and happy voyage.

INSPIRED BY THE MEMORY OF MY
GRANDMOTHER, MARY LOUISE WATT, AND HER
FAMILY OF ENGINEERS, SAILORS, HOME-MAKERS,
LOVERS AND ROMANTICS, AND DEDICATED TO
MY BELOVED WIFE SHEILA.

MAIDEN VOYAGE

CHAPTER ONE
A Wedding

"Jonathan Sketchley Adam, wilt thou have this woman to thy wedded wife, to live together after God's ordinance in the holy estate of matrimony? Wilt thou love her, comfort her, honour and keep her in sickness and in health; and, forsaking all other, keep thee only unto her, so long as ye both shall live?"

In the moment before he answered, Jon Ferris strove to seize and remember something of this magic, something he might carry with happiness into old age, to remember, remember, remember—for it seemed the doom of most people to forget, and he did not wish to suffer that doom. And—blessedly, magically—in that very moment of his wishing for it, it came: a scent of flowers, sweet and fresh, as if borne on a breeze, although everything was hushed and still, only the gleaming breathy whiteness beside him, her face inside that froth of lace, a pounding in his heart. The scent of flowers: he would remember that all his life.

"I will."

He was proud of his strong, dark voice; made it ring between the stone pillars and richly carved panelling of the church. He felt it was like a light in the darkness, as bright as the wedding dress, but strong and male and full of purpose. He was proud of all he had done and was doing; proud to have become not only the self he had imagined, but also a new entity, compounded of himself and this woman, a third being between the two of them, made of them and by them. Pride: it was a glorious thing. He would not deny he felt it or that he was thrilled to feel it.

"Philippa Louise, wilt thou have this man as thy wedded husband, to live together after God's ordinance in the holy estate of matrimony? Wilt thou obey him and serve him, love, honour and keep him in sickness and in health; and, forsaking all others, keep thee only unto him, so long as ye both shall live?"

A delightful thought occurred to her: she would never have to be called Wellington again; never have to bear the dreadful schoolgirl jokes about the Duke and meeting her Waterloo. And the dress was perfect, despite the haste; and her little sister Meg made a pretty bridesmaid; and in a few moments she would be out of this drab London church and trotting away in a carriage; then there would be the train-ride to the North, and the party in the big house, and their honeymoon by the sea; and then her new life would really begin.

"I will."

* * *

Philippa was first to wake. Pale yellow light stirred behind the curtains, filling the room with the promise of a sunny morning. Very gently, she turned to look at Jon, careful not to wake him. She smiled down at his face. It was peaceful, oblivious, yet filled with a kind of feminine warmth and softness she had scarcely noticed before. Her gaze moved to his shoulder: that was strong and masculine and she desired him again. For a moment she was tempted to roll her body upon him, but resisted the urge, and did not kiss the shoulder so invitingly bared beneath her lips. She lay back, happier than she could ever remember being in her life. It was neither a wild enthusiastic happiness nor a bright gaiety—though she had known both with Jon—but a wonderful, still balm of contentment. She had woken to the knowledge that they were married at last and safely together. No waking had seemed more wonderful to her than this one.

She moved her head, still not wishing to disturb him. A fine German clock in a wooden case seemed to look directly at her from the bedside cabinet. It was of severe design, as much an engineer's instrument as a domestic timepiece, but it ticked sweetly, as if joining the life of her happiness. Ten-past-eight: no wonder the sun was peeping in. A twitter of birds made her wonder what was going on beyond the window. She sensed a blue sky would be stretched above the town; streets still without traffic or pedestrians; a bright Northern wash of light so unlike mornings in London, yet with the same sense of roads running down to a river not far away, and the sea only a few miles downstream.

Newcastle-upon-Tyne: Jon's home town, now her home; the great industrial capital of the North with its coal-mines, shipyards, and factories. It seemed so quiet! So still and quiet, and his family's house so large and calm and gracious—although she sensed it could be a busy house too, and a happy one, with comings and goings of important people, captains of industry and their overdressed wives, jolly little maids with impossible North-country accents, perhaps even dark-coated foremen and workers coming to Jon's father for advice and orders. Then there would be Jon's elegant young friends, the designers and inventors and artists he knew, and even motor-carriages crunching and spluttering up the gravel drive.

This suburb was Heaton, just to the North of the city. There were some grand houses here, houses of rich people, and a beautiful park with a little river running through it called Jesmond Dene which had been laid out by Lord Armstrong the great gun-maker, and pretty open fields running down to the seaside, and trams to take you to the shops. Oh, she *must* remember all she could about Jon's home town, and not seem lost or stupid when his family talked about things and places—even though she had never been here before!

A strange Northern city, full of poverty and vice, they'd said in London, full of pits and factories and associated miseries. How ridiculous! Jon's family was rich. This house had central heating and electric lights. The welcome she had received from all the family and the servants had been warmer and brighter and friendlier than many she might have expected in London. Why, when they'd come out of the Central Station, they'd been driven here in a motor, with a policeman clearing the way for them through the middle of the town, and people raising hats to them as if they were Royalty! And what a city it was for engineers and inventors. She stared at the ceiling and tried to remember all the Newcastle 'firsts' Jon had taught her: the first hydraulic crane, the first breech-loading gun, the first electric lamp, the first steam turbine and the first turbine-driven ship—of course Jon's own family had been involved in that, she smiled. Even the first suburban electric railway ran close to the new house they were to occupy after the honeymoon. No wonder Jon was proud of his native city and the cleverness of Tyneside engineers; and he was one of them, no doubt with great work to do. She would be in the middle of it all, and match Jon's science with her own art.

It was really very modern. Perhaps this atmosphere was only to be found outside London, she mused. Her bright, quick mind sensed a provincial city of freedom, not stuffiness, not the old wicked ways of London society, but the change and movement of a new century, where clever individuals could make names and money for themselves by their own talents. Yes, she smiled to herself, this really was quite the thing—and all hers now. Even the birds sounded pleased about it. They were garden birds: a chirrup of sparrows and the song of starlings rather than the cooing of pigeons she had known when she had stayed in the country with her cousins, but they stirred the same happiness in her...and now there were church bells, quite close.

Of course: it was a Sunday morning! The second Sunday in May, Nineteen-Hundred and Four; the day after their wedding. She told herself she would always remember it; remember the bells and the birds and the happiness.

It no longer felt strange to say 'Nineteen'. They were into the new Century now, properly into it, and it seemed to stretch ahead like the blank pages of a thick and inviting diary, just waiting to be filled with exciting deeds. And she would do them. Philippa Ferris—Mrs. Philippa Ferris—would be among the important artists of the new era. There were so many roads to follow beyond Impressionism. Already that seemed old-fashioned to her. There were new ways to go, new ways of her own. Electricity, telephones, motor-cars, flying machines; power, speed, excitement: these were the passions which filled her as an artist; all the more shocking to her family when she was expected to draw flowers and animals for ever. 'The accomplishments of a young lady'—ha! She would have new accomplishments. This was the new Century: no longer strange, but real, around her, around everyone every day. It was to be celebrated, made sense of, developed, pushed forward to even more wonderful things. Art could be in its service, and it in the service of Art. Could they not see that? It was surely as plain as day. The old ways were gone, desperately out-of-fashion, never to be recalled. Why should they be? What use were they? It was the future that mattered.

This was one of the reasons she had married Jon: Jon the engineer, bright modern Jon without an 'h' in his name,

Jon whose father was a designer of ships on the Tyne, Jon whose family was steeped in the quest for speed and power, Jon who had been studying science and engineering in London when she had met him, Jon with his mind full of gears and wheels and turbines and the marvellous God-given power to understand power and make more power. Power that would whizz them round the world and make gods and goddesses of them. Power, power, power!

A gleeful smile came over her face: animated, intense, passionate in the stillness of the church-belled morning. How happy she felt to be wakened by church bells and yet not be in the grip of that old religion she'd fought about so furiously with her father. Of course there was God, but He couldn't be the kind of churchy God her parents believed in. How could He be that? God was the power that spun the world and directed the Universe: power, power, power, yes, the same power Jon could harness in his engines and she could spark out in her paintings. It wasn't blasphemy, it was glorious! And she'd told her father to his face, and her uncles, and her mother, and all the stuffy old Victorians who had stood in her way. God was the power and the glory, but you didn't have to go to church to meet Him, you didn't have to be frightened of Him, and He didn't have to stop you doing things. He made you do things, wonderful things, like painting in new ways and telling the truth. And God was love, not the wishy-washy preachy love they went on about from the pulpit, but real love: the love of Jon around her, inside her, right in the very middle of her when they were locked from lips to toes and poured sweet fire into each other, and the love of her kisses on his lips and the hot love of their rolling and sliding upon each other's golden skin, and the sweet peaceful love of sleeping and waking together, and all the happy glorious tender things in people's souls, and the wonder of Nature and the very essence of life. That was God; everything fresh and natural was God. That was what she and Jon worshipped. Why couldn't the old buffers see that? And why did they have to be so shocked when she talked like this? It was only the truth, and surely obvious to anyone with half an eye and an open mind. The truth was lovely, and the truth was.....she wanted Jon again. She moved her legs and turned over slightly and brought him awake with the tiniest pressure of her warm foot.

"Good morning, Darling." He said it before he opened his eyes. Then he did open them, wide and blue. "I love you."

"Good morning, Darling. I love you too."

They kissed each other's noses and snuggled together. He stroked the length of her back, over her buttocks, following the folded contour of her legs, and tickled her heels.

"Mrs. Ferris," he declared. "You have no clothes on."

"Good Heavens, Mister Ferris," she replied, running a finger from the dimple of his chin to the root of his penis and playfully tweaking the tip of it, "neither have you."

"Lucky then, is it not," he declaimed to the ceiling, "that we can be a second Adam and a second Eve on this bright morning as pure as the first morning of the World, here, in this, our Eden." He indicated the entire room with a lordly sweep of his arm, and let a rush of chilly air into the bed as they dissolved into laughter.

"A fine speech—but it's hardly Eden, Darling." Philippa snatched back the covers and snuggled into them. "Surely we inherit Eden when your father takes us to the new house. You say it's a fine little house. I do long to be mistress of it."

"You shall be—this afternoon."

"Mm. Kiss me, Jon. No, not there! No, it tickles…it tickles!" They snuggled together again. "Was this really your room when you were a little boy?"

"Yes," he answered, looking around the walls. He remembered a nursery frieze, long since taken down: the animals going two-by-two. "Yes it was."

"How romantic and poignant," she murmured, burying her nose in his neck. "Toy soldiers on the counterpane, and Sir Walter Scott on the bookshelf, and pictures of animals, and a map of the Empire, and little trumpets at Christmas time, and a rocking-horse…"

"Never had a rocking-horse, actually."

"I'll buy you one when I'm rich and famous—with my own money I'll have made in spite of everything that's gone before."

He put an arm round her, very tenderly.

"Is there no way we might talk your wretched parents round, now we are properly married and everything's going to be all right for us here?"

"I don't think so, Darling. It's not that they're against you. In fact Mother rather liked you. They're against *me*, don't you see? They think I'm wicked; or worse than that, they think I'm mad."

A shiver ran through her, and she remembered all the horrors of being disowned by her parents; how her father had actually beaten her, torn her dress, and thrown her across the hall of their big elegant house in London where it had seemed that such vileness could never intrude: the vileness of brawling drunkards and shabby servants and verminous prostitutes and ugly children and petty criminals and all the sordid life of the London back-streets from which she had always been shielded by wealth and security and what she had thought had been family love. To be pushed on to the street by her own father, and not allowed to come back into the house she thought was her own. To actually lie in the gutter in a torn dress, crying and hurt—actually in the gutter! The darkening afternoon, the nosey servants of the neighbours twitching the curtains but nobody daring to open a door or a window on to the deserted street; alone, crying, walking miles to her Aunt Margaret's house in St. John's Wood; Aunt Margaret eventually finding Jon; his rushing up in a hansom; their being together again. But to be actually thrown on the street: it was the stuff of bad plays and music-hall songs and she couldn't believe it had happened to her. To have her life broken apart, then so wondrously healed by Jon. She pressed her knees against him, curling them up into his stomach, and he caressed her back and her ankles, and she did not cry.

"Darling," he said with great tenderness, "there will never be any of that again." He kissed her bright hair, ruffling it into his face. "We'll be quite safe together, and you know my parents understand you and love you, and you shall be mistress of the new house in Jesmond and have your studio, and there'll never be any more cruelty or sadness or lies or misunderstanding for you to bear ever again."

"Oh Jon—I do love you."

And now she did cry.

* * *

13

"Goodness me," laughed Jon. "Mrs. Ferris in her clothes. I hardly recognise her."

The curtains were open now; sunlight filling the room, leafy trees waving outside, noise and bustle and a stir in the house beyond the bedroom door. Philippa wore a blue day dress, *broderie-anglaise* at the neck and sleeves, with a cream-coloured silk sash and kid shoes to match: the same colour as Jon's suit, the jacket so dashingly piped with brown braid.

"Mm, isn't it deliciously wicked? You'll always see me as naked as Eve whatever I'm wearing."

"I should hope I shall. Wouldn't want to lose that faculty."

"Well, you look quite the thing in your suit—even though I can see right through that, too."

They giggled and kissed and held hands.

"Are you quite ready for this, Darling?" Jon looked her very honestly in the eye. "They're all here you know, the family, the whole gang of them. Most of them are nice enough, but they can be a bit daunting. I'm afraid this Wedding Breakfast thing was Father's idea. He rather likes a show, and Mother pretends to be bothered and worried about everything but she's been looking forward to it madly really, ever since we decided to do it this way, and there'll be Sidney and Charles and their *fiancées* and a few fellows from the works…"

"For Heaven's sake Jon," Philippa laughed brightly, "don't be so shy of your own people! It's not as if my lot were here. Of course I'm ready for all this. They're taking us to their hearts—enjoy it! Your family have been wonderful. We couldn't have done this anywhere else. The Wedding Breakfast is a lovely idea. There now; your tie is straight."

"Good. We're all set then." Jon still did not seem to want to open the bedroom door.

"Jon, Darling," Philippa crept close to him again, put her arms around his waist, looked up into his blue eyes. "I think I know what it is."

Jon swallowed.

"Really?"

What a baby he could be sometimes, she thought, but a big and beautiful baby.

"Mm. You're embarrassed because we've had our wedding night in your parents' house, in your old room here where you were a little boy. We made love here where you used to go to sleep, with your mother and father just along the landing there, and the whole house listening to us. You came into me three times, and it was lovely, but you're embarrassed to think of it now with everyone waiting for us downstairs and wondering how you'll look."

Ridiculous, he thought. Where did she get her ideas from? Nothing like that had ever occurred to him. He was just tired.

"Don't be silly," he chuckled dismissively.

"It's not silly," she snuggled into his shoulder. "It's rather sweet actually. I understand perfectly. Really I do. I just know your family do too." She was clinging to him. "When my family disowned me for being an artist and for loving you, your family accepted me as their new daughter. They gave us

15

this house for our wedding night and they've found us a home of our own in this town, and now they're going to help us celebrate. I think that's wonderful. They love you, and they want you to be happy with me...and you will be." She stood back, looked into his face, held his hands, her smile hardening a little. "Anyway, you mustn't be shy now." Suddenly she was businesslike, almost cold. Something like embarrassment was writhing through Jon now, though not for the reason Philippa had imagined. He felt assailed and exposed by her piercing manner: simpering one moment, brash the next; and he had somehow hated her speech about how wonderful everything was. But he would not—and felt he could not—do anything about it. "We're married," she was continuing briskly, "and we're absolutely respectable, if that sort of thing matters to you. You know damn well it doesn't matter to me."

"Must remind you, Darling, Father hates swearing, couldn't tolerate it from a girl at all."

"Well in that case," she said with a sly smile, "you'd better wash out the filthy mouth of your damn little artist with a damn good kiss..." She moved her gleaming face up to his, licking her lips, "...and make it a bloody good wet one."

Laughter exploded their kiss apart, and she had to wipe his chin.

"You know," Jon smiled, "you really can be remarkably rude."

"Isn't that one of the reasons you love me? Anyway, I promise not to be rude downstairs, if you promise not to be shy."

"Very well. I promise never to be shy again. Watch." He seized Philippa with one hand and suddenly flung open the door with the other. A maid was scurrying downstairs to a clamour of people in the hall below. He marched Philippa to the top of the stairs. "Good morning!" he announced loudly to the upturned faces. "Mr. and Mrs. Ferris are coming down to breakfast."

A cheer went up, and glasses of sherry were raised. Sidney Charlton, Jon's friend who would have liked to be Best Man had he been given the chance, yelled: "At last we'll get at the devilled kidneys!" Someone else started to sing *For They are Jolly Good Fellows*, Jon's mother held her hands to her face wreathed in tearful smiles, and they descended to a chorus of clapping and cheering. Jon's father pressed forward, restraining his swelling emotions with a loud: "Welcome home, my boy. And welcome home, dear Philippa."

* * *

With the Wedding Breakfast cleared away—it had been more like a luncheon and everyone had sat late to it—the house remained full of guests. They had settled in little groups around the drawing-room with its recently-decorated lilac walls and large potted palms; they had spilled out into the hall and lounged on the sofa placed unconventionally under the grand staircase; they had invaded the conservatory, now lively with midday sunshine and animated conversation. Jon's mother Julia was a sufficiently accomplished hostess to realise the party was taking perfect care of itself, and she felt able to wander from room to room and relax into the spectacle of so many people clearly enjoying themselves in her house. It was not altogether what she had expected after so many worries connected with her son's marriage, yet now the feeling came to warm her heart as tenderly as the sun was warming the cheeks of her new daughter-in-law, holding leafy court under

17

the conservatory's ancient grapevine and arguing quite freely in favour of modern art and women painters—this to the director of Newcastle's most distinguished art gallery. Well, she was a bright one, thought Julia, and likely to stir up controversy wherever she went, but she'd be well able to look after herself at the same time. She wouldn't lose an argument—or if she did, she wouldn't care. Guests of this family would simply have to accept it. And Julia's fears that Jon would have his hands full with this tempestuous girl, which had so plagued her and ruined the last few months, seemed to evaporate in the friendly atmosphere of this party. With the knowledge that her husband was 'talking to' Jon at this very moment, she allowed herself to relax in the sunshine. And yet, and yet…ah well, a mother's fears. She would have to put them away. They would do no good now; for neither herself nor Jon.

William Ferris ushered his son out of the hall.

"You don't mind coming in here, do you, my boy?" He opened the door of his study. "I really must have a talk with you, man-to-man, so to speak."

"'Course not, Father. I say—you've kept this a wonderful room."

"Yes." William closed the great red mahogany door behind them, and the chatter of their guests was barely audible. Only a twitter of birdsong came in through the garden window "Yes. Harmony, balance, discipline, but thrusting forward to the future, not afraid of new things· that's what this room is all about. That's what we're all about."

William perched on the edge of his massive leather-topped desk. He was a powerful looking man, still in his prime at fifty-two years, taller and broader than his son, but with the same clear-eyed stare and open features. His moustache and his mane of hair—still worn unfashionably thick and long—had recently turned grey. This gave him the benign charisma of an old Professor, but his eyes were piercing and his expression shrewd. The strength of character and business acumen which had won him a fortune from marine engineering had been only refined by age. He watched his son looking again at the ordered bookshelves, the models of ships in mahogany cases, the drawings of engines, the Turner original.

"Oh, that reminds me, Father. Philippa's a great admirer of old Turner you know, despite being as modern as they come. I don't think she's seen this yet. She wants to go up the coast to Craster to see where the old boy stayed when he painted it. You remember the place."

"Yes." William cast about for a box on his desk. "We'll do that, or you can take her up there when you're at Alnmouth. Honeymoon at Alnmouth: wonderful choice, very peaceful, you'll have a delightful time. Remember our fishing-trips there? Never caught a decent fish yet. Must be ten years ago."

"Yes, Father."

"Ah, here it is. Have a cigar, Jon. I'm going to. If you ask me, this day's back-to-front with a party at breakfast time; feels like after dinner, somehow. Good idea though. I think it worked very well, don't you? You stirred your mother up of course, I can tell you. And Betty and the new cook were up half the night in the kitchen. She's spent some time in Paris, by the way, or says she has…the new cook, I mean, not old Betty. You wouldn't get *her* South of Gateshead. Well now, was your room all right? Your mother had Betty and the little maid do it up specially. Better mention it later, just to let them know you've appreciated it."

"Yes, of course. The whole place looks rather wonderful. It's good to be home."

"Capital, capital. It's good to have you back. There's brandy if you want."

"No thanks. Come to it, Father. What do you *really* want to say to me?"

"Well now, Jon," the older man settled into a chair, fiddling with his cigar. "It's not a lecture. Sit down, for Heaven's sake. But I do want you to know how I really feel about all this, and tell you something tremendously exciting which is coming up for all of us, especially for you. Anyway, we'll get on to that in a minute."

"Whatever it is, Father," Jon interrupted hotly, "I hope you're not going to voice some kind of disapproval of Philippa—like that dreadful argument we all had at Christmas. You see how wrong you and Mother have been about her. She's my wife now. I'll not sit and listen to more nonsense about her."

"Now that's unfair, Jon." William succeeded in sounding grim, hurt, severe, and warm-hearted at the same time: a devastating paternalism for any son, and Jon could only listen in silence. "That's jolly unfair, and you know it. We've never spoken nonsense about Philippa. Indeed, we've bent over backwards to make her welcome in this house—and continued to make you welcome too, when you didn't exactly do the right thing by us."

Jon whitened, and looked past his father at a picture on the wall: a steamship, somehow a symbol of success where he appeared to have failed.

"Do I have to remind you?" William was in full flow

now. "You neglected your studies in London, but continued to live there—at my expense, I may add. When you were supposed to be learning more about marine engines, you were…"

"For God's sake, Father!" Jon interrupted furiously. "The place to learn about marine engines is on the Tyne, not in London. You know very well the future lies with Parsons and his turbines. Reading old books in London is waste of time. Why, Parsons is a friend of yours—and mine."

"That's enough. You'll hear me out. Some of what you say is true, as we both know, but you should have the decency not to interrupt me or insult my intelligence. Now where was I?"

"You were berating me for idling about in London," smiled Jon.

"So I was." William, too, was unable to keep every twinkle from his eye. "Well, you cost me a small fortune, and damn near drove your mother mad with worry, carrying on with that bunch of artists and dissolute radicals. Then you took up with this outrageous and none-too-successful woman painter and got yourself caught—by her father, of all people—at some sordid studio *in flagrante delicto*, isn't that the polite way of putting it?" Any humour in William's manner had now been replaced by bitterness. "Well, that's how a lawyer would put it, and you wouldn't have had a leg to stand on if your behaviour had been dragged into court. At least she wasn't married, so you spared us that I suppose. Finally she's thrown out of the house by her narrow-minded father—not that I'm excusing such behaviour, as far as I'm concerned it was disgraceful. All the same, it didn't reflect very well on you, did it? Then to crown it all you get engaged—again at my expense—and insist on bringing her back home dressed up like a Countess, also at my expense."

"She had nothing to wear."

"That's what all wives tell their husbands, as you will discover."

"This *is* a lecture, Father."

"Hear me out I say!" William calmed himself and strode over to the window, looking out at the garden. "I'd like to know any other parents who would give their house over to a young couple for their wedding night after all that and entertain dozens of people like this. I've even found you a house. It's quite delightful, as you'll see this afternoon; in Jesmond, the coming part of town as you well know. People of quality will want to live there. There's a cook-housekeeper, a Mrs. Hutchinson: pleasant enough woman. I saw to it she got out of some trouble in the slums: a bad family but a good heart. We've placed her with you. She'll work like a Trojan. And there can be a lady's-maid for Philippa if she wants one when you come back from the honeymoon; her decision, of course. Not a bad wedding present, boy. I should say it was a splendid start in married life. I hope Philippa realises how much has been done for her and how much has been tolerated for your sake. I think we'd best call Philippa 'a spirited girl'; anything else would start another argument. She doesn't have much time for convention, does she? Well, that may not be altogether a bad thing. But she can be very unsettling, to put it mildly. You're lucky your mother and I are so forward-looking."

Jon found himself staring at the floor after all this. He knew most of it was true, and what might not be strictly true was an understandable outburst from an overstretched parent.

"Yes Father," he said. "I do know I'm lucky. You have been marvellous about it, and I know how upset Mother was when Philippa turned out not to be the sort of girl she'd imagined. I am sorry for the trouble. It's just, well, all that difficulty should be over now."

"It is boy, it is." William gave his son a kindly look. "Welcome back to the family. We do like Philippa, you know, even if I did say she was unsettling." He smiled, and put down his cigar. "Well she is isn't she? I dare say that's why you love her. She's a breath of fresh air—and sometimes that can feel like a hurricane blowing through a family, or through Society, if it comes to that. Don't think I approve of her father throwing her out of the house in London: despicable. But I can almost understand how he felt. I'd hoped you would also be large-minded enough to accept everyone's point of view in all this."

"You can't accept a girl being hurt when you're in love with her."

"No, of course not."

This admission brought a truce between the two men. Sunlight came into the room, sparkling its dusty corners.

"But I do understand." Jon leaned against a chair. "I always wanted love to ennoble my spirit—you know, make me a better man, as it was in the old stories."

"As it should be in real life."

"Yes. But for all that, I'm afraid I must have seemed ignoble to you and Mother. That's my tragedy as well, you know. I tried to do everything the right way, but at the same time live by what I believed in. Part of that meant defending Philippa and striking out for what we both believed was right, not tolerating narrowness or hypocrisy. Neither of us will be made a victim of it, and I shan't allow her life to be spoilt any more. I know she's outspoken and full of go and supposedly shocking ideas, but I love her and I want to look after her—and I shall."

"Good boy. I admire you for that." William turned to his son, his face animated with a new excitement, and he perched once more on the edge of his desk. For all his father's forgiveness, and the unquenchable good humour which sparkled between these men even in times of stress, Jon could not make out where this discourse was intended to leave him. One moment he felt hot and indignant, the next impotent and submissive, the next in spirited defence of his idealism, the next at a loss for thoughts. The only certainty seemed to be his father's strength of will. "All the same," continued the older man, "you're only twenty-three, you're suddenly a married man, and you don't have much of a career—not yet, anyway."

William watched his son, a ghost of a smile playing behind his grey moustache. The boy was no fool, he thought. He had been defiant over this girl, but that was natural enough. He'd also been weak, and he might have chosen a steadier wife, but deep down he was a good-hearted young man, clever and capable. If only he could keep his head, the future would be wonderful for him, quite wonderful.

"I had hoped to work with you, Father," declared Jon, "now that Philippa and I are to live in Newcastle." It was typical of the boy, thought William, to put the woman's name first. At the moment she came first in all his thoughts, no doubt. That might have to change. "Well, that's what I always wanted to happen." There was a note of nervousness in the boy's voice. Perhaps it was time to let him run off the hook—but the drama of what he had to say, the enormity of it, the wondrous, almost dreadful power of it, made him play a little longer on the invisible line.

"Yes." William let the smile broaden behind his moustache. "Yes, that's what I'd always wanted to happen too. I still want it to happen—and it will, in a way. But there have been some developments up here which may mean we shan't be able to join forces quite as we'd always imagined."

"Good God," Jon gasped, "you're not ill, are you? You're not going to retire or something…leave all this to me…not stay in business…?"

Now William laughed openly.

"No, no, Jon, nothing like that. I'm perfectly well as it happens, now that you mention it, and I intend to live to a mighty annoying age and work 'til I drop. No no," he chuckled, "it's something far better than illness or retirement. It's a job—but a job for which I've decided I am just a little too old, and for which you are just the right age."

"What?"

"Let me finish, please. Will you promise me, Jon, after all we've been through, that if I give you a supreme opportunity, you'll take it?"

Jon squared up to his father.

"Yes."

A surge of joy went through William.

"You'll not waste it, spoil it, or leave it unfinished?"

"I'll try not to, Father, not this time."

Tears of pride welled up in William's eyes. He knew he'd put the boy through a difficult time and he'd faced it well.

"Good," he laid a hand on Jon's shoulder, "because what I have been offered, and what I now offer to you, is, I believe, the supreme opportunity for any marine engineer at this time—especially one from Newcastle. You can stop looking worried. In a way, it's really quite simple. You won't have to leave your new home or your new wife. While you were away in London—under your very nose, though I don't imagine you noticed—Balfour's government voted the subsidies for the building of two new transatlantic liners: really big ones. One is going to John Brown on the Clyde; the other's coming here, to Swan Hunter. She's to be driven by the new steam turbines, Jon. Yes, Parsons' turbines, built in the Heaton works. You know what that means: she'll be faster than anything on the Atlantic, and Newcastle men will design and build her. You can be one of them, my boy; there's a place for you on the engine team at Swan's; Charles Parsons and I have seen to it for you. It'll be hard work, but I know perfectly well you'll be up to it—if you can just keep your head."

"It's…it's the *Mauretania*!"

"Oh, so you *do* know about her?"

"Doesn't everybody? She's going to recapture the Blue Riband from the Germans."

"Is she indeed? That's not in the plans—at least not officially."

"And I am going to work on her!"

"Ah," said William as the two men shook hands, smiling broadly, "that *is* in the plans then."

"Yes, Father. Thank you."

CHAPTER TWO
A New Home

A fine Summer afternoon settled in around the tall house. The last guests had gone and Betty the housekeeper was already supervising the tidying-up while her employers found hats and scarves and assembled at the front porch, where warm sunshine threw red and golden diamonds through stained glass.

"Do you have a motoring hat, my dear?" Julia looked quizzically at Philippa's summery boater.

"No. I was blown to pieces coming in from the station last night. I usually do like the wind in my hair, but not when I'm dressed up for a party."

"No, quite," said Julia. "Well, we can easily turn that into a motoring hat with one of my long scarves. Here—let me."

"Thank you." Philippa smiled as her mother-in-law spread the scarf over her hat, tying it round her neck and under her chin.

"Your hair is delightful, Philippa: that rich brown. I always think it goes so well with your eyes. There. You look as if you're going to ride across India on an elephant when in fact it's only a few miles through town."

"I look like a bee-keeper," Philippa chuckled, catching sight of herself in the mirror.

"Bzzzzz!" Jon appeared behind her with a tweed cap in his hands. "I can still sting you through all that." He placed a kiss on her neck. "Are you ready, Mother? Come on then—I can't wait to see this house."

The car was a de Dion Bouton. It crouched on the gravel drive like a strange reptile basking in the sunshine, which flared off its gleaming green paintwork and large, wide-awake-looking brass lamps. A rich scent of leather rose from the brown seats and the whole machine quivered slightly as the engine ticked over. Hoggett, the Ferris's chauffeur, stood proudly beside the car, strong sunlight making the most of his buttons and his large red face.

"It's a wonderful motor-car," squealed Philippa, like a girl being given a new toy. "It was lovely to ride in it last night, but it was dark and I didn't really see it properly. It looks so much more exciting in the daylight, as if it's going on an adventure!"

"Well done, Hoggett," said Jon, pulling on his gloves. "The beast looks ready for us all."

"Now, Philippa," William put on his tweed cap, "since we're going to your very own house, you'd better sit in the front."

"Thank you, Papa." She took his hand as he helped her into the seat. "I may call you Papa now, may I not?"

She looked down at William, one hand on her hat, the other in his, a lovely smile on her lips. No wonder his boy had fallen for her, he thought. The sunshine lit her gorgeous hair even through the veil of the scarf, and a shaft of light seemed to tweak her little nose, making her look utterly kissable. If he had met her at his son's age, he realised, he would have loved her, taken her, fought for her, and not given a fig for what people thought. Yes, 'Papa' was right: she had found a new father, and he a daughter.

"I shall be very honoured to be called Papa," he replied, squeezing her hand. "I know very well how much that means to both of us. Now then," he became brisk again, "you shall drive, Jon. I haven't seen you manage one of these recently."

"Thanks," said Jon, clambering aboard and patting Philippa on the knee. "Archie Barton had one in London: an Argyll. I had a couple of goes on it. Not as good as this one, of course. Child's play really, once you've started them up. There must be a way to improve the ignition."

"You'll have to be inventing one, Mister Jonathan," ventured Hoggett.

"You see who you've married, my dear," smiled Julia as she settled behind Philippa. "An inveterate meddler, a man who is infatuated with anything mechanical and at the same time permanently dissatisfied with it: that's an engineer for you. It's been just the same with William."

"Rather like artists," replied Julia. "We're never satisfied either."

"Right, Hoggett," said William from the back seat, "thanks for starting her up and putting the luggage in. Since there's only room for four, you can stand down 'til we return. I'll bring her home safely; I've watched you long enough."

"Very good, sir. Mind the brake, Mister Jonathan. It needs a fair bit of pressure, and you're fully laden. You'll need the low gear on Benton Bank."

"We're off then!" cried Jon, grinding the car into low

gear. It crept forward over the gravel.

"Cheer up, Hoggett," called William. "It's not the end of the road for you by any means. You'll be driving me and my wife as we grow older and these things get more complicated."

The car crunched out of the drive and on to Heaton Road.

"Hoggett'll be as nervous as a cat until Father brings this back in one piece," Jon told Philippa. "It's his pride and joy. Are you all right behind us there?"

"Yes, fine."

A breeze sprang up round their heads, blowing in scents of Summer: lime trees in flower, and early roses and wallflowers in the gardens of their wealthy neighbours. They turned on to another road and began to pick up speed down a steep hill. Jon put the car into its second gear and it ran more freely.

"Hang on to your hats!" he cried. "This is Benton Bank, Darling. Jesmond Dene's at the bottom."

"We must be doing thirty miles-an-hour!" shouted William.

"Forty—flat out down here!"

They whooshed into the dip at the bottom of the valley; Jon put on more power and shoved the engine into low gear as they roared up the other side.

"Hooray!" cried Philippa. "It's more fun than a helter-skelter!"

Soon the road had flattened out and they were down

to ten miles-per-hour again, chugging into the leafy suburb of Jesmond. Cyclists were out in force, couples with baby-carriages, people walking their dogs, children in sailor-suits and new dresses.

"What a lovely day it is," remarked Julia. "Everyone's making the most of a sunny Sunday."

They bowled along, the car steady under Jon's hands, his parents fallen silent in the back, sunshine spanking in on the brass fittings, the smell of warm and dusty roads mingling with the oily fume of the engine, birdsong fluting between the shouts of children pointing at the passing machine: all bathed in the hum of the breeze, the gentle growl of the car, and its comfortably sensuous swaying motion. Philippa's thoughts turned to her own happiness. How fortunate she felt to have escaped the horrors of the last few months, out of London and into this loving and generous family. Marrying Jon *had* been the right thing to do: she had known it all along. Now it was being demonstrated in the love and forgiveness she sensed was flowing from his parents, and in the simple contentment she felt in his presence.

She snuggled a hand along the seat and under his knee; it was met by the warm pressure of his leg. The thought of his body excited her, as it always did. The rolling motion of the car set up a thrilling quiver between her legs and around her hips, and her own body swivelled inside her dress as if eager to be free of all straps and buttons, and she felt ready to be stroked and teased by Jon; but a gentle, smiling stillness was also upon her. She felt she might have been married to Jon for years, but without the loss of happiness so many couples seemed to suffer with the passing of time. She felt she could go on like this for ever, in a combined stir of mild-mannered celebration and mounting desire. Yet at the same time she wanted change—not in the dramatic, strident way of which she had so often been accused, but real change along a natural course, a development of her life. She wanted to paint in this new house, match Jon's career with her own, indeed create a new third career which would be the endeavours they would both make together, in much the same way as their marriage seemed to have created a wonderful third being, an entity compounded of their two souls and bodies, incomplete without either and something with a life of its own which they could nourish. Perhaps that was how one felt about a child, she mused, yet did not feel the need for children, nor any desire to be a mother, not yet anyway. It was a desire she had thought about, but never truly felt. No doubt children would be expected of her by these people, but she felt no obligation to provide any, and knew Jon was not ready for fatherhood. He would have recoiled at the idea, she smiled, in his boyish way. And for the moment she was quite content with these three beings: Jon, herself, and this third entity born of their togetherness. She would paint in this new house, and when Jon was away at the shipyard she would be busy in her studio. Both their careers were in the ascendant. She recalled the drama of the morning, when Jon's father had led him out of the study and announced from the foot of the stairs that Jon was to work on the engines of the *Mauretania*, about to be laid down at Wallsend. The project was a gigantic one in every sense: the largest ship to be built on the Tyne, the biggest event for years in the North of England. Everyone would be enlarged by it: made richer and more famous. And she too would be part of it. As Jon built the new engines, she would build the new Art of the new Century. Together they were making history—even as they sat here side-by-side in the sunny breeze, rolling towards their new home.

"You'll have to ask Charles Parsons to put one of his turbines in a motor-car, Father," Jon's voice cut in upon Philippa's thoughts, "then we'd be whizzing along at sixty miles-an-hour or more—and quietly."

"Heaven forbid," laughed his mother. "You men are

dangerous enough playing in your shipyards, never mind on the roads."

"Not cold are you, Darling?" Jon turned to Philippa.

"No, no. I feel wonderful."

"Philippa, this is Osborne Road," explained William. "There's a fine church at the top: Saint George's, built by Mitchell the shipbuilder…"

"A rival," Jon whispered to her.

"…with a detached bell-tower in the Italian style, quite remarkable. Anyway, you see we're running up by the railway."

"That's the electric railway we were telling you about, my dear," put in Julia. "You're down to the coast in no time these days."

"The new part of Jesmond is being built West of here," continued William, "off to the left between the railway and the Town Moor. We'll be turning off left as well, not quite over the railway though. There, look—there's Saint George's, directly ahead. D'you know where you are, Jon?"

"Got it, Father. Lily Avenue, just off here." He swung the car into a quiet street. "Number Eleven, isn't it?"

The engine ticked and rattled as they coasted along the sunny side of the street, looking for the house. Then Philippa pointed and called out: "This is it. Here it is. Oh, it's delightful, it's lovely!"

Jon switched off the engine and birdsong came to their ears, loud and sweet, with a faint stir of distant traffic.

Number Eleven Lily Avenue stood quietly in the sunshine, as if contentedly awaiting its new owners. Shiny bottle-green paint gleamed around the windows, and a strong honeysuckle climbed up beside the door. Two storeys above, an attic window seemed to peer happily from under the ornately carved boards of the eaves.

"That'll be my studio," declared Philippa. "It's so wonderfully sunny up there; and it looks so secretive, like a window in a quaint old German town, but I know it'll be all new and modern underneath."

"Aren't they supposed to have a North light," remarked William, descending stiffly from the back seat, "studios, I mean?"

"Oh, supposedly so—but I love the sunshine, don't I, Jon? This will be perfect."

"Perfect," echoed Jon, already at the door. "D'you have the keys, Father?"

"I gave them to Philippa," smiled Julia. "She'll be mistress here—won't you, my dear?"

"We won't stay," announced William. "It does look very handsome. Good luck here, both of you." He extended his hand to Jon and seemed anxious to be away.

"You must come in," pleaded Jon.

"No, no, wouldn't dream of it. We'll be off. See you after the honeymoon." William kissed Philippa on both cheeks; Julia embraced her son and her daughter-in-law.

"Mrs. Hutchinson's not here today," she explained, readjusting her hat. "I thought you'd want to be alone. If you send us a telegram just before you're coming back I'll see she opens up for you."

"Quite right, Mother," Jon kissed her again. "Excellent of you. Thank you both."

"Goodbye. Goodbye."

Jon and Philippa waved from the front door; William started the car, hauled himself into the driving seat and pushed in the low gear.

"Goodbye! Goodbye! Good luck! Goodbye!"

They were gone, leaving the only the sunshine and the birdsong and the summery stillness of the little street with tall trees swaying above the railway at the end. Jon felt a sudden rush of loneliness; Philippa a surge of relief.

They went straight inside and found the house was hot, as if the sun had beaten upon it all day and left no corner of damp or chill to mar the warmth of its welcome. A vase of flowers had been arranged for them in the hall, and lightened its shadows with a heady scent. Yes, thought Philippa, it was a relief to have escaped Jon's parents. Lovable and generous as they were, there was something stifling about the way they had chattered all day about the neighbourhood and the new house and how to get here and what was in it—as if they were starting their own married lives all over again and forcing the new generation to take part in it. It had not been as she had secretly wished: stark and beautiful; a pure, simple walking to their new house, alone. It was understandable, she supposed, that it had turned out the way it had...but better to be on their own! Now she was here with only Jon, all she wanted to do was drink in his presence and absorb the atmosphere of their new home.

It could not have taken them more than five minutes to walk all over the house: upstairs, downstairs, through the cream-coloured and neatly-tiled scullery to the little back yard, out to hot sunshine at the front again, and back through the hall; spending only a moment in each room, taking its impressions swiftly into themselves. They were like explorers discovering a tiny island, and it was quickly mapped. Then they sat half-way up the stairs, sunlight pouring in through the windows of the porch, the banisters alive with the smell of new wax polish, the flowers gleaming on the hall table, dust motes dancing in the sun-shafts. Jon put an arm round Philippa's waist.

"Just realised, Darling," he smiled. "I never carried you over the threshold. D'you mind?"

"No," she kissed his ear. "It's old-fashioned nonsense. Rather insulting really, don't you think? A man drags a woman into a cave by her hair: same thing."

"Lucky I forgot my caveman's club then," he grinned, gently lowering a fist on to her head.

"I'm glad you didn't carry me over the threshold," she murmured into his cheek. "This is the new Century, and this is our new house, and it's ours equally, and we'll share everything we have and everything we do."

"I see," said Jon. "So every time you kiss my ear, I'll kiss your nose."

"That's the idea," she giggled.

"So I'll begin here," he whispered, sliding his fingers between the buttons of her dress, feeling the marvellous warmth and pulse and palpitation of her body, her breath coming hot on his face, her nipples hardening under his hands.

"And I'll begin here," she squealed, pulling his shirt open.

"We'll christen the house," he declared.

"Every room of it," she laughed.

Her light Summer shoes were soon waggled off and bumped down the stairs; she hauled off his boots and trousers and scrambled away from him, her stockings torn down as she went giggling up the stairs on bare knees. He caught her by the sleeve, pulling the dress from a gleaming shoulder. Laughing, panting, floundering under their own kisses, they stripped one another, wallowing their way upstairs in a chaos of clothes. In their new bedroom she stood in mock submissiveness as he lifted the last pieces of silk from her body—then they rolled upon the bed-cover, in and out of the great splash of sunshine which lay across it. Their love-making was as hot and bright as the blue sky beyond the window, and soon they were falling asleep into their own warmth, with the chirping of the birds and the distant rustle of the tall trees and the faint sounds of a quiet Sunday afternoon melting into their unconsciousness, lulling them to deeper sleep while the shadows lengthened and colours darkened beneath the velvet blue of a Summer evening.

The moon had rolled up beyond the window when Philippa awoke. She was deliciously comfortable, curled up backwards into Jon, whose legs were cosily crooked into the backs of her knees, an arm resting gently over her waist, his face buried in her hair, the faint stirring of his breath on her neck. How wonderful this was: to be naked with her new husband here in their own house with the curtains open and the Summer night breathing in at the window, and her own breasts and arms white in the moonlight. Yet even as he was folded around her, she was not thinking of Jon. She was thinking of her new studio on the empty floor above them, up the narrow staircase beyond this bedroom door; the attic room stripped to bare walls and a wooden floor, where moonlight would be sparkling in at the high, uncurtained window. She would whitewash the walls herself, and polish the floorboards when the housekeeper wasn't looking, and it would not be long before she would be painting there, with her brushes in tall jars on a shelf, an exciting smell of paints, and her slender body in her favourite blue painting dress, her hair tied back and a new canvas on her easel. What would it be, her first work in this new place? The sea, perhaps, or the river and its shipyards. Yes of course: the new ship! The racket of the riveters, the steam of the cranes, the monstrous machines, the clang and bang of creation, huge shapes arising, with the sun and moon bright in the same painting…the moon which looked down at her now. She stared back at it. The moon sailed high, higher than any ship; the leaves hung silently on the trees, all colours were no colour, but rich and dark and spangled with brightness as if candles and stars and jewels were cast across the vastness of the night, this deep, high night of the sailing moon. She felt the dance of history; the world singing to her private music, as if all futures spoke to her in languages of understanding, suddenly freed in the bright darkness, here in the little room with her husband sleeping innocently beside her. What would she not do, once she was alone in the silent room above their heads?

But, deliberately motionless, Jon was not asleep. He must not wake her, he thought, so soft and tender was she beneath his arm. He must not move it, nor shift his legs, nor change the pattern of his breathing into her hair. He could glance up at the moon without disturbing her. The same moon would be glinting on the river where he must go as soon as their honeymoon was over. The honeymoon, starting tomorrow, was now a distraction. He realised it with mere annoyance; without any of the anguish he had half expected to feel at the moment of admitting it to himself. The honeymoon was a distraction: it was simply a fact. He would spend a few days at pleasant, lazy Alnmouth, where the Duke's lands ran down to the sea. He would say he was happy with his beautiful new wife—and in many ways he would be—but all the time the river would be waiting, forty miles to the South, and the cranes reaching into the sky above the yard at Wallsend. He saw Mr. Balfour standing up in Parliament, his government voting the subsidy for the new ships; he saw dark-coated industrialists in London and Newcastle signing the contracts and shaking stern hands. He saw his father's friend Sir Charles Parsons and the sleek little launch *Turbinia* snorting down the Tyne with her new turbine engines whining under her steel plates; saw her startling, smoke-belching swoop between the staid battleships at the Spithead Review seven years ago; saw the Prince of Wales watching through a telescope; saw his father's proud face as he welcomed Sir Charles back home; saw their celebration dinner at the family house in Heaton, Sir Charles taking him aside and presenting him with his first set of drawing instruments. He saw a ghostly image of the gigantic *Mauretania*, as yet unbuilt, rearing up from her berth, the very berth they would be clearing at the bend in the river now; saw gangs of grey-capped workmen trudging down the grim cobbled streets from their terraced houses, so different from this one in well-set, flowery Jesmond. He saw himself in a new coat, plans under his arm, walking up the steps to the drawing-loft; saw himself in shirt-sleeves on the shop floor, the enormous engine castings above his head, the delicate vanes of the turbines spreading like the feathers in a peacock's tail. He smelled the reek of the river, heard the coarse cries of the workmen and the yelp of the gulls, saw the gaunt stone piers clamping the mouth of the Tyne. He saw the day—years hence—when the new ship would steam down the river for her sea-trials and seem to prise those piers apart, while every vantage point would be crowded with onlookers. It was as if a million things were speaking to him in the darkness, chanting in a thousand tongues the tales of childhood, murmuring through the trees a glory of suns yet to rise, whispers of winds yet to blow, and a water-gleam of songs yet to be sung. He imagined himself captain of a lonely ship run upon rocks suddenly grasping diamonds from the green ground and flinging them into his lover's hair, shouting down a sunbeam, dancing at the moon. Had he dozed for a moment, dreamed, stirred, and woken her? No—she was still asleep. However could he bear to tell her he would be happy to leave her and go to the shipyard so soon after they were married? How could he bear the creep and smack of that realization, and then transmit it—swiftly, harshly, or with agonizing slowness—to his wife…the wife he had so lately married to cement and celebrate their love?

CHAPTER THREE
A Honeymoon

The train rattled up Northumberland: vistas of green and purple hills to the West, glimpses of sea to the East. The hot weather had continued, sunshine pouring from a burning blue sky; the constant dazzle of light had made Philippa and Jon choose the shady side of their First Class compartment. They had swapped magazines: he was absorbed in *The Lady*, while she found nothing of interest in *Horse and Hound*. She folded it in her lap and looked past Jon's face at the procession of sun-struck fields.

She remembered the debate she had had with herself about bringing her sketch-pad and drawing materials, and how she had eventually decided not to pack them. Determined and disciplined, she would make an effort not to work during her honeymoon, although her imagination might be alive with ideas. There was what she was already calling the 'ship painting' to begin: it would have gigantic proportions, harsh angles, dark colours, and sunlight and moonlight on the same canvas. That, she felt sure, was a revolutionary idea in the spirit of the Age, indeed in the spirit of the future, and one which would bring her serious attention from the critics and perhaps even make her reputation. She was already sketching it in her mind—but would leave it there and not put pencil to paper until she was back in Newcastle. Then there were these wide landscapes of newly-discovered Northumberland, the heather-clad hills and wooded farms, somehow wild and cosy-looking at the same time, and all lit by a sun of unexpected ferocity. She had thought she might want to paint out here; now she was actually passing through the countryside and soon to arrive in Alnmouth—which would surely present more opportunities for an artist—the feeling was confirmed. Yet she would not break the promise she had made to herself not to work, could not break it, now she had deliberately left her materials behind. She hoped Jon would appreciate the sacrifice she had made for his sake.

Whatever was he thinking behind *The Lady*? *The Lady*, of all things! It was funny to see him reading it so carefully. Surely he couldn't be interested in the magazine when his new wife was beside him and they were swaying up the countryside to their secretive, romantic, exciting little honeymoon village beside the sea? Why, they had talked about this and planned it and looked forward to it for months before they were married. It had all worked out so perfectly despite the troubles their families had put them through, and now they were on their way, just as they had imagined during their darker days in London. Yet Jon didn't look excited. He didn't look animated at all, she thought. Oh, he could be so calm and quiet and self-absorbed, so infuriatingly self-absorbed! It was impossible to tell what he was thinking, that was the worst of it. People said he had an honest, open face, and she had always thought so too—but now the idea disturbed her. It wasn't a bad face, indeed it was a handsome face with the dashing fair moustache and the blue eyes and the fine nose she liked to kiss, but today it was a faraway face. He was thinking of something far away from the magazine and the train and the journey and from her. It was horrible; she hated the knowledge. She wanted to know, needed to know, had to know everything he was thinking. Her face surely told him everything when he looked at her. *When* he looked! Why wouldn't he look? He should look at her all the time, be able to show her everything that was going on in his mind without guile or effort. And here he was, looking at a wretched magazine and thinking of something far away.

"Jon," she tapped his knee.

"Darling?" The big blue eyes came up to her face.

"Jon—the window. Open the window, please. It's too hot in here."

"Yes," he answered, getting up to do it. "Better than the South of France. If it stays like this all week we'll come home as brown as berries."

"Jon," she said slyly, and took a breath to add 'what were you thinking about just then?', but decided not ask it. He might tell her the truth, ruin everything in a few words. She could not face whatever the truth might be; felt she didn't have to anyway. She would care only for the here-and-now. Everything was fine. The sunshine was pouring over her lover's hair. She would think of that.

"Mmm?" He turned from the window.

"I was just thinking," she went on, grasping at the words, "how…how lovely it'll be to smell the sea."

* * *

Alnmouth in 1904 retained the stone-built sturdiness it had displayed for much of the Nineteenth Century. Its long main street with the tall-spired church was built on a low hill between the river and the sea. The river Aln ran down from the Cheviot Hills, past the Duke's castle at Alnwick, and meandered its way across flat farmland to make the estuary and the little harbour at Alnmouth. A few fishing cobles rode the tide where the river widened and herons fished on the muddy flats; the old ferryman sat in his tarry-timbered hut, smoking his pipe and dreaming of when he might again ferry the bare-armed dairymaids with their churns of milk from the cows that wandered down to the river's edge on the opposite bank. The land and the sea were the livelihood of the people, and their wide vistas of grey or blue in storm or sunshine seemed unchangeable along the sandy beach or the bracken-covered dunes. Yet there had been developments in the last few years. Grand stone villas had been built at either end of the main street and around the riverside road; some of the smaller houses had been re-roofed and given stucco facings; most significant of all, a fine golf-course now spread between the houses and the beach. Hotels and guest-houses had opened; a large grocer's shop, cafés, and public houses had appeared in the main street as golfers and trippers had begun to arrive, bringing new flavours of wealth and holiday between the salt spray and the hayfields.

The station lay a mile inland, on a hill above the West bank of the river. Jon and Philippa left the train and rode down to Alnmouth in a pony and trap, larks singing above them, a fresh smell of the sea in their faces, just as Philippa had hoped. She pointed out the pastel-painted houses curving round the estuary.

"It's just like a Cornish fishing village," she exclaimed, "only bigger and wider and....."

"...and usually colder," laughed Jon. "We're very lucky this week."

"Aye sir," put in the bearded driver, "y'are that. The gud weather's brought a canny few fine folk up from Newcastle. You a golfer, sir?"

"Never played in my life."

"Aye well, if ye do fancy a game, I'm yer caddy an' aal. Ask for Mister Milburn."

"I couldn't hit a ball straight if I were going to be shot."

"Oh come on, silly," retorted Philippa. "An engineer like you, who knows about angles and deflection and all that sort of thing? You should be a natural golfer. Anyway Mister Milburn," she turned to him with a glittering smile, "I shall have a go at golf, even if my husband won't."

"Well that'll be summat, Missis. Right we are then." He pulled up at the ivy-covered porch of the Marine Hotel, overlooking the golf-course itself. "There's nae doot ye've picked the best place to stay. Enjoy yerselves noo." Handing down their luggage, he clip-clopped away, leaving the larks and the murmur of the sea to welcome them.

They were shown to a room, also overlooking the golf-course. They squeezed close together at the small window, resting their elbows on the sun-cracked sill and taking in the wide sweep of dunes, beach, and sea.

"There's Coquet Island," said Jon, pointing to a long shape seeming to float like an enormous whale just off the coast to the South. "Never been there. But along the other way, which I do know, it becomes very rocky and there's a little valley to explore running up off the beach. I'll take you there…but it's going to be rather quiet here, Darling. There's not a great deal to do other than walk by the sea and enjoy the peace. I hope you won't mind."

"Of course I shan't mind," she snuggled into his shoulder, kissing his ear in her playful way, "and I don't agree there's nothing to do here."

"Oh?"

"No. I'm going to shock Mister Milburn and everyone else by playing golf."

"I thought you might. They'll think you're a Suffragette."

"I am, in spirit. If I were still in London I'd be with them. I'll bet there isn't one woman member of that stuffy golf club down there"

"Probably not."

"And then there are all sorts of things to explore here," she smiled, tickling his neck. "Yes, all those places you told me about, and the rocks, and the beach…but let's start with this bedroom. There's a very interesting man in here."

Tickling him furiously, and pulling up her skirts, she drew him down on to the bed.

* * *

The Marine Hotel had few other guests, despite the fair weather and the attractions of the golf-course just beyond its windows. Those it could boast gathered each evening in the cosy, oak-panelled dining-room. A solitary waiter attended to a middle-aged Scottish couple in lumpy tweeds, a party of four Newcastle businessmen determined to play golf all day and drink all night, a fearsome-looking widow of enormous bulk recovering from some indeterminate illness, and Jon and Philippa. They felt—and were—the centre of speculation as they sat down to their first dinner.

"I don't think we should have dressed for dinner, Darling," whispered Jon. "Nobody else has."

"No—and don't they look bloody awful?"

"For Heaven's sake, Philippa! They can hear you."

They suppressed their giggles: not something to be achieved noiselessly over vegetable broth. Jon felt the Scottish couple's eyes fixed dourly upon him; Philippa knew the widow was staring at the bare dimples on her shoulders, and said so to Jon.

"Yes, and they're lovely dimples," he murmured, unable to look her in the eye, "and the best thing is, you have one on each side."

There were more noises with the broth.

"Of course *she* won't have any," declared Philippa loudly, and they both had to twist their stomach muscles to stop themselves laughing.

Between the broth and the fish, Jon ran his fingers over the woodwork beside their table.

"We'll have better panelling than this on *Mauretania*," he remarked. "Father said we'll be getting the very best craftsmen, even some woodcarvers from Palestine."

"Really?" Philippa was still unable to look at Jon in case they should burst out laughing. Instead, she smiled into the widow's unblinking stare. She wished something funny could happen in the room so they could appear to laugh wildly at it. The terrible certainty that nothing funny *would* happen made it worse. "So," she added, "your ship will be in better shape than one lady I can think of."

Jon stared helplessly at the fish. Even that looked ridiculous, the texture of its flesh somehow echoing the appalling tweeds of the Scottish couple. Surely he would burst. Somehow they controlled themselves and managed to eat. At length Jon leant forward and whispered:

"I wonder if they've guessed we're a honeymoon couple?"

"Oh," smiled Philippa, leaning back and raising her voice to the room, "I'm sure they've all guessed we're a honeymoon couple." There was complete silence, ghastly but wonderful. "Which reminds me. Waiter! Champagne!"

Jon had blushed, but recovered his spirit. Here was a wonderful girl—his wonderful girl, who didn't give a damn about anything except loving him. Wonderful! He would not waste the opportunity.

"What shall we drink to, Darling?" he asked loudly, straightening himself in his chair.

She played her wide smile to the open-mouthed audience.

"Why—to better panelling of course!"

* * *

They continued to cause a stir next morning when—true to her word—Philippa insisted on playing a

48

round of golf with the suddenly reluctant Mr. Milburn as caddy. She had taken a good deal of trouble with her appearance, to Jon's amusement and her own annoyance.

"Can't you see?" she had stamped her foot and rummaged through her Summer dresses, "I'm trying to look dowdy and masculine."

"Impossible," Jon had laughed. "Impossible, thank God."

"I should have brought tweeds."

"But you hate tweeds. You say they're stuffy and old-fashioned."

"So they are—but I should put them on for this, just to get past any old dragons in the Clubhouse."

"There won't be any old dragons in the Clubhouse. There won't be any women at all, if you ask me."

"Oh, I don't know." She had selected a brown skirt and her darkest jacket. "How about these?"

"Fine. But I don't know why you're bothering to look conventional. You're not conventional, I'm delighted to say."

She had put on her stoutest boots, leather gloves, and abandoned any idea of a hat. Instead, she had held her hair back in the snood she used to wear when she had ridden to hounds as a girl. She remembered having packed it somewhat doubtfully in her trousseau; now she had discovered why.

"There. I don't want to stand out *too* much."

"You will, Darling, you will," Jon had chuckled. "I can't make up my mind whether you're going skating, hunting, or up in a flying-machine."

Down at the Clubhouse, where Jon paid their green fees, there were whispers in the hall and peering faces from the lounge. The Secretary appeared. Without looking at Philippa he announced: "There are no rules which actually prohibit ladies' play." She sensed the word 'unfortunately' hung unspoken on his thin lips, muttered "pompous ass" under her breath, snatched a club from the bemused Milburn, and strode out to the first green.

For all her determination, golf did not come easily to Philippa. She was frustrated to discover she lacked the strength necessary to drive a ball very far down the course, and already knew she lacked the patience to set up and address the shorter shots and putts she might have managed. Jon, as he himself had predicted, played badly; but he didn't seem to mind and she took no notice of him when he laughed at his own mistakes, straightened his tie, and tried to learn from Milburn. She stumped round the course, nursing a smouldering fury and inflicting severe damage to the greens.

"Bugger me," said Milburn as a particularly heavy divot flew from her club.

"If you're not careful, Mister Milburn," she retorted, unabashed, "somebody will. Now pass me another club."

"Howay then, pet."

Her eyes blazed.

"Swear if you like, Mister Milburn. I've heard worse than you in London; but *never* call me pet!"

She returned to the Clubhouse in a foul temper.

"I shall never play golf again," she declared, pulling off her gloves. "If it's not a game for finicky fusspots," she dumped the gloves into Jon's hands and turned to Milburn, "it's a game for old men."

Jon didn't seem to mind being called a finicky fusspot, nor Milburn dismissed as an old man. They roared with laughter, which served only to further annoy Philppa. Jon took her to the café for lunch.

"You were magnificent, Darling," be grinned when the waitress had taken their order. "The whole place'll be talking about you. I love it, I love it. I love you, too."

"It's all very well being amused by me, Jon," she said darkly, "but I'm serious about breaking down these silly conventions. Somebody has to do it; in fact a woman has to do it. Men won't. Convention is quite natural to you; you were brought up in that sort of family."

"I can't altogether agree with that, my love." Jon looked hurt, and shuffled uncomfortably. He couldn't predict where this conversation might lead, but he did not relish the thought of saying something which would turn it into an argument. On the other hand, he felt that Philippa, of all people, should have appreciated her new family's openness and modernity. "I suppose we can be a formal-looking lot, we Ferrises," he smiled, hoping she would sense his discomfort and drop the subject.

"Well," she went on, "my family were hopelessly conventional anyway. I think all older people are. In a way they can't help it, but I'm young and I *can* help it…"

She continued in this way, perky and determined, watching Jon begin to eat his lunch. If he thought her silly or hot-headed, that was his failure to understand, and he'd have

51

to learn better or live with it. She was being true to herself. Drifting between the points she was making about women and Art came her realisation that this honeymoon was very strange. It had thrown up so many tensions and differences between them, powerful yet nameless. Their courtship—she hated the word but couldn't think of any other—their courtship in London had been fine; more than fine, exciting. Their wedding and their 'escape' to the North had been quite magical, and the new house was sweet and welcoming and a symbol of wonderful good fortune; but now the honeymoon seemed none of these things. It was dull or hectic, tense or empty. Perhaps she was being unfair to poor Jon, who loved her and had brought her into his family amongst all that fuss with her parents. Perhaps it wasn't his fault. Perhaps it was nobody's fault. It was just a fraught void between them. Did all newly-married couples feel like this? She hated the word 'couple', too They were not a 'couple', just one of all the other 'couples'. They were married, and in that sense had created a new entity out of each other, but they had remained themselves. She wanted to remain herself, to be utterly herself. She did not want to be submerged in marriage, to deny everything she was just becoming. The prospect was sad and terrifying and she wouldn't allow it. Her art would prevent it. She *was* her art. It would redeem her and make her anew, as brightly and strongly as the colours she would not be afraid to use in her new work.

"…like Matisse, who's working now in France," she was saying. "His colour is the subject of the painting as well as the way to express what it's about. D'you see?"

"I think so," said Jon, "but you'll have to tell me much more about the way modern painting is going, and how English artists can compete with the French, who seem to have it all sewn up—or all framed up might be a better way of putting it."

"Oh, I shall. You see the English have industry on their side while the French don't. We have all the machines and factories and shipyards, which I believe the new Art must spring from. France is still largely an agricultural society, apart from Paris of course, which as you know has always been a great intellectual and cultural centre. No no, we have the edge on industrial art…machines at work…huge new forces…"

This might be true, thought Jon. He had believed it was true when they had first met and so excitedly discussed their marriage of Art and Engineering, but now it sounded silly and impossible, and Philippa's soap-box manner was embarrassing to him—and all over a meaningless game of golf, which they had both hated anyway. Was this really the same girl he had loved so rapturously in London? Of course: the warm curvacious body, the luscious copper hair, the adorable nose, the bright eyes. If anything, she was more beautiful here in Northern sunlight. Yet that marriage of Art and Engineering, so recently sanctified, no longer seemed real. The ideal had evaporated in these curious days at Alnmouth. It seemed to him that she would never paint these pictures, never make the impression she so fervently imagined. Her hopes were too high, her plans too impractical for reality.

He himself had been thrust into a project so real it frightened him. Before this Summer darkened to winter, *Mauretania* would begin to rise, enormous and wonderful, raking the sky—and he would be at work on her engines. The reality of that was almost menacing; the prospect of it had transformed him. He felt a terrible yearning for solid work, for an end to plans and schemes and hopes and anxieties, for simple toil, for redemption through physical effort, for its clean and wholesome rewards. He wanted to pit his whole being, his bone and blood and mind and muscle, against hard steel. He would go to the foundries if he could, feel the searing heat as molten metal solidified into engine castings. He would sweat with his men on the shop floor and ride up the hull with

53

the riveters. On launch-day, if he could, he would work under the the hull, down with the sledgehammer gang, knocking her on to the greased ways, the great rivet-studded hull sliding back over their heads, coming alive on the water. That would be the glorious transformation of an idea into reality. Everything else, everything Philippa was saying, all seemed a false and hopeless sham built on dreams and uncertainties. He wanted no more of them. He would have clarity, definition, fact, a concrete truth he could grasp with his hands. Yet he must not love them more than Philippa. He must love her now as he had loved her at first. He would remember how beautiful she was, simply by looking at her again—and she was beautiful, with her richly coloured hair catching the light. He would think of that, and of her creamy skin under the jacket.

"…and look," she was saying, "here's another one."

"Another what?"

"Another motor-car, Jon. Just outside, look. Haven't you been listening? I've just been saying there are more and more of them every day now, aren't there? I didn't expect to see such a big and luxurious one in these parts."

A large tourer had pulled up outside the café. Its hood was rolled back to reveal a magnificent interior of gleaming controls and blue leather. Two men and a woman were descending, taking off their hats and goggles. They came in, jangling the door-bell, bringing a tang of fresh sea air and a tantalizing whiff of petroleum spirit, as teasing as the sunshine on their hands and faces. The excitement of wealth and adventure came with them into the little café as they took a table near Jon and Philippa, exchanging 'good afternoons'. Two seemed to be a man and his wife in their fifties, expensively dressed in light clothes; the third was a younger man even more fashionably dressed. He wore an elegant check suit with the latest kind of American collar and tie.

"Aha!" exclaimed the older man. "The lady golfer." He bowed handsomely to Philippa, full of smiles. "We couldn't help but notice you this morning. Good to see a young woman taking on the men."

He introduced himself as Gilbert Gough, with his wife Helen and his young cousin Robert, who kissed Philippa on the hand in the continental fashion. They were returning to London in easy stages from a motoring tour of the Scottish Lowlands. Arriving in Alnmouth that morning, they had watched the activity on the golf-course and would resume their journey after lunch.

"We're staying at the Marine," explained Jon as off-handedly as he thought would be polite. For all their glamour, there was something about these people he did not like.

"It's a beautiful motor-car," said Philippa, admiring it through the window.

"Yes, a wonderful machine," replied Gough. "Made in France, by the Renault company. The French have got a real industry going with these now, you know. I love driving it. I drive myself all the time; wouldn't let a chauffeur have all the fun. Next Spring we'll be going to Paris in it; there could be some fuss getting it on and off the Channel steamer. Anyway, this was a sort of trial. It's managed the run perfectly. The engineering is superb."

"My husband is an engineer," said Philippa.

"Really?" Gough smiled at Jon. He was a large man, full of enthusiasms and, apparently, the wealth to pursue them. "What kind of engineering?"

"Oh, bigger engines than the one in your Renault, Mister Gough. I am to work on new steam turbines for a passenger liner: the *Mauretania*. She's being laid down this Summer."

"Marine engineering, by Jove. Now there's a task. I could have gone into shipping, you know. Went into house-property instead. It's done me well enough. Now, take a city like Newcastle, just down the road here. There must be plenty of opportunity for property develepment there, I'd say…"

Helen Gough leaned towards Philippa.

"Are you enjoying your holiday?"

"Oh yes, very much. It's our honeymoon."

"Oh, how romantic! Congratulations, my dear." She beamed and re-settled herself. "What a wonderful place to come for a honeymoon: so quiet and peaceful. I do hope you'll be happy." She dropped her voice to a whisper. "But don't you find all this talk of engines and business rather boring?"

"Not at all. I'm a painter, you see."

"Indeed?"

"Yes, and I believe the future of Art lies in celebrating the great machines and engines and powerful forces which are going to shape our new century."

"Good Heavens, that is a novel idea. I dare say you could be right. Well, you'll be intrigued to learn that Robert is an artist, too."

"Yes, I am intrigued." Philippa stared at the younger man, languid in his check suit. He didn't look like an artist—but then neither did she, she guessed; and what was an artist supposed to look like anyway? She found herself the victim of the conventional attitudes she so despised. What did it matter how he looked? If he carried the same flame as herself, that was cause enough for celebration. "Well," she continued, smiling at him, "two artists in the same café: that *is* something—in England, anyway. Tell me all about your work, Mister Gough."

"Robert, please."

It transpired that Robert Gough was a commercial artist involved in the design and production of advertising posters. He was based in London but had frequent dealings with French designers in Paris.

"Oh yes, the adverts," enthused Philippa. "I love some of these new posters! Do tell me about the process. Do you have any French artists actually working with you, doing the paintings? Have you been inside the great Paris print works?"

Soon they were deep in easy conversation. The man who until this moment had said almost nothing now talked volubly about the intricacies of his profession. Nothing could have been more fascinating to Philippa, and she was instantly, helplessly attracted to him. At her wildest moment she could not have called him handsome, despite his elegant attire. He was small and rather swarthy, with thinning hair and a forgettable face, yet he held her with a magnetism so similar to physical beauty that to listen to him was almost like being in love. He was animated, passionate, energetic, charming. Philppa forgot everything but the thrill of meeting someone like this so unexpectedly, the joy of sharing enthusiasms, the hope that she might learn more about the latest techniques and so develop her own career. She knew she should feel guilty about this, sitting as she was next to her new husband who was chatting aimiably with the others...but she would wait to feel guilty. For the moment she was enraptured by Robert's tales of his frequent visits to Paris: the fashionable women parading their furs and walking their outrageously clipped dogs in the Bois de Boulogne; the motor-cars (there seemed to be more motor-cars in Paris than anywhere else); Robert's favourite café on the Boulevard Saint-Germain; the Arabs one would see in the streets; even the organ-grinders and hot-chestnut-sellers were romantic figures. Above all these were the paintings: old masters and new rebels in galleries all over the city. He was amazed that she had not been there already to discover 'what was going on', as he so casually put it.

Her mind reeled and raced, but as Gough continued his stories, a sense of disappointment crept over her. Her own career had allowed for nothing like this. With no formal training she had painted on her own in London, joined a group of artists, exhibited briefly with them to no particular effect, left to strike out on her own, painted a little more, and struggled on. She had made a few private sales of a few pictures—events she had had to regard as successes—but had never had her own exhibition, never found a ready market for her talent, and never made any significant money from it. This man seemed to have done it all, and done it with ease at an early age. He had been formally trained and had begun as a fine artist much affected by the Impressionists, but had had little success selling his work. He had then joined a firm of printers as a commercial artist and progressed quickly from there. He had simply been lucky, he said; the last twenty years had been a golden age for the printer, especially in France, and with better inks and lithographic techniques, it was bound to continue all over Europe. He insisted with a smile that his rich elder cousin had had nothing to do with his success. Illustrated advertisements were everywhere, but there was no doubt, he admitted, that the connection with the French poster artists had given his employers a great advantage and the visits to Paris an extra sparkle to his own career. It seemed to be the very sparkle that was missing from Philippa's. The opportunities seemed to have been denied her, and alongside her feelings of frustration came pangs of envy, hastily followed by a hot determination to do just as well if she were to be given the chance—or if she were not, then simply to seize it into her own hands.

The conversation became so intense that the Goughs felt it necessary to move their table closer to Jon and Philippa's ("I think it's the kind of place where such a manoeuvre is quite permissable," whispered Mrs. Gough) and they all took lunch together. At last they left to go their separate ways: the Goughs climbing back into their Renault for the drive down the Great North Road, Jon and Philippa strolling back to their hotel.

They had exchanged cards. Jon did not expect to see them again and said so as he guided Philippa round the riverside walk. Philippa made no answer, resolving silently that she *would* see Robert Gough again. It occurred to her, quite coolly, that she could have both these men in her life; both these men as kinds of husband: Jon as her husband in the flesh, Robert as her husband in the spirit. The two need never cross; she would never wish them to. She could never love the dark little Robert in the way she loved Jon's broad blond beauty, but she could love his passionate and artistic nature. It was the very thing she found lacking in Jon, yet loved him no less for it. Indeed she felt released into a new and simple love for Jon. She hugged his arm and smiled at him and they kissed under the Summer-yellow trees along the riverbank. How strange this seemed to her, how curious that in a moment's meeting with a stranger her love for Jon could be compromised yet strengthened. She should be ashamed of herself, she kept thinking. Yet it seemed so simple: the passions that stirred Robert Gough were the same as those that stirred her, so their union would be truly spiritual. It could also be businesslike. Yes, that was it: a union of professionals. It need never affect her physical desire for Jon, nor his simple and boyish devotion to her. After all, he had his work on the new ship; she should have hers. Of course, she reasoned to herself, the world would not see it that way. But the world would not know about it—not yet, anyway.

* * *

The next day was fine and blowy, and they walked to Craster. The sun was still shining, but the coastline was misted with sea-spray. It was a long walk: up the rocky beach, through the tiny fishing village of Boulmer, and along a cliff-top path alive with the butterscotch smell of full-bloomed gorse, the sparkle of sea-pinks blowing in the sunny wind, and the constant song of skylarks. A sharp North-Easterly, unusual in Summer, kept the spray in their faces and brought the roar of the sea on shore with the breakers, the white foam churned to brilliance in the sun. Philippa took off her hat and loosened her hair until it flew madly behind her.

"You look wild and beautiful," Jon told her, taking her hand, drawing her to him for a warm embrace, then admiring her at arm's length as she laughed into the wind. "You're wild and free and timeless, just like this place."

"No more poetry, Jon," she laughed. "I'm of *this* time! I'm right here, now, with you."

"Then thank God for it," said Jon, kissing her lips and turning their faces to the wind. "Thank God for you, and for us."

His doubts were gone; he could scarcely remember what they had been about. He had married this beautiful girl and brought her home: surely those had been the right things to do. He felt strong and lucky and capable of anything.

Just South of Craster the cliffs grew higher and a long point ran out towards the sea, seeming to be made of rust-coloured rock, pillared and creviced and alive with the cries of ice-white sea-birds.

"That's called Cullernose Point," explained Jon. "It's always full of birds. In Spring you can look over the edge and see them on their nests. Look at these, how they glide so well."

A heavy-bodied Fulmar soared past them, never flapping a wing as it rode the currents of air brushing up the cliff. It lazily followed the contours of the coast and vanished into the sun-haze of the South, another and another coming after it, each one an effortless master of the air.

"You know all these wonderful places, Jon, all these interesting things. I don't think I've ever been happier."

She was able to say it because, at that moment, she believed it was true. She knew she wanted other happinesses and different opportunities, but they need not spoil this, she thought. This was glorious, this was a genuine happiness of its own, and she had Jon to thank for it.

They stood for a while gazing Northwards at the spectacular ruins of Dunstanburgh Castle basking in misty sunlight beyond the village of Craster. The ancient stonework glowed in the distance, a mile of greensward rolling up to its towered gateway. It was a vista of soft blues and greens, the castle as pale as the vision of a dream.

"That is wonderful," breathed Philippa. "I can imagine it in the Middle Ages; flags and banners on the battlements."

"Queen Margaret escaped to France from there," Jon told her. "It was right at the end of the Wars of the Roses; there'd been a battle at Hexham."

"Can't you imagine the knights riding up to the gate, singing old French songs?"

"Yes, but it looks even better in late afternoon, when the stone turns pink and orange in the sunlight. You should see that."

"I'd like to see it."

"We'll come back then."

At length they descended into Craster and stood above its harbour, encircled by mewing Kittiwakes.

"Aha," Philippa pointed triumphantly to a stone house. "That's where Turner stayed, isn't it?"

"So he did."

"I've always wanted to see the place. Now I know why he loved this coast and painted the light so well here. He ended up painting nothing but light; that's what was so wonderful about him. People used to think he was an old sea-captain you know, with his gruff manner and his spyglass. They never knew he was a famous artist."

"Well, sometimes it's easy to be deceived by appearances."

They ate kippers in a tiny cliff-top inn with its view of

the churning sea.

"We'll smell of these for ages!" laughed Philippa.

* * *

On the last day of their honeymoon the telephone rang in the Marine Hotel. A maid scurried to find them.

"Oh Mister Ferris, sir," she gasped, "the telephone's going. A gentleman wishes to speak to you, says he's your father. We don't get many calls on the telephone, sir."

"Good Heavens. Is he all right? There's not illness or something, is there?"

Jon hurried into the hall and took the earpiece.

"Father—is that you? Are you all right?"

"Of course, my boy." The familiar voice was strangely distorted by the instrument. "I just wanted to make certain you and Philippa were well and that you'd been enjoying yourselves."

"Oh good—it's just that they don't often have the telephone ring here. They're new-fangled with it. We thought something was wrong. Yes, we've had a fine time, thanks. We've been lucky with the weather. Is Mother all right?"

"Perfectly all right. You *are* starting back tomorrow, aren't you?"

"Yes, unless there's any reason not to."

"There's every reason to come home, Jon. Sort yourselves out in the new house, then you'd better get down to Wallsend by the end of the week. They're clearing the berth at Swan's now. Stevenson the yard manager wants to see the engine team about the kind of space you'll need in the assembly shops. I thought you should be there with everyone else from Parsons'."

"Right-o, Father. This all sounds very exciting."

"It is. By the way." the voice had a chuckle in it, "did you know they're going to build a roof over the berth? Yes, an enormous glass roof with the cranes inside, and lights. You'll be working under cover. Softies!"

A sudden great flush of love welled up in Jon: love for his father, for his mother, for the life and happiness they had given him, for the support they had offered him over Philippa, for this great opportunity.

"I shall be there on time," he said. He felt a proud determination in his voice, but a waver of emotion too. "And Father…thank you for all this."

CHAPTER FOUR
To Work

Hot sunlight shimmered over the River Tyne, dazzling across the shipyards, factories and chemical works, lying oppressively on the roofs of the grim houses that rose above its banks, and glinting the water to the colour of molten steel. A midsummer tide lapped away from the new berth at the Wallsend shipyard of Swan, Hunter, and Wigham Richardson, dropping lengths of timber, hanks of rope, rags, cabbages, bottles, and a thousand other items of refuse on the filthy mud. An orange, still somehow shiny and perfect, bobbed in the swill just beyond Jon's boots.

He stood at the berth's edge with the rank smell of the river in his nostrils, squinting upstream into the haze of the Hebburn shore and doing mental arithmetic. *Mauretania* would slide out in that direction, rushing stern-first down the slipway into a foaming flood-tide. At nearly eight-hundred feet she would be longer than the width of the Tyne; that was why she would go down almost due South into this convenient bend of the river. With tricing lines to arrest her plunge, drag-chains, and a stern anchor dropped in the river, the engineers had worked out a launch run of twelve-hundred feet. Jon was trying to visualise it, to imagine the huge liner sliding off the ways to ride lighter and higher than she ever would again, the howling dance of the drag-chains, the cheering spectators, the straining tugs, the brown and white smoke billowing above the crowds on both sides of the river, the screaming whistles, the anxiety of waiting to see if she would stop in time. Yes, it would be all right—just.

"Aye, she'll be all right on a flood-tide."

It was the voice of Stevenson, the yard manager. He stood with hands in pockets, bowler hat over his shrewd eyes. Jon sensed he was being watched, assessed, criticised. While no-one had been openly hostile, he felt as lonely and uncomfortable as a new boy at school.

"Well then," Stevenson interrupted his thoughts, "have you seen enough down here, Mister Ferris?"

"Yes, I think so. Thank you, Stevenson. Not really my area, this part of it, but I can see you're clear for a tremendous job. Thanks for showing me over."

"Aye, it's a tremendous job all right, this one is."

They turned back to face the newly cleared berth. It was an awesome sight. Sixteen-thousand piles had been driven into the soft earth to support a grid of pitch-pine baulks. On top of that lay the floor of the berth: a vast deck of oak timbers six inches thick. It gleamed flat and empty in the sunlight, yet was already crossed with shadows, for over it reared the enormous iron and glass roof of the shed, where builders still climbed, shouting above the clang of their metalwork as the glistening panes were fitted. The two men walked back over the wide oaken floor. Everywhere the smell of new timber and oily machinery rose in tangy counterpoint to the stench of the river. Stacks of steel were already gathering in the yard, with more being unloaded from the spur of the Riverside branch line, where little steam locomotives puffed and clanked in constant comings and goings.

"Thanks again." Jon prepared to leave. On this, his first day, he would be expected back at Parsons' head office at the works on Shields Road in Heaton.

"All right, Mister Ferris. The lads all agree it's good to see some interest from one of Parson's gentlemen."

"Oh," smiled Jon, suddenly feeling easier, "is that what they're calling me? I don't know Sir Charles all that well, not really." Stevenson continued to eye him coolly. "I'm different, you'll see. I know I have my father to thank for this appointment…"

"Indeed," Stevenson broke in. "Your father was always well respected on the shop floor."

"Yes. Well, he was never lucky enough to get his teeth into a job like this. There never *was* a job like this, was there? I shall certainly make the most of the opportunity. I intend to get my hands dirty, too."

They shook hands. Stevenson watched Jon go for the cab that would take him back to Heaton. He was not in awe of young Ferris and his superior manner, but he knew his place. He wouldn't have allowed anyone else to treat him like a servant and call him 'Stevenson' without the 'Mister', but he supposed it was natural enough to the lad, and took no offence at it. He had seen his like often enough: young gentlemen-engineers with fine coats and white fingers and voices to match. They were best kept in the boardrooms and drawing-lofts; very few survived in the yards or made any pretence of understanding the workmen. Nor were they welcome. This one's father had been all right, stern but decent; rolling in money, of course, but honest and fair, not a snob. The lad might make out. He wouldn't encourage him, though.

Stevenson retraced his steps back down to the water's edge. For the first time in days a light breeze came off the river, bringing a fresh smell of the sea above the rank mud of low tide. Stevenson considered himself a plain, bluff man, but now he admitted a stirring of his heart with the breeze: a fresh smell of hope. There was new work on the Tyne again; peace for the warring families, their devil of poverty at bay for a while; food for the bairns; hope. He'd known it would come with the new century, and the war finished in South Africa, and the new houses being built, and the clever men like Parsons with their new engines. Clever men and big ships—it was a winning combination. Aye, the lad might make out. He wouldn't encourage him, though. He turned and stared up at the new glass roof. This building-shed was the biggest thing on the river. It would have to be finished soon: the first of the arc lamps were due to be fitted. When this Summer was gone and Winter afternoons began to close in on Tyneside, the work would proceed under the brilliant glare of electric light. Clever men indeed who could bend all power to this great endeavour. It was hard work, cruel work in the yards; always had been—but there was something about this job which made it new and marvellous. You could see it in the men, even before the keel was laid. Perhaps their kind and Ferris's kind could get on more honestly, see eye-to-eye, bury some of their differences of class and money and opportunity—and perhaps not. However marvellous the job, it was still cruel work in the yards. Aye well, young Ferris might make out, but he wouldn't encourage him, not too much. The orange which had bobbed prettily at their feet now lay stranded on the seeping mud. Stevenson raised his boot and pushed it under the slime.

* * *

The honeysuckle was in flower at Lily Avenue. When Philippa stood at the door to kiss Jon goodbye, its wonderful fragrance flooded between them; when she waved to him as he walked away, its ravishing mixture of red and orange flowers called desperately to her. This was a big day for Jon. He was going to Parsons' works in Heaton, then to the marine turbine shop which had been established just downstream form Swan Hunter's, and finally into the Wallsend shipyard for the first time, travelling by the electric railway that ran behind blue iron railings at the end of their street. The day was of no less importance to Philippa. She was staying in Jesmond. For the first time since their wedding, they were to be separated by his work—by her work also. As they waved in the sunny street, and the honeysuckle flashed its poignant sweetness into Philippa's senses, she knew she would spend this day establishing her studio. Jon turned for a final wave, and suddenly she was alone. She was surprised to feel a stab of combined anxiety and guilt. She had been used to being alone in London when she had broken away from her parents; yet she had never been completely isolated, living as she had in the bustling and crowded studio with her artist friends. Here, the genteel little street was empty and silent in the morning sunshine. Presumably, the husbands had gone to work; the wives would be inside or at the shops. By an odd chance it was also Mrs. Hutchinson's day off. Philippa felt responsible for the household of which she had been left in charge, and for the marriage to which it must become home. She felt guilty for planning to do nothing but set up her studio.

Yet why should she feel guilty? She told herself the houseold, such as it was, would look after itself. There was nothing pressing to be done; neither Jon nor anyone else was compelling her to do anything but please herself. She would not allow such thoughts, she smiled, pushing her thick hair back from her forehead, opening her blouse a little to let the sun warm her throat, leaning back against the hot doorpost, and folding her arms comfortably. She was sure young married ladies in Jesmond did not do this at their front doors, but she would not care, would be ruled by nothing but her own spirit. Jon knew it and loved her for it; she too would glory in it, and in the freedom to do as she pleased. Tradesmen would surely call later in the week; the housekeeper would be back tomorrow. She relaxed in the sunshine, absorbing the pleasures of her new home. Even at this hour the sun was bouncing heat off the broad flagstones of the pavements, and a large ginger cat was enjoying the warmth as it basked in a leafy front garden across the street. Another cat, a slender black one, tip-toed delicately along a fence, finding a place on a warm brick wall to sit and wash itself. Above it all bent a fresh blue sky, open and cloudless, with only the hint of a breeze. Contentment crept into Philippa's being; she shuffled her feet to become even more comfortable at the door and turned her face to the honeysuckle, smiling to herself. An electric train rattled down to the coast, unseen in its shadowy cutting behind the rhododendron bushes. Jon might be on it. She was alone…free.

She clattered up to the attic. This last flight of stairs was bare and unpainted, and she thought she would leave it like that: it was workmanlike and somehow exciting. Downstairs, the house had been cool and shady, but up here there seemed to be a trap of heat after days of sunshine beating on the roof. A sudden shock of realisation ran through her: the stairs reminded her of a dream she had had years ago, a dream of being frightened to go into an upper room she felt sure would be filled with cobwebs, mouldy furniture, monstrous spiders, and unspeakable terrors; but when, in the dream, she had forced herself up the stairs and into the room, it had been nothing like that, indeed rather open and friendly. So it was in the reality of this house. The attic was warm, dry, wide, and empty, save for the long wooden table she and Jon had carried up to be the centre of her workplace. Dreams could come true then, she smiled to herself, and in the most curious ways. Here at last was the friendly upper room—but in a strange city in the North of England. Here at last was her own studio, gained through marriage to her lover. How wonderfully curious life could be!

She sniffed the dry smell of warm, bare wood. Mrs. Hutchinson had seen to the scrubbing of the floor up here and it looked new. The walls had been washed down too, and the little gabled window—built smartly upright through the steeply sloping ceiling—sparkled as sunlight poured in. It was as welcoming an attic as anyone could wish for, and it would make an exciting studio. She felt a tomboyish glee in exploring its every corner, moving the table out of the sunshine, and deciding where her two easels would go. She would also need a chest of drawers, a hard chair and a comfortable one, and perhaps that old dresser from the scullery, or at least a long shelf. In the midst of her plans came the realisation that this was the first real room of her own. Her childhood bedroom at her parent's house in London had been furnished for her, and had always seemed dull and gloomy, its memory further scarred by the break with her father. She had been given pretty bedrooms whenever she had stayed with her cousins in Wiltshire and Sussex, but had always realised that other guests would occupy them when she was back in London. The studio to which she had escaped in Chelsea had been shared with friends. No, this really was the first time she could call it a room of her own. She stepped quickly across the boards and placed the palms of her hands against each warm wall, claiming them. She laid her cheek against a sunlit patch of plaster, closed her eyes, opened them again, saw the fascinating Jesmond roofscape through her window: slates and tiles, gables and chimneys, ivy trailing over high walls, another cat, blue sky, Starlings chattering in a tree. Her own studio! She would do great things in here. Her new life would stimulate new work—and this was the place to do it.

* * *

That same morning there was a new bustle at Matthew Watson's house in Union Street, just beyond the main road separating the town of Wallsend from its famous shipyards. Matthew was a quiet man of deep feelings, sometimes scoffed at by his workmates for being what they called a 'solemn-sides', but he was a reader and a thinker with a sense of history and was proud of the fact that he lived only a few yards from the line of Hadrian's Wall running to its Eastern end at the site of the Roman fort. And while this morning there might be little time for reflection, it seemed to Matthew that what was happening today was part of a great progession of history, of Man's endeavours to improve himself while old empires fell, new ones arose, and the world turned.

A marine carpenter by trade, he had secured work on *Mauretania's* berth, and—he allowed himself a grateful smile—this particular progression of history had not come a moment too soon. Although skilled and mature, he had been laid off by Armstrong-Whitworth's at the end of their last big contract, and in recent months had survived as a jobbing joiner. There had been plenty of work, but little status and less pay—when he had been paid at all. The families of Wallsend were too thrifty to spend much on broken doors and furniture which might be mended for nothing by the man of the house. Matthew had been forced to travel to the neighbouring districts of Byker and Heaton to be more certain of his money. But now he had secure employment at his favourite yard, at least until completion of the great ship, and the knowledge that a regular wage could be given to his wife Alice. She was always careful with money: a clean housewife and a good manager and a loving mother and Matthew only wanted the best for her. Recently, the best had been harder to give. Unlike many of the men whose families struggled against poverty in the surrounding streets, Matthew was no drinker and never gambled, but it had still been a struggle to place a few shillings in Alice's hand on a Friday night. There were three children to feed: Mary, their eldest at sixteen; their second daughter Ellen, who was nine; and little George, a noisy and demanding seven-year-old. It was Mary who had saved them, working in a milliner's shop for five shillings a week. The shop was in South Shields, but it had still been worth her while to spend part of this wage on a tram to North Shields and the ferry across the Tyne each morning and evening: a measure of how desperate the family finances had been.

Mary was a fine girl, thought Matthew: a hard worker with a bright mind, but not without a romantic streak, and one of different character from his own. She was gentle, but could have a wildness about her, fiery and determined, perhaps inherited through the Scots blood of her mother's ancestry. That was why, even when her daughter was a baby, Alice had called her Maisie. She did not seem the prim and proper 'Mary' she had been christened; she was Maisie, proud Maisie the bonny Scots lass with her black hair and fine skin and grey eyes so full of light. Well, thought Matthew, his pretty daughter could give up that job across the river now and have the leisure to find something closer to home.

"Yer away then?" said Alice Watson, standing at the door. "Got yer bait?"

"I have, pet." Matthew tapped his box of sandwiches as he stepped into the morning sunlight, his boots noisy on the pavement. "Canna tell when I'll be back. It'll be a funny day, the first day."

"G'bye Da! G'bye Da!" Ellen and George scurried round their mother as they got ready for school and eyed their father in his work clothes with a kind of awe. Matthew was thankful for work, but did not relish leaving his family. If he could somehow have stayed with them, on permanent holiday if such a thing had been possible, he would gladly have done so. The other men would have called him 'soft' and worse, but

73

it was the love in him, the love of his wife and children. Yet a man must work, he told himself. Without work a man was nothing, to himself and his family. He must leave then, and teach the leaving to his family. "G'bye Da," they moaned again.

"Goodbye now. Be good at school and look after yer Mam 'til I get back the night."

"Fetch us summat from the shipyard, Da," little George pulled at his father's trouser leg, "summat special for us."

"All right, son." Matthew bent down ad kissed his boy's hair. "Canna be sure what it'll be, like. I'll bring you something though."

"Will yer make us a wooden boat?" wheedled George.

"Aye, I might, when I get the time. I'll find out what the big ship's ganna look like and Maisie can draw it for yer. She's a good drawer is Maisie."

At this mention of her name, Maisie put her head out of the upstairs window, her black hair lustrous and almost blue in the bright morning.

"Goodbye, Da!" she shouted. "We'll have tea ready when you get back."

"Aye, there's a good girl." Matthew waved up at her. "Look after yer mother now."

"Take care, Matthew," Alice raised her hand in farewell, "and mind ye don't hurt yersel with all them new machines they've got there now."

"I'll be all right!" he shouted back, striding down the street with his toolbag and his bait-box, the sun in his eyes and new hope in the air.

* * *

Over the next few days Jon helped Philippa bring up the furniture she needed and she unpacked all her paints and brushes. Now the attic really was a studio, filled with the stimulating smells of paint, varnish, and linseed oil.

The hot weather continued, flooding the little house with the colours and scents of Summer. Mrs. Hutchinson busied herself with cooking and cleaning; tradesmen called to offer milk, meat, coal, and tea, the bright little green and golden tea-cart being a favourite of Philippa's, the jolly tea-man winking at her and promising to bring a specially decorated tea-caddy.

Philippa went into Newcastle and ordered two large canvases. They were delivered a few days later and she set one of them up on an easel, but did not begin the painting of the ship she had so long imagined. Instead she made sketches from the studio window of cats curled up in the sunshine, executed a quick watercolour of the front door with its honeysuckle, and even copied the patterns and colours from some of the bricks in the back lane wall, much to the astonishment of a passing neighbour. She could not bring herself to begin the large painting until she felt more settled…but when would that be? Still unused to the rhythms of life in the new house, yet fascinated by them, she feared she might never settle to what she knew must be her great work.

Jon left early each morning and was often not home until after six o'clock. Day after day Philippa told herself that these long hours were her own and that there was no reason to further delay the painting, yet she was ill at ease and frequently distracted by Mrs. Hutchinson, who would arrive on the earliest tram from Heaton and never leave until she had washed up from dinner. At first Philippa thought her a loud and common woman. She was tall and broad without being fat, and had an intimidating, almost masculine, appearance. She spoke in a coarse Geordie voice, using words that Philippa could scarcely understand and expressions that were a complete mystery to her. She seemed often to be in glum spirits, but the severity of her face was relieved by a pair of girlishly sweet cornflower blue eyes; and when the two women began to relax into their relationship of inexperienced mistress and hard-working servant, Philippa discovered a jolly soul could shine through those eyes. It was some time before she learned of Mrs. Hutchinson's rescue from abject poverty. Jon's mother had found her a temporary position as a maid with one of the wealthy Heaton families, and with promotion to cook-housekeeper, she had been sent on to Philippa and Jon. For this she was unreservedly grateful to the Ferris family, and extremely deferential to Jon, referring to him as 'the young master'. Philippa found this old-fashioned and funny, but realised she should never let Mrs. Hutchinson hear as much as a giggle.

Mrs. Hutchinson was full of energy, and her ceaseless bustle both entertained and bewildered Philippa.

"Noo divvent worry aboot a thing, Madam," she would say. "Aa'm in charge."

Indeed she was. Within a week she had established a routine to delight the most meticulous Sergeant-Major. Mondays were washing days. She would turn up in her oldest clothes, wearing a pair of ancient shoes without stockings and a scarf round her head. While water was heated in the gas-fired boiler, she would set up the heavy mangle in the back yard and hang a pair of washing lines across the back lane.

"What on Earth is that?" exclaimed Philippa on the first of these washing days as Mrs. Hutchinson strode through the scullery brandishing a heavy wooden stave.

"Why it's me owld poss-stick, Madam. The one Aa found here was a useless spelk of a thing. Aa brought this'n aal the way on the tram th' morning." With this she began to 'poss' the soaking bed-linen as if she were digging a mine shaft. "Mind oot for yer skirt and yer nice shoes noo," she added, suds flying all over the yard.

She worked the mangle like a seaman hauling in an anchor, then hung out the washing, making white billows across the back lane. But this was not the limit of her washday exertions.

"Mind Aa'm ganna scoot the yard, Madam!" she would call to Philippa, then empty troughs of soapy water over the yard, followed by buckets of clean cold water, 'scooting' it out with a heavy broom until the flagstones glistened and suds trickled away down the cobbled lane. "My, that was a morning's work and no mistake!" she would smile to Philippa. "Noo what'll ye be wanting for supper when the young master comes back?"

"You could call Mrs. Hutchinson a treasure—amongst other things." Philippa's smile to Jon over dinner was humourless. "You should see her work. She's got arms like a village blacksmith. In fact you should take her down to the yard; your ship would be finished in a month with her 'in charge' as she puts it."

"I'm glad she's doing everything for you. I do wonder

what goes on here you know, every day while I'm away. I think about you all the time. Anyway, Mrs. H. Yes, Mother found her a job you know, from terrible poverty. She's a remarkable woman. I'm glad you two get on all right."

"But that's just it, Jon. I don't think we *do* get on. I can't undertsand half of what she's saying—and I do think we might send things out to a laundry."

"Good Heavens, why, when we've got the indefatigable Mrs. H?"

Philippa clenched her fists.

"But you've no idea what it's like here on a Monday, Jon. There's no peace. I can't get any work done. The place is flooded out. You'd think she'd been in the Navy or something."

"Ah well you see," Jon explained with a careless smile, "it's something of a tradition up here. We do our washing on a Monday. Don't know why, really—but I suppose Monday's as good a day as any. At least she's keeping the place clean. And look at my shirts…" He held his shirt-front with a grin. "Splendid. I should just keep out of her way, Darling: go up to the studio or out for a stroll. I believe there's a very high-class grocer's just up Saint George's Terrace. They do marvellous hams and pickles and things—and cheeses. Now I think about it, we should have some. You might discover the shop on your next walk."

On Tuesdays Mrs. Hutchinson would be back to do the ironing, a process interrupted only by her running battles with the local cats. Next to dirt—or 'dort' as she called it—cats had somehow earned her particular hatred, and they approached the open scullery door at their peril.

"Geroot! Oot!" she would yell, rushing outside with rolled up tea-towel and heavy boot at the ready. "Aa'l skelp the buggers if they come in here! And Aa won't hear ye taking pity on them and feeding them, Madam. They've got dorty bottoms and they're covered with fleas an' aall."

Wednesdays were baking days, with Mrs. Hutchinson bashing dough on the kitchen table and the house filled with delicious smells. Although she was disturbed by the relentless fever of Mrs. Hutchinson's work, Philippa had to admit she liked baking days. She would steal into the kitchen like a naughty girl and eye the scones hungrily. Mrs. Hutchinson made twenty-four at a time: so great a number that she obviously felt no shame in eating three or four herself as they came out of the oven.

"Haway, Madam," she would say, holding out the tray of new scones, "help yersel." Then, when Philippa had taken a second or a third, she would flash her innocent blue-eyed smile. "Eee, Madam, we'll both be as fat as butter! Aa'll make rock buns next week. They're aal sugary and we'll be fatter than ever!"

Thursday was Mrs. Hutchinson's day off: an opportunity for Philippa to feel she might reclaim the house as her own. Yet she was assailed by doubts. Perhaps she was doing this all wrong. She had never been responsible for servants before; she wanted to be both firm and kindly but could not find the right tone. And this large, capable, earthy woman—who seeemd to be successful housekeeper, cook, mother, nurse, and wardress all at the same time—managed to annoy her at every turn. Mrs. Hutchinson wasn't a bad woman, thought Philippa, just coarse and cheery. At least she wasn't glum; that would have been unbearable. Perhaps Jon was right when he told her just to ignore the woman's work, engage in a little friendly gossip, then let her get on. All the same, orders had to be given and her own life led: the life of an artist, not of some surrogate daughter to this noisy woman. Oh, surely it would all work out. Philippa stared at the hot blue sky. Even the Summer seemed relentless this year. Surely it would all work out.

When Mrs. Hutchinson re-appeared on Friday—cleaning day—all Philippa's doubts and anxieties returned. The house was virtually dismantled for sweeping and dusting; then everything put back again by this woman who might have accomplished all the labours of Hercules in a single morning. After that came the business of the front step, which led to a crisis for Jon and Philippa.

"Mind oot, Madam," announced Mrs. Hutchinson, "Aa'm just ganna clean the front."

"It's very early, Mrs. Hutchinson, and I think I should like to take the sunshine here; just soak it up for a little while, you know." Philippa felt no need to explain in any greater detail why she wanted to lounge at the front door, smelling the honeysuckle.

"Haway noo, Aa've gotta wash the front step."

"Really," Philippa was keeping her temper, "I'm sure there's no need today. You washed it last week. Nobody else here seems to do it."

"Aye well, there's plenty of posh and idle folk in Jesmond and Aa dare say they think it's beneath them to have a woman washing a front step, but Aa wouldn't be associated with a hoose like that. Why in Wallsend they dee it every morning. Noo ye gerraway upstairs and dee a bit of yer picture and Aa'll wash the step and that'll be that."

"Wash the bloody step then!" Philippa stormed upstairs. "Just keep out of my way while you're doing it!"

She slammed the studio door. The woman was infuriating—and insolent. She would have to go. She would have it out with Jon, once and for all. She would! By the time Jon came home that evening she had calmed down sufficiently to make her point with a cool head.

"This business of washing the front step, Jon: it's ludicrous. We must be a laughing-stock in the street if anyone sees her sloshing water about."

"No, no." Jon's absolute seriousness was already exasperating Philippa. "No, I'm afraid you'll have to accept it, Darling. They do it all over Newcastle—at least in the poorer parts. Mrs. H will be jolly proud of our nice clean step, just you see if I'm not right."

"Yes, but we're not in a poor part of Newcastle, are we? This is supposed to be the respectable end, isn't it?"

Jon put down his glass of sherry. He would say what he had to say; there was no escaping it.

"Don't disappoint me, Darling."

"What do you mean?"

He did not look at her; felt her voice harden.

"What do you mean?" she asked again, very harshly.

"You know what I mean," he answered. "I hoped you wouldn't be snobbish about…well, people like Mrs. Hutchinson. It's not their fault, you know."

"Snobbish, am I?" Her voice was rising and Jon was wincing inside, but he told himself he would stand up for what he believed was right. Philippa would have to learn if she was to be happy—and he wanted her to be happy, despite this horrible moment. "Well, if I'm snobbish, you're just condescending. You seem to be at ease with the Mrs. Hutchinsons of this world and you think you're being nice to them, but you just sound pompous and stand-offish. You've got nothing in common with these dreadful people; don't pretend to just because your father employs a few servants. You can be paternal with them if you like, but I'm not used to such common creatures. Why should I be? They come from a different world."

"No, they don't." Jon faced Philippa with a new resolve in his voice. "We're all part of the same world—which you've forgotten because you're upset and angry. You must understand, Darling: the servants here and at the old house in Heaton or wherever we might live, they're all part of the family. Why, I grew up with people like Betty and Mrs. Hutchinson. They can be a little rough round the edges but they mean well. They're a part of our lives, and they look to us to, well, look after them. If it's all a bit strange and new to you, why not let me help? It's so easy, really it is."

"No, it's not easy; not with that dreadful woman in the house. What you seem to think is cheery and forthright, I call damned insolent. I've never had to put up with such manners or language."

"Well, your own language won't have endeared you to Mrs. Hutchinson, or anyone else of her class. She'll not think you're a perfect lady any more."

"Let her think what she likes," Philippa stood up, "and let her be damned! I'll swear at my servants if I want to, and I'll dismiss them if I want to, and I'll not be judged by scum like her!"

Somewhere, Jon found a calm voice.

"You'd do well to remember that it's 'scum like her' who keep 'people like you' in the way to which you've become accustomed."

"I don't have to tolerate this," she raged. "You can be as stuffy and as boring as my father—and that's saying something! And you don't understand what I'm going through here. You vanish into your blasted shipyard every day and I'm left here with that woman and there's no peace in the house. I can't get any work done for her shouting and beating about. I want rid of her!" She brought her fists down hard on to the table, and Jon saw a wild fire in her eyes. "I want rid of her, Jon. I mean to be my own woman in my own house!"

"All right then." Jon forced himself to smile. He was furious, but there would be no benefit in matching Philippa's anger with his own. There would be a better way. "All right. We'll speak to Mother about it. It'll not be easy—she set us up with Mrs. Hutchinson, you know; she thought she was doing the best thing. Anyway, we'll speak to Mother; she may be able to find someone else. I mean you don't see yourself managing here alone, do you?" Philippa did not answer. "So we'll speak to Mother." She made no reply. "Will that please you?" Jon was losing his temper. "Well, will it?"

"Yes!" she screamed, and rushed out of the room.

It took more than a day to recover from this quarrel. Jon was not sure they had recovered from it at all, but normality of a sort settled back into the house and he thought it best to show a brisk and open manner when he returned home.

"I shall speak to Mother tomorrow," he announced, "unless of course you'd rather…"

"I…I've been thinking, Jon," Philippa interrupted

with a tight-lipped smile. "Perhaps I was hasty about Mrs. Hutchinson." She would try again if only Jon wouldn't be stuffy about it; if only he didn't say something pompous and silly and take sides with his family; if only he could be warm and loving about it: hold her, kiss her, understand her, love her—then it would be all right. "Perhaps she might stay after all. I don't want to upset your family. They've been very good to me and I...well, I think I should try to get on with Mrs. Hutchinson. She is a coarse woman, I shan't say otherwise, and she's not the type of housekeeper I should have chosen myself, but she has her good points and perhaps, as you say, if I keep out of her way a little more...d'you think that would be best?" She looked appealingly at him. Would he see she was nearly in tears? Would he understand? Would he love her? He could mend all this or ruin her happiness in a moment. Could he understand? "Jon, d'you think...?"

"Yes, Darling." He smiled broadly from where he stood at the window, relaxed against the wall, half looking out at the evening sunshine, then looking at her fully, but not moving from the window. "Yes, excellent—and very sensible of you. I know her sort can take a little getting used to. I might have a word with her myself, tell her to mind her manners and pipe down a bit. How's that?"

"That's...very considerate of you."

'Oh, why does he not come to me and love me,' thought Philippa, 'take me, love me? Why does he not prove his love? Prove it, prove it!'

* * *

Matthew Watson's first job at the yard had been completing the oaken deck of the berth. Now, with a team of joiners and carpenters, he was enagaged in setting up three rows of massive wooden blocks which would support the gigantic hull. The keel would rest on top of the central row, the longest; the shorter rows on either side were to support the bilges. The positioning of these blocks was crucial to the initial stability of the growing ship. Jon arrived on the berth one morning to find two foremen, surrounded by a group of workmen, arguing over a plan. One of the foremen caught sight of Jon and called to him.

"Excuse me, sir! Are you one of the gentlemen from the drawing-loft?"

"No, I'm from Parsons'."

"Oh. Well, sir, we wondered if you might make sense of this plan. I canna see what they mean about these last few blocks."

"It's bloody wrong, man!" The other foreman looked as ill-tempered as he sounded, and thrust a dirty finger at the offending plan. "And thisun'll not know any better." He casually indicated Jon with flick of his elbow.

"You could be right," smiled Jon, feeling more than a little uneasy when surrounded by these hard, dark, angry men, but determined to stand his ground and help if he could. It was an encounter with the real, rough-edged, daily business of building the ship: he told himself to relish it. He had also taken an instant dislike to the second foreman, and sensed the presence of a bully. If he could defuse the situation, he should. "Let me see then. What's it all about? I'm not qualified to make any decsions about where these blocks go, but I might be able to read the plan for you."

"I can read the bloody plan meself," grunted the foreman. "Who does he think he is?"

"Give it over, Walker," demanded the first foreman. "No use in being pig-headed." He took the plan from the sullen Walker and held it out for Jon's inspection. "Here you are, sir."

"Let's see now," said Jon as cheerfully as he could, eager to calm the troubled atmosphere. "Well," he turned the paper a few times, "the rows look clear enough, but there's no scale on here, not as far as I can see. In my opinion it's not the proper plan of the berth floor at all, just a guide drawing. There'll be a properly-measured full plan somewhere." He returned the paper to the first foreman. "D'you mean to say you've been working from that all the time?"

Walker laughed, and muttered: "Bloody genius, isn't he?"

"No, sir," the first foreman explained. "There is a full plan, but Mister Coulson from the drawing-loft is off sick and we couldn't get hold of it today. We were given this by the clerk."

Walker stepped forward.

"I told you it was no bloody good! How can we do decent work when these buggers give us nowt but rubbish? I tell yer," he ranted on, "it's a conspiracy to ruin us all. Crooked bosses and daft clerks makin' us look stupid from the start. We'll be sacked if these blocks divvent gan in the right place an' I'll be given the blame, nee doubt aboot that! Give me that bloody thing!" He tore the plan from the other's grasp and stode off up the berth shouting: "I'll see who's ganna put this right!"

"I'm sorry, sir," said the first foreman. "I'll have to go after him."

Jon was left with the other workmen.

"Who's in charge here?" he asked.

"I am, sir. Matthew Watson."

"Right. I imagine you and the men now have some time off while those two sort it out." Jon shared the good-humoured smile that flickered around the group. "They could be a while…let's hope so."

"Aye, sir. We're not sorry to see the back of Mister Walker."

"I'll remember to keep out of his way."

"Right you are, sir." Matthew seemed reluctant to leave as the others drifted away. "Thanks for trying to help."

"No help really. You'd best wait for the right plan to turn up."

The two men found themselves alone.

"You an engineer, sir, up at Parsons'?"

"Yes. My name is Ferris. I'll be working on the turbines. At the moment I'm spending as much time as I can at the berth. I want to see her from the start, if you know what I mean."

"Very wise, Mister Ferris. I must say I'd like to see the turbines under construction 'fore they go in. Don't suppose I'll get the chance like. A marvellous invention of Sir Charles."

"Yes indeed." Jon liked this man immediately and warmed to his enthusiasm. "Very well, I'll remember you. If and when I'm able, I'll take you up to the works. Can't promise, but I'll do what I can if you really want to see."

"I appreciate that very much, Mister Ferris."

"Goodbye then."

* * *

Philippa had set up her large canvas for the ship painting. Its final coat of white primer was drying in the sunny studio, but as she stood at the window looking back at the easel she knew she could not yet begin the picture. Her ideas for its composition seemed to have evaporated. She had done sketch after sketch that morning, but not one of them had satisfied her. Now despair sucked out her resolve. The studio was so full of light, so full of her equipment and materials, so full of the blank canvas staring at her like a second window—a window on to nothing. The place was so full; her heart and mind so empty. She went out, banging the door behind her.

The sunny streets were still and empty, with only the passing of an occasional train to disturb the quiet middle of the day. The trains reminded her of Jon. She might ask him to show her the shipyard where she might discover a smell or sight or sound or texture to break her deadlock. Yet she shrank from asking. There would no doubt be practical difficulties in arranging a visit, but apart from that she did not really wish to go, to see his place of work, to be pointed out as the engineer's wife, to experience the actual noisome place that seemed to have claimed his heart. What heart?, she wondered. What heart, indeed! Her heels rang on the pavements, echoing emptiness. In the silent, sun-beaten Jesmond streets, she thought him a poor lover. She thought herself already an unhappy wife, betrayed by her own emotions, unable to find contentment with anything, a failure herself, failed by the man who had promised never to fail her. She walked back to the house. Only the honeysuckle seemed fresh, alive, and innocent, growing its own way at the door, unconcerned with human hopes and miseries, loyal only to the mysterious forces that ran within it, and blessedly ignorant even of those. Why, she thought, could humans not be like that? Then she opened the door, found the second post of the day, and picked up the letter which would change everything. It was from Robert Gough.

28,Cavendish Square,

London.

July 7th, 1904.

My Dear Mrs. Ferris,

I trust you will remember me from our fortunate, and I may say delightful, meeting at Alnmouth. I certainly should not forget you, nor the pleasure of our easy conversation.

I thought I should remind you that after the Summer holidays there is to be an exhibition of new advertising posters at the offices of my employers in London, and that a number of our French colleagues will be present. You might like to come down.

Certainly you would be more than welcome, and perhaps pick up a flavour of what is happening in our business. The actual date is not yet fixed, but is likely to be in late September or early October. I felt it wise to give you as much notice as possible, Newcastle being so far away. Of course I put no obligation upon you, but I feel certain this idea will interest you. Please let me know if you decide to come and it will be my pleasure to arrange as much as I can to make it a memorable visit.

I do hope you are well, and that your husband finds himself successfully engaged upon his great undertaking. Please pass on to him my very best wishes.

Yours most sincerely

Robert Gough.

The immediate effect of this letter was to send Philippa running upstairs, suddenly alive with enthusiasm. She threw off her hat and dashed into the studio, reading the letter over and over again at the sunny window. Now the studio did not seem a place of blank frustration, but once again the powerhouse of her imagination. Robert's approach was so bold and modern, polite yet easygoing, formal yet fresh: as bright and as forward-looking as her own mind. Dullness and misery were not her true temper; this was her true temper! Of course she would go and see the exhibition; she could stay with her artist friends in Chelsea and tell them about her successes—and it would be wonderful to see Robert again, and perhaps visit the house in Cavendish Square, such a good address. Robert Gough: the signature was in blue ink, very thick and dark. She stared into the blue where the pen had flowed over the paper, a blue enlivened by the gold of the sunlight pouring in at the window, with the very tiniest flecks of silver in the ink, as if some chemical had oxidised there and now lay on the paper to throw off a silvery sparkle. A new wave of smiles broke and flooded through her…blue, and gold, and silver!

* * *

"You've started it! Well done!" With an arm round Philippa's waist, Jon was admiring the canvas. It was now washed with a rich, dark blue. "It's a wonderful blue," he continued, "the blue of infinity. Brilliantly modern."

"We will see the ship head-on," explained Philippa slowly, "as if she's actually pointing at us out of the canvas. She is pointing North, so we are looking South, yes? To the left of the canvas the sun has risen in the East and all the highlights of the ship will be picked out in gold; to the right there's a blazing full moon, and all the highlights will be in silver."

Jon was filled with wonder.

"The fantasy of it," he breathed. "Unique."

"Yes," she smiled pertly, "it will be quite fantastic."

That evening after dinner they climbed the stairs again to admire the rich wash of blue, now seeming to have dried to an even more translucent hue, as if another piece of sky had been brought into the room to rival the midsummer light at the window. They stood there together, holding hands on the warm sill, looking out at the night. It was calm, with the first stars appearing. Tall trees were visible beyond the roof-tops, crowned with green and gold, their uppermost leaves just losing the last rays of sunset. The room reminded Jon of a storybook nursery, high up in some great house, where a little boy might kneel on his bed and stare out of the window, tempted by the swaying tops of golden trees, not wanting to go to sleep but marvelling at the stars, and wondering what the world was doing in the Summer night outside.

For the first time in days Jon felt at peace in his home. Philippa was warm and quiet beside him and tonight she seemed particularly beautiful, as if charged with a new vitality and wonder, her hair as rich as he had ever seen it. The hair was a delight and a fascination to him, the way it curved and was full of colours. It was so delicious a chestnut brown, but with red, gold, black, and even a greenish yellow in tiny strands of it against the light. Nothing seemed more glorious than its shining cascade enfolded in his arms. It swept in a perfect double curve from her creamy brow and fell about the rounded whiteness of her shoulders: shoulders he now kissed and kissed and kissed while Philippa arched her neck and smiled into the blue night. Then they relaxed, looked out again on to the roof-tops, and counted the sounds: the last train passing, a distant ship hooting on the Tyne, the Swing Bridge answering, someone playing a piano. It was perhaps two houses away, the tune scarcely recognizable. Jon hoped it might be Chopin; what could have been more perfect for this night than one of his nocturnes? But he could not tell. He could only let his thoughts drift with the music. Was it not strange to realise that there was always something beyond one's control, unknown and unknowable? Perhaps it was stranger still that people should wish it otherwise. How could anyone hope to control every aspect of an experience, why should they hope to? Yet he wished the music to be Chopin; wished for his own idea of perfection. Was it not embodied in his darling Philippa? A pain ran through Jon, the pain of her beauty and his longing. It was a pain he wanted to suffer for ever, yet feared he might never feel again.

CHAPTER FIVE

The Girl from the River

In August 1904, *Mauretania's* keel was laid. From this most crucial part her entire structure would spring. It lay like a rigid reptile on the central row of blocks, its height determining the distance between the still-to-be-created outer and inner skins of the hull. When Jon walked along the floor of the berth for a first look at the keel, he imagined it sprouting the steel ribs which would begin the ship's climb to the ringing glass roof far above.

Sun sweltered down on to the noisy floor as Jon made his way past groups of workmen, off the berth, and up to the drawing-loft. There, in that enormous room, the plans of the ship were to be enlarged to actual size, so that each part of her—ribs, plates, decks, companionways, and a thousand others—could be fabricated and added to the great structure.

"D'ye like it then, sir?" One of the workmen called to Jon as he passed. Jon turned to see a grey-capped smiling face, a dark arm saluting him cheerily then slapping the side of the keel with affectious as it pointed away from them like a colossal battering-ram ready to be rolled by Barbarian hands against the walls of some ancient city. "Canny bit o' work this, eh? It's not every day ye get to pat a big Mary on the bottom!"

"She'll have a fatter bottom yet!" grinned Jon in reply. No doubt of it, this job had lightened spirits all along the river.

Jon was lucky to arrive in the drawing-loft at a

spectacular moment. The vast blackboard-painted floor had been cleared and the draughtsmen's and tracers' desks re-aligned down one side. The place had a schoolroom atmosphere with its smells of paper, ink, pencils, and a hint of chalk-dust in the air; the women tracers standing around the edges of the floor in their long skirts and aprons looked like teachers about to discipline a school assembly, but instead there was an air of amused expectancy. A dozen strange faces peered in at the corridor windows and squeezed through the doors to witness the scene. Amongst them Jon recognized Matthew Watson and nodded acknowledgement to him across the room. Beside Matthew stood a slender, black-haired girl holding a large cardboard folder: clearly not a tracer for she wore no apron and looked about her with the anxiety of a stranger; at the same time Jon thought she looked capable and mature for her years, and that she shared Matthew's broad clear brow: perhaps a daughter or a niece being shown this almost ceremonial moment in the creation of the ship.

Today, the waistcoated and arm-banded draughtsmen were wearing incongruous carpet-slippers, to much giggling and ribald comment. Four of them appeared at the far end of the long room, struggling with what looked like a sagging flagpole. Jon saw it was a gigantic roll of paper. With some difficulty, this was set down and straightened, then, to cheers from the onlookers, it was rolled out like a parchment carpet. It crackled along the floor, Jon and a group of spectators on one side, Matthew and the black-haired girl amongst others opposite him. She had remarkable eyes, even at this distance: very pale blue, perhaps even grey. How uncommon, he thought, and beautiful…and suddenly she smiled up at Matthew and hugged his arm. Yes, a daughter or a niece, thought Jon, loving and demonstrative, too. He wondered, if he had had a sister, how she might have hugged his own father's arm: rather differently from this, he imagined, and no doubt in a better dress. This girl wore coarse clothes which looked too big for her, but her lot seemed better than many a working family's daughter: she had polished shoes while some had none, she was clean, and she looked happy. The girl glanced down again, tugged Matthew's arm and said something, pointing at the unrolled paper. Amongst the cheering and chattering, Jon could not hear what it was. He followed her gaze to the floor. Between them spread an intricate plan of *Mauretania's* bow section, reflecting light up at their faces: a flattened ghost of half the ship which would be quickened into life by the tracers, already preparing to enlarge sections of the plan to actual size.

The spectators were dispersing; Jon found himself squeezing through a door near Matthew Watson and the girl, protecting her folder from the crush of people.

"'Morning, sir," said Matthew. "It's a few years since I've seen that done."

"Good morning. Yes, a marvellous moment."

Matthew must have seen Jon staring at the girl's grey eyes, then turning swiftly away.

"This is my daughter Mary," he explained, "but we call her Maisie at home like." Jon looked again into the grey eyes. They were ill at ease, but not timid. "Mary, this is Mister Ferris, one of the gentlemen working on the engines at Parsons."

The girl bobbed a brief curtsey, awkward in the crowded corridor, doubly awkward with the folder in her hands. Jon sensed her dislike of being presented this way.

"How do you do?" said Jon.

"All right, sir." Like her father's, her Tyneside accent

was mellowed by an almost Scottish lilt. She was self-contained, perhaps outwardly unsure in the company of strangers, but calm inside, deeply quiet, peaceful. Sensing it in her made Jon aware that he lacked this quality—or lacked it now. He reflected that he might have been innocently happy once, before the sudden strains of a new career and a new wife, but could not remember it perfectly. The realization saddened him, then he determined to pay it no further attention. The girl was speaking again. "I work in South Shields," she added, as if compelled to say something else.

"Oh dear," smiled Jon. "Wrong side of the river." He wished instantly that he had not said it: aware that such banter was inappropriate, would be misunderstood by these people, and would mark him out as a member of his own class—an arrogant snob from the grand houses of Newcastle; remote, unfeeling, crass, and stupid.

"They don't think so over there, sir." She was rebuking him, but with a gentle smile. Perhaps he was not completely unforgiven.

"No, of course not. I'm sorry. It was meant as a joke, also that you might be better off with a job on this side of the river, like your father."

"Aye," said Matthew, "she would be an' all. That's what the lass is here for today. I'm ganna get her in at the yard here as a tracer if I can."

"Oh, very good, I see."

They were moving down the corridor, the other people dispersing to their work. Sunlight splashed in through the large windows; the din of the berth intruding; blue-black lights in the girl's hair and the loose dress drawn in to reveal her youthful figure; a stirring in Jon's groin. Matthew stopped.

"D'you think she's got a chance, Mister Ferris?"

"I—I really couldn't say. Not my department at all. But I hope so." Jon turned to the girl. "I truly hope so, Miss. Watson. I'm sure they'll be taking on more tracers: it's going to be a very big job—for all of us."

They were looking at each other, suddenly as equals. Jon felt himself absolved, but only just.

"Show Mister Ferris your drawings then. She's a good drawer, sir."

"Oh no, Da!" the girl protested. "Mister Ferris must be a very busy man. He won't want to be bothered with these like."

"Actually, I do." Jon saw the girl was blushing, and felt his own cheeks redden. "I should very much like to see them. My wife's an artist, I know what I'm looking at, or like to think I do."

Why, thought Jon, did he have to say something as silly as that to the girl; and why had he felt compelled to mention Philippa? Her painting would be nothing like this girl's drawing—just as she herself was nothing like this slender, pale, uncertain body in front of him. He should not have said it; should not have said anything.

"There you are lass!" Her father was holding the folder as she took out a sheet of paper. Jon expected to see a sketch of houses, ships, or the river; instead he was presented with a montage of finely-drawn human heads: a woman with loosely-dressed hair, a baby contemplating something at its feet, a little boy frowning at a playmate, two men with large moustaches, a soldier wearing a Durham Light Infantry cap. The portraits were like old-fashioned steel engravings and

98

perhaps laboriously done, but Jon saw that they transcended the conventional with a real spark of humanity in the faces. There was something else too, quite unexpected: a charm, a delicacy, a delight with almost the sweetness of a Watteau. Jon held the drawing for what seemed a long time, unable to say anything.

"…some of me family," the girl was explaining, as if she had now lost her shyness and was eager to talk, "me little brother, and two of me uncles." She looked up at Jon with absolute candour. "D'you think they're any good?"

"Yes, yes I do." He found his voice as he was handing back the paper and it was being returned to the folder. "Yes, they are very fine indeed. If you can draw as well as that you'll have no difficulty with the work of a tracer, although of course it's a different skill. Really," he smiled honestly, "they are very good. I'm most impressed. I'm afraid I can only draw diagrams, and then not particularly well." He saw the girl was pleased, simply and openly, and was smiling up at her father again. He drew breath to add what a pricking conscience told him not to say. "You might show me other pictures you've done—when you can, that is." He tried to say it casually, despite the beatings of his heart, "I hope you'll be good enough to let me know if you secure a position here. Your father can tell me."

"I'm sure that's very kind of you, Mister Ferris." Matthew was ushering his daughter away down the corridor. "We shouldn't keep you longer. Say Goodbye properly, lass, and be thankful!"

"I am." The grey eyes turned sweetly upon Jon again. "Goodbye, Mister Ferris."

"Goodbye…Maisie."

The grey eyes dropped and she turned and walked away, thin and delicate from behind, the luscious black hair rich above the poor dress. He should not have been so familiar, he thought. His father would have dealt perfectly with these people and been respected by them without this gauche insistence on a friendship with a strange young girl—a friendship which would only be regarded on all sides as improper. Yet he had not been able to help himself; and he realised he was happy. For God's sake, he thought, he had done nothing wrong; had spoken only the truth. Her drawings were remarkable and he did hope she found a job as a tracer. But he was stabbed by guilt. This truth was not the whole truth. At home he had a beautiful and high-spirited wife whose very different eyes would pierce his soul.

* * *

Philippa stood alone at the her studio window, hot sunshine pouring on to her hands from another open blue sky above the Jesmond roofscape. The cats were asleep in their comfortable hiding-places, the prim streets were empty of people and traffic, the birds twittered along the gutters: all seemed the same on another Summer afternoon—yet all was not the same. Jon had come home full of stories of some dreadful people at the shipyard: of workmen with struggling families and some pathetic girl who sketched in her spare time and was looking for work in the drawing-office. She didn't wish to know such people! Why should she have to hear about them? She wouldn't listen to any more about them! And there had been an evening of strained silence, not perfectly repaired by a stroll in the warm night air. Now Jon was back at the yard again. Philippa's painting stood on its easel behind her: completed, glowing, commanding her attention even when she wasn't looking at it. The sing-song cry of an invisible rag-and-bone man drifted up as he trundled his barrow somewhere through the back lanes:

"Rags, bottles, or bo-ens! Any rags, bottles, or bo-ens?"

How she hated it! Not the sound itself, which she had to admit was romantic in its own way, but the echoes it brought of working-class life by the river, a life of poverty and hardship lived in the 'low streets' she had never visited: a haunting, heart-squeezing distillation of everything she had striven to avoid for so long, and to which Jon seemed to be bringing her. She was convinced that by slow and devious means he was determined to involve her in the grimy concerns of shipyard life and the common people for which he seemed to have so much respect. She was certain they would not respect him, other than in a shallow display of deference to the superior classes. His concern seemed not only vulgar, but foolish. Well, she would have none of it! How glad she would be to escape to London for a while. She turned from the window. There was the picture: finished, glowing and glorious, utterly new and modern and absolutely her own. She would take up Robert Gough's offer, meet him, go to the poster exhibition, and arrange to have her own picture exhibited in a London gallery. A thrill of confidence ran through her: this move, surely, would free her from what she now dared to call the grim boredom of her marriage and set her artistic career on a new and glittering path. It was the right path too, she thought, inevitable from the moment she had claimed this bare wooden room as her new studio. She should not feel uneasy about taking it; after all, she was doing nothing wrong: visiting London and enlarging her circle of professional acquaintances was a natural part of her career. Yet a worm of guilt turned in her. Down at the shipyard—at this very moment of her resolve to go away, pursue her selfish ends, and see another man—was her new husband with his bright blue eyes and handsome face and tender mouth and simple, boyish love for her. She told herself she should be tender and simple, too; she should be loving and faithful and do her best to learn new ways and understand; but she turned to face the painting once more. A thrill ran through her body as she saw the steel-blue bows of the imagined ship thrust an almost frightening perspective out of the canvas, saw the dazzle of sunlight and gleam of moonlight she had created in this industrial fantasy suddenly, brilliantly, sweetly, defiantly, magically made real—and a mad glee came to crease her face, wiping out everything but itself and the pounding of her heart.

* * *

Maisie Watson clattered down the cobbles in her new shoes, facing into the warm wind which still came across the river from the South-West, bringing yet more Summer sunshine after months of heat. New shoes for a new job, and a new tracer's apron folded into her bag. She had been lucky, and she knew it, but there hadn't been much time or money for a celebration, just the satisfying knowledge that she wouldn't have to trail all the way over the ferry to the shop in South Shields, that now she'd be bringing another good wage into the family, and that she could hold her head up and say she was a junior tracer at Swan's working on the new big ship. Some job for a lass that was!

She turned out of Union Street towards the shipyard, joining the stream of workers making their early-morning way down to the river. Women were scarce in the crowd, and already she was having to get used to the cheeky shouts and jokes of the men as they passed her—but on the whole, those who saw she was making her way to the drawing-loft were cheerful and respectful to her. She was a working lass, and a lass in work like that would be proud and clever and haughty.

The wind blew against her face and neck; still warm, but with a sour edge to it, as if this heat had gone on long enough and a thunderstorm was needed to clear the air. A fresh wind off the sea would have been nice, she thought, and perhaps done something to clear her head. She felt as if she had caught a cold—'a Summer cold's worse than a Winter one', her mother would have said—and her throat was sore, not bad enough for the doctor, but she would have another disinfectant gargle when she got home, and perhaps a drink of port from Da's bottle before she went to bed. Going to bed was already an attractive idea, and she realised she didn't feel well enough to make the most of a day at work, but she couldn't afford to be off sick, not so soon after just having got the job. She hauled herself up the steps to the loft.

"Get a move on, pet!" said a cheery voice below her. She looked down between the wooden steps and recognized the dapper moustache of Mister Owen, a friend of her father's. "You look as if you're carryin' a ton weight in that bag."

"Oh, hello Mister Owen, I'm just a bit tired that's all. If you see me Da today will you tell him little George did get away to school on time, he was sick in the night like."

"I will, aye—but don't you go worryin' yersel too much about things at home. Yer Ma's in charge there now ye've got this job. Aa'll tell him though if I see him."

Maisie hurried on up the stairs, the clang of the berth seeming to beat in the back of her head.

* * *

"I shall miss you." Jon took the gloved hand and kissed it. "I shall miss you very much."

"And I you."

Steam wraithed up from the edge of the platform as Philippa turned to board the London train. She had not been in the Central Station since her arrival in Newcastle with Jon—and how long ago that now seemed. Today's hoot and rattle of the trains, the cries of the guards, and the shuffle of the passengers and the newspaper-sellers all seemed a noisy and awkward distraction from her ideal of getting away cleanly. She wanted a swift run down to London, and to be unfussily about her own business. Jon's insistence on seeing her off and the busy traffic in the Newcastle streets had made her perilously late.

"Do you have everything you need, Darling?" Jon was looking about him and tipping the porter who had stowed Philippa's dress-case and hatbox.

"Yes, I think so." She hoped fervently that the painting had travelled safely in its bulky package, sent on ahead by mail train. "You shan't worry about me, now."

"You know I shall."

"It's only for a few days. Wish me luck."

The guard blew his whistle.

"You must telegraph me from London!" cried Jon as the train moved out. "To tell me you're safe!"

He stood in the evaporating steam and saw her carried away down cold steel rails.

* * *

Maisie's new shoes, carefully polished, stood neatly together beside her bed. Her hat and her carpet-bag of work things hung on the door, but these ordered details belied the anguish and suffering in the small bedroom at Union Street. Maisie lay sweating near the climax of a fever, her face between the black hair as grey as her nightgown, Doctor Carr folding his bag.

"Be thankful it is not Diptheria," he said to Alice Watson.

"Is it Scarlet Fever then?"

"No, not that either. But your daughter is dangerously ill. If there's no improvement I'll have to take her to the Fever Hospital, but I really don't think that will be necessary. In any case I should prefer to leave her here for the night. She should be all right with good care."

"But for God's sake what is it, Doctor?"

"She has very severe Tonsilitis, but it's complicated by a high fever running through her whole body, as you can see. Her glands are swollen. She'll be in some considerable pain and swallowing and breathing won't be easy for her. But don't be alarmed, I think she's at her worst now and you should see some improvement in the morning. Call me back if she doesn't fall into a more peaceful sleep within a few hours.

Behind all this I think she is generally anaemic, too—very weak, Mrs. Watson. Now the fever will be contagious and you should keep the other children well away. I know that can be difficult with a large family in a small house but you must be strict. At the first signs of their feeling unwell you must give them this: the instructions are written on the labels."

"But that's another two bottles."

"I know. You can pay me when you can; I know you will. Your daughter should recover, Mrs. Watson, but she's going to need warmth and rest and good feeding to see her through next Winter. She could fall prey to something else and be worse even than this."

Carr had seen a dozen Wallsend families lose a child that way, but usually one younger than Maisie. Glandular Fever in a girl of her age could be fatal, but he had caught her at the crisis and he reckoned another dose of the quinine cordial he had left should reduce her temperature and induce sleep. The family was clean and the father had work: she had a good chance, but he remembered with bitterness that he had become a doctor to apply science, not take a gamble. All the same, he had learned that Chance played a powerful hand in these streets. These people, too, were wary of a young doctor: he knew they expected an old man with a frock coat and a military bearing, not a young man lately out of Medical School in Newcastle. Carr went downstairs with the mother; yes, the place was clean enough, the other children diligently sent to school. The girl had a good chance. At the door, the smell of the river came once more to his nostrils, and he longed again for a country practice. At College he and his friends had climbed the tallest buildings in Newcastle and looked to the North: the Cheviot Hills had loomed on the horizon of his homeland in the Borders; the cries of sheep and curlew seeming to reach from his imagination into the heart of the city. Today's yelp of scavenging gulls was a grim reminder that no country airs blew into these houses.

"Promise to call me again if there is no improvement," he repeated, "but your daughter seems to be a fighter. She must have felt ill for days before she collapsed."

"Aye well," said Alice, "the new job, you see. She wouldn't want to lose time."

"No. Well, she has been rather foolish. She will need to be off work for some time. I'll write a note to her employers of course."

"She'll lose the job, Doctor. If she doesn't go back she'll lose it."

"Better lose a job than a life, Mrs. Watson—but yes, I do understand how important it is. I really can't say how long she will be. Good feeding will speed her recovery, once she feels able to eat. I still think she should give up that job and look after herself at home if she wants to be   really well again, perhaps look for another one in the Spring. You must realise her constitution may not tolerate the stress and the cold of Winter if she is out working all hours. Well, good day to you."

CHAPTER SIX
Industry and Art

"It's a good port."

William Ferris filled two glasses. The fine Edinburgh Crystal turned the blood-red wine a bright ruby where it caught electric lamplight from his desk.

"I know it should be sherry before dinner, but I like port. Your mother still prefers that dreadful Madeira," he added with a smile. "What's Philippa's tipple?"

"White wine," smiled Jon. "Champagne when she can get it."

"Shame she couldn't be here for tonight's dinner and the good news," his father continued. "Shame she has to be away at all. How are you managing over in Jesmond there, just you and Mrs. Hutchinson?"

"All right."

"Yes, well don't get *too* used to being a bachelor again. So—you saw the telegram?"

"No, Father," replied Jon, unable to keep annoyance out of his voice. "I'm not all that high up in Parsons' you know, not exactly on the Board. I'm the new boy running round the yard."

"Well," smiled William, "give yourself time. Anyway,

Sir Charles showed it to me himself. A copy went to Swan's of course, direct from Cunard. Swans have the all-clear to build the after section to take the new engines, so you boys really will be able to fit your precious turbines after all. It's been a tricky few weeks. There's always a lot of foot-dragging about anything new, but you can understand how Cunard must have felt. If the new engines failed on the maiden voyage there'd be dreadful loss of public confidence and all that. So, you're under way. Cheers."

Jon took his port. Its colour still entranced him after all these years of knowing his father's tastes, and again the liquid jewel of it on this late Summer night was a poignant reminder of all his rich and happy boyhood days in this great house. Yet a buzz of annoyance fluttered at him as he drank and remembered, like the moth he could see beating the window: an unhappy creature of the night, determined to enter the lighted house from the unknown dark. He pretended his annoyance was about the ship.

"You would have thought Cunard had been through all that," he said, "with turbines already in *Carmania*."

"Ah yes, one of the 'pretty sisters', isn't that what they call her and *Caronia*? But that's just it, my boy: *Carmania's* been a testing-bed for the new engines. Cunard were not going to risk them in *Mauretania* until they knew they weren't going to burn up or shake to pieces or cost the Earth to run. The figures were confidential for a long time, but it's been shown that the turbines are not only faster, but more economical than the normal engines—as of course we might have predicted."

"But the truth is, Father, nothing but the new turbines *can* drive *Mauretania*. You know that."

"Of course. She's a giant, and she needs gigantic

power, but truth is not always admitted when there's money at stake. But really my boy, we're beating the air: the decision's gone through. Let's be pleased about it." William refilled his son's glass, with a shrewd glance into the blue eyes. "You *are* pleased about it, aren't you?"

"Yes, of course. And they'll be very pleased at the yard."

"You'll cable Philippa, will you? Let her know your job is safe?"

"Yes, I expect so. I…I don't always bother her with details of what's going on at the yard. She has her own career you know, chasing these opportunities in London and so on…" His voice trailed into an awkward silence as he felt a penetrating stare. Why did his father have to be so damnably perceptive? And was he now going to bluster, or look hurt and disappointed, or bring the spectre of an unhappy mother into the conversation?

"I'm sorry to hear that," said William, turning away to study the moth still fluttering at the window. "This is hardly a detail: this means you retain your position on an enormously important project at Parsons' and your career can move forward. Shouldn't your wife be interested in that?" William turned to face Jon again. "And tell me, if you *can* tell me, just what she *is* chasing in London."

* * *

Robert Gough had met Philippa at the station. He had not been wearing the check suit she remembered from their first encounter at Alnmouth, but a smart black frock coat. She had noticed how sleek his hair looked and that he had carried a pair of grey gloves in dandyish fashion. The artists she had known before her marriage had not dressed in this way; he seemed an uneasy mixture of an aesthete from the previous century and a businessman of the future, but within minutes of this second meeting she had decided that this was precisely the kind of man she needed to know now.

During their cab ride down Euston Road and Baker Street Robert had assured her that the painting had arrived undamaged and was safely inside his house before going on to Williamson's gallery. While he had talked easily of recent changes in the London streets and their contrast with new developments in Paris, Philippa had lost some of her original excitement at returning to the capital. It had been replaced by guilt. Newly married, she had thought, and already she was sitting alone in a London cab with another man, here at his invitation and her own selfish insistence, her trusting husband left alone at the other end of the country. There were people who would despise her for that; shocked by the improprieties of it. In her imagination she had seen them: Jon's father, his mother, certainly her own family. But what a stuffy lot they were, she had suddenly thought, and dismissed them from her mind, if not entirely from her soul. This business in London was perfectly natural—if not perfectly innocent. Was he leering at her? Surely not: he was friendly, but smart, cool and professional; this was a business visit, and he was—in the most gentlemanly fashion—escorting her to this very smart hotel in Mayfair.

"Would you dine with me tonight?" he had said lightly, almost as if her answer would not have mattered. "A small party at the house, a chance to meet some new people you might like: my partner Burton Sloane; yes, isn't it a funny name? You'd almost think he was an American with a name like that; now I put my mind to it I've no idea where he comes from. And there'll be his charming wife Emily, and another associate of the firm, William Rawlings, and his fiancée Daphne—at least I think they're engaged, one never actually knows with Rawlings, he's quite a fellow. You can show your painting to them: I've had it put on an easel in the drawing-room: looks very good. No really. One should say something better than 'very good'; it's a truly daring piece of work; it'll certainly set them talking at old Williamson's. To be perfectly honest, I'm not sure that's the right gallery for it, but I suppose you were lucky to get it in anywhere among the established places, it's so unusual. Well then, shall I send my motor-car at eight?"

She had agreed to everything with a smile, had climbed excitedly aboard the motor-car at eight o'clock, rattled North again into Cavendish Square, and was now seated at Robert Gough's round rosewood dining table, opposite her host and between his partner Sloane and his associate Rawlings.

Philippa reckoned that Robert Gough could be scarcely older than herself, but he had the manner of a much older man. She liked that; found him worldly and sophisticated and charming and clever; 'amusing' was the word that came to her. But there was something unsettling about his maturity, too. Behind his suave gaiety she found him rather old-fashioned; languid, yet formal and precise. He seemed to promise the excitement of success, yet was not himself exciting—despite her private wish that he should be.

It occurred to Philippa that the interior of his house was the perfect expression of her unease. The rooms had recently been redecorated from Victorian heaviness into the lighter mood of the new Century. She noticed the subtle shades of silvery greys blues and creams, she saw the curtains were of the softest translucent fabric, she recognized the modernity of the bright electric lights shining in French *electroliers* of bronze and glass, she appreciated the distinguishing elegance of their dining without a tablecloth; yet she could not deny that a certain stoutness of design remained in the house, nor could she fail to see that some rather stolid items of furniture had been retained. Was then the owner the same as his house: less modern than he seemed? He certainly was behaving rather formally: while his guests laughed and relaxed at the table, pouring their own wine and telling jokes, Robert remained cool and smiling, as if watching them all with a studied detachment. Was he watching her with the same coolness, or could she mean a little more to him than his other guests? For a while she thought not. She thought him almost too dainty to let himself go, to admit that he was with a pretty woman who was another man's wife and make something of that slightly dangerous excitement. An immaculateness had grow over him like a skin: it was impossible to imagine him with a hair out of place or an imperfect cuff—or another man's wife. And yet she was not sure that she wanted him to move an inch from his polite detachment…and beyond these thoughts, this was such an entertaining evening anyway. It had been a long time since she had enjoyed a party so much.

Burton Sloane, despite the queer promise of his name, was neither handsome nor witty; in fact, she admitted to herself over another glass of wine, he was downright dull. His wife Emily, though young and pretty, had almost nothing to say beyond some banal enquiries about life in a Northern town, but Rawlings was a tonic to Philippa's spirits. Robert had called him 'quite a fellow', and he lived up to the remark. His drinking had a Regency coarseness to it, and his naughty quips brought laughter to the table and a severe blush to Emily's face. He was rich too, and not ashamed to say so: he ran a motor-car in Town and hunted with his own pack of hounds in Northamptonshire. His fiancée Daphne—if fiancée she was—claimed to be a dancer in the latest experimental style with modern music, loose robes and bare feet; but in her low-cut, tight-waisted, and somewhat outdated dress, worn with old leather shoes, cheap jewellery, and garishly painted lips, she struck Philippa as looking more like a music-hall trouper, and a decidedly common one at that. Yet as she grew more drunk, Philippa began to imagine that despite the shortcomings of these people she was witnessing the birth of a new circle of talent: a brother-and-sisterhood of Art which she had often hoped to establish but had never yet made real. They were all talented people in their different ways, with the essential ingredients of money and influence and proven commercial success. Where she and her earlier artistic friends had starved in Chelsea, these might flourish in Cavendish Square. She would allow Robert to make love to her; at the same time she would allow herself to desire him. He was not so unattractive as she had once thought, with considerable style and real charm. And what kind of a lover would he be? She felt certain he would not be gentle; he was smooth, but not gentle. Vicious then? Lewd and coarse? No, but not gentle; neither fierce nor direct. He would be sly, with curious, deviant foreign tricks. She would not shrink from them; she would allow herself to be excited by them, grow into them, learn from them. The human body was a curious playground; she might actually enjoy his wicked tour of its every corner.

Then there was Rawlings. He was richer still, but she didn't imagine he had half Robert's influence in the world of galleries and commercial art. He would scarcely be worth seducing; he seemed besotted with the dreadful Daphne. But if Philippa thought his taste in women was dubious, she could only admire his taste in Art. Of all this party, it had been Rawlings who had best understood her painting. When he had seen it or the first time he had almost jumped: exactly the effect for which she had striven. He had appreciated the shocking juxtaposition of sunlight and moonlight and the brilliance of her perspective. Now, over the brandy, he was still congratulating her on her mastery of technique.

"…and I shouldn't wonder if it pulls off First Prize in a major exhibition, if you two know where to enter it." He looked with befuddled admiration between Robert and Philippa. "In fact," he continued, "I declare it wins another bottle of Champagne right away, if your man'll bring one up."

"Jules," whispered Robert, "another bottle of the Heidsieck." He turned to Rawlings. "You'll have me down to my last four dozen," he smirked.

"Don't be such a mean beggar. If she were at my place she'd have the whole cellar."

"I'll be lucky to manage another glass," Philippa laughed.

"You'll manage it," smiled Robert.

Jules brought the Heidseick and Rawlings stood up to pour it out, 'tinging' the glasses in showy style.

"There," he announced. "To a New Age of Art—and the new Mistress of the Age." They all drank to Philippa.

"Come on, Daph, let your hair down and give us a dance. They haven't seen your new one."

"Too squiffy," she giggled.

"You know," he persisted, "the *naughty* one."

"Definitely too squiffy for that!"

"Well damn it all, come and give me a cuddle then…in here."

He led her giggling into the drawing-room. Emily excused herself and followed with Burton Sloane in attendance.

"That just leaves us," Robert smiled at Philippa across the table without making the *risqué* comment about Rawlings and Daphne she half expected and wished for. "Of course there are also the remains of this very good Champagne." He refilled their glasses. "You've been a wonderful guest."

'A wonderful guest' indeed! She wanted more than this. She wanted him to take her in his arms, tear down her dress as she imagined Daphne's was being torn down, bare her shoulders and her breasts, cover them with kisses, stroke her ankles and her knees, bring the sweet and scalding fire between her legs, ruin her and make her whole. Yet she knew he would not, not yet, not so easily. He was fondling the Champagne cork.

"D'you know what they do with these in Paris?" he was saying. "They pop them in the top of a lady's stocking, just above the garter." Philippa burned with a sudden sense of her own thighs, calculated how far his hand must travel to find its way through her dress and petticoat. "But I think tonight, this one should go here." He tucked it rather primly into the mauve sash of her dress. It pressed uncomfortably under her ribs, with none of the pleasure his fingers might have given her. "I'll rescue that poor girl from the clutches of my drunken associate, and see you have a motor-car ride back to your hotel."

* * *

Philippa woke in her Mayfair hotel room with a

crushing headache. She rang for the maid and breakfast was brought to her room. Wearing her nightgown and *negligée*, she sat at the window drinking Indian Tonic Water and felt better. She realised she had forgotten the toll which London parties could take, and recent months in Newcastle had been very sober indeed. "Out of practice", she muttered to herself, and stroked a bare leg with her foot. Perhaps she should have rubbed *his* legs under the table. Had she made a fool of herself with Robert? She thought not. He had been very cool and proper, and she could scarcely blame him for that, so soon after her arrival in London and in the presence of his friends and colleagues. Next time she must make herself more seductive…then the next little Champagne cork like the one which lay on her bedside table might be dropped down between her breasts. She felt her breasts with her hands. They were firm and young: it should not be difficult to make any man desire her.

She took her bath, and rang for a half bottle of Champagne. She drank it as she dressed. It was less distinguished than Robert's Heidseick, but crisp and delicious nevertheless. The stir of fresh alcohol in her blood brought a warmth to her stomach and a new lightness to her step as she swept downstairs past the bobbing maids and the curt bows from the reception clerk and doorman. Yes, being back in London suited her well. She must visit more often, she decided with a smile, provided of course that Robert could be persuaded to foot the bill. That should not be too difficult either, she reckoned, emerging into the noise of noon. There, perfectly on time, stood Robert's motor-car, and in a few moments his chauffeur was driving her along Whitehall, over Westminster Bridge, and down to the Lambeth printing works. London continued to excite her, especially from motor-cars: they were noisy, but they moved so swiftly that one gained a new sense of the shape of long-familiar streets; one also felt like the queen of a strange civilization, visiting from another world where everything moved more quickly.

Before very long the brakes were grinding the car to a halt outside the works, and here was Robert in a dashing grey suit.

"Hello again." Robert took her hand and kissed it in that infuriatingly prim manner of his without any verbal endearment. Really, she thought to herself, she must have made a poor showing last night. He should have been in a froth of excitement at the very touch of her. "I do hope you enjoyed dinner and slept well." Better to have slept with you, she thought—and then wondered if she could ever bear to. No matter, she would have to make *something* happen. She gave him a glittering smile and linked arms, sliding her body towards his. Was there a hint of response? He held her arm tightly enough, but was pre-occupied with an apology.

"I'm afraid I can't show you the long-promised poster exibition, not quite yet, anyway. There are one or two you can see of course, and I'm sure you'll like them. There have been all sorts of delays, and this week we are having to complete an order for a soap company in Liverpool. We don't want to put the exhibition up half-heartedly. The delay may not be altogether a bad thing. When it does go up it'll be the talk of London."

"Don't worry, we are going to have a wonderful day," she announced, leading him up his own steps. "First you'll show me all over your amazing printing works, making sure I steal at least some of your artists' ideas for posters, then we will go to a very late luncheon at your favourite restaurant, which I'm sure will become mine. And you can give your chauffeur the day off; it's been wonderful to ride in your car but I really do feel like walking this afternoon. Will you mind? It's so warm the air will do us good."

The next hour opened Philippa's eyes to the possibilities of commercial art, and stirred new ambitions in her already seething imagination. Burton Sloane appeared, seemingly unaffected by his late night, and re-introduced himself with a charm and brightness he had failed to display over dinner. Philippa recognized it as the enthusiasm of a man in his natural element: the technical side of this business was the very essence of Sloane's life. Again she was seized by the notion of pressing these talented people into the service of her own campaign for self-advancement. It would be important to get to know Sloane and understand the mysteries of his machines and processes. She was genuinely fascinated, but even had she not been, she realised she would have stood for just as long and asked just as many questions and watched just as intently as he showed her various grades of paper and the latest typefaces from France and Holland. The teasingly astringent smell of the printing inks and the relentless noise of the presses—faintly insistent even in the opulent office suite where she was served French coffee—beat through her senses with an irresistible seduction. Here was a sweet and secure marriage of Art and Industry: so long desired and now presented to her by quirks of Fate she could never have imagined. Here was a route to success, wealth, and power. And it was a route she was determined to follow. These men made money out of a talent which had so far earned her none. She would not allow that state of affairs to last much longer.

"So you see," Robert was saying, "we are very much an international concern here. Amongst other things, the big presses you saw are from Germany, most of our ideas come from France…"

"And some of the inks come from your part of the world," Sloane put in with a smile. "The Richardson Company, somewhere in County Durham, near Blaydon if I remember correctly, Blaydon Races and all that."

"Oh, that's not my part of the world," replied Philippa airily.

"You're not happy up there?" asked Robert.

"I didn't say I wasn't happy in Newcastle. But I don't come from there, and I certainly don't belong there."

"Citizen of the world then, eh?" Robert smiled slowly. "Yes, you certainly are that—or will be. But I'm afraid I do have some annoying news for you." He put down his cup of coffee, and looked at Philippa with such embarrassed disappointment that she felt more pity for him than selfish anxiety over whatever this news might be. "I'm sorry to say that Williamson's won't agree to display your painting for longer than a week." His shuffle of discomfort gradually became a determined pacing up and down the office as he went on. "I can't say I'm altogether surprised but I am annoyed after making such careful arrangements. I'm annoyed on your behalf too. The work—and you—deserve better…but of course Williamson's were never right for you. They pretend to be a forward-looking gallery but they're ten years out of date. Your work's far too modern for them, and far too good. They're pretending to be shocked by an industrial theme from a woman painter and they're saying nobody will buy it because it's out of keeping with their established style. Well, thank God it is, that's what I say. So don't be downhearted. In fact you'll have the last laugh on them. Burton and I have a splendid idea to knock the stuffing out of Williamson's and anyone else who doesn't see where you're going—only if you agree, of course. We think your ship painting should be the frontispiece of our exhibition here."

Philippa drew a breath with a slight raising of her hand. Robert interpreted this as an objection and carried on.

"Yes yes, we know it isn't a poster—although I think it could nicely be made into one to advertise the shipyard, if they had the imagination to do such a thing—but that doesn't matter. In fact that's the point: we *want* to display original works of fine art—this one, anyway. It'll look marvellous right at the front of the entrance hall. Oh, by the way, it might be a good idea to cable your husband and let him know you'll be in London for another week or so, just while the painting is retrieved from Williamson's and all this is sorted out. Of course you shall stay on at the hotel at the Company's expense. Now where were we? Oh yes—everyone will see the painting right at the front of the exhibition, and I guarantee, I positively guarantee, that at least one of our rivals—and they'll all be here—will want to know about the artist, and it shouldn't be very long before they're commissioning you to do something for their own printing companies." He looked proudly across the room at the smiling Burton Sloane. "Unless of course we have commissioned you first." He grinned boyishly at Philippa. "What do you say. More coffee?"

"Thank you," she cried, rushing up to Robert and clasping his wrists. "Thank you, that's what I say!" She reached over to Burton Sloane and took his wrists in the same way. "Thank you both. You're both, you're both.....*darlings*!"

"We've been called worse than that," smiled Robert. "Well then, it's all agreed. Splendid."

Sloane hurried back to his presses, while Robert and Philippa celebrated with a look through a pile of recently produced posters. They advertised all manner of things from cocoa to railway excursions, and some were striking examples of the designer's art, but Philippa could think only of her own work and the new turn her career had taken. She was excited, but cool; and again her success seemed to have been effortless, as if it would have happened anyway despite all her planning and plotting. And if seducing Robert was no longer strictly necessary, then it could still be fun—and somehow harmless to Jon. Poor simple Jon. Whatever was he doing, back there in the North at that dreadful shipyard? She searched her soul for guilt, and was almost shocked to find none. But a sourness did come; a sourness of finding nothing; a sourness to spoil the pure flavour of innocent success she privately longed to taste.

They had lunch in a restaurant near Leicester Square, with much talk of Paris and the unspoken belief that they would one day enjoy luncheons in that very different city. For all her excitement, Philippa could still not feel completely at ease with Robert. His wit was clouded by sarcasm, and there was something supercilious in his manner which managed to annoy her even when she was most enjoying his company. Perhaps he was too much like herself. Below all this were depths she could not fathom. She gave up, and abandoned herself to the wine. She would enjoy what she could of him, and of all that Life might bring her.

Now they were walking back to Mayfair through an increasingly oppressive afternoon.

"I'm not sure you were right to walk," remarked Robert. "There's thunder in the air and we still have a long way to go: the other side of Regent Street."

"We can always shelter in a doorway," smiled Philippa. She almost hoped it would rain so she could tease him again with the closeness of her body.

They had barely crossed Berkeley Square and were still several streets away from her hotel when dark pennies of rain spattered the hot pavements. A rumble of thunder came over the roof-tops and in moments they were lashed by cold and drenching rain.

"You were right!" squealed Philippa, breaking into a run.

"And you were wrong. There *are* no doorways here."

Robert was not taking the rain well, shrinking from it and scurrying along beside her. She ran with a girlish determination, lifting her dress as her shoes splashed through instantly formed torrents. "Your hat'll be ruined," he added.

"Oh, hang the hat!" cried Philippa, snatching it off her head and blowing rainwater off her laughing lips. "Come on. It's not far!"

At last they gained the dripping portico of her hotel and hurried straight in. The vestibule was crowded with guests and visitors shaking themselves dry or waiting for the storm to pass before venturing out. They all looked askance at the hatless young woman and her rain-sodden escort.

"Mrs. Ferris will go directly to her room," announced Robert at the reception desk and hastily transferred the key from the clerk's hand to her own. Would he come up with her? Yes, he was at her side, mounting the stairs. Her heart beat more wildly. She could feel the rainwater inside her shoes, warm now; the heaviness of her wet hair soaking through the shoulders of her dress; a flush on her cheeks where beads of water still rolled. They came to the door of her room, shiny mahogany in the dim corridor. She turned full-face to him, grabbed his wrists again, suddenly noticing his hands were somehow dry while hers were still damp from her trickling cuffs.

"Come in with me—now."

"You know I must not." He sounded dull and resolute, but she saw his flickering eyelids and the flush on his cheeks matching her own, delightfully boyish. He was just shy! What fun it would be to take away his shyness!

"Yes you can," she grinned, lying back against the door. "It's right that you should."

A new fierceness came into his voice. He was just frightened, she thought.

"It is anything but right. How can you say it's right?"

She held on to his wrists, smiling slyly at him.

"You're a married woman!"

Her smile broke to a laugh.

"Must you remind me of such a thing, Robert? I thought you had better manners than that." He continued to stand in her grasp, as if uncertain whether to turn or to strike her. "Am I your first girl, Robert? Good Heavens, I never thought such a thing." She dropped her voice from a chuckle to a whisper. "This *will* be fun for you."

"No," breathed Robert sharply. "No, you must not."

"Oh but I must," she whispered, drawing his hands up to the mass of her hair and dragging his fingers through the wet strands of it, again and again until he hung his head and closed his eyes. "I must have what I desire…and I shall, shan't I? I shall have what I desire, shan't I?"

"Yes," he croaked, "I think you shall."

* * *

A few days after Philippa's departure for London, Jon caught sight of Matthew Watson leaving the yard and waved him a greeting. Matthew stopped.

"Was there something, sir?"

"No no, nothing, er, nothing particular. I just wondered how your daughter was getting on. I haven't seen her about."

"No, you won't have. Thanks for asking. She did get the job, but she's off sick now, still very poorly. She's had a fever. Doctor didn't even have a name for it, not a name me and the wife could understand, anyway."

"Oh, I am sorry. I'm truly sorry. Is she in hospital?"

"No no, she's past the worst now, up and about like, but she'll not be back at work for a canny few weeks."

"And the rest of the family are safe?"

"Aye, we're managing. It's very kind of you to ask, sir. Well, I must be away."

"Of course. Well, give my best wishes to your daughter."

This brief, formal, and somehow uncomfortable exchange left Jon severely depressed. He was quietly angry too, angry that illness should strike a happy, intelligent, and talented young woman just when she was set fair to improve her lot…and brighten his days at the shipyard with her clean freshness and lilting voice and quiet pride. He felt cheated, more so when he returned to the house in Jesmond and took his lonely supper, with only Mrs. Hutchinson's awkward ministrations from the kitchen. He must not be selfish, he thought. He had no right to feel cheated or depressed on his own behalf. It was the girl's own health that mattered, and the security of her family. What was it like to be ill in the dull streets of Wallsend, those small terraced houses, the back lanes with the ragged children and the outside lavatories? And she was so light of spirit, so tender, her eyes so full of hope; amid her poverty, so ladylike. Was all that to be lost now through a wicked turn of Fate? He would write to her, telling her he would do what he could to keep her position open during her illness, perhaps send a small gift to the family. What would they like? Sweets. Of course not: too childish, and they would be seen as condescending. Money? Certainly not, that would be quite wrong. No no! He must face the truth: of course he would have no power to keep her position open; the letter and the gift would not have a truly charitable purpose. He must not lie to himself, not so easily, not so soon, not ever. He was in love with her already, wasn't he? He should admit it, face it, then stop it. That *was* in his power to do. Everything in his own situation was in his power; there was no need for him to allow Maisie to take him over; every reason not be weak now, to be utterly different from how he had always been. But surely this was justified: he had come to know about her family, and now she was ill. No! It would have to stop; must never start. Stopping it would be quite easy. Philippa would be coming back soon, full of stories of her own success and he would throw himself into that, supporting his own wife instead of a family of strangers and their sickly daughter. His own wife, for God's sake! He must hold on to what he had. And he had so much, everything was going so well. Only another couple of days, then Philippa would be back, and with all her enthusiastic rushing about and her warm body and the tumble of her rich hair and her slender arms around him he wouldn't have time for anything else!

The next morning a telegram arrived to say that Philippa would be staying in London for another week.

CHAPTER SEVEN
Love and Marriage

"A filthy sodomite!" Philippa stared into Robert's eyes, then dropped her cold gaze down his body. "That's what you mean when you say you're incapable of loving me, isn't it? Love! What does your disgusting perversion have to do with love? You can't love me or even give me the crudest pleasure," she spat the words at him again, "because you are a filthy sodomite!"

He had admitted it himself, just inside her bedroom door. She had put her damp arms inside his jacket and held him around his waist. When she had looked into his eyes she had seen them fill with fear, then anger, then a kind of humorous but embarrassed resolve—and suddenly he had pushed her away, turning to the window and almost choking on his own words.

"You must not do this. I…I am not as you think. I may not love you. I can't love you, or any woman. If you must know, I love Burton Sloane."

She had recovered from her disgust more swiftly than she had expected. This was horrible, but she saw it was also another trick of Fate playing marvellously into her hands. She would conquer her revulsion and turn all this to her own advantage. She did not quite know from where she summoned the strength and guile, but suddenly both were there, at a turning point in her life and career when she could leap into her true character and make it an instrument of her newly forged will.

Robert was speaking again, in a high, self-mocking voice.

"There. It was easier to tell you than I had imagined. I should have learned by now not to be so upset by silly women. But you are different. I admire you. I actually do. And dear Sloaney, how he would laugh at all this."

"I might have guessed," she almost growled, re-arranging her sleeves and hair. "You and that unctious little man." She looked him up and down with renewed abhorrence. "I suppose you're well matched in a disgusting sort of way. I should have known, I shouldn't have been such a fool. But no matter," she affected an acid brightness, "I know now, and know precisley how and why to despise you."

"Really?" Robert had recovered himself, turned to face her, and was leaning with a kind of languid defiance against the window. "You can't find it in yourself to understand? An intelligent young woman of the world? I was wrong about you: I never dreamed you were so petty and provincial. It must come from living at the wrong end of the country."

"I understand perfectly well!" she snapped. "It's perverse. It's foul. It's horrible and you are horrible."

"It's merely a matter of taste," he went on, "and my tastes are my own business; but if you must have me justify them, it's quite natural."

"Quite natural? Quite *un*-natural!"

"No no, your fear of what I am comes only from your lack of understanding. Men have loved one another since

Antiquity, often with greater desire and tenderness than in your sordid flings between the opposite sexes. Some would call it the perfect love—but not everybody, as you have just demonstrated with the all-too common reaction. Modern society—so comfortable, so full of exciting things—is cruel and heartless and run by fools and bigots. So no-one must know of this. Particularly Rawlings and his crowd, and of course the many people I do business with. They would all be as narrow-minded as yourself, but alas I depend on them. I should be ruined."

"Yes, you *should* be ruined." She began to pace triumphantly around the room. "However, your nasty little secret is safe with me—but only for as long as it suits me. And how long will it suit me? That, my dear Robert, is entirely in your hands. Let's stick to our little arrangement. Why not? It's a purely commercial arrangement, why should I care what you do in your foul private life? My painting will be displayed as agreed, and of course it will excite great comment at your exhibition, won't it? Everybody will be asking about me. And, curiously, just as you predicted, a number of very lucrative commissions will come my way from your most distinguished rivals. You, of course, will feel obliged to outbid them with a very generous fee for my designing *your* posters. What are they for again? Soap? Cocoa? Railway Companies? It hardly matters. I'll do the work, it'll be good work, and you'll make certain it's accepted by your clients. I shall become very successful; again, it's only what you predicted. All your colleagues will say what excellent judgment you showed in taking on that girl. Of course I shall become *so* successful that I shall need a little flat in London; can't keep running up and down from 'the wrong end of the country', can I? How very expensive that might be for you. But you'll find me one, a good address too. And you'll do all this, Robert—because if you do not, I think the first people to learn of your peculiar habits should be *Mrs*. Burton Sloane, then Rawlings and his crowd, as you call them. There'd be a sort of rightness in that, wouldn't you agree?"

Robert, who had maintained his supercilious pose at the window during Philippa's speech, now advanced to the middle of the room, a mixture of pain and fury on his face.

"You are a viper!" he said.

"Good gracious," laughed Philippa, "such melodrama; so old-fashioned. Will you strike me then?" She showily presented her cheek. "Of course not. This is business, Robert, this is the Twentieth Century. And this shabby little episode, degrading as it might have been, has actually worked out rather well, don't you agree? I'm so glad I didn't let my obviously provincial disgust get in the way of common sense. We will continue our business relationship, though you, of course, will never touch me again. I shall stay in London for a few days while you arrange the details of hanging my picture and everything else we have agreed." She opened the door and held it. "And now you will leave my room."

Robert paused on his way out. He too had recovered, and his voice had a sparring note.

"Well, since we're in a mood for truth, what about your husband?"

"What about him?" asked Philippa blandly.

"A few moments ago you were ready to betray him."

Philippa held the door more widely.

"My husband, Robert, is a fool, and I may or may not betray him as I wish. But at least he is a normal man, thank God. Now get out of my room."

* * *

Jon's polished boots grated loudly on the dry cobbles. He had put on his oldest coat. The action had struck him as crafty and shameful but he didn't want to be noticed in these streets wearing a new one. How strange and snobbish, he thought. Had Philippa made him a snob? Of course not. He pushed away the self-criticism. Was he not merely excercising good manners, being considerate, doing this the least vulgar way, the proper way? He did not feel proper as he turned into Union Street with a gift for Maisie Watson.

It was Scottish shortbread, in a large tin decorated with a picture of Bonnie Prince Charlie on the lid and views of Highland lochs and mountains on the sides. They glowed green and purple against the painted tartan: a strangely poignant evocation of Scots Romance and the fresh outdoors. When he had glimpsed the tin through the window of Jesmond's most expensive grocery shop, Jon had suddenly known it was the most appropriate present he was likely to find. He had bought it quickly, almost furtively. If he was going to do this, it all had to be done now, this week, while Philippa was away. He saw plainly enough he was carrying more than a token of concern for a stricken family, he was delivering a gift of love. How quickly he had fallen! There was anguished pleasure in it, but he hated the self-imposed subterfuge and the knowledge that it was not a very honourable endeavour. If only Philippa hadn't rushed off to London so eagerly, and not been so obviously happy to stay away from him for another week, he might have felt more able to resist his new feelings. She could be quite cold and calculating, thought Jon, and sometimes quite indifferent to him. Maisie would surely not be like that: she would be warm and eager, less clever and witty and haughty with him, more friendly. Friendliness. That's what was lacking from Philippa, but what was lacking from him? He buried the unanswerable question, refusing to consider any blame himself. For the moment, with what felt like shameful convenience, he would blame his absent wife. She could be charming, fascinating, and madly desirable, but he realised already that their marriage had not been founded on anything like friendship. In his new responsibilities at the yard, in his new life in his own house, he wanted friendship as much as love. Were these the very things he was betraying now, even as he sought them through the glum streets of Wallsend to the accellerating heartbeats of new, illicit, and fatal attraction?

In the raw air with its riverside smells, he decided the letter had not been a good idea. He had written to Philippa, intending to explain his involvement with the Watsons and even make a brave confession of his feelings, but the small envelope posted to London contained neither. Maisie and her family were mentioned in a bland list of Jon's routine. His brief descriptions of the 'pretty girl' and her 'good parents' leapt like flames from the paper as he re-read them, but were shamefully less than the whole truth. They might mean nothing at all to Philippa, or she might deduce some gross infidelity. If he was going to deceive his wife, he wondered, why had he bothered to begin a lame explanation? If he was going to deceive no-one, why had he not been completely honest? Why, his footsteps seemed to hammer out, why was he here at all?

He returned his attention to finding the right house. He reminded himself that a gentleman did not carry a parcel through the streets, and this parcel was exciting some raucous comment from children playing outside their doors. Ahead of him stood a group of ragged girls swinging a skipping rope and chanting:

"There's a lad around the corner
got his eye on Alice Horner."

As he approached they stopped, and all he could hear was the cold ringing of a hammer on brickwork somewhere in the back lanes. It seemed to strike the chill of guilt into his bones, as clearly as fear and mistrust hovered in the eyes of the sullen children. Ignoring his discomfort he approached the eldest girl, who flashed him an unexpected smile.

"Hello Mister," she said brightly before he could speak.

"The Watson family," Jon smiled. "Which house is it, please?"

"The Watsons? Number Forty-Eight, ower that side."

"Thank you."

His boots crunched again over the cobbles; he could almost feel the stare of unseen eyes from the windows. When he reached the house and knocked his tension was mercifully relieved by a swift but gentle opening of the door, and he was looking at a mild-faced woman in a neat blue dress. He guessed it was Maisie's mother, and forgot his half-prepared speech as she stood smiling at him from the tiny vestibule, a narrow staircase climbing steeply behind her, the polished interior of the house quiet and orderly without the chaos of children he had expected.

"Mrs. Watson?" he managed, offering the parcel. "This is something for your daughter…and all of you. Thank you, no. I don't want to disturb your evening, I'm just glad to hear she's getting better more quickly than we thought…Yes, Jon Ferris from Parsons'…I hope she's soon recovered completely…Good afternoon."

It had not been an impressive speech, he decided, walking away. There had been no declaration of love, scarcely an admission of concern. Taken slightly aback by her Mother's news that Maisie was recovering with unexpected speed, and actually not wanting to see her, he had barely been polite. He had not done well and it would end badly. He found himself hurriedly avoiding the skipping girls when the eldest, having bent down to find something on the cobbles, stood up to face him with her same open smile and a chant which was not for the street game but a quiet prayer for him alone.

> "See a pin and pick it up,
> and all the day you will have luck."

The other girls shrieked and laughed but the shiny safety pin was placed silently in Jon's hand with a coy, angelic, upward glance. Striding back towards the river, he saw the cloudy afternoon shot through with a new yellow light high above *Mauretania's* building-shed, and heard seagull sounds borne on a faint warm breeze from the South.

* * *

Matthew and the other carpenters at Swan's were now engaged in making the vast and complex wooden cradle that would support *Mauretania's* hull during the critical stresses of her launch. At first it was cramped and dangerous work under the ship's very bottom. Here they laboured amongst the keel blocks on which she would rest throughout her construction. Below her huge steel plates and around the greased wooden ways down which one day she would slide, the work was made more hellish by the deafening clang of hammers and riveters on the inside of her hull. Then—as steelwork climbed from the floor of the berth to the distant echoes in its glass roof and shipbuilders bound for the higher decks rode in electric lifts which were only one of the modern marvels in this gigantic building-shed—came the delicate moulding of timbers to the curves of the stern and the rake of the bow.

"We call them the poppets," Matthew explained to little George who sat wide-eyed at their kitchen table. "The fore-poppet at the bow: that's the front of the ship…"

"I know that, Da."

"…and the after-poppet at the stern."

"That's the back."

"Aye, it is, and it'll have to support a lot of weight round the shafts. But the fore-poppets' the really clever thing. On the day of the launch it's got to give way a bit. When the back end goes in the water and begins to float upwards, the front end's ganna go downwards, isn't it? Well that's when the woodwork has to crumple a bit and break away to let the bow bear down without holding it too tight; but it mustn't be too loose either or it'll not support it properly and the whole ship could capsize."

George listened, rapt and impressed.

"Then we'd all look silly, wouldn't we?" concluded his father, reaching for his pipe.

"Haway you two," Alice Watson was intent on clearing the supper dishes. "They're building the ship down there and you're building it all over again up here. Now you get over by the fire."

George took a seat by his father's legs.

"Will you be the man who sees the woodwork breaks just right?"

"I doubt that. Most like I'll be underneath her, hammering in the wedges to raise her up off the keel blocks and on to the cradle so she'll slide down nicely."

"I canna wait for the launch day, Da. It'll be exciting!"

"Aye, it will. It'll be a holiday on both sides of the river; and you'll see the big ship slide down, you all will. I'll make sure you get good places to watch from. It's a long way off though, launch-day." Matthew looked wistfully into the fire, blowing gentle smoke at the chimney. "Canny bit of work to do yet like."

"Did Maisie draw the poppets?"

"No, lad, but she'll be drawing everything else they hold up—now she's back to work."

"Which reminds me, Da," Maisie came to sit at the other side of the fender, "you can have the last bit of Mister Ferris's shortbread."

Matthew shifted uneasily.

"That should be for you, lass."

"It was the best Scottish shortbread," said Alice from the sink, "very nice of that Mister Ferris to bring it for Maisie. A nice man altogether."

"Aye well, he might be", Matthew stirred more

uncomfortably in his chair, "but I'm not so sure my daughter should be ower friendly with a gentleman from Parsons', a married gentleman and all."

"Nonsense," stated Alice. "We should be happy for her."

"I'm not happy at all. My daughter's gone back to work too fast, she's been too fast in her friendship with this man, too fast altogether for my liking—and you're keeping her up in it!"

"Don't be upset, Da." Maisie leant forward with a smile. "Mister Ferris was just being kind giving us the present, and I do like him, but nobody's doing anything wrong. You're always saying yourself we should be thankful for how things are: I've got over my illness, you've got work at the yard, I've got work an' all, Mam's got plenty of food in the house for all the bairns, there's a bit of money left over each week…and well, you know, things are different in the world now, like. A lass like myself can hold her head up nowadays when she talks to a gentleman from a big house in Heaton and he can talk back with respect for her job and her qualifications and nobody's any the worse. In fact everyone's better off. It's the Twentieth Century, Da."

"Don't you start with that daft twaddle. How many times have I had that said to me in the last few years—and always by people wanting to make excuses for themselves. Hold your head up indeed. More like you'll be covered in shame before the year's out. I don't care what century it is, I don't care what you say, people's behaviour is just the same, and daft behaviour's daft whatever the date!"

"You're being too hard on her," Alice set down a dish with a decisive thump. "And leave off from worrying her; she's not well enough yet to take your kind of upset."

"She's well enough to idle about chatting to wealthy men way above her own class. Top boss's son, this one you know. Oh yes. Why only yesterday I saw them with my own eyes…"

"I was meaning to tell you, Da…"

"Aye, but you didn't, did you? You've been secretive. And anyway what's he doing hanging about the drawing-loft? He's supposed to be up at Parsons' working on the turbines. They haven't even been delivered to the yard yet—but *he's* there, isn't he? Sniffing around my daughter. Hasn't he got some fancy artist wife of his own?"

"She's in London."

"That makes it worse, you daftie!"

"Look. I was meaning to tell you all." Desperation had entered Maisie's voice. Her eyes darted from her father to her mother and across the room to little George standing meekly with his fingers in his mouth. "I want to tell you. I said I thought he looked sad and needed a friend. He said how much he wished it might be possible for us to meet somewhere away from work, when I felt well enough like, if such a thing could ever be possible, somewhere quiet for a talk."

"Somewhere quiet for a talk?" Matthew's voice rose with amazement. "This is unheard-of! And what did you say?"

"Well he was the shy one, you know." Maisie had calmed herself down as best she could, determined to state her truth. "He was being very proper. He didn't make any suggestions a young lady might object to. No, it was me. I said we might go along the sands."

"You might! And you might stand with your legs open like the hussies on the Fish Quay! This is beyond belief, woman! You're supposed to be the one with brains in this house."

"But you don't understand. He said if there was going to be any kind of meeting it would have to be with your permission. That's why I was going to tell you, to ask you. He insisted."

"And you think that's improper?" demanded Alice.

"I *do* think it's improper for a girl to go traipsing out with a married man! And she'll not have my permission. I've a mind to take my belt to her instead!"

Alice strode up to the fire and stood on the mat between her husband and daughter.

"You'll not do that to any of mine in my house, Matthew Watson. Our Maisie's done no wrong, and she won't neither. And if there's a chance for a girl of mine to better herself, she'll take it—with my blessing."

* * *

It was a Sunday. Train travel to the coast would be awkward and lengthy. Jon would have lied to his wife about this trip, but his wife was not here. Whatever she was doing in London would not stop him. He would be content to let the journey take its own time; enjoy everything that Fate seemed to have dropped into his hands; hands which held his first truly personal gift for Maisie: a fine lady's parasol carefully wrapped in stiff brown paper. He knew the shortbread would have gone round all her family, but the parasol would be for Maisie alone, and a lasting gift to date from this first wild and sweet encounter by the sea. He relaxed his hands, amazed they were not shaking, and turned his face to the sunlight streaming through the carriage window. Beyond the little train bloomed a brilliant morning: one of those cloudless days which could bring an almost Scandinavian Summer to the North-East coast. No breeze stirred the vivid blues of sea and sky, chill violet shadows held memories of colder days, gulls' wings flashed their Arctic white, but burning gold was poured upon the fields and streets and houses.

Set down at Tynemouth Station, shrill with day-trippers, Jon walked a route he had known all his life: down busy Front Street with its closed shops and on to the sea-front with the great black ruins of Tynemouth Priory directly ahead. How many times had he been taken down on to the coaly beach of Tynemouth Haven, shadowed by the huge North Pier and set with little boats? Here was the mouth of his homeland's river, exciting since his boyhood, pouring its industry and expertise across a world lapping at his very feet and stretching away to vast blue yonders all quite reachable from home, since home was the birthplace of adventures and clever people to make them come true. Here he had been told stories of monks and Viking raiders so far back in history he could barely imagine such things, and tales of his own family so close he could easily picture Uncle Edward nursing the engines of his Baltic trader as it steamed out beyond the twin lighthouses and his grandfather as Captain of sailing ships before that. But today, in these familiar places, he felt utterly different: somehow lighter, blessed with Summer sunshine where so often he had been chilled by Winter winds.

He turned away from his little beach of boyhood memories to walk Northwards up the Promenade. Above him burned a hot sun, to his left were the newly-built terraced houses with their spectacular view, to his right the North Sea sighed gently on to the rocks, ahead lay the glittering Long Sands running up to clear views of the distant lighthouse on St. Mary's Island and the promise of dark-haired Maisie Watson smiling at him with the sky so incredibly blue. A surge of delight ran through him. What had begun as a deliberate and guiltily-planned avoidance of truths and responsibilities now felt like a spontaneous treat. It seemed he was escaping to the sea with her, this day and perhaps always. It seemed he would know peace, and love, and sheer happiness. Whatever happened, he would never forget this joy-ride of hope and despair, of cruel circumstance, sudden good luck, and undeniable love.

Yet waiting for Maisie at Tynemouth Palace he did not feel so gallant. In the cool shadows of the dark building, holding his conspicuous gift and avoiding the stares of strangers, he suddenly wished for a less populated rendezvous: anywhere away from the theatre, café, and other tawdry attractions of this clumsy building with its bulging roof and towers like a great beached ship high above the beach. The wish itself was ignoble; he wished he had not wished it, and could be a completely innocent part of this holiday scene with the sounds of children bouncing up to the concrete terraces and always the faint whisper of the sea. He sensed the tide was coming in, with still no sign of Maisie. Would the tide of events, as inexorable as the sea itself, sweep them into shame and misery and drown any moments of happiness they might steal? It was more depressing still to realise that not all events were the external workings of Fate but the direct result of his own weaknesses, desires, and actions. Ages seemed to rise through Jon as he waited. It occurred to him that the proverbial drowning man whose past life flushed and gurgled across his brain never had the dubious luxury of watching his past being swallowed up as slowly as this. Everything he had been was about to vanish, but by the protracted stages of what would be seen as a shameful and scandalous affair. He was drowning in time and would be lost while the sea itself might rise and fall for ever.

"Hello there. You were hiding but I found you!"

It was Maisie, smiling at him. Maisie, in a blue dress and jacket with a hat to match, her footsteps ringing into the violet shadows of the terrace as she trotted towards him; her eyes another, paler blue as they shook hands in a polite but tender greeting, formal but stare-locked, reserved but passionate—and oddly different from that which either had rehearsed.

"It's wonderful of you to come today," Jon began. "I…I should really have called for you at home."

"No no, it's better this way. You know my father wasn't very pleased."

"Oh dear, I didn't want to cause trouble."

"Didn't you?" she giggled almost harshly, then her faced softened into a smile. "You still came, though. I admire you for that."

"And I admire you…very much."

"Anyway I don't mind a bit of trouble," she went on as if she had not heard his hesitant confession. "It'll all settle down like when he sees we're good friends."

Jon wished their meeting had not had to begin with news of the trouble it was causing. He held out the parasol.

"I brought you a present: for a lovely sunny day."

She took it tenderly, with a smile of thanks.

"I'll unwrap it in the sunshine then; we're in the shadows here. I'm going to love having this, I can tell even through the paper. Come on, into the sunshine. Come on, let's have our walk."

Down on Tynemouth Long Sands they felt heat and light bouncing off the beach, cooled by the prospect of a brilliant blue sea. They stopped and looked at the horizon, flat calm and sliced by dazzling gulls' wings.

"D'you know what I always think down here?" Maisie swung her arms into the blue light.

"Tell me."

"I always think we've left our troubles on the land behind us, and there's nothing out there 'til you get to Denmark."

"You love the emptiness of the sea," smiled Jon. "You're really a mermaid."

Maisie took hold of Jon's arm, steadying her weight against him.

"Are you all right?" he asked.

"Yes."

She was reaching down and behind her, deftly pulling off first one shoe then the other. Her feet gleamed white and bare. New tides of desire rose in Jon. This slender girl stood barefoot beside him, her ankles smooth, her heels unblemished. How lovely might she be with bare legs, bare arms, entirley naked in hot sunshine?

"I didn't bother with stockings," she was saying. "I

knew I'd want to paddle today. I'm well enough now, you know. I won't catch cold, not on a Summer's day like this anyway. D'you mind us going in bare feet? Is it improper like, now I'm with you?"

"No, of course not. You could never be 'improper'. Anyway, you look delightful with your parasol and your feet are very pretty."

"First time that's been said," she replied with a laugh.

"I'm sure it won't be the last. It's very modern for young ladies to go barefoot, on certain occasions anyway. There's a woman from America who dances with bare feet: Isadora Duncan. Some people find her very shocking, and I suppose she has been, but there's something rather beautiful about what she does. Anyway, she's started a craze for elegant young woman to dance without their shoes."

"Why there's nothing new in that. Me Ma and me've always taken our shoes off to dance. I suppose we've been lucky to *have* shoes to take off. You understand about affording things, don't you? It's been a struggle sometimes, but the bairns in our family have always had shoes, even us girls."

"You have a sister?"

"Aye, Ellen, and there was another one called Alice. She died though. Diptheria. Me Ma said she'd gone to Wonderland, you know, like Alice in Wonderland. I believed that for years. I sometimes wish I still could."

"It can't have been easy for you."

"Nothing's been easy for us."

Jon stopped their walk and spoke to her face.

"This isn't easy either, is it?"

"No, to be honest it isn't, but come on. Come on." She started their walk again. "We'll get through it, you and me. We'll be happy."

They went down to the sea, rippling in over firm sand. Water foamed around Maisie's ankles. She gave a little squeal then smiled up at Jon. "I've got no shoes or stockings on but I feel as if I've gone up in the world. Canny, eh?" She stood in the wavelets and looked directly into Jon's eyes. "But I'll have to talk proper if I really want to get on, eh? You know, not say words like 'canny' and that."

"Well," Jon looked embarrassed, "now you mention it....."

"I don't mind. You could teach me the proper words."

"I wouldn't presume to."

"You could though." She walked him on along the sea's edge. "And I don't mean just words, like. I mean behaviour and things, you know: manners, and how to be a lady."

"You *are* a lady, and there's nothing anyone can teach you about good manners. Some people have no idea about manners, but good manners are perfectly natural in other people—like you. You are sweet and gracious and anyone who met you, anyone from the King to a shop-girl would have to admit it."

"I *am* a shop-girl," she declared, grinning at his

embarrassment.

"Trust me to say the wrong thing."

She laughed aloud.

"Well I *was* a shop-girl 'til I got this job. Now I'm a drawing-loft girl, so I suppose that's going up in the world."

"It certainly is," said Jon firmly, "and only what you deserve. You're very good."

She was looking down at her feet again, swishing them through the tiny wavelets.

"But if I was really good I wouldn't be here, would I? I wouldn't be walking on the sands with a married man."

Jon stopped, rooted to his last footsteps by pangs of anguish.

"Dearest Maisie, that tortures me, you know. If I make you unhappy I promise I'll never see you again. I'll never do anything improper between us."

"No, no, no," she wailed. "You make me happy, very happy. And we're not doing anything wrong, not really. That's what I told my father. I told him I thought you were sad, and needed a new friend, and I could help you after you'd helped me. And you are sad, aren't you?" she ran on, "You are unhappy, aren't you? There is something wrong between you and your wife at home, isn't there? I just know there is. Oh, don't tell me if it's wrong to tell me. I won't do anything bad and come between you if it's not meant to be…"

Jon stopped her with a hand on her arm.

"I think it *is* meant to be, and you know it as well as I

know it."

They stared at each other in the hot blue shadow of the parasol.

"What I really want to do in all this, Maisie, is make you happy…which must have been said a thousand times before in situations like this, but this time it happens to be true."

"Well, nobody's said it to me. And you want to make yourself happy too, don't you? Be honest." She found herself beyond anywhere she had intended to go in words. "Eee, I've never talked like this to anyone before. It's terrible." She looked down. "But somehow I just know it's right."

She had no more words. Jon sensed the beginnings of tears in her eyes.

"It is right, Maisie, I know it too. Lift your head up, and don't be ashamed of anything. I think you are a wonderful person; the best I've known. Let's walk again."

Their crisis over, she brightened once more.

"To be honest I haven't been happy like this for ages," she began, "but I can remember when I last felt like it though." Wistful smiles were playing across her face. Jon was delighted to see her innocently joyful again. "I was just little. I cannot have been ten year old. I was in the country with one of me uncles and his family. He had a farm out by Morpeth somewhere. He had money like, and he used to take us bairns for a few days when it was Easter or Whit or a special holiday. Anyway, this day, I think there was just me, and me cousins were nice to us all day, and we went walking across the fields and into some woods and out again on to someone else's farmland so we could see the hills all the way up to Scotland. It was like the back of beyond to us bairns, but it was lovely like. Then back at the farmhouse, me uncle showed us a Hedge Sparrow's nest. He knew exactly where to go and he parted this bush with his big hands and there was the little nest with tiny eggs in it and they were a beautiful bright blue, like bits of sky fallen down into the nest. I remember thinking that: like bits of blue sky. It made us so happy, but it made us wanna cry an' all, afterwards I mean, when I remembered it and wished I was out there in the country again."

"That's wonderful, Maisie," said Jon. "I could say your eyes are like little bits of sky, but it wouldn't be original now."

Maisie looked down at her feet again.

"You don't have to be original," she said quietly.

"Not with you, no. It's very relaxing."

"…as long as you don't say I've got eyes like eggs."

She turned a teasing smile up to him before she burst out with a laugh. They stopped walking and Jon put his arms around her waist. He drew her slender body to him, holding her lightly as she looked down again and put her hands on his shoulders, not defensively, but girlishly, in friendship as much as in love. He kissed her warm brow, then held her more tightly as she nestled her head into his neck, warmly and cosily, as if they were children snuggling together under a blanket in a quiet room of a peaceful house, not outside with an open sky and hot sunshine and the beach full of day-trippers. It was their first kiss, yet he was almost unaware of its momentous importance. He thought he might now kiss her on her lips, while she thought she might stroke his chest and kiss him on his lips, but neither made the move to do so. They stood in a wordless embrace as a wave came in, gently swishing over their ankles, wetting the hem of her skirt and his boots. But then as the wave receded, as she dug her toes into the sand and as they held each other more tightly, it was impossible to resist. He found her mouth with his lips; she pressed her breasts against him. After the next wave they stood apart, searching each other's eyes.

"I can hardly say what I'm thinking," Jon began in a tremulous voice, "but I do know you're a wonderful girl. Everything you say and do is fresh and honest. I love that in you, Maisie."

"Look," she declared. "Look at me standing in me bare feet on me own beach where I've walked since I was a little girl. I'm not pretending, I'm not deceiving you or myself. I've always believed if a girl stands at the water's edge with nothing between her skin and the sea she can only tell the truth. I don't know where the idea came from but it's a goodun and I'm feeling it now and anything I say's going to be the truth."

She threw her shoes back up the beach, folded the parasol, dropped it on the sand, pulled off her hat, and stood in full sunlight: blue-clad, dark-haired, bright-eyed and resolute.

"I'm telling the truth. I love you and I know you love me. We cannot change it—and we don't want to, do we? It'll work out well, I promise, but only if we tell each other the truth, always."

No more words were spoken. The sun burned down, the waves came up the beach, the shouts of children mingled with cries of seagulls and sounds from the crowded Promenade. Jon and Maisie felt the eyes of the world upon them, but at the same time a new security and trust. He reached out his hand; she took it in hers. Together they walked up the beach, saying nothing.

* * *

A fine Summer evening hung over the Tyne, calm blue air with a hint of dusty pink already settling in the West where the river wound away into dazzling bronze light. The factory hooters were sounding the end of the working day and feet were tramping away from from quayside and shipyard, but the prevailing mood was of stillness, a soft-textured peace in the air to match the faintest hissing of the calm sea as it lapped the beaches at South Shields and Tynemouth beyond the piers. Maisie sensed all this at once as she came out of the drawing-loft, stood for a moment at the top of the wooden stairs, and felt the cooling air on her face.

She set off down the steps with a light heart: going home, a few minutes early, too. She'd take little George down to North Shields if it stayed nice like this; they could walk along the Fish Quay and look at the trawlers and sit for a while watching the big ships come in up river. She swung along towards the gate, looking at the sky, scarcely noticing the group of dark-coated men gathering at the gate: of course, the workmen's meeting. Her father had told her a young man had been injured while working under the hull and there was to be some complaint made by his foreman. She didn't want any strife to come into the yard; times were good, she couldn't imagine why some of the men wanted to stir up trouble with the bosses, they were all in work on a grand new ship and getting paid. Accidents were bound to happen; there was no need to make matters worse with blame and conspiracies.

"Ho, ye in the skirt! What's it worth, lass?"

She spun round at the lewd cackle, didn't recognize the leering face, but noticed Walker the foreman, whose long features she did know, standing behind the man who had accosted her. Normally, she felt well able to shrug off bawdy comments and coarse cheek; she'd had little to put up with really, she thought. There were two ways to deal with it: she could look the man straight in the eye and let him know she thought he was no better than a piece of muck, or she could just walk on and ignore him. She'd done both in her time at the yard and been left well alone, but there was always some cheeky lad or dirty-minded older man to be put in his place. And suddenly, on this lovely mild evening, she felt vulnerable: afraid of the workmen's dark plotting, afraid of Walker's surly troublemaking, afraid of the crudeness and rudeness, above all afraid of her own emotions. She'd just walk straight past looking at the cobbles and get on home.

"Divvent waste yer wages man," she heard Walker say to the other, his voice deliberately rising as she passed. "To my mind there's loose women, then there's prostitutes, then there's gentlemen-engineers' sluts!"

CHAPTER EIGHT

The Decent Thing

"I'm sorry, Mister Walker." The grey-faced youth shepherding his workmates shuffled in front of the foreman. "This is all we're getting."

"Don't look so scared. It's not your fault." Walker scowled at his threadbare audience. "It's the fault of the bosses, the fault of the system that injures boys and intimidates men, the fault of the very structure of our lives we all have to labour under. It's fear, ignorance, and oppression, and it's given us eight men. How many hundreds work here, and what have we got? Eight men. What bloody use is that?"

"You tell us, Mister Walker," shouted one of the men. "You called the meeting."

"I'll tell you right enough. When eight men become eight-hundred, when eight-hundred become eight-thousand, when eight-thousand become a whole class striding forward in a workers' movement, that's when there'll be a change. That's when you'll get decent wages and better conditions here in the yards and a better life out there in the town."

"We're doing all right for money. We canna complain."

"You can—about injuries like Jamie's, plainly caused by a negligence and an uncaring management."

Defiance rippled through Walker's listeners.

"It was nowt but an accident. They happen now and again."

"Aye," Walker seized his opportunity for renewed vehemence, "and they'll go on happening until we change things for the better."

"I say we're doing all right."

"You mean money, don't you? Well, if you're happy with the wages you get you're dafter than you look. But arguing about money's a different matter. I'm not talking about money. I'm talking about power: power to change your lives, to give your wives better homes and your children better food and education; aye, and things you've barely thought of but which could be your right: pensions and hospitals for all, strong unions of tradesmen getting fair pay and fair treatment in disputes, with dole money to support you when you're out of work—not that there'll be much unemployment. Why, the yards and the factories will be booming when they're all brought under state ownership. Aye that's right: you won't be working for private companies with selfish bosses, you'll be employed by the state, paid by the state: a fair day's wage for a fair day's work in safe conditions, properly inspected and regulated. And you won't bring your bait in a tin, Edward Bowen," he pointed at one of the men, "you'll eat in a works canteen, paid for by the state."

"You mean free dinners?"

There were laughs all round.

"No man! But proper food and proper rest times to eat it. D'you not see? This place could be transformed. There'd be no more dangerous practices like working in the cramped and unsafe conditions that caused Jamie's accident. Now who will join with me to protest about dangerous conditions in the yard and start this great endeavour?"

No-one offered Walker anything but objections.

"It's always dangerous in the yards, man. You know that. You've just got to look out for yourself and be sensible."

"He's right, Mister Walker. No point in stirring up trouble when there's nowt wrong. Nobody's been killed on this job; nobody properly hurt for years. It's a canny safe yard, this'n. I'm not complaining."

"And he's right and all. I'm not ganna be some sissy who moans about a bruised finger. I'm building a ship, man, not breaking up Society!"

"But don't you see, you blockheads? This could be the start of a Worker's Revolution."

"Oh aye, a revolution. Didn't they have one of them in France a hundred year ago and end up cutting each other's heeds off?"

"Aye, they did." Walker replied without a smile. "But the trick, Mister History Teacher, is to cut the right heads off and then make sure there are no bloody little corporals ready to turn themselves into new tyrants once you've got rid of the first lot."

"Mind out for Napoleon Walker then lad!"

"That's right, laugh. Laugh if you like. You can afford to laugh this week, this month, this year. But when this ship's built, what'll your futures be, eh? What about your bairns growing up in the same bondage and poverty that's ruined all of you?"

"Ruined, are we? Who says like?"

"I say, and wiser men than me," Walker went on undaunted, "wiser men than any of us here. There are thinkers and writers and politicians in Germany and Russia who know what the future hold for us. They're planning it now. I tell you, there's revolution coming. It'll start on the Continent somewhere—probably in Russia—and we can be part of it, but only if we understand now…"

"I'm not listening to this!" came a shout of derision.

"And I'll have nowt to do with a bunch of foreigners," stated another. "Russia's losing that daft war with Japan, and they're building battleships in Germany…"

"Ours are better like," came an assertion from the ranks. "We'll be putting British turbines in *Dreadnought*."

"A good thing too. And it's a hell of a long way from Russia to Wallsend! I've always said I'll have no dealing with bloody foreigners."

"Me neither. I'm off—and my advice to you, Joseph Walker, is to keep your hands busy and your mouth shut. Goodnight to you."

The men strode away, leaving Walker with his young deputy.

"They don't want to listen, Mister Walker. They just want to gan home to their wives and bairns."

"Aye, and the pub and the chapel and the music-hall and the whorehouse and every other institution that keeps them prisoners of their own ignorance. They want to quench their passions, not use them; and using their minds is too much trouble an' all. They don't even want to think."

"No—'cos they don't want a Workers' Revolution."

"Oh yes they do, lad." Walker took a sudden hold of the youth's lapel and spoke fiercely to the thin face and frightened eyes. "They want a Workers' Revolution right enough; they just don't know it yet. And when the time's right, we'll bloody well give 'em one, just you wait and see!"

* * *

"Well, here we are again," Philippa was pulling off her gloves, "back home in our little three-storey staircase of a house." She gave Jon a humourless look. "How've we been doing?"

"I've managed," replied Jon evenly. He was racked with so many emotions: disappointment, annoyance, guilt; above all a terrible soaking sadness, an inescapable realisation that this reunion held the promise of nothing but anxiety and sorrow. "I should ask how you have been doing."

"In London? Very well, really," she rattled on. "Williamson's gallery won't hang the ship painting properly so it's going to form the first display anyone will see in Robert's own exhibition at the printing works—some time in the New Year I believe, perhaps even earlier. It can't be soon enough for me. It'll be a great opportunity for me and my future work. Robert and his partners think I'll have a whole new career designing advertising posters. They really are the coming thing, plenty of money in them too. Goodness me," she twisted around Jon to face the hall mirror and struggled to take off her hat, "I'd forgotten how tight we are for space here."

Jon thrust his hands in his pockets to steady himself, wanting to shrink from this ordeal yet determined to initiate it.

"If you're not happy to be back, Philippa, you can tell me. I was going to say you can tell me without offence: not exactly true, but you can be honest and tell me anyway. You should be honest. If you've developed a taste for London life again I can't stop it, I can't really object to it, although plenty of people would say I had a right to. They would think you had behaved badly in rushing away from me so soon."

"Ha!" Would she be cruel, witty, acid? Would she share any of the sadness seeping through Jon? "How judgmental you are. One might almost say how pious. But then again, have you anything to be pious about? Haven't you been developing your own career while I've been away? And God knows what else you've been up to; I certainly don't. You haven't been quick to tell me anything—apart from that letter you wrote about some wretched workman and his sickly daughter."

"Yes," Jon drew a shaky breath, "the Watsons. They are good people."

"They'll be common people. That doesn't mean they'll be good. It certainly wasn't a good letter, Jon, but I read between the lines. You're in love with the daughter."

She had taken off her hat and tossed it on to the hall table. Now she lay back against the wall and folded her arms. Jon looked at the wallpaper behind her head, opening his mouth, searching for breath and words.

"Don't bother, Jon. You don't have to say anything. It's perfectly natural for a silly boy like you to fall in love with a pretty young girl you think needs looking after. I suppose it's even natural for someone as ridiculously innocent as yourself to put it in a soppy letter to his wife. The only amazing thing is that you've fallen so quickly. Well," she turned to the mirror again, tidying her hair, "perhaps that's not so amazing."

Jon found his voice.

"I wrote that letter to try to be honest with you, to let you know what was going on up here while you were away."

"To be honest?" She laughed aloud. "Honest? You haven't been honest at all, but then you didn't have to be. You make a few shy references to some silly girl in one letter and I can deduce the whole sordid affair."

"My relationship with that family is not a sordid affair."

"It will be shortly."

"What about your sordid affairs?"

"What about them? If I don't mention mine, you can carry on with yours. Is that how it's going to be?"

"I should never have sent you that letter."

"No, no, you were only being honest weren't you? Doing the decent thing; except even then you couldn't come right out with it. I had to discover it myself; not that it took much wit or wisdom."

"It hasn't taken very long, has it?"

"What?"

"To discover we are less than the ideal couple."

He was met with a bright, cold laugh.

"Really Jon, do you actually believe there is such a thing? And would you want to be part of it anyway?"

"Yes. With you, I would have."

"I don't like your past tense—but at least it's tantamount to an admission of guilt." She bustled past him. "Oh for God's sake Jon—and for our own sake—do we really have to endure one of those old-fashioned marriages where two people are locked together in some artificial social and domestic life, denying their own tastes and desires and needs? You should value your independence as I do mine. I'm sure you have things you want to do on your own, or perhaps I should say without me. Perhaps you've found someone else you'd like to do things with, or perhaps only *one* thing."

She had a wicked gleam in her eyes as she stroked her dress smooth over her breasts: a mixture of reproach and amused cruelty. Jon was stabbed by guilt and disgust. She was condemning him, but enjoying her own sarcasm while she did so. She paused, expecting some defence or riposte, some admission or denial which, moments later, she must have realised she would not be given. In his wordless refusal to justify himself or do further battle with his wife, Jon realised their marriage was ruined and silently pronounced it dead. Its soul, their once-absorbing love, had been destroyed. The void that was left was scarcely worth fighting over. The only debate would be what to do with the corpse, which all the forces around him might not allow him to bury. The prospect filled him with horror, but Philippa's persistence strengthened his resolve. The crueller she became, the easier it would be to nail down the coffin.

"…and now if that dreadful woman you insist on keeping here isn't outside bawling her common head off at stray cats, perhaps she could bring me some tea. I certainly don't relish making my own…or in your *ideal couple* does the little wife slave away in the kitchen while the strong and clever husband goes out philandering?"

* * *

The enormous skeleton of *Mauretania* continued to rise in her building-shed; a forest of ribs thrusting up into noisome air and clad as they climbed in plates of steel. Visitors to the berth were now given a real and impressive sense of a ship, especially as they watched a gigantic pneumatic cutter wheeled along the scaffolding to cut the portholes.

"But it's her length, man, her length", observed Stevenson to Jon one day. "Look at her: seven-hundred and ninety feet, and you cannot see round her curves. Awesome, man. There's been nothing like this on the ocean—ever."

And it was true. This ship was bigger than anything built on this river; bigger than anything in these men's lives. An epic of steel and of human endeavour, thought Jon; her very size and vast importance must overshadow everything else here, which was why Walker's agitation in the yard would come to nothing. The enormous endeavour must overshadow Jon's own miseries, too, he thought. He must be soothed and fufilled by it. Every day he must leave his bitterly ambitious wife at home; leave her shrill or silent, judgmental or scheming, and immerse himself in the loveliness of work. He must leave his desire for Maisie too, leave it in another compartment of his being, and be swallowed up in the grand progress of history, the rise of his career and the parallel rise of the gigantic ship…or, he told himself, at least he must try.

Every day now, the overhead cranes were lifting enormous steel plates to the ribs of *Mauretania*, while portable furnaces heated a seemingly endless supply of rivets. On his visits to the berth, Jon was fascinated to watch the riveters paired on either side of the plates. Their noisy work, brutal and dangerous, was also nimble and athletic, imbued with the trust and security of a team. Glowing rivets were shaken out of the furnace and flung into the catcher's thick leather gloves. Transferred to tongs, the rivet was aligned with the rivet holes and knocked home. Then the holder-up would brace himself against the rivet head while his mate inside the hull would flatten the other end. Within seconds the cooling metal would contract, and another strong joint would bring *Mauretania* a little closer to watertight completion.

Would he have been happier as a riveter, thought Jon as he craned to watch? Doing something clear and definite, doing it well, having the satisfaction of making something without struggling to cope with the thinking behind it, getting a wage, and going home to a simple security? No, that was ridiculous. Life was not like that: neither a riveter's life nor his own. The position and quality of his own life had been made by Fate; he had then continued to make it what it was by his own actions. And anyway, he told himself, there was nothing wrong with his work. He was succeeding at his post in the turbine works and popular with his colleagues. None suspected he was anything other than happy at home with an attractive and talented wife. Yet Maisie knew instinctively, and had been the only one honest enough to say so. Was that not why he could love her so well, so rightly? But work, work—he would make that his cure. The precision of his instruments, the beauty of the mathematics, the delicate assembly of the shining vanes which would spin power through the ship and across the ocean, the wealth and security of his family, his mother's trusting smile, his father's steady gaze. He must strive to bring it all back to his new home, drive out his own weakness, and honour his marriage.

Walking back one evening through the neat streets of Jesmond he decided he could give himself and Philippa and everything they had hoped to establish another chance. He would simply see no more of Maisie and her family unless it should be by accident. It was a dreadful thought to him, but in reality it should not be too difficult just to move his life and activities back to where they were before that fateful meeting in the drawing-loft. He had little reason to visit that part of the yard now and would strive to keep himself at the engine works as much as he could.

He hurried through the front door with a bright 'hello' and found Philippa coming down from the studio. In their conversation over supper he brought the Watsons under discussion and said quite truthfully that he had not seen Maisie for some time and that he was unlikley to have much more to do with her family. He had kept the shakiness out of his voice, and tried to banish any particular emphasis on Maisie as a topic of conversation amongst the various others he introduced over the table.

"Oh, them." He was amazed to find Philippa showed little interest. Had she any idea what he had gone through to establish and then declare this resolve? "I remember you said that girl had some talent for drawing."

Was she interested then? Was she going to challenge him, accuse him, probe him? Or had his deliberate blandness—so shameful to himself and so far from what he really felt—carried them through this conversation into the future he was trying to build.

"Some talent, yes," replied Jon. "I don't suppose

anything will come of it," he lied with an eager smile. "I want to see what *you* are drawing up there."

"Oh, just fiddling with ideas. I'm really getting ready for the London work."

"Of course: this splendid exhibition with your ship painting in it."

"Yes, although that's largely taken-care-of. I really mean the work I want to do for Robert's company. He simply must see my poster designs before he hires anyone else."

"You mean you're going to work for him?"

"Well, on and off, yes."

"And you're going back to London?"

"Of course. I shall have to—and soon. There's something unsettling in this letter from Robert."

"He writes to you?"

"Yes: business matters, letting me know what's going on. It's very good of him. But in this letter he's talking of working with French designers again. Well, I want to get in first. I shall take my new designs down next week."

Jon felt truly torn. By returning to London so soon, Philippa was knocking away the foundations of what he was trying to re-build for them both. By leaving him alone, she was allowing the temptations of his seeing Maisie to flood back.

"London again next week." To summon strength, he tried to sound like his father. What *would* his father have done in a situation like this? He imagined he would never have allowed it to develop in the first place. "London again," he

163

repeated, realising he sounded like no-one but himself.

"And I may even go on to Paris and stay a while to see what's going on there." Philippa's enthusiasm was infuriating to him; yet at the same time could it not be a wonderful release? No! While she hurried on, opening long vistas of time he could spend with Maisie, he must stick to doing what he had convinced himself was the decent thing. "You see, what with the *Entente Cordiale* and everything it means, there couldn't be a better time to go, could there?"

"Actually," Jon put down his napkin, "this may *not* be the best time to go. It's not long to Christmas. It'll look very bad if you're away then. The family won't like it. I'd like us to be together, especially for Christmas."

"Would you really?" She was being hard and sarcastic again, as if she had seen right through him and found nothing but a hollow intention. "Well," she stood up to fill a glass with port, "we don't always get what we want for Christmas, do we?"

"I had hoped not to have to argue about this," Jon heard his own voice quivering again, "but if you must go back I think you should leave it until the New Year. Your exhibition's opening then, isn't it? That would seem the right time to go. At least put on some sort of show here over Christmas."

"Some sort of show?" Now she was indignant. "I suppose you mean for the family. But deep down you don't want some sort of show, you want the show to close—but you're so weak and spineless you can't even make an end of a marriage you should never have begun."

"Shall we divorce then?" Jon felt a brutal release to have said it.

164

"Certainly not! This marriage may be finished, but it isn't over, not by any means. It's a very convenient base for everything I wish to do at the moment, and if you had any adult sense you'd see it could be exactly the same for you. I don't hate you, Jon. I have simply fallen out of love with you—as you have quite plainly fallen out of love with me. This must happen to thousands of people. Why not to us? We should be thankful it's mutual. As far as I am concerned we can continue to live here and do what we like outside the house."

"But is nothing to be saved?" Despite the swelling of release in his heart and the wild possibilities opening to him, he would try once more. "That's no way for us to live, Philippa; no way for anyone to live—and the family certainly won't understand."

"To the Devil with your family! I should never have entered it, but since I have, I am going to make the best of what there is. If you would open your eyes you'd see the best is quite good. There is plenty to be *saved*, as you put it. We have wealth together, and success in our own fields. I know you like this house and this place; it's not what I should ideally choose and I certainly don't intend to spend the rest of my life here, but I can tolerate it for the present. Look around: we live well. A divorce would certainly do my career no good, nor yours I imagine. You can go and play with your big boat and I shall develop my own career. There are all kinds of opportunities. And let's be clear about something else: you may come to my bed when you feel the need and I'll come to yours when the fancy takes me. You remain a handsome young man, and you've already discovered I'm not frigid—anything but! The family won't be looking and, as people will keep saying, it is, after all, the Twentieth Century. I say we can make the best of it."

"You haven't noticed, you haven't wanted to notice,

but that's what I have been trying to do—although along very different lines."

"Well you've made a piss-poor job of it. We could both get on perfectly well and even enjoy this sort of marriage if only you'd see what an opportunity it is for both us."

"I am beginning to see."

"Good." She drained her glass. "I have decided to leave for London tomorrow. For the sake of the respectability you hold so dear and to keep your pompous family happy, you may see me off at the station." A strange new smile came to her lips. "There's a new show opening in London this Christmas: *Peter Pan*, it's called. It's about a boy who never grows up. Every time I pass the theatre I shall think of you."

* * *

Jon walked alone out of the Central Station. Where would Philippa be now? Settled in her compartment? Crossing the bridge high above the Tyne? Gathering speed towards the South? He recalled with sorrow how different their first parting here had been; how he had shouted 'you must telegraph me from London to tell me you're safe'; how this time he had shouted nothing after his polite 'goodbye'. Today had been a sorry show indeed, he thought. While Philippa seemed content to carry on a sham for her own purposes, the whole business was just hideous to him; but he shrank almost as much from the dissolution of his marriage as he did from the impossibility of continuing it.

Yet here in the clamour of Newcastle swelling around

him, here in the place of his own birth, here came a strange balm to soothe and enrich him and fill him with a kind of hope he had not expected to feel this day. Here under the great station portico stood the Cullercoats fishwife, up from the coast with her creels of herring and crabs. She was doing brisk business: handing her customers paper-wrapped fish and pocketing silver coins somewhere deep in her traditionally pleated skirt.

This woman with her weatherbeaten face and coarsened hands, her hard life and her stoicism through it, seemed a world away from Philippa's life—but an easily-accepted and lovable part of Jon's own. He realised he had more in common with her and the life going on around her than he might ever have with his own wife and the kind of life they had tried to establish together. That was his tragedy, but also his salvation. The world of the fishwife was tough, but there was warmth in her resiliance and tolerance in the good-humoured Geordie banter he could hear as he passed into the busy streets. He found solace in the reality of his homeland; took courage from the vitality and industry of which he seemed a natural part. He had discovered with horror that there was little or nothing natural about Philippa's behaviour, at least not within their marriage. It was not entirely her own fault, his own nature and actions must be partially responsible, and they had both made the same terrible mistake. Yet whatever his resolve, whatever her tolerance, he knew they could never bridge the chasm of their differences. On his home ground with Maisie there would be no chasm. However tremendous the difficulties in making a life together—and he almost reeled from the briefest thought of them—their love would be buoyed up on mutual understanding.

The life of the city thronged and rattled around him, but his imagination had settled far beyond its streets on some distant Northumbrian beach. If only they might stand one day together beside a quiet sea and watch the cleansing, all-consoling tides about their ceaseless washing of the Earth; have misery and waste sucked out, and rise from drenching storm to endless calm. In a kind of waking dream he could not recall having experienced before, he seemed to watch old ships with unknown cargoes sail into the sunlit haze of sea and sky. Maisie was beside him; they were holding hands, their sweetest memories safely stowed, their strongest hopes ready to land them on whatever empty isle or teeming continent they might reach in swift and smiling navigation, beaching all for secure rebuilding on a sparkling shore. They would sleep in the sun, and dream more blues than in a conscious spectrum were allowed, while warm pools waited and flooded afresh, afresh with cleansing, all-consoling tides. Then they would wake to embrace in universal light slanting over the Earth's round shoulder, bared and lovely for the sun's caress.

CHAPTER NINE
Silent Night

"So yer off spending money again?" Matthew Watson eyed his daughter adjusting her hat.

"Only a bit of Christmas shopping, Dad." She looked lovely, he thought, pulling on her gloves like a proper lady. "I'll be going back into town next Saturday with Mam, but I want so buy some secret presents today. You know, surprises."

"Well don't be surprised when you've no money left." Her father's reproach came with a good-humoured smile.

"It's all right, Dad, I've been saving up. I'll be back for tea-time."

She trotted through the door to catch a tram to Newcastle, making no mention of the beating in her heart or the letter in her handbag.

It had been delivered anonymously to the drawing-loft. On the landing of the loft, each girl had a peg and small cubby-hole for bags or a change of shoes, and there she had found an envelope addressed formally to *Miss. Mary Watson*. Even before she opened it, she had known it would be from Jon.

She read its single page again and again as she sat in the swaying tram. His wife had gone away once more to

London. His marriage was an empty shell. He could not be sure what would happen now; all he knew was that the love he had found with herself was rich and true. If she could truly love him against the odds, odds he could not pretend were all in their favour, and bravely face the difficulties he could not deny, there was some hope for their future: a future he desperately wanted to share with her. He knew they had both tried to stay apart and but that to keep doing so was against all their instincts. Would she bring him joy and do him the honour of meeting him in Newcastle on Saturday? She stepped off the tram into busy Northumberland Street.

There were colourful Christmas decorations in the big shop windows, notably Fenwick's department store, at which wealthy-looking mothers were standing with their children, who seemed oblivious to the passing rattle of horses and carts, trams and the occasional motor car. Already they were filled with the excitement of the season, captured in the gleaming red and silver trappings of the shops made brighter by contrast with a cold grey sky. It was amazing how much busier the town had become over recent Christmases, thought Maisie. The new century had brought new things to buy and new ways of advertising them and people seemed to have more money, but with it had come a brashness which took away some of the glow she remembered from her childhood Christmases. She would make trips to town with her father when it had been darker and more dimly lit and they would always go through the fascinating Grainger Market, walking this very route she was taking now.

There was Grey's Monument at the junction of the big streets. As always, she looked up at the statue of the man who had led parliamentary reform and imagined his magnificent view over the town. She didn't pretend to know much about Parliament but she knew from her history lessons that it had needed reforming and that Grey had been the great man to do it. There seemed to be a need of great men now and not too many of them about, what with seething politics abroad and unrest in the yards and factories at home. If the world was run by women, she reminded herself with a smile, it would be a more sensible place.

Then she was threading her way into the vast covered market and for a moment forgot her thoughts of history, politics, and modern times and even the nagging worries and tremulous excitements about Jon which she had been carrying all the way on this journey. Here she was inside the Christmas world of her own childhood: cosy and dramatic, rich and threadbare, exciting and soothing all at the same time. The aisles of butchers' stalls were thronged with shoppers looking at geese and pheasants, sausages and eggs. Here were the cheap clothes stalls and the tiny toyshop like a jewellery-box of childish delights. Here were the fruit shops with ordinary apples and oranges alongside special things for Christmas: figs from the Holy Land and dates from the desert. The familiar box had French writing on it and pictures of Arabs on their camels, and she always felt as if a scene from the Bible was somehow made real with that box: baby Jesus had been born in the stable just out of the picture and the Three Wise Men were coming over the dunes on their camels carrying dates with exactly the same sweet sticky taste as these. She could never remember a Christmas without a box of dates in the house and she bought one to take home.

Then she was outside under chill clouds. She was a grown woman, walking beneath sooty buildings, treading old cobbles in Twentieth-Century boots, heading into a less familiar part of town to meet her lover. Baby Jesus had grown up and died for our sins and every time you sinned He suffered all over again and it was your fault, but you could be forgiven if you went to the priest and confessed how bad you had been and promised never to do it again—at least that's what her Catholic friend Veronica believed, or something like that. She wasn't sure what she herself believed, or what anyone believed. She knew what was wrong and what was right, whether or not God or Jesus or anybody else had anything to do with it. She knew what was right between people living now, today. She knew what was fair and honourable between men and women; she knew the power of true love could not be evil—or she told herself she did as she walked down her historic streets towards the steam-wreathed ship-hooting river, under the great lantern tower of her Cathedral and its famous 'clock with the fiery face' from the Geordie song. Would Veronica do this, knowing it would be what she would call a sin? And if she did, would she then put it all right by a visit to her own Cathedral at the opposite end of town? She strode on, deciding she couldn't tell what Veronica would do, since Veronica wasn't in love.

Jon was outside Pumphrey's Coffee Shop at the appointed time, just as he had promised in his letter. A stab of anxious excitement went through his body as he saw Maisie's trim figure cross the cobbles towards him, but he also recognised another emotion: pure joy. With her short-stepped run in her polished black boots she seemed to turn a key in his soul, opening doors to a magical future. At the coffee shop's door she was girlish and bright and as her fresh smell of soap rose in the chilly shadows above the clasp of their hands he was filled with desire to kiss her; but to kiss here in the street, full on the lips: no, that was not done, she would not expect it, it would not be proper. Instead he kissed her hand in the continental way—and that indeed seemed right as she responded with a glittering smile and a movement he hoped was something like a shiver of pleasure. It was a whisper of sunlit re-birth even in the deadly midwinter cold. Had it always been the same for lovers, thought Jon, this strange renewal of life from death, this gain from loss? So slow, the longed-for harvest against the terrible rushing of time and circumstance; but here, through the very fist of Winter, a flower could smile and a seed be sown.

"I hoped to God you would meet me," he said quietly.

"How could I not meet you after your wonderful letter?" she smiled at him.

"I'm not sure it was so wonderful."

"You're a brave and honest man."

He took her inside to fragrant warmth, up a broad staircase to an unexpectedly gracious room where cold lucheon was spread on a central table and waitresses bustled about with teas and coffees.

"Let's go to the window seat," he said. "I was brought here by my mother before I went away to London and I always remembered it as my favourite little piece of old Newcastle…"

"…And now we'll always come here together," she smiled.

"We certainly will."

For some time they sat quietly on the high-backed upholstered seats, as if cosily in a railway carriage. They looked down into the old-fashioned street with its mysterious yards and fascinating alleyways, or up to St. Nicholas's where gilded weathercocks flew cold Northern air, but mostly at each other, as if searching eyes for a glimpse of soul to be revealed here, now, at this pre-ordained meeting on what to them had already become hallowed ground. Maisie drank more coffee and looked back at Jon.

"I came here ready to say all kinds of things to you," she confessed, "but now I canna think straight to remember

173

any of them, except I just want to be with you. What were you really going to tell me today?"

"That I love you truly, Maisie," he declared, "that I've struggled terribly over all this, first with Philippa coming back from London then going away again. There was a time I tried to make another go of our marriage, you know. I really did try not to see you again."

"I knew you would try that." Her smile over the cup was both provocative and mild. "Didn't work, did it?"

"No it didn't. Even if it had worked from my point of view—which, loving you so much, it just couldn't—she would have ruined it all again by going away as she did, saying what she said, making it quite plain her idea of marriage to me was some kind of sordid, lustful, business arrangement. More business than lust, I can tell you."

"You don't feel any lust for her now, like?"

"No!" He was defensive against her strange smile. "Are you teasing me?"

"You're nice to tease, Jon, just sometimes…Oh Jon…" she put down her cup, looked with agony into his face, "…I didn't mean to hurt you. Oh, that's terrible. I'll go on hurting you with me saying daft things at the wrong time."

Jon had recovered and took her hand again.

"No, no. The only way you hurt me is…like a phrase of Chopin." There was a long pause, filled with chatter from the room, the aromas of coffee and food, the distant clatter of the street below. "No, with you I am not hurt, I am regenerated—by finding the one person who can redeem me, forgive my sins."

"What sins?"

"You know very well. But my greatest sin was in marrying Philippa: the worst thing I ever did—for her as well as for me. I never intended to make her unhappy. I thought I loved her. I genuinely wanted to give her a good life. I was dazzled by her good looks and vivacious ways, and by her undoubted talent. I'm not taking that away from her. She's a remarkable woman in many ways; I'm sure she will become a very successful commercial artist. But continuing to live with her is intolerable now…now I love you and know what you feel for me. But am I justified in breaking rules I've always lived by to secure my own happiness?"

"It's our happiness."

She sounded pert; Jon could only sound desperate.

"Some would say we have no right to happiness; that people like us are born to endure separation."

"They don't have to." She hated to hear the anguish in his voice, to see the clouding of his fine face.

"They do," he went on, "because breaking laws and morals brings misery. But I ask myself over and over again: should we not go through the misery into something better? And what would be left if we were to deny each other? Nothing but greater misery and empty memories."

"That's right." She smiled and took his hand. "And it's not wicked to love me just because you've married the wrong woman."

"Oh, it is wicked. It's a sin, and you know it."

She didn't know where she found the strength to

carry on, here in this public place, but she smiled at him again and held tightly to his hand. He was too good a man to lose, she had kept telling herself. Now she would tell him. The strength was there, inside her. She must give it to him so that he, too, could be happy.

"It might be a sin in the eyes of the law and the Church and all these people here and everybody else but I also know it's right. It is, you know. I told you I knew it was right on the beach that glorious Summer day. D'you not remember everything we felt, everything we knew was true? All the same though," she folded her arms forcefully back on the table, looking older and more stern, "I didn't just come here because you wanted to see me. I came to say something as well: to give you a chance to give me up."

Jon looked shocked but she went on.

"Not for the reasons we've been talking about; for another reason. I don't belong in your world, Jon. I know what your family would think of me."

"What rubbish!"

"No no, be honest now, like you've been honest about everything else. I know what your family would think of me: some common working lass from the river."

"That's not true."

"Oh, grow up Jon man, of course it's true! I'd never grace one of your family parties in Heaton."

"You'd be the most graceful thing there."

"But the maids you've got and the people you meet in that Jesmond house of yours, they'd all be laughing at us looking and sounding stupid and ignorant."

"They'd be the stupid and ignorant ones, Maisie. We talked about this on the beach, didn't we? I said then you are a lady and you always will be. We both have to be above such nonsense. Anyway, I don't care what my family think."

"You will one day, and I don't want you to be ashamed of me."

"Ashamed? I couldn't be ashamed of you. I could only be ashamed of myself if I let stupid snobbery and narrow-mindedness ruin what we've got between us."

"Well," she looked out of the window, sighed, and put her arms back towards him across the table, "I just wanted to give you the chance. I think you're a brave and honest man. I'm giving you the chance to give me up. That'll need a different kind of bravery."

They looked into each others eyes again and—completely unexpectedly, but sweetly and gloriously—a strange, soft laugh was in danger of bursting out between them.

"There's no chance," grinned Jon, "no chance at all." Then he took her hands and looked at her delicate fingers and his voice sounded serious again. "It is true. For the first time I've found the one person I can truly love: you. You are the very centre of me; everything I am is now for you. Would it be right to waste this marvellous union of spirits just for some rotten convention? The marriage is over. It's nothing but a paper bond, and that bond will eventually be dissolved, whatever she says now. And my family can think what they like; one day they'll come to see what a good and lovely person you are and they'll have to acknowledge and accept our love or they can all go the Devil. But now, only you can save me."

"All right then. We'll save each other, won't we?"

"I wish…" Jon looked down into the street again, "I just wish you could come home with me, now."

"I canna come home with you Jon, you know that." She put her hands over his. "Not just yet."

* * *

On Jon's next visit to Newcastle he joined Christmas shoppers in Fenwick's and climbed the stairs to the Ladies' Fashions Department.

"Oh, yes sir," the little shop-assistant was pleased to make an expensive sale, and her customer's charm had been infectious, "the lady will be very warm under this one. It'll make a lovely Christmas present, sir."

"I hope so."

"It's a grand box as well, isn't it, sir?" They shared their glee as a large round box, decorated in green and gold, was placed on the counter. "A new hat for the new year!"

So here he was again, carrying a parcel through the streets, full of plans, full of love. The hat was large and stylish, made of rich brown fur he thought would go so well with the blue coat Maisie wore. He would re-wrap it when he arrived home, and place the Christmas card he had already written inside the box on top of the tissue paper covering the hat. He thought the card itself was a triumph of symbolism. Instead of the robins, fur-clad children playing in snow, churches, sleighs and stained-glass windows that featured in all the stationers' shops, he had found a card with a picture of a great galleon sailing a golden sea, banners and pennants streaming from its masts. It was shown laden with gifts and above it silver clouds parted to reveal angels with trumpets. The galleon was the ship whose building had brought them together, the gifts were his gifts of love, the angels' songs of joy were for them. This Christmas would be the start of their great voyage together, through stormy seas perhaps, but at last—through love and understanding—into wondrous calm. And accepting this hat and this card, she would let in his love after so much drought, and his love would flood her, but with such gentleness, such honesty, so many more hats, and so much more than hats. But this was a beginning, at the end of the old year and the start of the new. When she wore it and laughed, he would know innocent happiness. This year he had bought her a new hat. Next year he would take it off to kiss her hair.

* * *

On the dark afternoon of Christmas Eve Jon went from the engine works down to *Mauretania's* building-shed. His supposed mission to report on the progress of her after-section in readiness for delivery of the lower turbine casings was secondary in his mind to a hot desire to see Maisie—a hot desire shivered through with doubts and uncertainties. He hoped desperately to see her, wish her a Merry Christmas with love, and give her the hat. He could not just leave it in the loft for her, did not want to leave it with just a note, he had to see her and present his gift face to face. It would surely be better this way—but when she took it home would she acknowledge who it was from, or despite their resolve and declarations, must his love bring deceit and

179

discord into her family as it had brought ruin into his own?

There rose the great hull under a blaze of electric lights which was itself like some benign radiance from gigantic Christmas decorations, but any homely associations were dispelled by the incessant rattle of the riveters and the brutal clang of heavy hammers on enormous steel plates. Elsewhere, Christmas Eve might be given up to a sense of excited anticipation and impending festivities, but here in the berth work continued apace through the rapidly darkening afternoon.

It took Jon longer than he would have liked to accomplish his task, writing the notes he had been told to make amongst a tangle of pneumatic hoses and pipework cluttering the vast after-section of the hull through which he had to clamber. As always on these sorties, he was accompanied by Stevenson the yard manager, a man much concerned with safety procedures and Board of Trade regulations. Jon imagined that he himself might constitute an infringement; sparks of his suspicious unease fanned into blushes under the glare of Stevenson's sharp looks and critical manner.

"Christmas parcels, have we, Mister Ferris?" Stevenson eyed the bundle of box and briefcase under Jon's arm. "Someone's a lucky person. Mind yourself as you go through here."

What did they really think of him in the yard? Did they know about Maisie? What was happening at home? Would he cause his father more disappoinment and his mother more anguish? What was happening at the house in Union Street? Had he done only wrong, brought trouble instead of joy this Christmas? Christmas: he was both riven with guilt and sparkling with delight, his spirits tossed in hectic contrast to the stolid bulk of the liner growing around him, rooted to her keel-blocks and seeming as heavy and immobile as a mountain. But one day she would float, majestic and free, alive with warmth and splendour, her magical vitality spun by awesome power. He himself would play a tiny part in bestowing that power upon her and the world. It was a time to admit pride and feel joy, to leap from the sins of deception to the holiness of love, to fling defiance in the face of death and dullards and anything which might stand in the way of regeneration. Out of this bleak midwinter new stars and suns would surely rise for Maisie and himself. As the ship would float into immeasurably wide seas, so their love would flower into freedom—or so it seemed to Jon as he turned at Stevenson's request.

"See here, Mister Ferris." Pride had also affected Stevenson's voice. "We're about midships here. She's pretty solid aft of us, double bottom and bilges sealed up now, just about ready for the turbine casings. If you look aft it's a grand view: you can see one of the holes where the shafts will go out."

Jon squinted at the flare of artificial light, many yards distant down the curving steel floor.

"Oh yes, I see! It's like light at the end of a tunnel."

"Aye, there'll be four of your shafts running down there, and a foaming wake beyond them one day—and plenty noise where we're standing now, I imagine."

"A turbine is surprisingly quiet, Mister Stevenson."

"I have yet to see such a thing," Stevenson's admission was tinged with awe, "nor properly imagine how it goes. Steam roaring through great silver vanes of a thousand windmills: it's like a dream."

"It's an engineer's dream, Mister Stevenson," smiled Jon, "and you've imagined it with some brilliance. A thousand windmills indeed; but now imagine the power of twenty-thousand windmills, pushing water faster than dusty grindstones ever turned."

"Aye, it'll be champion. Well, you can make your report to the engine works with satisfaction, I think. Mind yourself as you're going down. A merry Christmas to you sir, and your family."

"And to you, Mister Stevenson."

By the time Jon had negotiated the hazards of steel and timber to make his way out of the hull, noises in the berth had abated as workers prepared to 'knock off' for Christmas Eve. All along the Tyne, hooters in factories and shipyards signalled the beginning of the holiday and the steady homeward tramp of feet began. Jon walked up towards the drawing-loft. Would Maisie be coming down those wooden steps? Would this be his chance to deliver his present and wish her love and happiness for Christmas?

The blank, unlighted windows of the drawing-loft revealed plainly that its staff had been sent home early. So Maisie would not greet him with the pleasure and surprise he had so long anticipated. His carefully arranged expedition had come to nothing. Would his honesty make a merry Christmas for any of them, or by admitting his feelings and acting upon them was he spreading only woe?

He sat forlornly on the bottom step. Up and down these wooden stairs trotted the drawing-loft girls, Maisie with them yet so unlike them. Alone among her workmates she wore her coat with a ladylike grace, from her alone rose a faint clean perfume into the chill air, her pale skin and bright eyes now the light of his world in all its garish darkness. He missed her vital presence, longed for even a glimpse of her, yet admitted to some cowardly relief that tonight, after all, he did not have to run the gauntlet of the other girls' giggles, the downcast sneers of the workmen, and the silent but barely-concealed accusations of an illicit love-affair, of deception, of adultery. Had his efforts to fight down his desire and abide by his old rules been merely weakness? Had he made any effort at all? Philippa had made the effort: with a few harsh words setting him free; with a few others trapping him in their loveless marriage, refusing even to consider divorce. Would he always be alone in darkness, waiting for circumstances to change? At least he was on the very wood down which Maisie's light feet must run, and could grasp the very handrail stroked by her fingers. That alone seemed a privilege, and would have to suffice as his Christmas treat—if he allowed himself to believe he deserved one.

This was no use, he told himself, and prepared to go. It would be a long ride home on the train. He stood up—but was immediately frozen to the spot as a new and unexpected sound came to his ears. It was music. Somewhere in the now-quiet shipyard someone was playing a concertina: a lone workman sending his comrades home with a seasonal tune. But this was no rousing hymn, no jaunty carol; this was *Silent Night*: sweet and slow, note-perfect, echoing faintly around the gigantic ship, up to the enormous glass roof and down to Jon's small figure. It was the twinkle of stars and teardrops, the tingle of skin and frost; the melody so rich and swelling, the sentiment so tender and mild; and here came the heart-rush of emotions with the music of hope and salvation, redemption and love. The blessing of love above all: love in the frozen blue night, love across the whole Earth, love beneath the changeless stars.

* * *

In Union Street the carol-singers were assembling around lamp-posts, catching what brightness they could from the gaslight to aid the efforts of the little boy with a lantern, borne proudly on the end of a pole too long for him to manage. They were catching a few pennies from shipyard workers homeward bound as well as whatever they might be given through front doors. Maisie was watching from an upstairs window.

"Look at him, Mam," she giggled, "the lad with the pole. It's far too big for him!"

"Canny voice though, or one of them has."

"Little George'll be going out with them next year."

"He wanted to go this year like but I wouldn't let him, not with all the coughs and colds about and one daughter just over the fever."

"Oh for Heavens' sake, Mam, I'm all right now. Don't spoil the singing with worries. I'm all right and everything else is ganna be all right. Just wait and see."

"I wish I could be sure of that, lass."

Maisie put her arm around her mother.

"Let's just listen, Mam."

The song was *Silent Night*, the voices slow and sweet. Maisie's thoughts of were of Jon: the warm feeling of his hands around hers in the coffee shop, the way he kissed her hand with shy grace and controlled passion, their silent walk up Tynemouth Long Sands in weather so different from this dry, cold, Christmas Eve with its black sky and frozen stars. So far she hadn't found him a Christmas present. She could afford something out of her wages, but the joy of her plans was rubbed off by the sadness of having to do it in secret: Mam and Dad weren't ready for the whole truth yet. She hated being deceitful to anyone, most of all to people she loved in her own family; at this time of year it was somehow even worse. But she would buy Jon a New Year present after this difficult year was over: something to symbolise a new start in a surely better year, something fresh and never used before, something just waiting to become Jon's and be used and enjoyed in a glorious future.

Little George came to the window and looked down into the street, cocking his head as he listened to the carol. At first he hummed along to the tune, but the very strength and purity of the voices seemed to silence the child and his little fingers crept into his mouth, his wide eyes staring into the gaslight, as if drawing wonders from a well of sound and shadows. His face, thought Maisie, was a picture of innocent delight; and knowing he was her lovable little brother would have to be her Christmas treat—if she allowed herself to believe she deserved one.

* * *

"Such a shame dear Philippa can't be with us…and at Christmas, of all times…well that's what happens when women give themselves careers; never held with it myself…there's enough to do at home…running a family should be the woman's career…I suppose that picture of hers will make some sort of success…painting pictures? No money in that…"

The chatter went on around the great dining-table. This was the first uncomfortable Christmas dinner Jon could remember. All his life, Christmas had been a simple, honest, reliable, thoroughly enjoyable holiday. The wealth and importance of the Ferris family had never seemed to spoil its innocence; family crises had never intruded upon their traditional celebrations. But for Jon, and for all of them, Christmas 1904 was different.

Down the river in Wallsend what would Maisie be doing now? Would her family be having their Christmas dinner at this very moment? He raised his Champagne glass in a silent toast to her, staring into the wine-gold crystal, becoming part of its tiny, sweet and lovely world: a world of happiness and bubbles. There were worse things to be than a Champagne bubble. You grew from a mysterious fountain on the side of a sparkling glass, rose in a stream to a fragrant surface, and escaped into eternity…but no Champagne bubble knew the joys of loving a woman, nor the privilege of being loved by a woman as rare as Mary Watson. He would raise a silent, secret toast to her now, sweet Maisie only a few miles away, due East down the river. Now, which way was East from here? Yes, just to his right and a little behind him.

"Jon dear!" His mother's quizzical look across the table was mixture of amusement and alarm. "What on Earth are you doing?"

"I'm…er…I'm listening to the bubbles."

CHAPTER TEN
Unveiled

"Merry Christmas!"

Philippa raised her glass to applause from the small crowd gathered in the foyer of Robert Gough's printing works, the sleeves of her new silk blouse rustling expensively, electric light falling on her bright hair.

"And a very prosperous New Year," smiled Robert as the toast dissolved into chatter around the newly unveiled ship painting. Its daring perspective and strong colours now dominated the foyer and were still exciting comment from the critics, businessmen, and other guests at Philippa's London debut. "Well," he continued, "it's going to be prosperous, isn't it?"

"I'm sure it is," she replied eagerly, "thanks to all you have done here."

"What about all you have done there?" Robert indicated the painting on its display easel. "None of this would be happening without your vision."

"We will do well for each other," she stated coolly, "but I know where thanks are due, and I do appreciate all this, here at the beginning of our collaboration. You have given me a wonderful opportunity, and I'm so glad you decided to launch the painting before Christmas rather than wait until the New Year. It's been very exciting."

"I'm delighted you've enjoyed it."

They raised their glasses and drank again.

"So tell me," continued Robert. "What does your new success feel like?"

"It's my *first* success, to be honest," she admitted, "so all the more reason to thank you again."

"You'll embarrass me."

"I doubt that. But I feel…glowing, really; pleased with myself, quite shamelessly pleased with myself…and, well, hugely relieved. Is this what success should feel like?"

"Yes," he smiled again, "Lovely, isn't it?"

"Lovely," she grinned.

"Good. So never let anyone tell you success is overrated or that its trappings are worthless. It's true that success can play tricks on you, sometimes exact a cruel price, and often vanish, but while it's happening its wonderful. And the spoilsports are wrong: success isn't hollow, it's full of delights. You shall partake of them."

"Frankly Robert," she laughed, "I'm too sozzled to partake of very much more. I seem to be wandering through a dream."

"Don't worry, I have to stay on here to the bitter end, but I shall see you are returned safely to your hotel…where you may drift off knowing your dream is coming true. It really is coming true when the critics leave early. Charles Bosanquet hurried back to *The Times* half an hour ago. You have nothing to fear there. Kershaw of the *Standard*—who always writes his critique *before* he attends the private view so he can spend his time boozing and gossiping—has just gone: presumably to change his copy; and after all his whisky and Champagne—or I should say after all *my* whisky and Champagne—he'll have the Devil's own job coming up with something better than his usual 'remarkables' and 'praiseworthys', but he'll manage it. You'll have good reading at breakfast tomorrow."

"Good Heavens," she giggled. "I'll be lucky if I can see straight at breakfast—whenever I wake up for it. But it has been marvellous, Robert, simply marvellous. After all that's been happening back in Newcastle, I honestly didn't expect another London Christmas for a while. It's been a lovely surprise."

"Well," Robert took her hands, "I hope our latest celebrity has room for another surprise. After your London Christmas, what about a Paris New Year and a commission to do some posters?"

* * *

Through the first weeks of the new year the North of England was bathed in mild weather. Dry and bright days were not uncommon in a Northumbrian January, but this year's 'false Spring' seemed more surprising as a sparkling sun poured through bare branches. Stark streets along the Tyne took on Summer hues. On his morning journeys to the engine works, Jon felt bathed again in a comfortably familiar Scandinavian climate, although as far as he knew the only member of his family to visit Norway and Sweden had been his Uncle Edward on that Baltic steamer. Was it possible to inherit memories? Walking through Newcastle he saw again the brightness of medieval centuries brought brilliantly to life in his own time; the dazzling colours of an illuminated manuscript on towers and spires and those gilded weathercocks flying chilly air while mild sunshine softened everything in his dreaming afternoons. Then the light was like an angel sighing over the town, her great wings casting shadows of warmth as soft and shapeless as the memory of a dream, and his love for Maisie was as fine and courtly as that in any ancient Romance, yet as real as the tortured grind of wheels on cobbles, as modern as the gleaming vanes of the turbines under construction   below his glass-sided office.

As he walked through the town and past shops announcing their January sales, he was tempted again to buy things for Maisie, to shower her with gifts, to dress her up in the finest clothes: something he had never felt for Philippa, even in his earliest days with her. Philippa had been smart and fashionable, always elegant and sometimes seductive, but rarely sensual and never sweetly welcoming. Maisie's body was slender and beautiful, waiting to be dressed in clothes she would wear with grace, and no richness would corrupt her simple goodness. Each purchase of a dress or a coat would be a joy, and the clothes themselves treasured as special tokens of love. Yet he could not go buying things without her there; these joys would have to wait, like so many others, for fufilment in a clean new life they had not yet attained.

He thought again of the fur hat, still wrapped magnificently and kept in secret for her. Since Christmas there had been no opportunity to see Maisie and present the hat, but the gift should not be delayed much longer. Now he had heard from Philippa that she was going straight to Paris after the successful launch of her painting, the way was clearer than ever. She had had what Jon regarded as the temerity to send him newspaper cuttings of her good reviews. Estranged though they were, he felt she was asking for his approval and a distant celebration of her success. As he walked through the sunlit North, all he felt was a noting of her success: a fact amongst others of a London life he realised he was no longer able to imagine, and wondered vaguely whose fault that might be. He was not yet free, but his chains felt loose.

So it was that Jon arranged another late afternoon visit to the berth, hoping Maisie had found the note he had left in her pigeon-hole and that somehow she would be able to stay behind unnnoticed, or at least without exciting too much comment. Jon loitered in shadows from which *Mauretania* reared her gigantic blackness into the lights, themselves stabbing from the wider blackness of the sky above her building-shed. One day, he told himself, their meetings would no longer be clandestine, one day when everyone knew the truth of their love and accepted it, and their new lives had truly begun. But on this January night they were still in the dark and twisting tunnel of subterfuge.

* * *

Paris in Winter was bright and cold. Philippa was invigorated by the brisk and sunny air, so different from a gloomy London of foggy streets and stuffy rooms. She went along the wide boulevards and through the great buildings with Robert Gough as her attentive escort. They seemed to have buried dislike and mistrust and found a genuine friendship alongside their business arrangements, cooler and more distant than either might originally have hoped for, but secure enough to guarantee a mutual enjoyment of the city's pleasures: vast or intimate, rediscovered with Robert's delight or encountered for the first time with Philippa's glee.

From her elegant hotel on the Avenue Wagram near

the Arc de Triomphe she was met by Robert in a new Renault motor-car. He had hired it for the occasion, and they drove all over star-shaped Paris. As the city she had imagined from Robert's descriptions in the Alnmouth tea-room unfolded its reality around her, she realised how far she had travelled from her quiet Northumbrian seaside honeymoon with another man. What was her husband doing in those glum streets so far away? The thought scarcely troubled her. She must admit her failed marriage was a fact of her life, but today it seemed a fact of considerably less significance than the rich blackness of her new muff, the modern style of her motorised progress down the Champs-Élysées, and the possibilities of her commission to design advertising posters in the greatest capital of Art.

They were here on business, but Robert continued to play the generous host and tireless guide. He despised the tourist haunts of opera and cabaret, Cathedral and monument, but insisted on a full afternoon in the Louvre, where Philippa was fascinated to see paintings she had read about for so long. Modern paintings in smaller galleries they visited excited her more, and at a startling exhibiton of photographs she began to form new ideas for her posters. All the time she was aware that this great city held precious knowledge and experience: sometimes blatant, sometimes secretive, some force of inspiration between shabby street and splendid palace. Through its vast weight of history and its ceaseless artistic endeavour this culture pressed on. Alive in Winter sunlight sparkling through the trees or caught in the glamorous necklace of lights springing up every evening along the Seine, here it was, spread before her in this banquet of joyous and teasing opportunities.

"And you," smiled Robert over their *crêpes*, "the great modernist, do you like the Tower?"

"Yes I do. It's magnificent."

"It's been open for nearly twenty years and nobody here seems used to it; de Maupassant said its restaurant was his favourite place for lunch because from there he didn't have to look at it…but by then he was potty old man, of course."

"Well, I love it," enthused Philippa. "I love everything: the delicious smells in the food shops, the way they wash the streets every morning, the beautiful ironwork on the railway stations, the photographs—especially the photographs. I had no idea photography was so advanced here; one hardly sees a camera in England. Photography is going to become very important in your business, Robert, and I think in my work, too."

"Yes, I'm sure you're right. You'll have an opportunity to discuss that tomorrow with Marcel, our young manager at the gallery."

"Oh yes," Philippa flashed an excited look over her cognac, "am I really going to go round the print works?"

"Not unless you absolutely insist. The printing's done in a new place on the outskirts of the city, just a factory really. No, the best thing to see is the gallery. It's a vital showcase for our work. Most of what they display are French designs, naturally enough; we are one of just a few foreign companies they deal with. It hasn't been easy to break into the continental market, especially since the French are so good at posters anyway."

"Coals to Newcastle, eh?" smirked Philippa.

"I wasn't going to use that expression, but you'll re-light our furnace here by carrying some glowing brilliance *from* Newcastle."

193

"Really Robert," she smiled, "you do stretch the metaphor. Anyway," she finished her drink, "it all sounds marvellous and you're giving me a tremendous time."

"I promise you'll have another good day tomorrow. By the way, d'you want a contract for doing the first posters or shall we just shake on it?"

Philippa gave her most glittering smile.

"Let's have it all written down, shall we?"

The next morning the Renault took them on to the Left Bank, down the Boulevard Raspail, and into the Luxembourg Gardens. Here Philippa was led briskly through the cold air, admiring the statues, noticing the processions of schoolgirls with their nuns or governesses, and recoiling from the unexpected contrast of tramps waking from unwashed and alcoholic oblivion into clean sunlight on their benches. Robert took her to lunch through the narrow medieval streets of the Latin Quarter. Braziers burned at tables outside the café, but nothing could match the warmth and temptation of comforting food and drink to be enjoyed in its dark and fragrant interior. Then at last she was taken to the gallery on the Rue Saint Jacques, and Robert ushered her through its new glass doors.

Marcel was a thin young man, his hair dark and long around an eager and intelligent face. He welcomed Robert and Philippa with great courtesy, and showed them the displays of advertising posters with much pride. She saw at once the innovative design, high technical quality, and brilliance of execution she would have to match if her designs were to stand alongside these, displayed as they were with a sense of importance and reverence to equal anything in the fine art galleries. Robert hovered, quietly investing Philippa with the exotic qualities of a visiting genius. Then a secretary appeared, insisting Robert must hurry into the office and answer a telegram from 'Monsieur Sloane in England'.

"Well", Philippa smiled, alone with her guide, "this really has been a delightful experience—and I must say you speak perfect English, Marcel."

"Thank you. It is necessary for me to do so because the Americans and English who come here refuse to speak perfect French, or indeed any French."

"I know," she giggled. "We're awful about languages, aren't we?"

"But you, Madame, could never be awful in any language. You are a very talented and beautiful woman, and adventurous also, I think. And to speak again of delightful experiences…" He passed a glance slowly down her body and up again to her eyes. "…I hope we may share more."

Philippa gave him a steady look, and licked her lips.

"I hope so too."

"Tonight!"

"That," she glanced at the door, "may be difficult."

"I shall come to your hotel."

"No." She stepped forward. "No. You understand that would never do, not with Robert here…but, well, now I come to think of it, Monsieur Gough and myself have a purely business relationship, and his dream of a delightful experience is certainly not mine. You have no idea what I'm talking about, have you?"

"Madame?"

"You are not, shall we say, 'intimate' with Monsieur Gough?"

Marcel shrugged dismissively.

"I do not understand what you speak, Madame. Monsieur Gough comes to Paris occasionally, I see him here, I know him only as a great gentleman of business."

"Thank God for that." She brightened with a wicked spark. "Well now, I think perhaps we could enjoy an evening together."

"Oh, there is none of your English 'perhaps'; it *will* be enjoyment for us. All this afternoon I have desired to kneel to you…"

"Dear me," she strolled over to the window, "how extravagantly romantic."

"…but not, you understand, as an English knight to his lady, oh no. I mean to kneel to you as a French lover, and you shall welcome me *à la Narbonne*."

"Really Marcel," she affected an innocent smile, "now it is I who have no idea what *you're* talking about."

"Oh but you shall. You shall find it most pleasurable, I assure you." He was urgent again, and stepped close to her. "Return here to the gallery alone. I shall be waiting for you."

* * *

Maisie crept back up the final flight of stairs and

opened the door into the drawing-loft. The big room appeared afloat on dazzling moonlight. It held remains of warmth from its heating pipes and from a day's sunshine which had poured through the enormous skylights, now showing a translucent midnight blue above her head. The place was empty and still, yet could not have seemed more alive: vibrant with the smells of chalk and ink and a faint and lovely fragrance rising from enormous sheets of paper rippling over the blackboard floor. Maisie stood entranced in the doorway. This was where she worked every day, but it had never looked or felt like this: a benighted Cathedral of Industry, a mysteriously warmed Winter grotto, fit place for a lovers' meeting.

Jon was nowhere to be seen, but she would wait as requested in his note. Before her spread the plans of *Mauretania* being enlarged to actual size: pieces of the huge liner coming to reality on this very floor. Under this enchanted night sky, it was easy to believe the dream-ship might suddenly, magically, frighteningly struggle up off the paper into a startling third dimension through barred shadows, black under blazing moonshafts. She gave a little shudder: not afraid, but awed by the drama of this vast space. Where was Jon? She ached to see him: a real ache, a real tension in her body, tingling now as desires she could not and would not control took posession of her. She walked out across the loft, the broad floor as tempting as a beach, a meadow, or a ballroom. Her boots rang very hard on the boards and echoed up to the skylights; she bent down to unbutton them and pull them off. She felt freer and more adventurous without boots, but her black stockings offended her fairytale mood. It took only a few moments to roll them off her legs, step forward out of her own shadow, and skip with bare feet into the middle of the floor, the dry paper crackling slightly under her heels. This place of all places, she thought, was the place to go barefoot—and feeling the swish of her skirt against her legs, watching moonlight flash on her toes, she danced to the sweetest, dreamiest waltzes she could imagine, her arms resting on silver shafts of light, her feet swishing in and out of the moon-squares.

A noise like a gunshot tripped her into terrible shock. Another and another! Her heart leapt up, her hands flashed to her face to stifle a scream. Another and another and another! Her eyes popped, her skin was drenched in a sweat of fear. Another and another and another and another! But they were not gunshots—they were handclaps. Someone was clapping, now faster and more softly, now it stopped…and out of the shadowed doorway stepped Jon, his arms spread wide. Maisie flew to him and clung like a terrified child.

"I'm sorry, I'm sorry, Darling," he crooned, stroking her hair. "I'm so sorry I frightened you…but you looked so lovely dancing there. You looked so sweet and lovely. I wanted to give you a standing ovation!"

She grinned up at him.

"I nearly died, man!"

They found their smiles and kisses in their own shadows.

"I didn't know if you were a ghost," she went on.

"No, I'm alive, thank God. You're the spirit: the spirit of ecstacy and freedom, loveliness and innocence. Tonight you're not of this world, you're pure spirit."

"Get away! I was just having a bit dance."

He held her from him.

"Don't stop," he smiled.

"I canna go on now you've caught us," she chuckled. "I feel daft."

"No, no," he took her hand. "Come on." He steered her along the floor, the patter of her naked feet in strange counterpoint to his firm stride across the paper. "This is it—look." He held her ready to dance.

"What d'you mean?" she laughed.

"Look down…no, here. See?"

"No."

"The ballroom. This is the plan of the ballroom. We're standing on it now."

"Oh," she softened in his arms, "I see now."

They took a few steps of a private, sacred dance.

"It's all ours tonight, darling Maisie, just as it will always be, as far as I'm concerned. One day I'll see you dance in the real ship when it's built…First Class to New York."

They stopped, the tiny waltz running its course quite naturally into a tender embrace, where they stayed for long moments, swaying slightly, stroking each other's hair.

"I have a present for you," he whispered. "That's why I had to see you tonight. It was meant to be a Christmas present but now it's a New Year present. It's just over there…"

"Not yet, please. Just hold me here, Jon."

A delicious warmth crept between them. Jon's hands found a place at the base of her spine where her dress seemed thinnest and the curve of her back most inviting; Maisie's fingers found the nape of his neck and began to caress the skin above his collar. Stopping for a moment to look at each other, they caught the glint of moonlight in their eyes—and fell to kissing, hot and fiercely in the black and silver night. Their rhythm now was not of the gently swaying dance, but of a slower, deeper union. It was almost unconscious, this pressing together of their bodies; neither felt the other had broken a spell of tenderness, neither wished the other to stop. Maisie slid her arms inside Jon's jacket, feeling the warm silk of his waistcoat over his long, strong back. Words welled up in them, yet neither spoke nor made a sound. Jon felt Maisie's breasts against him, stroked the line of her shoulders, and rubbed that place at the base of her spine, feeling his whole body vibrate with desire for her, sensing her gentle response in each warm pulsation of their embrace. This was so different from how he had felt when making love with Philippa: no haste, so sense of conquest, no need to overcome embarrassment or perform a ritual. This was friendly, sweet, and untroubled; they could stay like this without guile or doubt until their bodies determined the next move.

Jon's fingers found a tiny parting on a seam of Maisie's dress where it stretched over her back and she giggled when he gently pushed a finger into it, tickling her spine through her petticoat. She wore no corset; her smooth skin must lie just beneath this linen. The thought was wildly exciting to him. If only he could feel the tingle of her flesh, touch the very essence of her. Now a fire ran through him, as if blood and heat were pouring into every part of his body, carrying his desire for her to his fingers, his lips, and the hot tightness at his groin. And this new wildness was matched in Maisie. She kissed his neck and giggled more throatily, wriggling more tightly into his arms, burrowing with her nose and lips into his chest and shoulder. While Jon's fingers explored her back, his other hand was lifting her skirt and stroking her thigh. How wonderful, she thought, that only moments ago this leg had been lonely and secretive in a black stocking; now it seemed fully alive for the first time, revelling in the touch of another wonderful human creature. It was such a funny thought that she started to laugh, but as she caught sight of her leg braced firmly alongside Jon's—the long pale shaft of skin gleaming in the moonlight, the bare knee flexed, her silvered foot on the floor—she felt suddenly serious, holy, wonderful. She saw her toes pointed on the paper, each bone in her ankle modelled by the silver ripple of light. She felt akin to all women of ancient times and to everyone alive this night, ready to be fulfilled in her future. She realised now why nakedness was necessary and pure; how this love could not be sanctified while a single scrap of clothing remained between them.

"Take my dress off, Jon," she whispered, placing her hand on Jon's at her back and thrusting his fingers more deeply into the split seam. "I love you, Jon. I want nothing between us now. Take it off—tear it off if you like."

But Jon was gentle, awed, reverent. She stood very still, smiling as cloth and buttons parted beneath his hands. It did not seem to Jon that he was simply stripping this girl of her clothes; he was baring her spirit with her body, freeing her into a new life. He too felt the need to throw off every patch and thread of covering—and found her pulling at his belt. For one piercing moment he remembered the wedding night with Philippa and his boyish, gleeful baring of her breasts; how she had guided him between her legs, gasped with pleasure, then turned away—but this was not the same, could not be the same, would never be the same. This was so easy and natural. Now he saw Maisie's throat and breasts washed in moonlight. He kissed her nipples and stroked her waist and gently moved his fingers into the strong, dark, mysterious hair. He knelt to caress her back and kiss the white skin below her waist. He heard her quiet, simple laugh: a smile made audible. He felt her stroke his head and take his face in her hands, raising him up to look once more into her eyes. The expression on her face was sweet and soft yet brightly wide-awake. She was proud and pleased to be naked in front of him; he too to be open to her gaze and tender fingers. She held his penis gently while it swelled and rose and as she let it stroke her skin they felt free and delighted, wild with desire yet childishly happy. They sank to the floor, tumbling slowly through the moonbeams. He stroked her hair and told her it was all different colours in the silver light. She said his teeth were gleaming. She was delighted he should come into the very middle of her, the very centre of her body, where it seemed her very nature was rooted. He felt the hot lapping of her body round him and the wild sweet fire consume him, thrusting it, giving it, sharing it, rolling warm and happy into relaxation, her hands cradling his head, the moonlight showing her peaceful smile.

"You *are* like a mermaid," said Jon at last, relaxed and warm yet wakeful and lively, remembering how he had called her a mermaid at Tynemouth. "You're a beautiful mermaid lying on a white beach."

"I've got legs though." She stirred them over the whispering paper.

"That's right," said Jon. "Real mermaids *do* have legs when they come out of the sea."

She kissed his nose, brushing his face with her hair then looking critically at it.

"Mermaids are supposed to have golden hair."

"That's just in fairy tales. There must be black-haired mermaids as well."

"All right then." She swished her hair down his chest,

playfully tangling it in his groin, then kissing her way back up to look pertly in his face. "I'm your black-haired mermaid—with legs." She waggled them into a moonbeam until he caught her feet in his hands and kissed her lips as he touched each part of her.

"And with toes…and ankles…and knees…and a bottom…and a lovely long back…and shoulders…and a neck…and a chin…and a nose…" He kissed it. "And a nose." He kissed it again.

"Too much nose," she whispered.

They laughed and rolled on to their sides and cuddled together for what seemed long minutes. He had never imagined this night would be so wonderful, their loving so playful. His joy was beyond anything he had expected—all from this beautiful, strong, tender girl who loved him with such honesty.

"D'you know why we are so comfy?" asked Jon at length, unable to keep a laugh out of his voice.

"No." Maisie propped herself up on one elbow. She had expected to feel cold by now, but didn't. Some moments ago she had feared she might feel soiled or ashamed or frightened or something less than the decent person she had always hoped to be, but she didn't. She felt exactly the opposite to what people would say of her: she felt filled with honour and grace. She felt joy, too. There was laughter in her eyes. "Come on then, tell us why we're so comfy."

"Because we are in the linen store—or more properly *on* the linen store."

"The what?"

"Look." He rolled over and traced a finger across the floor under her nose. The words *Linen Store* showed clearly on the plan. She grinned and smoothed the paper with her hand.

"We've rumpled a fair bit of linen then, haven't we?" Their warm bodies shook helplessly while she giggled. "I'll be up all night doing the ironing!"

They recovered.

"Can I have my present now?" she purred.

"Yes of course…but it's not going to go very well with your mermaid outfit."

* * *

Philippa was thankful her long winter coat was fur-lined, yet it scarcely prevented a constantly shocking coldness billowing up around her legs as her boots rang on the chilly pavements. A Winter night in Paris: this really was a desperate adventure, she thought, finding her way alone to the gallery with a husband deserted, one lover abandoned, and another to be met. She was passing the stares of strangers: some hostile, some amorous, all unsettling. What did she look like? Did any of them see through to her wicked intent? But what was wickedness anyway, she thought? Wasn't it all just the fun she deserved? She should allow herself to relish these unconventional experiences—and she would! She snuggled her scarf more tightly at her throat and nursed her muff. It might be madness, she thought, but it was wickedly wonderful madness!

She saw Marcel in his shirtsleeves, lit by the yellow lights of the gallery. He recognised her, opened the glass door, and she walked straight in. He kissed the hand she took from her muff, turned off the lights, and her led her to the lounge where they had been that afternoon. Now it was warm and seductively lit, and Champagne stood in an ice-bucket.

"You are ready?"

"You will see," smiled Philippa, tossing the muff on to a chair and taking off her hat. She sat on the end of the *chaise-long*. "You were going to kneel to me," she reminded Marcel. "Now here I am."

He sank to his knees, unbuttoned her coat…and found gleaming nakedness against the black fur.

"Magnificent," he whispered, "magnificent!"

"It was ticklish, to be honest," she giggled quietly, "and rather cold."

"But now you will be very warm, I promise." He was caressing and kissing her breasts and shoulders and stroking her waist, whispering as he went down her slender whiteness. "We will make love *à la Narbonne*. As you have already anticipated with such panache, the lady reclines on a low bed, the man on his knees before her—and she draws him in, curling her legs behind. You see? It was the method preferred by Madame de Narbonne, a great courtesan."

"You are a great talker," she whispered.

"But only to explain how we might enjoy *le meilleur penetration*…the best."

"I think…" she gasped, "you have explained it…"

she locked her boots behind his waist, "…very well!" She had felt nothing like this great shivering heat before. "You will have very sore knees," she murmured through her smile.

"It will be worth it," he said, holding her firm and pointed breasts.

* * *

Philippa took a new French brooch from her blouse and placed it in her jewellery case.

"Did you hear someone's found the biggest diamond in the world? All Paris was talking about it."

"No doubt," replied Jon, "but since it was found in South Africa it will remain a British possession, so all Paris can talk its head off."

"I had forgotten how pompous you can sound. And must everything we say degenerate into an argument?"

"No," he said coldly, "but it is likely to do so if you maintain bitterness in our lives by insisting on this empty marriage."

She spun round on her chair.

"What has happened while I've been away, Jon? You're suddenly calm and assertive. I just can't get to you through some new sense of responsibilty." A sly smile played over her lips. "Don't tell me: you've got the slum-girl pregnant."

Jon's silence fanned a blaze of fury in her eyes.

"That's it!" she exploded. "That's it, isn't it? That's what's behind your new brazen attitude, your blind stupidity. You've taken her to bed, here or some foul place of her own. God, you sicken me!"

"Why should anything I do sicken you? You don't care what I do."

"Oh yes I do!" She sprang to her feet. "Especially when it involves some filthy common people from back streets I want nothing to do with."

"You need have nothing to do with any of this. Just leave me."

"Come on!" she blazed into his face. "Do I have to slap it out of you like some stupid boy? Have you been sleeping with the bitch? Have you got her pregnant? Well?" She could barely keep her hands off him, then turned away, restraining herself with clenched fists. "God Almighty! Do I have to suffer these insults behind my back?"

"No you don't," he stated calmly, "but I won't discuss her in this way. We have discovered true and honourable love and I will not abandon her."

He felt as much as heard the scream spread across her face.

"But you are married to *me*!"

He sat down. He wanted no more fights with Philippa. Why did she want more with him?

"Haven't we been through all this? You said before

you left for London you would be content for us to do things independently. That was your idea of how to carry on through what was left of our marriage."

"My idea was not to condone some ridiculous and sordid affair which can only drag you and your precious family into the mire—and me, by implication, with them."

"Never mind all that. Why will you not agree to a divorce? You can cite what you like. I've either done it or will do it."

"Well now, the adulterer speaks. There's a fine admission of guilt. It's the sort of confession that should get you locked up—but it won't get you a divorce, not until it suits me, anyway. A divorce would be very modern and convenient for you, wouldn't it? And your offer is so very frank and up-to-date of you, isn't it? Well, I rather like being a married woman—for the moment, at least. And that very generous settlement your father made: we don't want to lose that, do we? Or put it another way: *I* don't want to lose that. It will fund me very nicely while I establish my new and independent life."

"How can you be independent if you openly sponge off someone else's money?"

"A wife doesn't sponge off a husband, Jon. He keeps her…or d'you only want to keep a mistress?"

"No, I want to make her my wife."

Philippa blazed again, waving her arms as she strode around the room.

"That is the most ridiculous thing of all! Some common girl from the slums of Wallsend. What does she possess that's bewitched you?"

"She hasn't bewitched me. If anyone ever bewitched me it was yourself, in ways of your own which can never affect me again. This lady possesses only good-humour, decency, and grace."

"Lady? Grace? Such fine words, but what blind nonsense! How could you?" Philippa gave him a look of feigned incomprehension, then turned away. "Perhaps I begin to see how you could: because you're made of the same cheap and nasty stuff."

Jon bore the insult with the calm he was determined to maintain.

"The only cheap and nasty thing in any of this is your own brittle, grasping nature. It may have ruined this marriage, but it won't ruin my next one."

"Oh, but it will, Jon," she spun back to face him, red and hectic. "I'll ruin everything for you—just see if I don't!"

CHAPTER ELEVEN
Strangers

The Hamburg steamer wallowed across the bar between North and South Shields piers and pushed into calmer, coal-black waters of the Tyne. Its few passengers were at the rails to watch their progress up the river. As they passed the gaunt ruins of Tynemouth Priory and the seagull-swarmed teeth of the Black Middens rocks, their attention was diverted by a blast on the whistle and a slowing of engines. The First Mate opened a door on the bridge to receive megaphoned shouts from Lloyd's Hailing Station, a tiny hut on the end of a jetty.

"What ship are you and what is your home port?"

"Can't these English read a ship's name at this distance?" muttered one of the men at her rail.

"They are a nation of officials," replied his smaller comrade with a smile, "like the Germans. Even the obvious must be written down."

"They do not yet know that what is written down must soon be torn up."

"You and I will tell them, Anatoly."

"*Maria-Theresa* ex Hamburg!" boomed the Mate above their heads.

"What is your cargo?" returned Lloyd's Hailer.

"Wines and spirits," answered the Mate through his own megaphone, "timber, clocks and instruments, passengers."

"Pass to your berth," came the reply, and the steamer's engines were rung to Slow Ahead once more.

"So, the little Englishman allows us to proceed to his country," grinned the bulkier Russian passenger, "but our German Captain takes us there anyway."

Vladimir Andreyevich Druginin slapped him heartily on the back.

"You already appreciate the play of European politics, Comrade Melnikov."

* * *

Summoned once more to his father's study in the big family house, Jon felt small, cold and alone on this dark Winter afternoon. He might have faced anger with some resilience, but to witness shame, disgust, and pity in his father was almost unbearable.

"We have become strangers, Jon." William tossed his evening newspaper into the waste-basket. Jon could see the civilised and homely life he had enjoyed for so long being thrown out with rubbish in the same way. "Could you not tell your mother and myself about this girl?" Jon made no reply. "Obviously not," William went on. "We had to hear of it from gossip at the yard."

"How," Jon swallowed, "however did it reach your ears? Have you been spying on me, Father?"

"No, damn it, I have *not* been spying on you! Will you insult me with such a thought on top of what you've done already? But what does it matter how it reached my ears?" William thrust his hands into his pockets to stop flailing them in fury and took to pacing angrily about the room. "What difference does it make which lecherous workman saw you go up those stairs? Who cares which Wallsend wife tittle-tattled some sordid version of what you did in the drawing-loft? I don't give a damn who embroidered the tale in the back streets, but when I hear lewd gossip about my own son in my own offices and Board Room, then I feel shame. Shame. D'you understand what that means?" William paced up to Jon in a towering rage. "Well, sir?"

"Yes, Father."

"I should hope you do. The good name of this family is now a laughing-stock in the pubs and gutters. These people we employ, from the meanest labourer to the most pompous manager, they all look up to us as examples of decency; and what do they have to look at now? Some philandering wastrel son abusing his privilege, destroying his marriage, and carrying on with a girl from a respectable working-class family—in her very own workshop in the supposed season of goodwill!" William spread his hands in a gesture to silence the beginnings of Jon's objection. "Whatever the truth is, whatever your own suffering or real motives, whatever we think—that's what *they'll* think. The laughs are very loud, Jon, at a time our class cannot afford to be laughed at by workers. It's ironic to realise that drinking yourself to death or whoring your way round the Fish Quay would have been more acceptable, and probably more easily forgiven by the general public. And never mind the general public. Once more, your mother is in despair. You are rightly ashamed."

"Yes, Father." Jon hung his head but found his voice. "Your soiled version of what Maisie and I mean to each other is less than the truth...but I *am* ashamed."

William walked over to the window.

"Well, much good it'll do you, or any of us. Feeling bad about this will not repair the damage you have done. But swift and sensible action will."

'This is the end,' thought Jon. 'He will ask me to give up Maisie and I shall refuse. I shall be disowned and cut out of the will. We'll have to go to France or South America. It could be worse. I'll live as an engineer, Maisie will be my wife when Philippa agrees or dies of fast living. Until then we will be poor exiles, but at least we'll be together and I'll have made some stand for love of her.'

"A divorce at once, a divorce."

"What, Father?"

"I said a divorce—or are you deaf as well as daft?"

"She won't agree to one."

"She will when she's been persuaded—by me. Sit down."

William returned to his desk and sat on the edge of it. Jon remembered the excitement of his father giving him the *Mauretania* job from this very same position of relaxed command—but now it seemed he had failed in every way and could never redeem himself. He would forever be the weak and erring boy, an embarrassing disappointment to a successful father now pushed to the limits of his tolerance.

"I'll deal with your awkward wife for you. I used to have the devil of a reputation as a ladies' man," William went on with an odd smile, "not in quite the way *you* think. I was supposedly famous for handling the spirited women. 'Any shrews to be tamed or harpies caged? Send for Ferris!' That's what the College fellows used to say. Your mother, I might add, was in neither category. If there was any taming to be done, she did it to me, wonderfully and with love. When I lacked sense—as we all do sometimes—she made me see it, and I've never looked back without delight upon our years. She made me and made this family."

"But that's it, Father," Jon spoke up, "that's it exactly. I know I've been weak, but with Maisie I can be strong. She has 'made me', as you put it, or she will. She certainly brings out the best in me—although you can't think this deception is my best behaviour, and I don't either. But I certainly shouldn't have gone this far if I hadn't been sure; neither of us would. We *are* sure, quite equally. You have no idea how long and how hard we fought down these feelings between us—again equally, independently. We tried to stop it, but we couldn't. Stopping it would be the ultimate wrong, whatever transgressions we have already committed."

"All right. Why, if you felt like that, did you not come to us about this girl? Did you think we would not understand problems in a marriage? Did you think we would have no sympathy with our own son in love? Have we failed you so badly?"

The suggestion was torture to Jon.

"No, Father," he answered. "Surely it is I who have failed *you*…in failing to be honest. But I hid the truth at first because, well, I thought it was a sin—which of course technically it was. Then I tried to deny it because I couldn't quite believe it myself." He managed a faint smile. "Even when I knew there was no escaping our genuine love, I shrank from making it public. I thought I'd already caused enough trouble in the family with Philippa. Maisie and I would have brought it out into the open ourselves, and soon. We could really do nothing else."

"What?" William interrupted. "Is there a child?"

"No."

"You mean 'not yet'. Well, for everybody's sake try and keep it that way."

"Child or no child, Father, we want our love to be public knowledge, publicly accepted."

"It won't be. I'm amazed I have to remind you that you're not only breaking the rules of marriage, you're defying the conventions of two classes. Since you seem determined to do both, you should have faced the truth earlier and told it. Your persistent weakness and stupidity always undermines the security we have provided for you."

William saw his son squirm.

"Don't interrupt me with another excuse. There isn't one—however unsuitable a wife Philippa has been. In the eyes of the world there are no excuses, but there are obviously *reasons* for what has happened. Some of them might be good reasons. I see a ray of hope for you in this new girl of yours. That's why I'm taking this attitude, and you're damn lucky I am. You're quite right in thinking you've brought enough scandal into the family. But if you meant to tell us, and I believe you did, it's a devilish mischance that gossip from the yard reached us first. Anyway, you and Philippa must be divorced. I shall tame your shrew, which obviously you've never been able to do. Then you must marry this girl."

'I am safe,' thought Jon, 'but not entirely forgiven.'

"That is exactly what I want to happen, Father," he said.

"What you want and what you get can be two very different matters—but the fact that you're determined to marry her, even though there is no child from this scandalous liaison, suggests good motives to me."

"We love each other completely, Father. If only you could meet her and see the goodness in her, you'd recognise at once my terrible folly in marrying Phillippa and hers in pursuing me…" Jon found himself pleading in a tone of voice he had not intended to adopt, but now he felt unable to hold back. "…She and I are just not right together, but Maisie is sweet and honest, honourable too, gracious in every way. I long to improve her life, take her away from her poverty, but not away from her roots and her decent family. I shan't ruin her or force her into a life that's not natural to her. That's why I've done all this. It's had to be in secret—or I thought it did, because of Philippa, for what I thought was the family's sake, in a way for everybody's sake. I have tried to be strong. If I've been weak it's been my own fault, not Maisie's."

"Very well," William slid from the desk and paced the room again. "Various people have been at fault. We have indulged you, Jon, and look what happens. We accepted an unconventional wife, but we won't accept an unconventional mistress. You'll marry her."

"Of course I want to marry her, but Philippa won't divorce me."

"So you say." William selected a cigar. "Have you given her sufficient grounds?"

Jon looked down.

"Of course you have. Well," William seemed to brighten, as if a load of worries had slipped from him, "it's more usual to pay off the girl, but in this case we'll have to pay off the wife."

A match rasped beneath the cigar and flared yellow in William's face. Jon's eyes shrank from the flame and searched the corners of the room for a soothing darkness.

"How refreshingly modern of you, Father."

"You should put some effort into sounding pleased instead of sarcastic."

"I am pleased. I'm delighted."

"No doubt. It's always delightful when somebody else pays your expenses." Fragrant cigar smoke billowed between father and son. Jon sensed his comfortable family life might be preserved after all. At the same time he recognised the prickling of scruples—which did not seem to be troubling his father. "By how much do you think you will be forever in my debt. Well come on, you know her tastes. How much d'you think it'll take? Ten thousand pounds?"

"Good God. That's a fortune!"

"It's several fortunes. You think it's too much to be rid of her?"

"You could try five, or three."

"And haggle? Or are you thinking what I throw away on Philippa comes out of your inheritance? Oddly enough," William blew smoke at Jon, "it will."

"I'm just trying to save you money, Father."

"That'll be the day."

"I know this is all very unpleasant…"

"You've said it, boy! But I can think of many more unpleasant varieties of hot water—not to mention boiling oil—in which I could justifiable let you drown, or at least wallow purgatorially for a while; but you've been honest with me and I'm going to be honest with you."

It occurred to Jon that his father must be like the American millionaires who crossed the Atlantic on the ships he built: powerful patriarchs doing deals in vast sums of money, controlling their business empires with ruthless efficiency, dominating their families, buying off intruders who didn't fit. Jon had writhed under his father's curiously aimiable tirade, but now he felt a glow of awe, admiration, above all pride. If part of his conscience thought this ignoble, another found it irresistable.

"I've never really liked Philippa," his father was saying, "and I shan't be sorry to have her out of the family. As far as I can see, apart from indulging whatever carnal lusts sprang or festered between you, she's done nothing but make you wretchedly unhappy—and I don't like to see my son unhappy, even if he's deserved it from time to time. So I shall pay to rid us of her. I can afford it. You need not look so desperate; we both know she'll take the money and go."

William studied his cigar with a magnificent confidence Jon could not share.

"But just suppose, Father…suppose she doesn't take the money, out of spite."

"She will. She may be spiteful, but she doesn't strike me as being burdened by scruples or high-mindedness, and she's not a fool." William drew on his cigar again and looked at his son. "D'you think I am?"

"Of course not, Father. I don't know what to say."

"That's because you think it's despicable."

"No."

"Yes you do. Despite what you've done and what you've said, and despite your obvious joy at my not thrashing the hide off you, deep inside your basically decent mind you think its shameful and despicable to pay off a woman because you're tired of her or because she's not exactly what you thought she would be or because you've found someone younger, prettier and more innocent. Part of you still thinks it would be noble to desert this girl and go back to your wife, then spend a lifetime pretending you had done the honourable thing. But I tell you now, Jon, that would not be noble. That would be your greatest indecency, greatest dishonour, and greatest folly of all. I believe you love this girl in ways you never loved Philippa—perhaps because when you met Philippa you were too young to appreciate these other ways; I don't know, I can't pretend to fathom every corner of your soul. But I do know that if this girl loves you as I suspect she does, you must make a success of it. You must! Lose this one and you'll be lost forever: lost in regrets, in yearnings for the past, in shameful feelings worse than you've suffered already. I know it and you know it. I also know you still think my scheme is despicable. Perhaps it is. So you may despise me now, but you'll certainly thank me later and for the rest of your life."

Jon looked away.

"I don't despise you, Father, but I hate all this business. Philippa should divorce me without your having to pay her."

"Of course, but you've just told me she won't. This is the expedient way."

"It's shameful."

"There you are, you see: precisely as I said."

"I'm ashamed of *myself*, and of all the terrible trouble I've brought into the family."

"All right, we've been through that, but we've spoken enough of shame. Now you should rise from it into something you can be proud of: a secure marriage with a good woman. If you are sure Mary Watson is that woman, I support you."

"Thank you; and I am sure."

"But you're still unsure about my methods, aren't you?"

Jon said nothing.

"That's because you are romantic and I am practical. In fact I'm both, as you should have realised years ago. If you learn to combine the two, as I have done, you might find the results very successful. But never mind that at the moment. Today I'm being practical, and you don't altogether like it, do you? You still believe no price should be put on happiness—even though the price I'm paying may secure it for you. But I tell you a price is put on happiness every day, Jon. I thought you would have discovered that already, simply by working at Parsons'. Ten thousand pounds, five, even three would transform a factory or shipyard worker's life for ever beyond his wildest dreams. Properly invested, it would provide his family with generations of wealth and security. You can say I'm spending it to please a hopelessly romantic son and clear his scheming wife out of my family, or you can say I'm investing it in our future. Take your choice, but accept it's the most practical way."

"It won't be wasted, Father."

"Whatever you do, Jon, don't dare to talk to me about waste. Now go and speak to you mother and explain what we have agreed."

Jon was at the door when he heard his father's voice again.

"Did you expect me to punish you, rather than help you?"

"Perhaps." Jon turned once more to face the elegant figure wreathed in cigar smoke.

"But it wouldn't have mattered if I had, would it? You're invulnerable."

"Invulnerable?"

"Yes. That's what you feel, isn't it? Invulnerable, through love."

"Yes."

"Good."

* * *

Vladimir Druginin and Anatoly Melnikov found rooms in a North Shields boarding house. It was a lengthy walk to *Mauretania's* Wallsend building-shed, towering ahead of them as they trudged up-river.

"I want to see the streets and houses here," explained Druginin, "smell the atmosphere. Don't worry, my tall friend. When we are employed at the shipyard we will take the tram."

"Like we did in our Moscow days, eh?" Melnikov smiled down at his smaller, slender companion.

"Yes, but you must not expect to find those pretty girl students you so enjoyed looking at on the Moscow trams here. There are many things you must not expect here."

"Oh?"

"Indeed," Druginin went on, warming to his subject as he walked. "To begin with, you must not expect quick or enthusiastic responses to what we have to say."

"Why not? They are oppressed workers."

"Perhaps, but the workers here don't aspire to revolution."

Dismay clouded Melnikov's face, and annoyance raised his voice.

"Then we will be beating our fists against frozen iron, or worse, dealing with academics and intellectuals; and remember, Comrade Lenin has no time for them. I remember his exact words: 'There can be no advance until the workers themselves are saturated with revolutionary ideas.'"

"That may be so," replied Druginin calmly, "but we must admit the character of the country in which we find ourselves, then turn it to our own advantage. The workers here have no concept of proletarian equality; if they did, most would reject it. They aspire to wealth and middle-class life. They don't want to destroy the ruling classes, they want to join them. There's a huge lower-middle class here. Most of the workers we will meet believe they can be part of it by working hard and making money. Of course there'll be a few hotheads, but as you must learn, my dear Comrade, hotheads in England are doomed."

"Then before the workers can be inspired," stated Melnikov, trudging purposefully beside his friend, "the aristocracy must be destroyed."

"Perhaps," Druginin gave him a cool smile, "but the lower classes don't especially want to tear down the aristocracy. They enjoy looking up to it. You must understand that even the meanest and poorest Englishman sees himself as a country gentleman with a house and garden, cheerful servants, and pretty china. Oh, the great houses will decay, the estates will be broken up, the ruling classes' own decadence will destroy them in time—but that could take another century, even longer. The Labour movement here is very strong, but it's an old-fashioned, genteel kind of socialism seeking parliamentary reform, talking endlessly, voting on everything. The men want better propsects, the women want votes, they all want better drains and more holidays—but, as I have heard Americans say, 'that's about it, kid'. There will never be a revolution here like the one already started at home."

"Then we are here to destroy a great symbol," declared Melnikov, vehemently indicating the shipyard cranes ahead. "By subverting work on this ship we will sabotage a vessel of international capitalism, and the rich swine who sail in it will all be drowned!"

"No no no, my big and dangerous Comrade," Druginin chuckled aimiably. "You are not subtle. We won't sink the ship. We will help to build it. But while we are here we will also build something of far more importance: the greater revolution, the world revolution—even if it will not take the form Comrade Lenin would prefer. England is a good place to work upon it. Do not forget that Bolshevism was born in England. Remember two years ago when the Congress had to move from Brussels to London? I was there when Comrade Lenin's followers became the majority, the Bolsheviki: a great moment."

"Of course," grinned Melnikov. "I am proud of you. You are very intelligent."

"Yet we must use greater intelligence still. Here there are no peasants living like animals in our dark and vast Motherland, where the golden splendours of the Tsar's capital seem like Heaven-on-Earth, where the Tsar himself seems like a god. Of course these workers are oppressed, of course they are denied the power of International Socialism, but they hardly know it. They can save their pay and take their families to London on the train. They can nod at their king on the racecourse and call him Teddy."

"This same fat and self-indulgent king," put in Melnikov, "arranged for the Tsar to have his hats and boots made in London."

"Precisely. Our peasants are not permitted to know such things, but the English workers think it 'very jolly'. They see the King and the Tsar as members of a club they themselves wish they could join. So here, the revolution cannot start in the fields of the peasants or the streets of the workers. It must be nurtured in the salons of the rich, while the parliamentary system must be shown as hopelessly ineffectual so the workers have no hope left *but* revolution."

"Everything you say inspires me," replied Melnikov, renewed ardour increasing his long pace along the cold street. "We carry the fight against capitalism into the very forge of British industry! Again we are soldiers in the greatest war ever waged!"

"Indeed," the small man smiled grimly at his ebullient companion, "but there must be a shorter war within the longer; more violent and of more immediate effect. Such a war is coming anyway, but we must do all we can to accelerate it."

"What war is this, Comrade?"

"The war between the rich nations: England, France, Germany. Russia may also fight in this war, but it will be a sacrifice worth making—because this war will ultimately be a war between ruling classes in which they will fracture one another's political structures and destroy their economies. Then the workers will rise from its ruins in true revoloution, free from serfdom at last. That is what we are working for here." Druginin felt the glow of admiring glances. "You like my speeches, eh, Anatoly?"

"Comrade Lenin himself would admire every breath."

"I am not so certain of that, my trusting friend," Druginin smiled, "but I promise to keep making them to you. As for speeches to others, in this country we must not climb on walls and shout at street corners. We must work calmly, from inside."

"Yes, yes, I see," Melnikov strode excitedly ahead of

his smaller comrade, then stopped to allow him to catch up, "but how? How?"

"First we must settle into jobs here, learn more and better English, befriend powerful men."

"You will do it Vladimir Andreyevich."

"And you will help me, Anatoly."

* * *

Installed once more in a London hotel, Philippa summoned Robert Gough to lunch.

"It's on me," she smiled, settling ostentatiously at the central table of the Grill Room.

"I couldn't allow such a thing," Robert protested politely.

"'The lady does not pay'; is that what you're thinking?" Philippa studied her menu. "Well this lady is putting it on her hotel bill, and paying that too."

When she had ordered for them both and the waiter had gone she gave Robert another glittering smile.

"You mustn't worry about accepting little treats from me; after all, you gave me a splendid time over Christmas, and you'll be paying me for designing these posters."

"That is an entirely different matter: a business arrangement."

"Ah yes," murmured Philippa, "we must remember we are very good at business arrangements. Do you have my contract ready?"

"Er—I don't actually have it with me, my dear."

"Then you may send it round here this afternoon, or I'll come to your office and sign it. There is also the matter of my flat in London." She took up her glass of German wine. "I do like this hock."

"Too sweet," snapped Robert.

"Oh, but that's what I like about it," she purred, "and you're surprised. You thought I was sweet enough already."

"No fish for me," Robert waved at the waiter. "Take it away."

"The flat." Philippa drained her glass. "I can't keep running up and down to London, and you did say you would find me one."

"I said nothing of the sort."

"Oh, but we agreed. You must remember."

"Rooms in London are increasingly expensive," Robert stated quietly.

"I'm sure they are, but you must also consider the price of not finding me some. Surely you want the unsavoury details of your personal life to remain our little secret."

Robert narrowed his eyes and clenched his fists.

"You won't blackmail me," he whispered hoarsely.

"I hope I shall not need to."

He squirmed beneath her impudent stare.

"If you must raise unsavoury details, you might consider those which have come to light about your miss-spent time in Paris."

"Into precisely which details have you been prying?" sneered Philippa.

"Marcel, I hear, is an able seducer of women."

"Very able."

"Did he seduce you?"

"Most enjoyably—although to be honest I should say the seduction was mutual. I have developed a particular technique with young, virile Frenchmen. I understood such matters were of no interest to one of your kind, but since you seem to have heard the details, why ask me about them?"

"You behaved scandalously under my very nose!"

"Or the nose of your spy, whichever pathetic employee was depraved enough to be watching—or is depravity your own department?"

"I discovered it only through a chance comment. I was told…"

"Don't bother. I don't care if Marcel told himself. In any case, what can it possibly matter to you how I am entertained in Paris or anywhere else? Your tastes are noticeably different; you should allow me mine. Good God, am I doomed to be surrounded by pompous, pious, hypocritical men? Marcel was a refreshing relief."

"You mean his animal behaviour?"

"Come come, Robert, no animal could possess his intensely human sophistication, or my delight in it."

The clink and chatter of luncheon going on around them only heightened the discomfort of their icy silence.

"It seems I disgust you," Philippa continued at last. "Have you forgotten how you disgusted me?"

"That's hardly the point," scowled Robert. "I took you to Paris to further your career, not indulge your wantonness—and least of all with a valued colleague. Marcel is a married man with children."

Philippa laughed openly and turned some heads at nearby tables.

"Well that's hardly the point either; and what's this sudden respectability? Was he not, only a moment ago, 'an able seducer of women'? Anyway, I'd have thought a Frenchman's morals were the least of your worries." Philippa got into her stride and poured herself more wine. "No no, my dear friend, business associate, professional mentor, and all the rest of it, your principal worry is how to keep *your* morals out of your friends' gossip, out of the papers, and out of the courts—and I have the answer." She raised her glass in a toast to her own schemes. "Apart from all the other things we agreed, you simply find me—and pay for—a delightful little *pied-à-terre* right here in London. Then what you consider to be my scandalous liaisons can be conducted well away from your precious Paris dealers, although I may pop over the Channel now and again to brush up on technique: our new French allies certainly do have things to teach us."

Robert stood up, threw down his napkin, and stalked

silently from the table.

"Remember it has to be a good address," Philippa raised her voice to his impassive back and her glass to the whole room. "Mustn't be seen slumming, must we?"

* * *

Druginin and Melnikov emerged from the shipyard office slapping each other's backs and waving salutes at their new workmates. Cunning eyes watched them from shadows of the great hull.

"I couldn't have dreamt it, but it's true."

"What is, Mister Walker? And what lingo's that? Are they Swedes or Danes?"

"They're Russians, man—and I've never been more pleased to see foreigners in my life. We can do nicely with some of their particular trade."

"They'll be carpenters, or they wouldn't have been signing on with Mister Charlton."

"Carpenters—aye, they might be. They can be road-sweepers for all I care. I'm not interested in what they build, it's what they're ganna tear down that interests me. You know what they do best in Russia, don't you, or are you so daft you don't know what's come in under your very nose? Well I'll tell you what they do best in Russia: revolution!"

CHAPTER TWELVE
Talk of Revolutions

Mauretania continued to rise and expand inside the echoing cavern of her vast building-shed. With work on the turbines now progressing, Jon found himself spending less time at the yard and more at Parsons' engine works.

Each morning on the train from Jesmond he would open his briefcase and take out Maisie's New Year present: a leather-bound book embossed with *Diary for the Year 1905* in gold lettering. He ran his hands over the diary without opening it, imagining her buying it from the most distinguished stationer's in Newcastle. He reckoned it must have been an expensive purchase out of her wages, especially after the financial strain of buying presents for her own family. He thought it an apt and tender token of their love, a subtle and meaningful match for the hat he had bought her at their first Christmas.

How extraordinary, how wonderful it had been. Alone in the city, for years on separate streets, sharing only anonymity among all the strangers' glances—and then their fateful meeting through the building of the great ship. As leaves had fallen, love had held them; then in frozen, leafless Winter they had learned that love was much stronger than they had been. Now they must not hesitate; whatever love's pain, love's rapture would also be theirs. Whatever the events of this dread Winter, their new Spring would come. So, thought Jon as the train rattled down to the river, let these lightening mornings with their clouds as mysterious as silent swans herald an end to separation. This coming year of 1905 would be *their* year, *must* be their year.

He looked out of the window at the backs of dreary houses, the blackened brick of walls and bridges, the glum hinterland of factory, railway and dock. Philippa was in London again, giving no notice of her return. He told himself he should feel released, but felt only trapped. He longed for this coming Saturday and for future Saturdays with what he felt must be greater passion than the commonplace desire of a worker for the week-end. He and Maisie had established a pattern of meeting at Pumphrey's on Saturdays. Walking through the crowds of Newcastle to a cosy rendezvous felt safer than encounters at the shipyard, where they must risk suspicious eyes and wagging tongues. When Philippa was living with him in the Lily Avenue house he lied about working at Parsons' on a Saturday; when she was away he didn't have to lie. He was not always sure what lies Maisie told her family, only that he wanted an end to lying. The deceptions were ignoble, but the meetings at Pumphrey's were joyous. They felt secure in the warmth of the upstairs room and the seclusion of their favourite window seats, looking down into the narrow street of the bustling Cloth Market or up to the Cathedral weathercocks that might be symbols of a gilded future—if only that future could be reached.

They had made their decisions, now they must make their moves. So this grey morning Jon did not replace the diary in his briefcase with his usual wistful reverence; he opened it, studied his schedule of meetings, and began to lay plans for what he imagined would be the most difficult meeting of his life.

He must face Maisie's father—and with better grace and courage than he had displayed when facing his own. He must make some kind of formal application to Matthew Watson and confess his determination to marry Maisie. That would surely clear the air between the families and bring his intentions into the open. The stumbling-block, the hurdle, the hideous iceberg of impossibility floating before him was, of course, his continuing marriage to Philippa. In its sordid shadow, he might be seen as nothing more than a philandering adulterer. He could not allow them to think that, for Maisies' sake if not for his own. But how could he make them understand? How was he to tell the whole truth and retain some honour in the eyes of a new family who might already detest and despise him? Maisie would do it so much better, but the responsibility of this encounter would have to be his own. Of all the ordeals his love for Maisie had brought him, he dreaded this the most.

He looked at dates when he might be at the yard and able to meet Matthew on that neutral ground—or would it be better to turn up at their house? No, of course not, a doorstep encounter would surely not be polite. Damn it, he thought, none of it was polite. Yet it had to be done with honour. Should he just write? No, it had to be face-to-face. Which were the possible dates? Empty pages stared at him, the creamy paper inviting better thoughts than his own this morning. He had wished to fill these pages with beautiful memories, not traumatic appointments.

He looked out at the grey sky. Was the weather still cold enough for Maisie to be wearing her hat? Was she wearing it at all? Had it caused comment, created more difficulty for her? He suspected she would never wear it to work. It would be kept for special occasions and their meetings at Pumphrey's. He longed again for the cosy window seat and the shared fragrance of their coffee. He imagined mornings with her as his lover and wife, grinding delicious beans brought specially home to peace and birdsong, flowered cups, the calm of honesty, the clink of trust.   Trust: it was a rare and precious thing and he desired it greatly. As he left the train and the noise of the engine works pressed around him, he felt no-one trusted him at all—except Maisie. Would she be at work now, too?

* * *

Two days later Jon was to be present at the rotation test of one *Mauretania's* turbines. He had decided to invite Matthew Watson. It would be an opportunity to witness something by which Matthew should be fascinated: the delicate vanes of the engine turning over before they were hidden in their casings and deep within the ship herself. Jon's invitation had honoured his promise made on that day in the drawing-loft, the day he had first met Maisie with her father. Now he must meet him without her and tell his wonderful but terrible truth.

On the appointed day the men stood together as part of a small assembly in the engine shed: suddenly hushed as the test was prepared.

The great turbine sat in its lower casing of cast iron. Its upper casing was not fitted and the array of glittering metal vanes could be seen clearly. Their diameter grew as they extended down the shaft; a shaft that would eventually turn one of *Mauretania's* gigantic screws and drive her through the water. A belt running from a stationary steam engine had been fitted to the shaft protruding from the turbine's smaller end to replicate the effect of steam propulsion. As the onlookers waited, pipes on the stationary engine emitted faint wisps of steam as it stood heavily in its corner of the shed. How old-fashioned it looked in comparison to the sleek, gleaming, modern machine it was to drive.

"Of course they won't run it too fast here," Jon explained to Matthew. This felt like small-talk. He was nervous and ill at ease. He wanted to tell his truth to this man and face its consequences, but knew he would not do so until he could take Matthew aside after the test. For the moment it was easier to speak of engineering. "They've left the top casing off so they can watch the revolutions and see if the bearings are holding the shaft straight and solid…and they'd better," he added quietly, "we've spent enough time worrying about them."

"What if the bearings aren't right?" whispered Matthew.

"The whole thing thrashes itself to pieces and someone gets the sack."

An electric bell was rung; the shed fell silent. Then pressurised steam was released into the engine and its belt began to turn the turbine's shaft. In moments the vanes were whirring and glittering in beams of sunlight that poked in from the high windows.

"Runs nice and quiet like," observed Matthew. More noise came from the puffing and clanking of the old steam engine than from the sweetly turning turbine, but a dramatic stir of wind was set up in the shed. "She's turning over some air, though."

"She certainly is." Jon was watching with a sudden intensity. "I honestly didn't expect that; in fact I'm amazed. Look what's happening at the the back." Dust, shavings and scraps of paper were being blown to the end of the shed. Coats were ruffled. The speed of the revolutions was increased and a workman's cap blew off. Jon watched, entranced. "I never thought there'd be such a push of air…and that's only doing, what, two-hundred rpm? Less, I'd say."

"Better when the top casing's on," suggested Matthew.

"It will be—and the air coming out will be compressed even more."

After only a few minutes of the test the steam engine was slowed and the speed of the turbine's revolutions dropped. A chatter of voices rose from the watchers as they began to disperse, but Jon stood still, a faraway look in his eyes.

"This is going to win us the Blue Ribband, isn't it?"

"Pardon?" Jon returned his attention to Matthew.

"I said this is going to win us the Blue Ribband."

"That's the idea: over to America and back before you can say Charles Parsons."

"Have you met the great man, Mister Ferris?"

"Yes. He's a friend of my father." Jon was struggling to manage this conversation. His mind was elsewhere, his thoughts and imagination jumping wildly from his anxiety over facing Matthew about Maisie to a future he had glimpsed so unexpectedly in the stream of air rushing from the turbine. He forced himself back to the present. "Parsons. Yes, he gave me a ride down the Tyne in *Turbinia*."

"Lucky lad, eh? Some of us have to make do with the Shields ferry."

"Well, I remember it was a special treat. It was my Birthday. We went out between the piers; doing about twenty knots. That was nothing to what she did on that famous day at the Spithead Review, but I've never travelled faster on water. It was tremendously exciting."

"She was taken to Paris for the 1900 Exhibtion, wasn't she?"

"That's right. It must have been a terrible ride down the East Coast and through the Channel; she's not the most stable boat in the world."

He wondered how he could be chatting so easily and so aimiably to this man when his whole mind and spirit were in such turmoil. His love for Maisie and his intentions had not yet been mentioned but they must surely be within a few moments; and now there was his new idea, an idea of terrible proportions in his imagination. Once again his attention was dragged back to the present.

"There'll be no probems like that on the big Mary; solid as a rock, eh?"

"She should be. We'll do everything we can to keep the vibration down as well. A lot will depend on how the screws behave in the water. Not actually my department."

"I told my little lad, George," Matthew went on. "I said 'Something that goes up and down has to stop and start again, but something that goes round and round can go faster and faster.'"

"I couldn't have explained the benefits of a turbine better myself."

The shed was clearing, the engineers consulting sheets of paper and their test instruments. Jon strove to keep a tremor out of his voice

"May I take you aside for a moment, Mister Watson?"

They found an empty corner of the shed, stepping through a sunbeam into quietness. Was that a good sign, wondered Jon momentarily, or were the shadows that lurked in this corner of the building to be his omens? Suddenly, Matthew turned squarely towards Jon.

"Don't think I don't know what this is about and don't think I'm ganna make it easy for you to say whatever you ganna say."

"Indeed, Mister Watson." Jon swallowed heavily. "You know then that I love your daughter."

"I know you're carrying on with her and she is with you. I have every right to thrash her and despise you before I knock you down. Men have been shot for less."

"I can understand how you must feel, but you do not have those rights." Jon heard himself sounding pompous, but went on as honestly as he could. "We love each other truly—which is why I am facing you now."

"You haven't been too quick about facing me."

"We had to be sure of our love."

"Love! Is that your word for it? You're a married man. Do you love your wife?"

"Not any more. It's been very difficult, very unhappy." Now Jon was saying it, he felt able to say everything else. "We have fallen out of love."

"And am I to trust such a man with my daughter? A man who marries then falls out of love and carries on a secretive affair with an innocent girl? An adulterer and a liar?"

"I have told no lies."

"Except to your wife no doubt!"

"Perhaps. But those times are over. My wife and I are to be divorced. I shall give everything I have and everything I am to Maisie."

"Aye, and what are you?"

"You must judge me, and I'm sure you will. But I hope you will come to trust me."

"Trust you?" Matthew took hold of Jon's coat. Unexpectedly, Jon felt no fear. He studied the face now so close to his own. It was anguished, but somehow remained a good face. Noises from the working riverside came into the shed; Jon had a momentary vision: the beauty of the ship they were creating against the ugliness of human misunderstandings. "Trust you? I could have you dumped in the river, man! But if I choose to let you stay alive, how are you ganna prove yourself?"

"Have I not proved myself already? Can you imagine what I have had to face from my own family?"

"Oh yes," Matthew dropped his hand from Jon's coat, "I was wondering when we'd get round to that. 'Posh young master from the big house in Heaton carries on with common girl from the shipyards.' That's the tittle-tattle in the back streets; you're lucky the newsboys aren't crying it outside the Central Station."

"You know Maisie is anything but common."

"Aye, but her father's common. She comes from a common family—or that's what your lot'll be thinking."

"That's not what *I* think."

"Are you a Socialist?"

"I could be."

"A traitor to your class!"

"Yes, I am certainly that."

"Aye, but we're not talking big politics, we're talking family politics—which is much trickier."

"You're right, indeed."

Matthew paced about in the shadows. His anguish hurt Jon; a hurt he could not express here. Must he always cause hurt to people he loved and respected, to his own family, to the wife he had once loved and the woman he now loved so much more, to this decent man whose decency he had offended? Yet at this very moment he saw chinks in the wall of darkness. The anguished father was beginning to admit them.

"You might be a good man, Mister Ferris, but you might not be good for Maisie."

"You loved her first. I'm not yet a father, but I understand how one must feel about his daughter."

"Maybe you do. You're very perceptive and open-minded, more than I thought you'd be, but you're still not the man I wanted for my daughter."

"Then I am sorry to be a disappointment, but I'm the

man she's chosen—and I'm proud to be."

"It'll not go easy for you both you know, however you manage it. Even if you got your divorce and married my daughter decently, your life wouldn't be easy. You come from different worlds, man."

"The world is changing—and we feel like changing it even more."

"That's just daft talk. You're a young man in love and you feel like that. I felt like that when I fell for my Alice." Matthew turned to the shadows. "I don't hate you for falling in love, but I'll hate you if make my daughter's life worse than it's been already. There might be love and decency in you, but it'll be beaten out of you, beaten out of you both. The world's like that, man, not like you imagine it from the big house in Heaton." He strode up to face Jon again. "And I don't want decency and love and happiness beaten out of my daughter!"

"I'll see she has the best life possible. I'll give her everything."

"Oh aye, money. That's always very acceptable, but your money may not be enough in this case."

"I don't mean just money."

"I know, I know. I understand you better than you think. I don't hate you, lad. At first I thought I liked you. I might still like you. I might even come to respect you. You've been honest, I'll give you that, and brave in your own way I suppose. I can imagine how you've been feeling. I've brought up a daughter, more than you've done, and you might be the man to take her way from me, or you might not. So I'll do nowt—for the moment, anyway. My wife sees a chance for Maisie's happiness and I might see it too, but I don't see it yet.

So you'll examine your conscience and your manners, and you'll do what's right for Maisie. I don't mean what's right for convention. You've already flouted that, haven't you?"

Jon breathed heavily.

"Yes."

"In every way?"

"Yes."

"I thought so. You'll not bring a bastard into this world, not with my Maisie!"

Jon could feel his neck trembling, but he stood as tall as he could and made his declaration.

"No. We will be married. Our families will be united. Any child will have our name and our love." Then, before anything else could be said, Jon stepped even closer to Matthew. "I must ask you: do I have your blessing, Mister Watson? Do I have your blessing?"

"No." Suddenly, the stocky figure was walking away, looking hurt, aggrieved, yet defiant. "Not yet. I'll see how you go."

Jon found the determination to call after him.

"Thank you, Mister Watson. Will you shake my hand?"

"No, not yet."

Jon was left alone in the shadowed corner, the world of work beating on outside.

* * *

It was a cold Spring in London with flurries of snow; lingering grey days lit for Philippa by the glow of praise for her *Mauretania* painting. There were notices in the newspapers and the art magazines; it was talked about by critics in the circles that mattered to her and to Robert Gough. Even the general public showed an interest; groups of people could be seen at the windows of Gough's offices where poster-sized reproductions of the painting were displayed.

"Look at them," said Robert. "That's a good response: ordinary people, crowding at our window. You have every reason to be delighted."

"The interest of ordinary people is delightful in its own way," drawled Philippa, "but ordinary people do not commission artists. Where are my contracts, Robert?"

"All in good time," he replied with annoyance. "Meanwhile, amuse yourself with these."

He tossed a ring of keys on to the desk.

"Oh," she smiled with brittle intensity, "the keys to my kingdom. How very timely: I was just beginning to find London hotels a little dreary."

"And I was finding them intolerably expensive."

"Must you always be vulgar about money? You're not putting me somewhere cheap and nasty, are you? You know that won't be acceptable."

243

"You'll find your new flat on Cheyne Walk most acceptable, I assure you."

"Oh," she gave him another of her bitter smiles, "by the river in Chelsea! How very Pre-Raphaelite. Art has moved on since that lot were there, and thank God it has, but I daresay Chelsea will do."

"You will make it do. You will find your contracts in the post shortly and you will execute the work quickly and without fuss…"

"Stop panicking, Robert," she said darkly, snatching up the keys. "There'll be no fuss—provided, of course, you keep your side of our little bargain."

"Our little bargain is no bargain, it's cripplingly expensive."

"Not as expensive as a court-case; or would you prefer to be kept at His Majesty's pleasure? It could be arranged on a conviction for buggery and gross indecency."

"Just leave me, will you? I have a very busy morning."

She moved to the door without looking at him.

"There's something else I'd like, Robert." She put on her gloves. "A camera, a modern camera. See that one is sent round to the Chelsea flat, will you?"

* * *

Chilly weather persisted in Newcastle. Maisie's fur hat

did not seem out of place as she walked through the glum streets, but in the warmth of Pumphrey's she took it off. Jon felt that the shine of her hair and flash of her eyes could be tokens of a long overdue Spring.

"I have good news, Darling. Philippa has a place in London…and I spoke to your father."

"I know. He told me."

They ordered coffee and talked about her father. Once again, now he was with Maisie, Jon felt capable of anything.

"He refused to shake my hand—for the moment anyway, but there's hope. He understands, I know he does."

Maisie took Jon's hand across the table.

"We'll have to carry on whether he does or not," she said.

"Of course—but I want him to."

"He might understand." Maisie held her coffee cup in delicate fingers Jon wanted to kiss, but she was being practical. "He probably does understand, but what you really want is for him to approve of you, don't you? You want him to say 'come on, lad, come into the family, marry Maisie, and everything'll be canny'. Well, he may never get to saying that. He may never genuinely think it. My family's not for you Jon, and your family's not for me. There's just us. We mix perfectly, but the families don't."

"Class differences. I hate all that business."

"Aye, that's it: social class. We can love each other

but our families can't. Just see that and accept it."

"There are revolutions going on right now about class differences," said Jon vehemently. "It'll be better one day."

Maisie put down her cup with a teasing smile.

"Are you a revolutionary, then?"

"I'd like to be. Not for politics, but for us."

"Revolutions don't come easy. I remember that from history lessons."

"But today it's different, my Darling. It's a new century, new machines, new ideas. We should move into a new world where we can all respect one another, be rid of the old prejudices and hatreds."

"Well," Maisie's cup was raised again and her eyes twinkled over its rim. "I never thought I'd be marrying a revolutionary speech-maker. I'll buy you a soap-box for a wedding present."

"Are you always going to laugh at me?"

"Aye, if you give us cause to."

They chuckled, held hands again and looked out of the window. The words 'marrying' and 'wedding' brought them images of a future they were determined to grasp. Each in their different ways, they felt it was coming within their reach.

"Philippa's in London", Jon repeated. "We'll be approaching her about the divorce shortly."

"We?"

"I mean me and the family; actually I mean my father."

Jon did not relish their conversation drifting towards the distasteful subject of persuading Phillippa to agree to the divorce, but Maisie seemed pert and confident today and able to make light of anything.

"There'll be a revolution there, right enough," she was saying. "She won't like the idea of being 'approached'."

"We already know she doesn't," replied Jon with bitterness in his voice.

"She'll only want a divorce when she's fine and ready. I can understand that. I wonder if I'm a bit like her."

"God forbid," said Jon.

"No, seriously." Maisie had that teasing smile again. "I think I must be. She's determined to hang on to you and I'm determined to take you away. I think you like determined women."

"I like *your* kind of determination, sweet and lovely Maisie, not her brash and vicious kind. No no, she doesn't want to hang on to me; she wants to hang on to the marriage for her own wicked purposes, whatever they are at the moment. I'm not even sure what they are. She'll want other things in London now, not me, but she'll still make life difficult."

"Well I'll make it easy," Maisie was smiling differently now, with warmth and tenderness. "I'll make it easy if I can. I love you, Jon. I'll do anything to keep your love, to keep us happy like we are now."

"You just have to be yourself, Darling," said Jon.

"And we both have to survive the revolution, whatever this revolution is."

They smiled, held hands, touched knees under the table.

"Odd thing," said Jon at length, "the last time I was at the shipyard I met some Russians who were talking openly of the revolution that's begun over there."

"Oh? I haven't seen any foreigners about the loft."

"I think you will before too long. I spoke to one of them afterwards: a very intelligent man and a highly-skilled carpenter. When it comes to the fitting-out he'll be doing the woodcarving on the panelling in First Class I should think."

"Now I heard there'll be woodcarvers coming from Palestine to work on the ship. That's a long way to come, isn't it? Mind you, plenty of Arab sailors around South Shields. I used to see them when I worked there."

"It seems everyone wants to work on *Mauretania*. We certainly did, didn't we? I liked this Russian chap; remarkably good English."

"He'd best stick to his chisels." Maisie drained her cup. "He and his 'comrades' will get nowhere with their daft twaddle here…unless they've already infected you with it."

"Now you sound like your father."

"Well he and I are both right then. A workers' revolution in Wallsend? You know as well as I do all the workers want here is to keep their jobs and take their pay and go to the pub afterwards."

"Now who needs a soap-box?" Jon grinned. "You're right, of course. England's not the place for that kind of revolution. It'll never happen. But the walls between classes will come tumbling down. They won't be torn down by people like these Russians, but they'll crumble enough to make our future life better and the lives of our children. Anyway, I'll tell you this, Darling: I saw something revolutionary the day I spoke to your father."

"You won't see *him* carrying any red flags."

"No no, I mean something I saw when the turbine was tested."

"Yes? What was that?"

"Well," Jon attempted to demonstrate with his hands, "when the turbine spun round, it pushed so much air out backwards you could have driven something forwards with the force of it…I mean if the air could have been properly contained, properly engineered to come out with even greater force. Instead of being an engine driven by steam it could have become an engine using air to drive itself forward: an air-engine—can't think of another name for it—an air-engine. I can't think how it could be made to work on just air, not yet anyway, but it could be, somehow. You wouldn't need a shaft or turning screws or anything other than the turbine vanes themselves, pushing the air out so fast the whole thing would surge forward."

Maisie looked at him steadily.

"They'll call that idea hot air and worse. I'd keep that idea to yourself; just get on with building the ship."

"It was the most exciting thing I've ever seen."

"Why no, that's supposed to be me!" she laughed. "Anyway, look outside. It's snowing again."

Suddenly, Jon took her hands more forcefully than ever.

"Will you come and live with me in a new place in Tynemouth?"

"I...I don't know." She looked at the snow beyond the window. Beyond that she saw a whole new life and the difficulties of taking up that new life; and she saw the simple step she could take that would make it all possible, the simple step that would also be a terrible step. She turned back to Jon. "Do you have a new place in Tynemouth?"

"No, but I can get us one. It'll be us together, Darling: not in your parents' house, not in the house that was my home with Philippa, but somewhere new, just for us."

"That's a big move. I'll think about it." Her eyelids flickered. "To be honest, I'll think about nothing else now."

More snow fell through the chill dusk: grey snow from a greyer sky, cruel gift of a harsh world, cold and unlovely. The lovely things were here in the warmth, here inside. Outside they might appear to be young lovers, but they felt old. They had terrible problems and drastic circumstances. But inside they felt timeless and that not everything conspired against them. There was the warm fire and these comfortable seats at the window and the rich aroma of comfort. Jon lifted his cup in the lamplight. To Maisie he seemed beautiful, vulnerable, strong, tender, and sparked through with an agonised passion to match her own. She felt calm and frantic, exhausted and charged all at the same time. They looked at each other with the kind of emotion beyond expression in words. It might only be expressed in music—and music did seem to soar and sing and rage and whisper though their very souls until they could do nothing but fall into each other's arms. She took his hand across the table.

"I have to go home," she sighed.

"I know."

Heavy wet snow was falling into already slush-filled streets. Now came the all-too familiar feeling that she was losing everything. If she allowed herself an extravagance of expression she thought it was a kind of death, a death of the spirit. Not a single shaft of wintry sunlight offered salvation; no magical effect of frost enlivened the scene with hope. There was no hope—only the prospect of his return to the remains of a loveless marriage. Then she felt there might be hope. Let him hate the deathly partings as much as she did; let him find no love anywhere but in her arms.

They had made themselves late. They walked uncomfortably through the sodden streets; the short distance to the Central Station seemed lengthened by coldness, their progress impeded by the umbrella they shared until they could put it down inside the noisy, echoing building where big snowflakes still found their way under the glass roof curving far above their heads. They kissed not too lingeringly but with a divine warmth, her slight perfume and luscious eyes filling his world.

"This isn't right," he declared. "I hate to leave you. If we have to keep parting like this I should at least take you to your door." But the coward in him was still afraid to take her to her door, glad of the distance and the train and the circumstances that kept their meetings away from their families.

"I know," she whispered close to his face. "I hate to leave you, too. I always do. But one day we'll be together and never leave."

The train for Jesmond arrived. They kissed and Jon stepped up into the carriage. The bang of the door was cruel in the coldness, echoing pains in Maisies' chest and stomach. She discovered it actually hurt to leave her lover in the snow, to see his stylish coat disappear into the shabby railway carriage and then to watch the whole train disappear into a wintry greyness of fiercely swirling flakes. It hurt. It wasn't an extravagant expression, it was a physical fact. A new glumness settled over her and seemingly over the whole city, like the discovery of an illness. One day she might lose him like that, in a cold walking-away. Tonight's bleakness was almost unbearable. If there had to be snow, she wished for better snow, for Christmas snow; better than that, for fine Summer weather to come with this coming Spring, for new life. By the time she reached her own home she felt as if she had navigated through a deadly storm. She wanted no more partings like this, no more partings at all. She would go and live with him in Tynemouth, whatever her family thought. It would be a huge move for her, the outward sign of an inward revolution, an utter change in her life—but she would be the determined woman whose brightness and resolve he so admired. She would keep the good humour that made her so happy to see him laugh. She would agree to live with him in the new place in Tynemouth. Whatever the cost to her reputation, she would do it. Tonight they might seem to be in a terrible Winter, but she would go to live with him...then what a beautiful Summer it would be.

CHAPTER THIRTEEN
A Threat and a Promise

"Where the devil is your wife, Jon? I called on her today and your faithful Mrs. Hutchinson told me she was in London again."

William Ferris challenged his son in the quiet, mahogany-and-stained-glass atmosphere of the gracious house in Heaton. Invited to dinner with his parents, Jon had been consumed by the sadness of realising once again that the secure home of his boyhood had become an arena for family discord. It was inevitable that the polite reserve employed at the table would be replaced by confrontation in the drawing-room. Yet here was hope of a resolution.

"I think she's likely to be in London for some time, Father. I received this letter from her telling me she's acquired a flat down there."

"Ha! Back to her sordid haunts with a riff-raff of artists and scoundrels."

"Not quite. I think you'll agree this is a decent address in Chelsea."

Jon offered the letter and William took it with an ill-tempered snort.

"So she's making money, or using yours."

"Not mine."

"What, have you cut her off?"

"Not exactly, Father, but she has always insisted on being of independent means. I believe she has—well, let's call them 'supporters'—in London."

"You mean she's a kept woman with a parade of lovers? I trust they're not keeping her so well she'll refuse my generous offer—if I could get it to the damn woman. I suppose I'll have to write. I should have preferred to do it face-to-face up here in her own home."

"I don't think she regards Lily Avenue as her home any more. It's horribly sad, but she's drifted away."

"And who allowed that to happen?" William glowered into his son's face. "Your mother and I provided you with a delightful house that should have become a happy family home, but you couldn't keep it together. I wonder how hard you tried."

Anger rose in Jon...

"Very hard, Father."

...and was matched by William's temper.

"But not hard enough! You couldn't keep your eyes and hands off this new girl." William sank into his chair. "Oh, I'll stop blaming you. We've been through it all, have we not? It takes two people to make a marriage Jon, but only one to destroy it."

Jon turned to face the window with its closed curtains.

"We've both destroyed it," he said.

"Well don't dare pretend to be sorry she's gone." William resumed his calm and practical manner. "Anyway, she's not entirely adrift, is she? She's still connected to you by marriage. I understand she's keen to keep it going for her own peculiar purposes, and will be until she accepts my divorce settlement. I shall make it in due course if you give me that address in Chelsea. If she won't accept through our solicitors I'll go to London and see her there. Now, what are you doing these days at Parsons'?"

It was easier for Jon to sit down and talk to his father about developments in the turbine works and the progress of the ship at the yard, but he made no mention of his revelation at the rotation test. The idea of the air-engine was too outrageous, too seductive, too powerful to be introduced to his father just yet. Anyway, he told himself behind the bland conversation, he had not thought it through, not at all. The rotating turbine might produce a thrust of air to push itself forward, but unless steam or some other source of motive power could be manufactured neatly within the turbine itself, the idea was scarcely a departure from what existed already. The concept had to be of a self-contained engine that could be fitted into any vehicle, independent of any boilers or furnaces. Something inside the turbine casing would have to spin the vanes. But what? Whatever that might be, the idea itself was wonderful and revolutionary and Jon thrilled himself with it all over again…yet the thrill was ruined by the knowledge that he would not tell his father tonight in this house, not share the excitement. It would all have to be put away and kept away. It would sound ridiculous and Jon felt ridiculous enough already. At last, inevitably, he mentioned Maisie and confessed their intention to live together. William's mood darkened again.

"It's appallingly bad form to take this girl to what was

your marital home."

"I know that. I thought you would take that attitude, and I agree—though perhaps not for exactly the same reasons. Anyway, that's why I intend to buy a new place for Maisie and myself in Tynemouth."

"And live openly together?"

"As openly as this wretched hypocritical society will allow."

"You will flagrantly keep a mistress? For that's all that'll be seen of this, you know, however noble your intentions. They won't look noble at all. You'll outrage two families. Why not wait until the divorce?"

Jon stood up.

"There may never be a divorce, Father. Despite your scheme and your generosity, Philippa will *want* to outrage two families, to harry us all into terrible situations. But Maisie and I can't waste our lives waiting for some vicious woman to change her mind."

William smiled and took another cigar.

"Spoken like your father. Goodnight, my boy."

* * *

With the bow sections of *Mauretania's* hull almost complete, work proceeded towards her elegant stern. Timbers of the stern cradle climbed higher to form the after-poppet supporting the steel plates that would be so vulnerable on launch day. Vladimir Druginin and Anatoly Melnikov were put to this work. It was not the fine carpentry to which they aspired, but they knew if they accomplished it well and kept their jobs at the yard they would eventually create some of the woodcarving that would so distinguish the great ship's interiors.

As Druginin had predicted, they had little success as propagandists for the Revolution. The hot-headed foreman Walker had called another meeting and introduced the Russians to their workmates, but no great speeches were made and no enthusiasm was shown. The general feeling was that Marxism seemed dull or dangerous and best left to foreigners. Walker's gleeful declaration that 'the foreigners are right here, right now, and ready to help us' fell on deaf ears.

Jon was at the yard to take further measurements for the shaft bearings. Negotiating the obstacle course of timbers that supported the stern cradle, he recognised the Russian carpenters from their first encounter. They were taking a break from work, their tool-bags at their feet, and were pouring tea from a can into metal cups.

"Tea, Comrade Engineer?"

The taller man held out a cup. This was an extraordinary gesture; no English workman would have made it to a visitor such as Jon in these circumstances. Jon felt it would be churlish to refuse. In any case, he had been drawn to these men after their first chance meeting. They had seemed high-spirited and keen to be friendly. Their working clothes were not quite those of the average shipyard labourer; their peaked caps of foreign design gave them a tinge of the exotic. Whatever jobs they had found here, Jon sensed they had the spirit of artists.

"Thank you."

The tea was black and strong and heavily sweetened.

"Mathematics!" The smaller Russian grinned, pointing at the columns of figures on the folded page of Jon's notebook. He seemed to enjoy pronouncing the English word again. "Mathematics."

"Ah yes," Jon returned the smile. "Measurements."

"Measurements!" The taller man whipped out a carpenter's rule from his pocket and held it aloft with a laugh. "I measure also."

"Yes, we must all very careful measure," smiled his friend, raising his cup. "To good measurements!"—and the three men drank.

Druginin, who had proposed the toast, had more and better English than Melnikov.

"In Hamburg we measure very careful. Our work was to make model of ship in wood...before big ship built in steel."

"Oh yes," said Jon. "That's interesting. They did that here. There was a wooden model of *Mauretania's* hull, one-sixteenth scale. Let's see now, that would be, er, forty-eight feet long. I know it could carry four men. They were testing for the most efficiently shaped hull. It had an electric motor; went up and down the river here for months. I wonder where it is now," he added almost to himself. "It must be in the yard here somewhere; I've never seen it. Oh, I'm sorry," he returned his attention to his listeners. "I don't speak any Russian. I hope you understand my English all right."

258

"All right, yes of course," replied Druginin. "You speak very good English," he added with a mischievous smile.

"Very witty. Yes, I've had a lot of practice."

"Tea, Comrade Engineer?" Melnikov lifted the can again.

"No," his friend instructed him, "this time you say 'more tea'."

"Ah," Melnikov smiled at Jon. "More tea?"

"No thank you." Jon returned the cup. "Yes, it's a pity the English are only good at speaking English. I'm afraid Russian would be quite beyond most of us; we're lucky if we master schoolboy French. But woodcarving," he pointed at the bags, "now there's a great skill. Woodcarving crosses all frontiers. You have some very fine tools there."

"Oh yes," said Druginin. "Anatoly keep chisels with him always."

"I stay with them always," grinned Melnikov.

Jon looked down into the bags and pondered, with real admiration, the souls of men who stayed with their tools. They had travelled to foreign countries, no doubt facing hardships and difficulties, yet had not fallen from grace with their craft and the tools of their craft. There was a nobility and a loveliness in that. He saw the smooth handles projecting from their canvas roll, the invisible faces of the chisels presumably sharpened and oiled and protected. He saw the mallets and rulers and a heavy brace-and-bit, its assortment of drill-bits no doubt also carefully oiled and wrapped. And all the time as he pondered the devotion of these men to their craft, his own idea of the air-engine was turning in Jon's mind…turning, turning…as he thought of everything they had talked about, every image that had come into his mind of the models and the woodcarving and the cranking handle of the brace-and-bit…turning…turning…

"Would you do me a favour?" He looked steadily at Druginin, "Would you lend me your brace-and-bit?" He was faced with a blank look. He pointed into the bag. "Your drill brace-and-bit…the tool…with the crank."

"Ah!" There was a moment of recognition, the men muttered something in Russian, Druginin held the tool aloft. "Where do you need hole?" he smiled.

"No no," he must control his voice and his excitement, Jon told himself as he spoke, "just to borrow the tool…to turn something."

"I bring it to you."

Of course—they would not lend or leave their tools. How presumptious he had been to ask. Was this all folly, a crazy dream, a diversion in all their lives that would lead them only to confusion? Yet the men were pleased and willing. They were cradling the tool, showing him its smoothly-turning well-oiled action, nodding and smiling. Jon knew, in a heart-racing moment, that he would trust them and share something tremendous with them.

"You promise to bring this tool to me when I need it?"

"I promise, Comrade Engineer."

* * *

Sunshine sparkled off the River Thames as William Ferris strode Westwards along its embankment. He could have taken a cab but preferred to walk. It had been some years since he had visited London and he was intrigued to discover its new developments. The capital struck him as noisier and more crowded than ever, but the famous thoroughfares were cleaner than in the days of his youth and the new century had brought some attractive new buildings. Most notable of all was the increase in motorised traffic. Motor cars—which not so long ago had appeared as bizarre machines for the eccentric or laughable toys for the rich—were now tolerably efficient vehicles. More and more thronged the streets as a real challenge to horse-drawn transport. 'Give it a few years', William mused, 'and there'll be no horses in town at all.' London looked and sounded modern. Shop-window displays were colourful and inventive, and bright, new advertisements had sprouted all over the city. The posters brought Philippa more forcefully to William's mind: did she not design some of these? Odd work for a woman, he thought, but there was no denying her talent.

William found himself in Chelsea sooner than he would have liked. He realised how very distasteful it was to run this sorry errand on behalf of his son. The things he and Julia had gone through for the sake of their boy, and now this: taking money to a woman, demanding she remove herself from their lives—dreadful. He forced himself along Cheyne Walk and found the right door. The once very elegant house had been made into flats; still desirable and expensive property, guessed William as he pulled the bell…all under a soft, powdery blue London sky that he thought should have had a better mission to bless. He saw the sky was the colour of Julia's dressing-room wallpaper: one of the newly-fashionable pastels his wife so admired in their home. Wives! He had been lucky with his all these years and done right by her. Why could his son not have been lucky with a wife; or if not, at least have behaved himself?

The door was opened by an elderly housekeeper wiping her hands.

"Who shall I say, sir?"

Philippa appeared in the hall, dismissing the woman brusquely before William could answer. She was wearing a pale blouse and skirt with fashionable shoes, her richly-coloured hair tied up. She looked slender and full of vitality; as attractive as ever, thought William. She would have to be faced here and now.

"Good afternoon," he said coldly.

"I hope it will be. Come in."

She led him through the hall to a spacious back room where French windows were open to a garden. Unexpectedly, the terrace was dominated by a modern camera on a tripod pointing at a huge canvas on which was painted an avenue of trees and a depiction of Pegasus swooping down to the road. What looked like a brand new bicycle was propped up incongruously against the window. The scene was so extraordinary that William was immediately distracted from what he was going to say.

"I'm pleased to see it commands your attention," said Philippa with a faint smile.

"The painting? Yes, the winged horse is quite spectacular."

"I'm glad you think so. It will be my advertising poster for Pegasus Bicycles; a photographic poster, quite the latest thing. My model will sit on the bicycle in front of the painting and I shall photograph him. He's due quite soon." She sat down in almost queenly fashion, very composed and commanding. "So now we've discussed my business we should discuss yours."

"Very well." If he found her good-looking and talented, William quickly confirmed his judgement of Philippa as brittle and charmless. At the same time, her enthusiasm for her work—almost incredible in the uncomfortable circumstances of this meeting—was somehow endearing. Is this how Jon had been endeared? William pushed the thought away. "You received my letter?"

"I did."

"And do you feel able to accept its terms?"

"Perhaps."

He thought she was being intolerably sly. He hoped she would not push him to a display of ill manners.

"Then you might have accepted them by letter and saved us the embarrassment of this visit."

"I might have but I chose not to. Are you embarrassed?"

"You know that I must be, Philippa. This is all tremendously unpleasant. It would have been less so if you had agreed to a divorce from my son in the normal way."

"What's normal about a divorce? Anyway, you weren't embarrassed to mention a very large amount of money in your letter. Five thousand pounds to be rid of me smacks of desperation, not embarrassment"

"For goodness sake, Philippa, you must know that nobody in the family would ever have wanted this. You force my hand to offer terms; you cannot deny they're extremely generous." William did his best to compose himself. "Now, will you admit your marriage to my son is over? Your delay is ignoble."

"Ignoble?" She tossed her head. "And what has been noble about your son's behaviour? Jon cheated on me with some slut of a factory girl." William maintained a stolid expression. "Well? Don't tell me you approve of her!"

"I approve of anyone who can bring my son happiness through love and decent behaviour. We may not have given her credit for doing so, but she appears to have displayed those qualities."

"Love and decent behaviour?" Philippa sprang to her feet. "This is fantastic. Your provincial hypocrisy is unbelievable!" She waved her arms. "Any decent behaviour in the marriage came from *me*, struggling to cope with Jon's selfishness and immaturity in that little prison of a house while he went out to play with his engines and found some common creature to dally with."

"It's not the mere dalliance you like to think it," stated William with a deadly calm. "They hope to marry."

"And I hope to make them wait...but if she's stupid enough to marry him in the end I hope she'll discover what a useless husband he is. Your son has failed in almost everything."

"You think so?" William gritted his teeth. "Well thank God he failed to give you a child."

"Lucky, isn't it?" Her eyes sparkled madly. "You'd

have had to disown the little brat. You wouldn't have wanted any remnant of me left mewling and puking in the great Ferris family, would you? If I want children in the future I'll see they're fathered by men I can truly admire."

"Enough of this, please." William clasped sweating hands behind his back. There was nothing else to do but stare her in the face and re-iterate his offer. "Will you or will you not accept my offer of five thousand pounds to proceed immediately with a divorce? You may sue, Jon will admit adultery."

"So he damn well should!"

Disgust rose in William. He had tolerated her abuse of his son, he would suffer her censorious manner and her bad language—if only he could secure an agreement and leave he would tell himself it had all been worthwhile.

"Do you accept this offer?"

She sat down and put on that teasing, maddening smile. His heart was actually pounding, like that of a foolish boy in trouble. The knowledge that she had upset him so much only aggravated his annoyance. At the same time, against his will, he found himself beginning to revise his earlier judgement. She was anything but charmless; she oozed charm, the most dangerous charm.

"Well now," she drawled, "yes, actually I *do* accept. It makes very good sense, good business sense. What do I care what happens to your stupid boy and his workhouse tart? I'll use the money for more worthy endeavours."

"Very well. I thank you for your answer, though hardly for your manner of delivering it, and if I were you I'd examine your conscience before you call any of your endeavours 'worthy'." William felt exhausted and prepared to leave. "I originally intended this very distasteful business to be dealt with by my solicitors. I am sure you regret as much as I my decision to meet you face-to-face."

"Certainly not…and don't go." Her smile made William squirm. "I don't regret our meeting at all. It's rather cleared the air, hasn't it You thought the human touch would be more civilised, more polite. How typical of you. I'll take your money, but not in the good grace you've been hoping for. I resent being chased out of this family before I actually want to go, but as I said before it makes good business sense."

"You're not a fool." William couldn't resist the parting shot. "You see the sense of five thousand pounds. You appear to be an accomplished businesswoman. I'm sure you'll manage perfectly well."

"I intend to. You really are very small people in a very small town. I shall move on to bigger and better people and places."

William turned his back on the insult and his face to the door.

"Good day to you."

"And you're confident Jon will manage perfectly well without me, aren't you?" Her teasing voice followed him down the hall. "You believe he is well rid of me. I'm sure *he* thinks he is, and he'll enjoy his freedom at first with that shop girl or whatever she is. But you haven't heard the last of me. Jon cheated me and failed me and I'll have my revenge when it suits me."

Blue sky poured its sweet light through the door, London lay beyond, and beyond London lay William's escape from this sordid exchange and freedom for his son. He had only to take his train home, but he felt compelled to turn once more to face the slender young woman who had so changed all their lives.

"There's nothing admirable about you, Philippa, but there is something fascinating. Did you fascinate my son?"

"Oh I do hope I did," she smiled wickedly. "He *looked* fascinated—until he felt some need to play in the dirt. Then he just looked silly."

Her expression was triumphant.

"No-one could ever say that about you," said William drily. "You will survive this well. I'm almost pleased for you."

"Thank you, ex-Papa Ferris. You and I should have been better friends. You understand women."

"My son does, too; he does now, anyway. You taught him a lesson: how to find a better girl who will love him properly. I suppose I might thank you for that. At the same time, I know perfectly well you took advantage of his innocence, as you are taking advantage of my money. Jon is a capable engineer, rather gifted in fact, but he is not worldly."

"I did try to *make* him worldly," she parted her lips and licked them, "pleasures of the flesh and all that."

"You will hear from my bank and my solicitors—after which I trust we will not hear from *you*. Goodbye."

William strode away into the street but heard Philippa calling after him, her voice full of the smiles of exultation and money.

"Oh no, this isn't goodbye, merely au-revoir!"

CHAPTER FOURTEEN
Big Secret, Little House

The offices of Parsons' Engine Works, so busy during daylight hours, were silent as darkness fell. Yet the darkness and silence were not complete. Lights burned in a first-floor window and footsteps beat across the cobbled yard. Jon walked as noisily as he could to make a deliberate show of approaching the night watchman at the gate.

"Good evening. I thought you should know, if you see lights in the offices, it's only myself working late."

"Nee bother, Mister Ferris." The watchman brandished his lamp and truncheon. "I'll keep an eye out for any prowlers."

"I'm sure you will. I'll be leaving in a hour or so."

Jon strode back to the building and entered its shadows with a mixture of relief and tension. He realised once more—as he had realised over and over again since beginning this escapade—that he had never done anything so outrageous or dangerous in his life; but so far, so good, he told himself. He climbed the echoing stone stairs with an increasing heartbeat, he came to the Boardroom corridor…and a figure loomed from a doorway.

"I have been waiting," whispered Vladimir Druginin, "long time."

Jon recovered from the shock. "Your patience will be

rewarded," he said quietly. The Russian was here, on time, unobtrusive, just as agreed. So far, so good. Jon opened the Boardroom door. "In here, please. You have brought the tool?"

"Of course."

Jon switched on the electric light. The long mahogany table sprang into gleaming view. The imposing fireplace frowned down upon empty leather chairs. Pictures of steamships adorned the panelled walls and the familiar model of *Turbinia* sat in its glass case at the end of the room. In this very room he had been welcomed into the Company with his father's support and Charles Parsons' blessing. How long ago that seemed! How he had fallen from grace, yet found new love and new life! The place was a polished cavern of wealth and power: dignified, almost overbearing and pompous, yet also a cradle of vast excitements and new ideas. Now Jon had a new idea of his own. He glanced again at the model of *Turbinia* and hoped the neat little ship on which he had once ridden with boyish glee would be a good omen for tonight's desperate endeavour.

"Thank you for your help." Jon closed the door behind Druginin's long coat. "Do you know anything about the laws of physics?"

"Certainly."

"Then you may already know that one of Newton's Laws states that to every action there is an equal and opposite reaction. That's how a rocket works."

Druginin was wide eyed.

"You are to build rocket?"

269

"No," Jon smiled, "something else, but the principle would be similar…and this is what we need to prove it would work."

He moved to a side table where a small model of one of *Mauretania's* turbines was attached to a wooden plinth. The tight array of gleaming metal vanes reminded him, as they always did with a smile, of a crowded flutter of ladies' fans. Days earlier he had entered this room alone and checked that the model was not too heavy and that the vanes spun easily on their bearings and that the base of its plinth was smooth. He had found it covered in green baize and that it slid quite easily along its polished table. It would be the perfect demonstrator—if the vanes could be turned fast enough. Now he heard himself explaining this to Druginin in a soft voice, a voice he might use to calm and reassure a frightened child, and it occurred to him that he was the father and the idea was his child. He smiled again. It wasn't a very original metaphor; how many inventors had claimed paternity since that first Eureka was shouted in ancient Greece? But he did feel he had created something as new and as wonderful as a child. He curbed his pride as he carried the model from the side of the room on to the long, central table; he hadn't made any of this work yet, and the Russian had to be told what was happening.

"When I saw one of the real turbines being tested, there was a tremendous rush of air streaming out behind it. The vanes were churning up the air like a ship's screw churns up the water, then they were pushing it out of the back of the turbine. I suddenly thought if a turbine could be built that didn't drive a shaft but just made more and more air rush out behind faster and faster, the force could be so great it could drive the whole thing forward."

"What thing?"

"Well, anything the turbine was fitted in to. A boat, a motor-car perhaps, even a flying-machine."

Disbelief stood in Druginin's face.

"I know, I know: the weight. It would have to be made very light. I believe it could be. Anyway, this form of propulsion, the turbine, it's the most exciting engine in the world and it was created here. My idea could be the next stage. That's what we're here to prove tonight."

"Why do you do this in secrecy? Why with me?"

Jon felt unable to list his reasons; he saw only a litter of obstacles and a parade of sceptics that included his father and even Maisie.

"There are too many other things going on," he said dismissively, "and I'd never be believed. Anyway, nothing is proven yet, not even to myself. That's why we have to do this."

"And me?"

Suddenly, Jon felt able to tell the truth.

"I trust you. You have no reason to laugh at me or hinder me. I think you understand we are both outsiders—and you're the only person I know with one of those." He indicated the brace-and-bit held suspiciously under Druginin's coat. Of course it wasn't the whole truth. Matthew Watson would have such a tool, but that route to this moment would have been impossible. Facing Matthew about Maisie had been traumatic enough, approaching him about this would have seemed ridiculous. And Jon sensed there had been too much talk already. He wanted to get on with this and get out. "This is a working model," he continued briskly. "It's all to scale." He grasped one end of the steel shaft between his finger and thumb and turned it gently. The glittering vanes spun slowly. "Pretty, eh?"

"Like Christmas toy," said Druginin.

"Shall we give the world a new Christmas present?" Jon could not keep the glee out of his voice. "Right. Let's turn it round."

"But steam goes in other way," objected Druginin as he indicated the narrow end of the turbine, surprising Jon with his knowledge of the engine.

"Indeed it does. You understand. That's why the vanes get bigger as they go down the shaft. As the steam loses its energy it needs bigger vanes to work on and the final vanes are the biggest of all. See? But we're going to turn it round. Instead of these vanes blowing air out of the wide end of the turbine, they're going to rotate the other way and suck air in."

"Why?"

"So we can blow it out of the narrow end with greater force. Imagine all that air compressed by the turbines being forced out of a narrow tube at the end. There's not an outlet tube on this but it shouldn't matter. We'll do it now. We'll use your tool as a crank. Jam the bit on to the end of the shaft here. Go on, jam it on hard."

Druginin did so, standing at the end of the table with the crank like the starting-handle of a motor-car. Jon, standing to one side, held the model lightly by its plinth. He looked down the smooth expanse of shining mahogany. It was clear; the long table was a path of light. He suddenly saw there was nothing in his way, nothing but his own hesitation. He had hesitated far too much in life; tonight he would strike out bravely for his future.

"Now, if you please."

Druginin turned the handle of his brace-and-bit, the vanes spun, a wind stirred into his face.

"Faster," ordered Jon. "Faster, faster!" The vanes spun madly into a blur of silver light. The blast of air increased behind them. Jon felt a what he had longed to feel, what he had hardly dared to dream he might feel: a slight pressure against the braking action of his fingers. "Faster! More, more!" The vanes hummed madly, air streamed into their faces. Jon's mind raced. It was happening, it really was! Should he hold on? Should he let go? It was happening…yes, yes! The shout of glee was coming up into his throat…"Right!"

Jon lifted his fingers from the plinth. The whole model slid away, driven down the table by its own action. It travelled a yard or so and slewed to a stop. Jon heard a laugh and realised it was his own. He looked at Druginin through suddenly misted eyes. The Russian was beaming.

"It moves!"

"Indeed it does. It's the air that moves it. Congratulations, Mister Druginin!" Jon clasped the Russsian's hands. "You are the first man to drive the Ferris air-engine!"

They shook hands furiously.

"Let's do it again." Jon was garrulous now. "You see what happened? Every action has an equal and opposite reaction. The air pushed backwards and the whole thing moved forward. Oh, I know the efficiency of it is ruined here by friction and weight and all kinds of adverse conditions—but it *moved*! You *saw* it move—and that was just with the power of one man with a hand tool. With some other motive power it would turn faster and drive anything. D'you see?"

"I do! I do!"

They were ready to run the turbine again. Jon held the plinth, Druginin cranked the handle furiously, the plinth was released—and once more the model slid away down the table.

"And will you build this, Comrade Engineer?"

"No, not me, not yet." Jon was relaxing, running fingers through his hair. "It needs a vast amount of work, work I can't do yet. The timing is terrible. I have my job here; I have found a new woman I love, and there are endless problems with my wife and family. But I do have the idea. I have to make many calculations, draw detailed plans. I shall draw them, then one day the machine *will* be created, and there'll be a new engine for a new world. But first we must live in *this* world." He turned to face Druginin. "Now you've heard my confession, will you swear to secrecy about this?"

Druginin gave a beguiling smile.

"Your secret love, or your secret invention?"

Jon could not suppress a chuckle.

"Both, actually."

"I have no reason to betray you, Comrade."

"Very well." Jon produced the wad of bank-notes that had troubled his pocket all day. "For your trouble tonight."

"It was no trouble."

"And to seal our promise. No word to anybody. Will you swear to secrecy about this?"

Druginin took the money without much emotion, almost as if he had been expecting it. For a moment Jon felt he had not bought any security at all...then the Russian gave another of his beguiling smiles.

"Oh yes," he said quietly, edging his way out of the room into the darkened corridor, "this will be great secret, certainly."

* * *

"Mr. and Mrs. Ferris, is it?"

William Robson, Estate Agent and Valuer, met Jon and Maisie at the door of the house for sale in Percy Street, Tynemouth.

"Yes," answered Jon, smiling at the obvious misconception and at his bravery in correcting it, "but the truth is, we're not actually married yet."

"Well, good morning—and I trust the happy day is not far off. A ring to go on that pretty little finger, exciting times, eh?" Robson decided to stick to business. "Aye well, let's have a look around Number Twelve, shall we?"

A funny pair, these two, he thought. They were hiding something. Was she pregnant, getting set up in a house before it showed? They'd better hurry up with the wedding, then. Or was she a mistress? Aye, that was it, he was a waster with a wife in Heaton or Jesmond or further out in the county, sowing his wild oats with this lass from the factories—well, perhaps not a factory, a decent shop-girl, a little more gracious and better educated than most, but beneath his class, and damn lucky to be getting a house bought for her. They'd never get on of course, in this house or anywhere. He might have the breeding and the money and she had the nice little figure under that dress, but this sort of marriage could never work. She'd be like a fish out of water with his folks and he'd be looking for new tart in a year or so. Never mind, they were business, and looked like good business. Robson held his clients outside the door for a moment. Percy Street had been built as a neat terrace many years back in the last century; small houses but with handsome, round-arched front doors and tidy windows; a quiet location off the main thoroughfares, only a few hundred yards inland from the ruined priory, the pier and Tynemouth Haven. Today it was bathed in freshness and a smell of the sea.

"Very attractive, don't you agree? Vacant property as you see; not many for sale in this street. Those that do fall vacant are usually to let…and of course you're just behind the shops in Front Street along there. It'll make a handsome little purchase for your first home."

Robson knew perfectly well that the street was somewhat run down and not currently fashionable. He knew that vista of the sea at the end of the street, so appealing a surprise today, could become a chill, grey wall of despair. Number Twelve was unusual, done up rather expensively, out of its class, an oddity, a bit like these two themselves. Perhaps that's what they wanted: something different, somewhere quiet and out-of-the-way. But he would say good things because they would believe anything he said if they wanted the house; the man would, anyway. The lass was a different matter. For all her quiet manner she'd be as sharp as a needle.

"After you, madam. I always say assessing a property needs a lady's eye."

Inside, the house managed to look welcoming even when empty, with sunlight coming in to warm the fresh paint and new wallpaper. Money had been spent here; the previous owner had done well and was moving on. The place was ripe to be snapped up—but by these two? The lad kept asking the girl if she liked this, if she liked that, and she was being coy and quiet and looking around with faint smiles and nods and it would be the same old story: Robson would have to sell to the woman.

"Come and have a look upstairs, madam. You're going to like what you see." He held them again outside a door, his hand on the unusual and rather expensive porcelian handle he would point out later. "Now then," he opened the door, "what do you think of that?"

"Oh, look at this, Jon…"

As Robson had expected, this brought a squeak out of the girl.

"…it's a proper bathroom!"

"It is indeed, madam." Robson got into his stride. "The current owner must have spent a canny bit on this, and through that other door is a modern lavatory. I doubt there's another bathroom and WC in this street; most of them'll still have their tin baths and outside netties. You'll be making a very sound purchase, sir: a solid, older property, nicely modernised."

"Thank you, Mr. Robson. The house is most attractive." Jon turned to Maisie, "Just as we'd hoped, isn't it?"

"Fine," continued Robson, doing his best to interpret Maisie's quiet smile. "Well then, I'll leave you to look around for a while, get a proper feel of the place without me hanging around like a wicked old uncle when young people have their minds to make up. I have some business to do on Front Street and shall be back within half-an-hour to see you out and lock up. Of course there's no hurry for a decision. I appreciate you may have other properties to inspect, though I doubt you'll find anything quite as nice as this one around here. You have only to contact me at the office. Well now, au revoir for the moment, as they say in France."

Robson left them in the front parlour and Jon turned to Maisie with a whisper.

"I'm sure they don't say that in France, not in that accent anyway."

"Jon," she took his hands with a quiet smile, "we're alone in our new house. It *is* going to be our new house, isn't it?"

"If you like it sufficiently."

"I do, I do! I've always dreamed of having a proper bathroom. When I saw it I was going to say it'll make a nice change from the tin bath in front of the kitchen fire but I didn't want to seem like a girl who came from a family who only had a tin bath—not that he didn't know, like. I'm sorry you've got him to deal with. I've had enough of him already with his red boozer's nose and his oh-so-jovial manner."

"He's all right, just a bit pushy."

"He saw right through us, man. And don't pretend you didn't notice. You're going to have to get used to that, you know: people seeing the differences between us."

Jon held her hands tightly.

"We've been though all that, Darling."

"No we haven't. We've hardly started to go through it. If we live here together, if we live anywhere together, there'll be worse than him to deal with."

"You'll rise above such nonsense. You already have."

"Well," Maisie breathed more easily, "I know I've already got plans for the bathroom." She smiled with enthusiasm and stepped daintily to the front window. "Oh yes. If I can draw plans for a big ship I can draw them for a little bathroom. Oh, Jon my love," she hurried back to him and took his hands again, "I love this house already, I love you, and I want us to live here. I love that fanlight over the door; I love the smell of the sea and the look of it at the end of the street, we're so close to it, and the old cliffs of Tynemouth, and the sands down there. It'll be canny living in a street named after the Dukes of Northumberland. It's a beautiful place and it'll be a happy place for us if we manage things the ways you say we can. But are *you* happy here, never mind me for a minute, do *you* like it?"

Jon had scarcely seen her so wide eyed.

"Yes," he answered happily, "I think it's a wonderful find."

"Be honest now, it's not the sort of place you've been used to."

"Thank God it isn't. It's a glorious fresh start."

"Yes, I think it will be glorious. But tell me something Jon, tell me the absolute truth, here, now, before we go any

279

further. Did you feel like this when you went to that other new house?"

"You mean in Jesmond, with Philippa?"

"Yes, that's what I mean." She saw him drop his eyes for a moment, saw a pang of emotion flicker across his face. "Give us the truth now."

"No. No, the truth is I felt different. The first day in that house was all set up for us by the family. I wasn't really free, I suppose neither of us were. She soon wanted to be, of course. The business of the house was exciting in its own way, as you can imagine. We'd just been married, there was plenty of money about, I had my new job, she had her painting project, but it was all arranged for us; not free and truly happy like this. No, I didn't feel like this. I feel wonderful with you."

"But you did love her."

"I did then, yes, but not as I love you now. My love for you is better, because you are a better person, and you have made me a better person."

"Thanks for saying that, and meaning it."

"I do mean it—and something he said when he pointed at your finger makes me determined you should have an engagement ring now, the finest we can find for you, as soon as possible."

"Oh no, Jon," she protested. "We talked about that before; you know what I think about that. It'll cause a right stir. You're not divorced yet. I'll wear one when everybody knows we're going to get married, when it's all settled and all understood by my family, and by yours too. If I wear one now it'll cause a real fuss at work with everyone asking who's the lucky man and all that."

Jon held her hands tightly.

"*I'm* the lucky man and I want the world to acknowledge it, and acknowledge you as my fiancée. Anyway, we must be formally engaged. I want us to be. If you're worried about the ring you could accept an engagement ring from me and not wear it at work."

"Oh, now that *would* be daft," she said vehemently. "I'm not going to have an engagement ring and not wear it."

"All right then; be brave and *do* wear it. You've asked me to be brave, now I'm asking you."

"Well," she stepped back with a smile, "I know what you're like about special presents for me. The ring mustn't be anything too expensive; nothing so big it's going to put peoples' eyes out when they see it."

"Oh," he retorted, "I think it must be. I want everyone's eyes put out."

"Are we having our first argument?"

"No," he smiled broadly, "we're making another great decision: to get formally engaged. Watch me. You'll notice the Jane Austen language and down-on-one-knee stuff has been thrown out by this forceful young man of the Twentieth Century." He stood to attention theatrically, taking Maisie's hand and bowing over it as if about to kiss the fingers of a continental baroness. "Miss. Watson, will you do me the enormous honour of becoming my wife?"

The humorous play-acting was over in a moment. This was real. She rushed into his arms and hugged him tightly, burying her face in his chest, kissing his neck and cheeks and lips.

"I will, I will, of course I will! I love you more than anyone in the world and I want us to be together for ever."

"We will be, Darling."

"And I'll wear your ring. I'll wear it proudly."

They stood together for long moments, kissing gently. At last she kissed the tip of his nose and looked around the room.

"We've got engaged in an empty house that isn't even ours yet," she stated, "but I don't mind that. It's another strange circumstance, part of all the others we've had to go through to get together. And it's made the house sacred to us, hasn't it?"

"Yes it has." Jon held her tenderly, looking around. "I rather like it like this, bare and empty. It still manages to be cosy. We'll make it cosier still, but it's rather good like this, don't you think? It looks like a place in which to make love." He put an arm around her waist and felt the slender shape under her dress. "A place to make love naked in every naked room."

"Not now, man!" She laughed madly. "We'll have to behave. There's less than twenty minutes before he comes back!"

"All right," he smiled. "I'll put my hands behind my back and pace about like Collingwood on his quarter-deck."

"No you won't. You'll keep your hands round my waist; no lower, mind…" she squealed, "…or higher!"

Jon lowered his hold again.

"There now." She wriggled her waist and narrowed her eyes at him. "Twenty minutes keeping your hands there and you'll be nicely numb."

Jon chuckled into her neck as he kissed her gently.

"That's one of the things I love most about you: your sense of humour. Which reminds me: I don't think Philippa ever cracked a joke with me, at least not in your way. I couldn't possibly be happy with her. I can only be happy with you. She was witty, not funny."

"That's me right enough. I'm very funny, me. Anyway, Geordies have a better sense of humour than Londoners. We will make love here though," she added with a sparkle in her eye, "when you've done the deal with Mister Robson and the place is ours and before there's any furniture in or anything. We'll dance through the whole place, and if you like I'll wear nothing but my new engagement ring." She giggled delightfully. "It'll be like that winter's night in the drawing-loft."

"I shall remember that all my life. That was magical."

"This will be too."

He kissed her again.

"Do you really like the house, then?" he asked quietly.

"Yes, I really like it—and I like what you're doing for us. It's a very big thing, Jon, you and me coming here. You do know what a big thing it is that you're doing, don't you?"

"Yes. I'm doing it for you, for us, for our whole

future and our children's future."

* * *

Druginin and Melnikov sat late in their lodgings, making tea, eating biscuits, drinking beer, eating sausages, listening to noises from the benighted river, and talking. Sometimes they felt their real lives, their true lives, resided in the companionship of these talks. There was work, there was sleep, there was the rest of life, there was Russia and the rest of Europe behind them and England before them, but this was their real life: their talk. They spoke of everything from their childhoods to the curious circumstances of their present situation, huddled around bottles of beer in a small lodging-house on industrial Tyneside in the early years of a new century.

"German beer is better," remarked Melnikov.

"Don't say that to the workmen here," Druginin warned him with a smile, "you'll cause a riot."

"…when all we want is a revolution. Very funny, Comrade."

"I am learning English humour. It is not coarse. It is rather subtle."

"Like you, eh?"

"Subtlety has its uses. You remember when I went to meet the engineer that night and when I came back I told you I had not made any decision about it?"

"I remember," said Melnikov.

"With great subtlety I played the character he thinks I am, did what he asked and took his money. Then the situation—and it is a remarkable one—required a few days' thought, some subtle thought. I have spent those days wisely and now know exactly what we must do."

"I am excited to hear this," smiled Melnikov, pouring more beer. "I know you will launch a great scheme."

"It is already launched, my friend. We have only to guide it to a successful conclusion." Druginin took his glass and settled himself more comfortably in the shabby armchair. "This machine, this air-engine of his imagination: I was prepared to reject it as a mad enthusiasm, unworkable, useless to our cause or anybody's. But I tell you it is perfectly viable. Not in his hands, of course. He is an enthusiast, but his intellect is inferior. He thought it necessary to explain the laws of physics to me and to confess his love for a woman who is not his wife. His capacity for industry and business dealing may also be deficient. He is, above all, an innocent. Yet I believe he has created, or rather imagined, a machine that could change the world and that will certainly be of value to us."

"So—this Englishman. Is he a genius?"

"He may be a genius. Like many a genius, he may also be a simpleton. That would make our task easier. I told him I had no reason to betray him but I have every reason. This machine could have great military value. Even before it is built, the very possibility of such an engine could accelerate the coming of war. That is precisely what we want, is it not? Have we not said this many times? So, plans for the air-engine must be sold to the Germans who will give us money towards our cause, build the engine faster and better than the English ever would, and use it as a military threat. This quiet Englishman with his pleasant face and secret girl, he is not the one to make the most of this." Druginin sat forward to emphasise his point. "The Germans!"

"You are so clever, my friend." Melnikov laughed with glee.

"I must not be too clever," Druginin continued with his quiet smile. "I had also thought of selling it to the Americans, who have more money…but the time is too soon for the Americans. The war will be started in Europe, presumably by the Germans, so the plans must go to the Germans."

"In all your cleverness," Melnikov was pouring more beer as he spoke, "have you ensured that such plans exist?"

"The Englishman will draw them. He told me himself."

"When will he draw them?"

"Soon, I imagine. He is a slow thinker; he proceeds by flashes of inspiration. He laboured over telling me that he has to solve some problem of a propulsion agent, invent some means of turning the turbine within its own casing without having it linked to another source of power by shafts or belts and without having steam forced through it from a boiler. I understand that this will ensure his air-engine becomes a self contained unit which could be attached to any vehicle. That will be the crucial development, the essential difference that will make this superior to any existing turbine. There will be some way of doing this. I can't think of it myself. We'll leave such work to geniuses, then more practical men such as ourselves will make use of the result. Anyway, he will eventually solve this problem and draw the plans. Then we will be able to proceed. Of course it will not be a straightforward sale. He will be difficult to bribe. He is a good man, utterly sincere, and honourable behaviour is natural to him."

"To Hell with all good men," grunted Melnikov.

"No no, a good man can sometimes be useful. And honourable behaviour and sincerity can be most effective. I have occasionally employed them myself."

Melnikov chuckled into his beer.

"And you will employ them again to win his confidence?"

"Oh no."

"Then how will we get the plans?"

"We will steal them…or I should say *you* will steal them."

CHAPTER FIFTEEN
Red Hot Air, Ice Blue Stone

The house at Number Twelve Percy Street, Tynemouth, was duly sold to Jon. He took possession of the deeds and showed them to Maisie as proof that their future together would be a reality as well as a dream. Then he gave her a key, and suddenly she felt she had been granted access to a whole new world.

It would be a new home with the man she loved; a different house of which she would be the mistress; a place for love and for happiness and for the rest of her life with Jon. The idea of it all ran constantly through Maisie's mind and even through her body, making her tingle with the hot surge of excitement and shiver with the chill of anxiety. This was also the leaving of her childhood home, a rupture with her parents, a drastic break from her family and the only life she had known—until this new life with Jon had surged into her being.

She would be engaged, but it was hardly a conventional engagement after a conventional courtship: the kind of courtship her family would have expected, the kind she would once have expected herself. She would be married, but not yet, perhaps not for a long time. She would be living in that little house with a still-married man, 'living in sin' as her Catholic friend Veronica would have put it—and not just Veronica, everyone would think the same. Everyone was so narrow-minded, nobody seemed to understand how sweet and beautiful and perfectly natural and completely right it was for Jon and herself to be so in love like this, how wrong and unhappy his first marriage had been, how mistaken people could be about his character. But everyone would come to understand. They would have to. If they didn't, she would tell them herself, *make* them understand. Oh, it was wonderful! It might be frightening but it was wonderful; surely it would all turn out right if she was careful and honest and explained the truth to everyone who needed to know it, kept things to herself when she could, and enjoyed every moment of this excitement with Jon. Over and over again she told herself that this decision would be the best one she had ever made.

The mixture of excitement and anxiety consumed her every moment. At busy breakfasts with little George getting off to school and her father getting away to the shipyard, she thought his face was rather clouded these days, his mouth very glum. She knew it was because of her and she felt a sting of bitterness at bringing disapproval and strife into the family. But was it really all her fault? Was it not natural enough for a girl to love a man and go off to marry him? Aye well, she didn't have to remind herself too often he was married already—but could they not see this was the start of something better for both of them? Of course it was the end of something too: her departure from the little house in which her parents had struggled so hard to keep her safe and happy would be the end of secure family living in these decent, well-kept rooms she had known all her life.

When Maisie told her parents the house in Tynemouth had been bought and that Jon would be ready to take her there as his fiancée, there was a final agonized exchange of raised voices, accusations of wanton immorality and downright stupidity subsiding into sullen silences. The air in the kitchen was hot with flushed faces and anguished looks; it was her father who kicked open the door to relieve the stifling atmosphere. But no fist was raised to Maisie, no hand of restraint laid upon her. She realised, with an unexpected terror, that her mother and father were really going to let her go—go her own outrageous way, into whatever happened. If they did not understand her completely, then surely this proved they loved her completely. She wanted to cry but wouldn't, not in front of her father. He still had to be shown his lass was doing well for herself, not bringing shame but going up in the world. Her mother understood better, or pretended to, and saw Maisie off to work with a smile. Did it have to be a sad smile? Aye, she supposed it had to be, for the moment.

She kept herself busy in the drawing-loft and got on with the work. It was progressing quickly, yet there was still more and more to do. While *Mauretania's* hull rose steadily beyond the drawing-loft windows, in here the tracers were already enlarging plans for the superstructure and interiors. It was detailed, fiddly work: easy to get absorbed in, also easy to get tired of. Maisie couldn't afford to make mistakes in her drawings and bring attention to herself, not these days. She kept her head down, wondering how many of these women knew what was going on in her life. She reminded herself, though she hardly needed to, that workshop gossip ran round this place like wildfire, and very coarse and vulgar it could be, too. How many of them knew? And what did they know? Notes and packages in her pigeon-hole, Jon's visits to the yard, her trips to Newcastle, the workmen jeering at her, her father's meetings with Jon, the new house in Tynemouth, her mother trying to keep order at home: it all added up to something suspicious if you wanted to look at it that way, and these women would. There must be talk already and there would be more. But what, who?

That Rosie Sullivan two desks away: she would know something. A clever Irish girl, so good at her sums she could have been in the Accounts department, she was forever nosing around the other desks listening for gossip and too often over Maisie's shoulder passing it on to Ellen Robson.

Everyone knew Rosie Sullivan had what they called 'long ears'—and a long tongue between them, added Maisie to herself. Rosie wasn't particularly liked and she knew it and didn't care and she'd be quick to expose anything damaging she could find about any of the other women.

If it wasn't Rosie Sullivan it would be Peggy Dowling, big sister from a brawling bad family at the other end of Union Street. How she'd got a respectable job as a tracer in here Maisie couldn't guess—unless she'd lifted her skirts to the supervisors. The rumour was she'd lifted them to other men in the yard; not that any decent man would want anything to do with a Dowling girl. Their hair was none-too-clean and they had a smell about them, though it seemed Peggy had had to tidy herself up a bit to get and keep this job. All the same, Maisie could see her shoes were never properly polished, the hem of her skirt needed stitching up, and as soon as there was a sniff of warm weather she would do the unheard-of thing by coming to work in a blouse with the sleeves cut short and buttons open down to her petticoat—and that wasn't clean, either. She was a disgrace to the drawing-loft but was brazen about it when she'd been told off. Peggy led a little gang of the noisier, naughtier girls from the loft and Maisie knew they'd be the first to throw stones at anyone who could be made a victim.

On her days off, Maisie could think of nothing but how she might meet Jon or how she might spend time in the house at Tynemouth making it ready as their new home. Sunday became the highlight of her week, for on Sunday afternoons—sometimes with Jon, sometimes alone, letting herself in with her new key—she would visit the house and begin to clean it, arranging curtains and the few kitchen utensils her mother could spare. For both Jon and Maisie, despite their widely differing upbringings, Sunday had always seemed infected with a kind of grey anaesthesia. For Jon it had been the ritual of church and a family lunch, the day enlivened in recent years by the advent of the motor-car and the Sunday outing. For Maisie it had been chapel and the drudgery of the kitchen; she too had tried to freshen the day by her insistence of a walk on the beach or along the pier in search of…she never knew quite what. Yet the emptiness of shuttered shops and closed factories dominated the noontide streets; the last drunkards would be turned out to argue beyond slammed doors; then afternoons of children turned out to play while exhausted parents slept or snoozed, snatching moments in bed or in armchairs before the threat of the toiling week ahead stole the remains of their day of rest. Now Sunday afternoon was charged with emotion as never before, and sacred as her time at the new house.

It was not always possible for Maisie to spend as much time as she would have liked with Jon, but while Philippa remained in London they could at least meet at Pumphrey's when time and circumstances allowed.

"Yes," Jon confirmed, "she's still in Chelsea—doing well at her poster business, I suppose. She's talented and clever and there'll be good reasons for her to stay in London."

"D'you think she'll come back to the Jesmond house?" Maisie looked anxiously into her cup of coffee.

"Well, as you know, she made a great fuss of wanting to keep a foothold up here. Many of her things are still in the house. They could be sent down to London if she wanted them; they'll have to be when the house is sold."

Maisie listened to him, his words punctuated by a disturbing rattle of traffic from the street below and the unsettling chatter of other lunchtime visitors to the upper room. She was always uneasy when they were talking about Philippa, even in this businesslike way. At the same time she wanted to know, needed re-assurance that the ties of Jon's past were loosening.

"Will it really be sold?" she asked pleadingly. "Will that really be the end of her bothering you up here?"

"Yes, I hope it will be. I don't like being there now there's nothing of me really left in that house. In my heart, I've moved to Tynemouth with you already."

Relief brought a smile to her face. The traffic and the chatter seemed friendly now.

"That's a lovely thing to say."

"It's only the truth. I hadn't really put it into words before. The house in Lily Avenue is actually very nice, you know. It's a good place to live—if you're with a good person. My good person is in Tynemouth, or will be shortly…" They held hands. "…so it doesn't matter how nice Lily Avenue might be, there is nothing there for me. My father wants the house to be sold; after all he bought it for myself and Philippa together, not for her alone. I think the arrangements are that she stays in London, the Jesmond house is sold, and the divorce goes through that way."

"You mean your father is in charge of the arrangements and you're not exactly sure what they are?"

"Yes, I've left the arrangements to him, and no, I'm not exactly sure what they are. It's better that way." Jon paused and looked out of the window, their favourite window in Newcastle, down into their favourite street. He wanted to keep this place sacred, their haven of peace and security, but the strains of their present circumstances intruded. "You think that's a weakness?"

"No."

"Other people would. They'd say I should be sorting all this out myself."

Maisie took his hands again in her familiar and delightful gesture of support.

"You've done enough for her already, my love. I can say that to you now, can't I: 'my love'? I really can say 'my love'. As far as we can tell, your father's been very good at dealing with her. Let it happen, let her go."

"By God I want to," said Jon. "It's she who won't let me go so easily."

"I think she will when she sees it's all over between you and she finds new interests in London. New interests and herself—that's what she cares about more than anything, isn't it?"

"You've got her character right there."

"So let's not talk about her any more today. Let's talk about you."

"About us," smiled Jon, kissing her hand.

"You first then."

She watched him draw a quick plan of the air-engine on a sheet of paper unfolded from his pocket. She heard him explain that this was how it looked now, this was as far as he'd progressed with the design, but that it still needed something within its casing to spin the vanes of the turbine, 'a source of motive power', he called it. She said it was no good looking at her like that, she didn't have a source of motive power up her sleeve, unless it was a waggly finger ready to tickle him. And he was too trusting, she told him. The best inventors worked alone, didn't share their brilliant ideas with other people, especially not with odd refugee Russian carpenters. He argued it was teams of people, not solitary thinkers, who made inventions into viable products. She remined him he still had plenty of solitary thinking to do before this invention could be anything more than a drawing…and never mind the air-engine, would he like to meet her for fish-and-chips?

"Sunday lunch?" he smiled.

"No, my love," a flicker of unease crossed her face, "I'll have to be at home with Mam for that—until I move. No," she brightened again, "I meant Saturday night supper on the Fish Quay. You've never had fish-and-chips down there, have you?" She gave him a naughty smile. "It might not be quite the place for the likes of you, but it's always been a real treat for me and the bairns. I'll take you."

"If you're sure it'll be all right."

"Why shouldn't it be all right…unless you're too snobby to be seen with me down there?"

"No, no, Darling," Jon replied quickly. "I didn't mean that. I meant if it was all right for *you* to take *me*. Shouldn't *I* be taking *you*?"

"Oh," she laughed brightly, "you mean me paying for us? Haway man, Jon. A big cod-and-chips from Purdy's shop is one-and-six. I can afford three shillings. You're worth more than three shillings," she added with a gleeful wink. "And you know what everybody says these days," she affected an upper-class drawl, "'this *is* the Twentieth Century'. Why, women in America are buying motor-cars for their men."

"Are they indeed?" replied Jon with a laugh. "Some kind of women."

"Your kind of woman. You've got one. Come on, it'll be fun. There are no rules down there, you know—apart from the rule that says you don't let some cheeky bairn jump the queue."

He suddenly saw her as the cheeky bairn herself, now developing into a lovely womanhood that still retained happy strains of that cheek. It was not rudeness or impertinence, it was release of her true self, a part of her growing-up—and he was making it possible. He felt pride. He saw in a moment that he had a mission in life beyond his work; he was already engaged upon it, had been since they met. He was thrilled to believe he had found a true and valuable purpose: to love this girl properly with tenderness and understanding, to use whatever influence and wealth and power he might have to free her into a new and fulfilling life. He thought that if anyone ever told his life story, this would be the most important fact of it, this is what it would really be about. Yes, he had worked on a great ship, he had invented the air-engine, but above all he had loved Maisie Watson, been loved by her, and set her free. He seemed to realise for the first time, in a flash of reflection, that he had provided Philippa with little more than his body and a new studio. She had been swift to use both with a bright, temporary enjoyment—and then left in pursuit of new excitements. This would be different. He would provide Maisie with his complete love and everything his life could give her, and she would never leave him. Here, upstairs in Pumphrey's, she saw none of this in his face. He just seemed to be laughing. She could not tell that he was planning, with deep joy, another event to follow Saturday on the Fish Quay.

"All right," Jon smiled. "But if you buy me supper, I'll have to buy *you* something. In fact I've already bought you something but it'll keep until after the fish-and-chips."

"You can buy us the lemonade. That'll be threppence

each, and we'll need it after the hot fish."

They laughed, held hands again, and relaxed into their seats high above the busy Cloth Market, the Cathedral weathercocks once again winking down a gleeful brightness on their endeavours: seemingly so simple, yet charged with such passion.

"Lemonade and fish-and-chips," said Jon with an amused smile. "It sounds exciting."

"It will be; you'll see."

* * *

North Shields Fish Quay at night was rough and disreputable, loud with the brawls of sailors and the shrieks of prostitutes, pungent with the smells of the herring boats and the smokehouses. The trawler harbour was transformed from the bustle of its industrious, moneymaking daytimes to a gaudy, shadowed, dangerous hinterland where policemen walked three-abreast, down from drunken evictions at the notorious Low Lights tavern to pickpockets and loiterers along the quayside wall—and beyond it, the ceaseless river darkling its way past the wealth and the poverty and the pride and the shabbiness to the open, all-cleansing sea.

The Fish Quay could never be genteel, but this mild Saturday night it looked innocent enough and seemed to promise a sense of holiday fun. The sky was still full of light, some boats still passed up and down the river on a flood tide, it was too early for the drunks and the fights. Ragged children dangled their lines and hooks off the black timbers of the quay; a better-off family was strolling the waterfront, showing their children the moored boats. An old seaman sat on a bollard, looking wistfully upstream past the Shields ferry landings to the looming cranes of the shipyards.

"He looks almost too picturesque to be true," remarked Jon as he and Maisie walked the uneven planks of the quay. "I wonder what he's thinking?"

"Perhaps he's waiting for a huge new ocean liner to come down the river." Maisie snuggled a smile into Jon's arm as they walked. "He'll get one before too long: I was drawing parts for something they're calling the Verandah Café yesterday. It looks just the place for afternoon tea half-way to America, very posh." She squinted into the red and yellow of the West. "Our yard's just up there."

She turned her attention from the vista of river, cranes and factories and led Jon back to the street of ships' chandlers', sailmakers' and fishmongers' shops that ran behind the Fish Quay towards the noisy pubs of North Shields. The narrow shop that sold fish-and-chips was doing brisk business to a crowd eager to carry away a steaming, tasty supper.

"D'you get the smell?" asked Maisie, tugging Jon's arm gleefully. "Nothing like it, eh? No taste like it, either."

She led him in and they joined a none-too-orderly queue to face an orgy of heat, noise, smell and activity as the two burly fryers in their greasy caps and black aprons poured baskets of chips into bubbling vats. Dangerous clouds of steam roared behind the high counter as water on the freshly-rinsed chips met the boiling fat. Children and adults alike stood fascinated as filleted cod and haddock, dripping with milky batter, were plunged into pans of sizzling fat. The shop was a boiler-house of belching, fat-laden steam and jostling, unruly children, but it was a place of exaltation to Maisie and she let Jon see it in her face.

"Like a ship's engine-room," she beamed. "D'you not think?"

"Perhaps—on a very oily tramp steamer."

"Oh," she smiled. "Mister Snobby Engineer, is it?" It was lovely making fun of him like this, here in the hot shop when she'd got him on her own ground, his hands awkwardly in his pockets, his face reddening with the steam and perhaps a bit of healthy embarrassment. "They'll keep the engine-room on *Mauretania* tidier than this but they won't eat as well."

"Actually, stokers on the Atlantic do eat pretty well. They fry leftovers from First Class on their shovels. Did you know that?"

He thought he sounded pompous and wished he hadn't said it, but she didn't seem to mind, she was so excited by being here. She was joyous; it was part of her escape from drabness into excitement. He had made it possible, just as his first meeting with her that fateful day in the drawing-loft had struck the spark of their love. How amazing life had become since she had so innocently shown him those tender, acutely-observed, remarkable drawings of her own. He let his pleasure in her glee take over from his awkwardness in this raucous shop. He would enjoy the whole business as the treat she meant it to be; then he would present *his* treat—about which he would say nothing at the moment.

"I didn't know that, to be honest," she was saying, then pointed laughingly over the counter, "but look, they've got a stoker of their own here."

A woman had appeared in a fat-smeared apron, her hair tied up in a cloth, carrying a small shovel of coals. She opened the iron door of the boiler furnace and threw the coals into the roaring red cavern. A blast of scorching air rushed from behind the counter and struck Jon and Maisie in their faces.

"Cod-and-chips twice!" yelled Maisie into the heat. "Over here. I want bigguns, mind, and I want salt and vinegar put on!"

"Giz a minute, pet!"

The furnace door was slammed shut and the woman began shovelling chips into paper bags and wrapping scalding fish in sheets of old newspaper. Maisie turned to Jon and wiped her face.

"Why, the red hot air nearly knocked us over," she grinned. "It's like an oven in here anyway, even with the boiler door shut."

"What did you say?" Jon fixed her with a stare.

"I said the hot air…from the boiler door…I was standing too close when it rushed out."

"Hot air." Jon smiled deliciously, allowing a mixture of excitement and contentment to wash over him and slow his voice. "Of course. It rushed out. That's the answer: hot air!"

"Two cod-and-chips!" The woman thumped hot, paper-wrapped packages on to the counter. "Three shillings, pet."

Maisie paid and took the packages and elbowed her way out of the shop with Jon. The newspaper oozed heat and grease and vinegar and when it was opened the salty fragrance of the fried fish rose temptingly into the cooler air.

"Use your fingers!" Maisie was helping Jon unwrap his chips. They found a quiet niche in a smoke-blackened wall and leaned against it, looking across the river to lights just coming on in South Shields, and Jon was talking rapidly now with his mouth full.

"…hot air is the answer: that's what'll drive the turbine. It really *will* be an air-engine. Air will be heated in the casing itself, it'll expand and force the turbine to spin, and that's what will drive the engine. Once it's turning it'll suck more air in anyway and that will be compressed and heated and keep the force going."

"How will you heat the air?"

"I don't know," confessed Jon between chips. "I don't know yet."

"Coal or coke?"

"No, no," he rattled on, almost making her laugh. It was wonderful to see what had happened to him so quickly, she thought. "You can't carry a coal fire inside this engine and I don't want one stuck on the side with pipes going in and flues going out. No, no; some kind of burner inside, using motor-spirit perhaps, even paraffin; something like that. It's a brilliant answer, Maisie. Darling Maisie—and I remember now you mentioned it once before and I didn't make the connection."

"Mention what?"

"Hot air. You said something about hot air that day in Pumphrey's when I first told you about the air-engine, but we were really talking about other things; anyway, it seems I needed to watch you feel the hot air as well as hear you mention it before I could make the connection. In fact you made it for me. It's perfect. You are perfect. This is the best fish-and chips you ever bought. I love it and I love you!"

They ate the hot, fresh, salty fish and Maisie was delighted to hear Jon talking on and on with such excitement.

"*Mauretania* will steam down here. There'll be tugs on her but she'll be under her own power: turbine power," he added with a boyish grin. "There'll be thousands of people lining each side of the river that day."

"Aye, I know," said Maisie. "You'll not get a pin between them on the Fish Quay here. What a day. We'll both see it. You might be aboard her for the trials."

"I doubt it very much. I'm not that important at Parsons'. I don't know where I might have to be on the day she goes out, but we'll watch together if we possibly can."

"You're so excited you forgot the lemonade," she laughed. "I'm glad you're so excited," she added tenderly, putting her hand on his arm.

"We'll go back for the lemonade when we've finished this. You were right, it's wonderfully tasty. And I am excited. Hot air is the answer, and it came from you."

"Me and old Purdy's fish shop…" Then the laughter died from her voice and she muttered "Oh no, oh no…"

"Oh yes, yes, yes!" came a jeering female voice.

Jon looked up to see a gaggle of young women advancing towards them, all in cheap hats, one dressed more loudly than the others, her red-cheeked face and bright eyes convulsed with a vicious glee.

"Well now, here she is!" The women continued to bear down on them like a squadron of crows. "Maisie Watson with her fancy man—and ooh, very fancy he is, too. There's money in this!" They hesitated and stared with sharp looks but they hardly stopped. There was a clatter of narrow boot-heels on the cobbles and a swish of sleeves as they jostled past Maisie, deliberately bumping into her. She felt a stab of fear and saw revulsion in Jon's face as the women came and went with a flush of cheap perfume and rude giggles and a voice kept purposefully loud. "…and he might be good looking but he must be a daft bugger, slumming on the Fish Quay with the likes o' her."

Their cruel laughter faded as they trotted away, tossing backward glances. Maisie went rigid. Jon put an arm around her.

"Don't let them upset you, Darling. It's just stupid street gossip."

"Oh yes", sniffed Maisie through a sob, "that's what it is. But it's not stupid, it's real. That's Peggy Dowling from Swan's. She's in the loft with me. I'll have Hell to face now."

"The drawing-loft girls didn't know about you and me?"

"Grow up, man! You don't think I've gone round telling everyone, do you? But she knew. Now they'll all know."

"So, what does it matter?" While he held her she could feel Jon doing his best to comfort her, but every word just annoyed her more. "Some stupid, common girl," he was saying, "who has no idea of what we have together, of who we are, of how life is going to be for you outside that drawing-loft. You said I have to face this kind of thing, but you have to as well. Just ignore them, or tell them what you think of them. They're like classroom bullies. It's jealousy at the bottom of it. You're too good for their sort and they can't bear it. Don't let them get you."

Infuriated by her own vulnerability, she wriggled free, stopped her sniffs and hardened her voice.

"They'll get me their own ways, I know they will. That Peggy's from a family of bad'uns, really rough."

"Now don't be silly. They can't hurt you."

As he said this he knew it wasn't true. They could hurt her, had hurt her, and would hurt her again. He had said it to comfort her; also because he had hardly known what to say. He hesitated to speak again, but she was in full flow of upset and anger.

"Oh yes they can!" She clung to his arm again and shuffled him away from the wall down to the dark edge of the river. "She's a hussy and a gossip and she'll make my life difficult when she tells the whole shipyard I've been seen down here with you. They'll all know I'm going to be living with a married man. They'll all know I'm not even engaged."

"Funny you should say that, Darling…"

She wrenched herself away from him once more.

"There's nowt funny in this."

"No, I didn't mean that." He was smiling at her, taking her hand again. She felt unable to resist him and suddenly never wished to and she fell softly against his chest.

"I mean about being engaged, because..." She felt his blue eyes upon her, bright even in the growing dusk. "...you *will* be engaged. You'll be engaged tonight, and you can show everyone your ring and walk proudly through the world and never let anyone take our love away from us."

As she looked up at him, a new beating in her heart, she was distracted by a distant hooting on the river. Another ship was coming downstream on the flood tide. She felt as if her soul was being carried out of herself; far out to sea perhaps, somewhere she had never been before, then brought back carefully, held firmly but laid down gently in a new home. Jon continued to speak; she heard him keeping his voice slow and steady as if to manage his emotions.

"I was going to do this tomorrow, in the new house actually, in that bare front room before the furniture changes it, but I'll do it now, here, beside your river, *our* river."

In a moment he had produced a small box from his inside pocket and opened it beneath Maisie's wondering eyes. She saw a gold ring set with a large blue stone, larger than anything she had imagined. Before she could speak Jon was talking again.

"I've had this in my pocket for a few days," he was saying with a smile in his voice: tender, but restless, with an almost agonised joy. "I didn't know where else to keep it completely safe. Now it must go on your finger—if you're sure you like it."

"How could I not like it?" she gasped.

"Well, I know the sapphire blue isn't quite the grey-blue of your eyes..."

"...more like the bright blue of yours," she said.

"Perhaps, but I did think you should have a blue stone—for your Scots ancestry, apart from anything else."

"Oh yes, yes. It's beautiful," she managed through a sob she couldn't control. "It's so beautiful. It's the colour of Heaven."

Jon held her tightly and whispered into her hair.

"Yes it is. And in the old legends blue was the colour of constancy, and we'll be constant for each other, won't we? We'll be constantly in love."

"Oh, there's no need to question that." She was recovering into a firmly rooted joy. She could speak now and tell him her truth. "I know that's what you want and what you need. I know better than you think. Yes, I'll be your constant wife—and lover."

"I love you now and always will. Let me put it on for you."

It took only a moment to slide the ring on to Maisie's finger, but she felt it was a long moment, extended by frothy waves of happiness inside her, the darkening air of the riverside, the lights of South Shields twinkling across the black water, the churning of the approaching ship, the clear seaward light still in the Eastern sky. Jon's voice drew her back to his embrace.

"I guessed the size, but the jeweller said it can be made bigger or smaller if needs be."

"It's perfect." She was jovial now and felt full of fun. "I'd expect nothing less of an engineer."

"I'm just a good guesser."

"It's beautiful. It's absolutely beautiful. It must have cost a fortune." Then she felt the ring was heavy: richly, glamorously heavy, exotic and opulent beyond anything she had ever owned. "I've never worn a ring before, not even as a bairn playing with buttons and washers and things. It's heavy."

"You'll wear it lightly with your true, womanly grace."

He took her hand and kissed the ring so new on her finger—then she could not stop the tears coming, and the ship hooted again and surged past the Fish Quay and Jon held her as she shut her eyes to tears of happiness and opened them again to her new life.

CHAPTER SIXTEEN
Moving

The fact of her engagement, made so gloriously evident by her new ring, gave Maisie the courage to announce her move from Union Street to Tynemouth. Yet her courage was tempered with anxiety. She wanted to avoid an evening fractured with arguments and a night disturbed by tears, so she was careful to make her announcement on a bright morning when little George had left for school and her father was on his way to work.

"And am I supposed to be pleased about this?" Matthew grumbled his way out of the kitchen. "Is this something to be proud of?"

"Don't be like that, Da. I'm engaged!"

"Aye, to a married man. What does that say about you—and about us?"

She realised there would be no escape from the conflict and that she would have to protest.

"Jon's first marriage is over," she stated firmly. "He'll be divorced and we'll be married. And for now, I'm engaged. Look."

She held out her hand; her father brushed past it.

"Aye, there's no missing that ring. He'll have spent plenty of his father's money on that. It's almost indecent."

"Don't you say that!" Alice turned sharply on her husband. "It's a beautiful ring for our beautiful daughter."

"It's like something a man would give to a kept woman."

"That's a horrible thing to say to the girl. It's not like that at all. It's a beautiful, elegant ring, a ring for a lady if ever I saw one, and our Maisie's wearing it graciously. Can you not see it's lifted her spirits, man?"

Maisie forced herself to keep smiling.

"You'll see a wedding ring next, Da."

"One day—if you're lucky." Maisie thought she had never heard such bitterness in her father's voice. Then she heard cruelty and shame, and she had never heard those together in her father's voice either. "Until that day you're my daughter living in sin."

"Don't use that expression in this house!" shouted Alice.

"It'll be an expression used all over town and there'll be ruder ones than that, I'm telling you."

"Listen to me, Da." Maisie sat down, wishing that just sitting down might make everyone happy again. "I love you and I love Mam and everyone in this family. I'm not breaking it up. I'm engaged to a loving, kind and generous gentleman who will marry me and give me a wonderful life: a life of things I could only have dreamed of 'til now. He'll bring good things to all the family, you'll see."

"I don't want his money."

"I don't mean money, Da, and you know I don't. I mean decent help and opportunities in all kinds of ways. Look what he's done for us already."

"Ha! I don't want to look too closely at what he's done for *you*."

"Less of that!" warned Alice. "Hear the lass out."

"He's been kind and decent to us, Da." Maisie went on, desperate to keep tears out of her voice. "He's shown kindness to you at the yard, I know he has. Anyway," she found her voice had strengthened in its own glorious way, "he's loved me and he's made me a real woman. I'm growing to be the full person I was always meant to be, someone special, someone different."

"Now it's the sin of pride!"

"Yes, Da, I am proud, but it's no sin. I'm proud of Jon, I'm proud to be his fiancée and I'm proud of my decision to go and live with him. He's provided a new home for me, he loves me, and he's a fine man who will do great things. I'll be proud to be his wife. You don't know the half of his cleverness and his ideas. So when the new house is ready I'll be going and I'll be proud to be going—and I wish you could understand properly and be happy about it!"

Just as she felt she could hold back her tears no longer, her mother stepped forward.

"You'll go with my blessing, girl."

Maisie saw the sad but kindly smile of acceptance, yet she could not feel entirely blessed. As she left the kitchen she saw her father's head was bowed with something worse than defeat. It was bowed with shame.

Jon was astonished to receive a telegram that told him Philippa was travelling back to Newcastle that very day; a day on which he could not possibly be absent from Parsons'. By the time he returned to Lily Avenue she was already in the house with a horse-drawn van standing clumsily outside.

"Yes it's true, Jon. I'm moving all my things...not that I have so very much to take with me," she gave him a brazen smile as the porters carried her final cases into the van, "but I couldn't have fitted my trunks and spare canvases and all the studio things in just a cab, could I?"

"Why now?" asked Jon. "Why today?"

"Why not? I wouldn't have thought you'd have any objections. Are you not pleased to be rid of me?" She turned haughtily to the porters. "Have these things taken to the Luggage Office at the Central Station. I am booked on the seven o'clock train to London; name of Mrs. Ferris." She turned back to Jon. "Well, I am still Mrs. Ferris—just."

"We had better go inside," said Jon.

"Don't want to be seen fighting on the street, do we—or isn't that where you belong these days?"

They went up to what had been Philippa's studio, high above the neat gardens and cobbled back lanes of well-set Jesmond. They had both known such excitement in this pale, clear, sunny room once so full of ideas and endeavour. Now it held only discomfort.

311

"No great harangue, Jon, please. It's been a hard day and it isn't over yet; up from the crack of dawn and going back to London tonight."

"You could have made an easier journey of it, stayed overnight."

"Don't pretend you'd have liked me to stay the night here." She fiddled with her gloves.

"Don't pretend you would have wished to." He looked out of the window.

"Well, once-upon-a-time I should have wished to. I did have an idea to keep this place on as my Northern studio, but not now. I see my future is in London."

"You mean you've seen the sense of what my father has said—and given."

"I'm not sure I like your sharpness, Jon. The new sense of security this woman seems to have given you is rather brusque and unbecoming."

"I suppose it's a result of no longer being in your power," said Jon as evenly as he could. "And that's sheer hypocrisy, coming from you; there's nobody sharper or more brusque than yourself. I don't know how you dare say such things."

"I suppose I dare say them because I am no longer in *your* power…"

"You never were," Jon interjected harshly.

"…and as for your father," she rattled on, "yes, he has been most generous, and I have accepted his generosity and his terms—but in a way it's dirty money. You wouldn't let this marriage run its course; you had to do the dishonourable thing."

"*You* speak of dishonour?"

"Yes. Falling out of love is sad, but it doesn't have to be dishonourable. Finding someone else can be awkward, to put it mildly, but even that doesn't have to be dishonourable. Buying off an unwanted wife *is*. We'd have gone our separate ways soon enough, Jon. You'd have had your factory-girl eventually—but no, you had to go crawling to your father and beg him to get rid of me for you."

"It wasn't like that."

"That's what it looks like from here. Actually, I rather admired your father. He's a handsome man of handsome character. He deserved better offspring. It must have been awful for him, dragging himself down to London to face me on behalf of his weak son."

"If I've been weak with you, I've found new strength with Maisie."

"Oh, how wonderful for you. The little boy thinks he's grown up at last. Don't make me sick! But if you have found any strength you'll need it, because despite your father's money you're not entirely rid of me—even in that new place of yours at Tynemouth."

A new anxiety stabbed into Jon.

"You know about that?"

"I have my spies."

"I imagine my father told you."

"Haven't seen him since he came to Chelsea."

"Well," Jon shrugged, "the house in Tynemouth is common knowledge anyway."

"*Common* being the appropriate word. Up a back street somewhere, I understand. Not quite jolly old Jesmond, is it? And I suppose you'll be taking that dreadful housekeeper with you. Still doing your shirts, is she? Of course not: you've found a prettier little skivvy to do the washing for you—and marrying her, too." She gave him another bitter smile. "You are plainly comfortable with that class of person."

He decided he would not be baited. He would ignore the insults and refuse to join the sorry fight.

"Since you ask," he stated quietly, "Mrs. Hutchinson has been found another situation; I'm not sure where. And you're quite wrong about the house in Tynemouth. It's delightful. There's a view of the sea."

"How nice for you seafaring types. A love-nest, eh? I can't imagine what a love-nest looks like."

"I'm truly sorry you can't, Philippa."

"No," she looked round the empty studio with a faint and honest smile, "we didn't quite make one here, did we?"

Jon, almost against every instinct, began to feel sorry for her.

"Will you believe me when I say I hope you'll find one some day?"

"Yes," her smile broadened, and he remembered how

startlingly attractive she could look, "I believe you, good-hearted Jon and all-round-decent-chap—or that's what people who aren't married to you might think you are."

The cruel wittiness of which she seemed so proud might make reconciliation impossible, but he would try. He didn't know exactly why, but he would try.

"So," he managed to keep anger out of his voice, "since you recognise that I wish you well, will you shake my hand?"

"Certainly not." The reply was pert and bright-lipped. "If anything, I shall come back into your life and cause you hurt and harm, just as you've caused me to suffer hurt and harm."

"You haven't suffered in love." Jon clenched his fists and his teeth. "You're incapable of it. You only know lust. You are a mine of selfishness."

"Is that what you think? Perhaps you're right. It seems I was made to look after myself. Somebody once called me a viper. Well, I'll be back to bite you—but this time I'll make the move when it suits *me*!"

"We've had this conversation before," said Jon with a sudden calm, "when you came back from Paris. Remember? You threatened to ruin everything for me and my new wife…"

"The stupid girl isn't your wife yet!"

"No," Jon tried once more to ignore the fury between them, "but she will be; and she is anything but stupid. But neither are you. You know perfectly well that you agreed terms. If you want my father's money, you must let the divorce go through—after which Maisie *will* be my wife, and any stupidity will then be your own in pursuing this angry feud over nothing."

"Nothing? You committed adultery with a slut!"

"And I'm sure you continue to behave like one in Paris and London or wherever the fancy takes you. But it no longer matters, Philippa. Whatever you think of me, I don't hate *you*. I have no need to hate you. I have found true love. I thought I might find it in this house, but I didn't. I found it elsewhere, when I wasn't even looking. I hope you will too, one day."

"True love!" she stamped over the bare boards of the studio and down the stairs. "Romantic nonsense! Well, Jon, whatever we had between us may be over, but it isn't finished—not yet."

* * *

Port-holes had been cut in the vast steel walls of *Mauretania* and, as Maisie put it, the hull was beginning to look like a proper ship now. In the drawing-loft, she was enlarging the plans for the four funnels.

"It's a canny feeling, doing the funnels," she explained to Jon during one of their walks through Newcastle. "It makes it even more of a proper ship, like; and it's nice to think that one day the steam from *your* engines will be coming up through *my* funnels. Mind it's a big job. The funnels are enormous. They give you a good idea of the size of the ship. Lay them on their sides and you could drive a tram through them."

"Is that so?" Jon looked at the trams, carts and motor-cars rumbling through the streets. "I hadn't realised that. You really think you could get a tram through them?"

"Well, a motor-car anyway. What are you thinking of? You've got that 'thinking' look of yours."

"I'm thinking how marvellous it might be if we could actually lay one of the funnels on its side and drive a motor-car through it—just to impress everyone before the launch. All the newspapers would want a photograph of that, showing how enormous the ship really is, especially in America. They like big things in America; always impressed by that kind of publicity stunt. It's another one of your great ideas."

"You had the idea," she smiled. "I just had the thought. But don't go making a nuisance of yourself with the managers. With us coming together and all, your best idea is to keep out of trouble and just do your job."

"That's what you're doing, is it?" he replied with a tinge of bitterness.

"Yes, I suppose it is," she sighed. "I'm keeping my head down from the likes of Rosie Sullivan and Peggy Dowling."

He took her hand.

"Have they given you any trouble?"

"No, just dirty looks—and some jealous ones. Their eyes popped when they saw the ring."

"I was wondering how that would go down."

"It went down like a big blue stone!" Jon was relieved to hear her laugh. "None of the girls in there have ever seen a ring like it. Most of them have been very nice about it. They think I'm marrying a millionaire."

"I wish you were," Jon chuckled. "We could do with a million or two."

"I like us just as we are: me with my drawings, you with your inventions and your ideas."

"Ideas to fill an ocean liner," declared Jon to the crowded street, "money to fill a rowing-boat…if that."

"You know," said Maisie, hugging his arm, "I just love to see you happy like this."

"We are rather marvellous together, aren't we?"

* * *

A long period of warm, dry days made Autumn seem like a lingering Summer. A golden stillness lay over the city and the river, leaves held their green, late flowers bloomed in the Jesmond gardens. The honeysuckle at Number Eleven Lily Avenue continued to climb vigorously beside the door and offer its last few flowers to mild sunlight. Jon remembered how warm and welcoming the house had looked on his first day there with Philippa, how prosperous and inviting it had appeared as they rolled up to the door in his father's motor-car; now, as he left it for the last time, alone and on foot, he felt a curious pleasure to see it looking very much the same. Only he and Philippa had changed. The house seemed to bear no scars of their unhappiness. The Estate Agent's *For Sale* board cast an ugly shadow across the front window; but that would soon go. The property was likely to sell quickly. There was nothing about it to hint at pain and loss and failure. As it stood securely in Autumn sunlight, it had no atmosphere of sadness. Philippa had carried that away with her; Jon hoped desperately that he was not carrying any of it with his own departure. He had resolved to put a drastic marriage behind him and carry only good things to Tynemouth for Maisie. The new owners, whoever they might be, would inherit no ghosts of wickedness or tragedy. Jon closed the door and silently wished them well.

Jon's belongings and most of the furniture from Lily Avenue had gradually been transferred to Percy Street and when he was not at Parsons' he was busy making the Tynemouth house ready for Maisie's arrival. Although they continued to see each other as often as they could and to spend Sundays arranging and re-arranging their new rooms, Jon knew Maisie would not make her move until she judged it best to leave her family. He felt these days to be filled with quiet excitement, the restrained turmoil of a transitional period that would end suddenly and leave him in exciting but unfamiliar territory somewhere beyond his youth. "It was the end of my old life when I came here," he told Maisie one day. "Now it will be us together, for ever." As he said the words he found a diamond-hard core in his growing determination. He would show the world he could make and maintain a successful marriage. He would not merely enjoy his rapture and relax into contentment with this girl, he would strive for their happiness.

The Autumn days at Tynemouth were shot through with yellow sunlight and good humour. Jon was ready to engage a maid but Maisie was adamant that she would have no servant in the house and would run it herself.

"We never had a maid at home," she protested. "We could never afford one! No, maids don't go to Wallsend, they come from Wallsend, from families like mine—and I'm not having another Wallsend lass here." Her objections dissolved into her own laughter. "Maybe in years to come, when I'm getting old and tired, you can find a maid for us, but 'til then I'm going to be a proper wife and housekeeper myself, not have some poor girl slaving on under my feet when I want to do things my own way."

"All right," Jon relented with a smile. "She wouldn't last five minutes with you anyway. And speaking of things done your way, I see you're doing a fine job in the bathroom."

"Now you keep out of there," she warned him with a cheeky grin. "there's wet paint in there."

"I know," said Jon, holding up a rose-coloured forefinger. "Pink."

"That bathroom's the best thing in the house and it's going to be the prettiest room you've ever seen. I'll be spending a lot of time in there."

"If you lie in the hot water long enough you'll come out the same colour."

She was pleased he was learning to tease her, as she sometimes liked to tease him. It was part of their growing together, but she knew she had to love Jon with tenderness and care. He had been hurt by another woman; he had been hurt by his own sensitivity. She must come to him not only as the romantic girl she knew he adored, but as the real woman he must learn to accept. So it was, that one grey-clouded Sunday when she knew Jon would be expecting her at Tynemouth, she arrived at the door. She was not in the old clothes she wore for painting the bathroom, but in her best coat and hat, carrying two suitcases with another bag slung across her shoulder.

As the door opened her heart beat faster, and not for the first time that morning. She had meant this to be joyous, but saw Jon realise she had been crying. She forgot what she had intended to say, what she had been rehearsing all the way on the train and with every tiring step from the station. All she said was: "I'm here now and I'm not going back. I'm never going back."

She was inside now with her heavy bags on the floor. Jon had closed the door and was holding her tightly, sweetly, happily. For the first time in many months she felt safe. He was kissing her tenderly, then fiercely, then softly again as he realised she was almost asleep in his arms.

"I've been so tired," she said, "so frightened."

"I know, I know," was all he was able to say.

"But I'm here now and we'll be together always."

"Always."

They stood for long moments in a silent embrace. She remembered she had planned to pull off her shoes and stockings and make her first steps into the house with bare feet. Just as she had stood at the edge of the sea that Summer day on the Long Sands, declaring her love for Jon with cold water round her ankles, so she would step into the house on this special day with nothing between her skin and the sacred ground of their new home—but that gesture, which she had imagined Jon would understand perfectly, seemed contrived and pointless now. She was already in his arms, all she had taken off was her hat, and Jon was caressing her hair.

"Come to bed now," she heard him say, "right now, my Darling, before you unpack anything or we do anything else. Come on, right now." He took both her hands and kissed her engagement ring. "I can imagine what you've been through, but there'll be no more tears today. This really is the start of our life together."

She stepped over the bags on to the stairs, but held him there, kissing his face.

"I will come to bed with you, Jon, but not just as your lover now. I'm coming to bed as your wife-to-be and your partner in this house and for the rest of your life…and," she managed a weak laugh, "I'm so tired…it's been so long…so full of worries…"

"Come on then," he said tenderly, leading her upstairs, "let's just sleep together…and I mean go to sleep properly."

So, as the day darkened to afternoon, they held each other in that absolute sharing of trust which allows untroubled sleep. Cuddled comfortably in Jon's arms, Maisie hoped not to dream. She wanted only the curtained darkness of this Autumn day with the distant sound of the sea crashing into the cliffs beneath the old Priory. The wind and weather and all their worries could stay outside. In here, they would give each other peace; there would be no cruelty or selfishness. Safe and trusting sleep would be their true love-making on this quiet Sunday in the small house with the sound of the sea at the end of the street.

CHAPTER SEVENTEEN
Red!

In the small bedroom, newly furnished for their new life, Jon and Maisie made love with passion, vigour, and honesty—but not every night as each had privately thought they would, at least in these first days together. For them, everything was permissable in this house, or would be; it was a haven of intimacy, secure but free, simple but sensuous. Often they just lay together in quietness and realised this was the true expression of a love deeper than desire. There was the delicate wonder of her young shoulders and the high, delightful breasts; there was the dark power of his strong body and the clear light in his eyes; they could electrify each other with the faintest touch; her skin was smooth, his arms were strong—but they could relax into delicious sleep. Then there would be morning light at the little window, grey or white or blue, and a new chill in the room until they got up and lit the fire. They cuddled gently, holding their warmth.

"Don't you think we are very modern," said Maisie from her pillow, "both going to work every morning, you to Parsons', me to Swan's? Most women stay at home doing the housework."

"Drawing a ship is better than dusting a parlour." Jon held her warm waist with a smile.

"I'll do the dusting on Sunday," she put in quickly.

"We can live this way while there are no children," he added.

"We shouldn't have children until we are married, should we?"

"It would be better that way, for everybody's sake, especially the children's sake."

"That's all right." She cuddled into him more tightly. "I don't mind waiting. Do you mind waiting?"

"No. It's the right thing to do."

"You'll still love me if I make us wait?"

"Of course, Darling. There are ways to avoid having children."

"I know." She stroked him with a gently rising giggle. "I know when it's safe for us and when it isn't. I'm not daft you know."

"You are most certainly not daft."

"I never thought I'd talk like this to anybody."

"I never thought I'd have anybody like you to talk to."

He found her smiling into his face

"It's safe this morning, Jon…as long as we don't make each other late for work!"

* * *

Every morning, when the fire had crackled some heat into the bedroom and they were dressed, Jon replaced the engagement ring on Maisie's finger. It was a tiny ritual with a huge significance, a repeated betrothal he was determined and delighted to make. Then, with the ring gleaming on her finger, she would put her hair up. After their early breakfast they would leave for work together in the unconventional way Maisie had recognised, taking the train to Wallsend, separating only when Jon walked towards his engines and Maisie towards her drawings. But in the evenings she would usually be home before Jon. He might find the exciting spirits of paint and turpentine mingled with tempting smells of supper.

She was decorating the inside panels of the bathroom door. There were seagulls riding a windy sky at the top, then a brown Eider Duck sitting on her downy nest with the black-and-white drake standing behind, and on the lowest panel a Hedge Sparrow approached its nest of sky-blue eggs. The draughtsmanship was as accurate and detailed as Jon would have expected from Maisie, but the real glory of the door-painting was its colour. That sky behind the seagulls was luminous, the feathers of the Eiders seemed warm and strokeable, the leaves around the Hedge Sparrow's nest were many shades of sunlit green and secretive shadow. The three paintings, superb in themselves, made an exquisite piece of decorative work—and Jon was full of praise.

Of course it was a stabbing reminder of Philippa's ship painting, although he did not say much to Maisie about that. She already knew Philippa was an artist and had created a painting of *Mauretania* in the Jesmond house. While Jon did not elaborate on this, he could not forget Philippa's excitement in creating her attic studio nor the drama of the ship painting and how he had been genuinely astonished at its audacious composition and brilliant execution. Maisie's painting was a very different work of art. It was not for herself. It was for the house. It was a gift of love.

In these Autumn days Jon felt consumed by a constantly regenerating love for Maisie. As he walked to the Engine Works beneath windy skies, or sat in the office with a rainy blackness scuffling at the windows, he would think of her in the Tynemouth house or at her own work in the drawing-loft, so tantalizingly nearby. One afternoon there was a tremendous thunderstorm over the Tyne. Jon stood excitedly at the office window, enjoying the blue flashes, liking to believe he had sent them to Maisie, letting the crashes of thunder echo their passion from cloud to cloud—but then it was just a miserable empty afternoon as he sat to work. He felt cold, alone, and not very grand. He recognised, with a smile of gratitude, a deep need beyond his great want. If she would come to him now, to his cold thin sides, they would surely make music from the wind's desolation. The sky cleared to a frosty blue-black and he hurried home. They would build their fire from the star-sparks that flashed in that unfathomable vault now they were together as part of its vast unity.

In this rhythm of sleep and love and work and home, Maisie realised she was thinking of the house as a ship, as if its walls had girders of steel and the staircase was a companionway from saloon to cabins high in a sturdy superstructure. Was it aground like Noah's Ark on its hill-top, or moored securely in this little street? It was solid, yet seemed to sail through sun and wind and swing to its own bearings under the stars. And in this house that was a vessel for her imagination she found she was happy: simply happy painting ceilings, polishing brass handles on the windows, fitting out shelves and cupboards, discovering new spaces, stowing her few treasures, painting the bathroom door, making ready. Perhaps, when they had been here for years, there would be times to sail away, to journey over seas wilder than the serene blue of her imagination and find adventures far from this or any harbour; but for now she was dropping anchor into calm waters, dressing her ship, hoisting flags of pride to stars that seemed no longer cold. She was on her maiden voyage, the voyage of a lifetime. And again the morning light came in at the window and her engagement ring was slipped sweetly on to her finger and her hair was put up and they had breakfast and took the train to work and in the darkening Autumn evening she left the drawing-loft for Wallsend Station and for home.

She wished the Winter would not come, she wished the leaves could be forever green and gold and that she might go walking through the stately streets of Newcastle in a new hat, her dress swishing above her polished shoes. She would imagine that dark birds flying in a windy sky would bring Jon's spirit to her as he watched her swing along in Autumn elegance. But she did not fear the change of seasons; Summer would come again and clouds would be white. She rustled through some newly-dropped leaves, wanting the warm-eyed harmony he brought.

Strong arms came out of the shadows behind her. They held her with a terrifying strength. She knew at once she could never escape the animal ferocity of their grip. Panic screamed into her throat but before she could shout a hand was clamped over her mouth. It was a woman's hand. Her own hands were forced behind her back and she was marched over the boot-scraped cobbles into a pool of gaslight. Her jacket was pulled off her shoulders and a rope slung round her waist, lashing her to the lamp-post while another rope came to strangle her neck and another replaced the hand on her mouth. It bit fiercely into her bleeding lips as she tried to hold it off with her teeth.

Her blouse was torn open. With a madly beating heart and rising disgust she thought her breasts were going to be exposed. Then she thought these women would snatch off her ring and steal it. In her terror and panic she swore silently that they could do what they liked but they would not get the ring—and she clenched the fingers of her bound hands as

327

tightly as she could. They could strip her naked in the street but they wouldn't get the ring. She thought they were going to pull down her skirt next...but instead, through a maddening cascade of frightened tears, she saw Peggy Dowling standing in front of her.

"Well now, Missy, who's the red woman, eh? We know your posh fancy man's a married man. We know you've gone to that house with him, brought shame to your own folks. Why look at that: we've made the pampered little darling cry! Well if your own father won't belt the skin off you, we'll turn it red!"

Another woman stepped forward with a can of paint and a brush and in moments a drastic, shocking cross was slapped across her breast from her shoulders to her waist. She caught the strong paint fumes between her gasps and sobs, felt its coldness soak rapidly through her torn blouse on to her skin.

"Does he like your black hair, pet? Well he can have redhead now, like!"

Her hat was wrenched off and the cold paint slapped on to her head. It ran slowly past her ears on to her shoulders as a final thrust of paint daubed her skirt between her legs. "Red there an' all!" they yelped, throwing down the brush and scurrying away, screaming their laughter into the shadows as the dropped can of paint rolled to silence on the slimy cobbles.

* * *

"You are Jonathan Sketchley Adam Ferris?"

"I am."

Why was a policeman at his door? What had happened? What would have to be faced now? Maisie was late. He knew it was going to be about Maisie.

"And Mary Watson, formerly of Union Street, Wallsend and now of this address is your fianceé?"

"Yes, yes! What the devil is it, man?"

"There has been an assault, sir. Miss. Watson is safely at Wallsend Police Station. There is a doctor with her now. I must ask you to accompany me there at once. We have a cab waiting—and the lady will require a change of clothes."

Through the agony of the journey the policeman would tell him almost nothing. When they eventually arrived at Wallsend, Jon rushed into the Police Station only to be stopped by a grim-faced man, soberly dressed to match his expression.

"Mister Ferris? I am Doctor McEwan."

"I must see Miss. Watson immediately. What in God's name has happened? Are you the family doctor?"

"No," droned McEwan, "I sometimes attend on Police matters. The Constable sent for me and thank goodness you have returned with him." Jon found his manner infuriating. The few moments it took them to walk into a private room behind the Police Sergeant's desk seemed extended to an age and their progress delayed at every step as the doctor spoke with no trace of emotion. "Her clothes are ruined, but the Police will no doubt require them to be kept as evidence. There are no serious injuries, nor has the woman been violated..."

They entered the room and Jon saw Maisie sitting on a chair clutching a grey blanket round her throat. Her boots and black stockings showed beneath the blanket, her other clothes had been piled on the floor. Her hair hung down raggedly and was defiled with shocking streaks of red paint. Her face looked grey and bruised and her eyes reddened with tears, but she was not sobbing. She managed a weak smile as Jon went to her and held her shoulders. The anguished look on his face almost set her crying again.

"Don't get too much of a shock, Jon," she said quietly. "I'm all right, really I am."

"I'm here now, we'll get you home."

He looked into her eyes and thought he would explode with love and anger while the doctor continued his passionless report.

"...of course there is some bruising to the mouth and a cut lip. We are fortunate that no paint ran into the eyes. I have bathed the areas of skin affected by the paint as best I can; some has come off with methylated spirit but it will probably need turpentine, and not too much of that to irritate the skin—after which it must be washed immediately with soapy water. The hair should be removed..."

Maisie clutched the blanket and looked up with sudden vehemence.

"Aye, cut me hair off, will you? You've seen a naked woman tonight, now you'll see a bald one."

Jon knelt at her chair.

"It's not that bad, Darling, really it isn't: just a few strands down either side…oh, and…well, a bunch at the back. When you put your hair up again no-one will ever notice."

"Cut it all off," she barked. "I'll start again without any trace of that street scum in my hair."

Jon turned to the Sergeant.

"Do we know who did this?"

"You know well enough," answered Maisie abruptly. "It was them cows from the drawing-loft."

"We have Constable Harker's report, sir." The Sergeant produced some sheets of paper. "We can take a statement if the lady is willing to set down the truth of what took place."

"I've had enough of all this." Maisie's voice was wavering now. She had held herself bravely until Jon had arrived; now she was ready to cry again. She looked up piteously from the blanket. "Take me home Jon, just take me home."

The doctor offered them the use of his cab and they were set down quickly at their front door, the benighted sea swishing at the end of Percy Street. Jon set the water to boil and they hurried to the bathroom.

"I want you to take my clothes off, Jon." Maisie stood bravely in his arms. "Everything off now. I want the feeling of my man undressing me, not them women…I mean *those* women. From now on I'm going to speak like a lady if I can, I'll be a good wife to you, you'll be proud of me…."

"Darling, Darling, I am proud of you. I love you. I've

loved you ever since I first saw you and I always shall."

Now her determination seemed to fade and tears were not far away.

"...and I want you to take me to bed—when I've had my bath. I want a proper cuddle, mind. Now you bath me, Jon, and wash my hair for me in our pretty little bathroom here I tried so hard to make nice for us."

"You *have* made it nice. The paintings are going to be wonderful."

They were home and together. Everything in their house would be cherished and enjoyed to counteract the revulsion of crime and pain and the vile world outside. They had escaped, they were home. He washed her hair under the taps of the sink, gently at first then as vigorously as he could with his own shampoo. Somehow, she softened its masculine fragrance to a sweet perfume. Most of the cruel red streaks came out as the doctor's spirit was washed away, but some of the paint had set hard and she said she would cut it out herself.

"I'll not cut all my hair off," she promised. "I just said that because I was so furious. I'll just cut the red bits. You don't want a bald woman, do you? I'll do it carefully."

"It should grow back quickly," he replied, hoping to reassure her.

Naked in the bath, now filled with soapy water, she looked small and vulnerable, splashing herself with her hands.

"Hot running water, eh?" She smiled girlishly through the steam as Jon knelt at her side. "Not everyone has that. It's like on a ship, First Class."

Almost overcome by love and tenderness, he washed her gently, hoping the warm bubbles would soothe her and diminish his own sorrow.

"I never wanted to hurt you," he said. "I never wanted to bring you pain. It's the last thing I ever wanted to do."

"It's not your fault. I wanted to be proud, I wanted to be looked up to and envied and this is what I got for it. It's not your fault, my love—and that's what you are: my love."

Her sweetness, her girlishness, her mixture of innocence and determination almost brought him to tears. He did not want to let them fall; her own tears had been enough tonight.

"That's what you are, too," he managed.

* * *

The next morning Maisie was up as early as usual and preparing breakfast almost as if nothing had happened, but they both knew they had been through a dark terror they could scarcely name.

"How's the hair, then?" she asked Jon. "Be honest."

"It's all right." He could see uneven lengths of hair but no trace of red paint. If there was a shorn patch at the back of her head it was not immediately noticeable. "Really, it's all right. You've done it very well."

"You don't see the difference if I keep it up like this."

He was more upset by her torn lip and bruised mouth and was overcome with anger.

"I'll move us back to Newcastle," he stated with sudden vehemence, "or out to the country, Corbridge or somewhere like that where these people can never hurt you. I am responsible for this and I shall put it right—or at least make sure it never happens to you again."

"No, no." She sat down to face him across the kitchen table. "Don't you see, that would be giving in to them? That would mean they've won. No, we have to stay here, in this lovely house you bought for us. It's our home. I'm not going to have us driven out by a stupid cow like Peggy Dowling and her lot. I'll face her and all her kind. I'll face them all with pride in my husband and my new life."

It was true, he realised. She was brave enough and strong enough. Behind her gleamed the newly blacked kitchen range with its warm ovens, polished brass fender, coal-scuttle and fire-irons. While he had made her queen of his heart she had made herself queen of this little house—and she wasn't going to abandon her throne.

"And there's our work," she went on, "yours and mine on the big ship. We've got to finish it, see her launched and steaming proudly out of the Tyne."

While he listened to her, fighting back the tears of his own emotion, he thought what a wonderful girl she was, so gentle yet so resolute, and how amazingly fortunate he was to be loved by her. Yet the cruel attack that had brought them even closer in love still reeked of unfinished business.

"At least we can have these women charged with assault," he said. "They could probably go to prison for what they've done to you. I'd be happy to lock them in myself and

334

throw away the key."

"No, no, you mustn't do that, please. You'll bring the Dowling's down on us like a pack of dogs. I told you they're a bad family. They'll say I had their daughter put in prison and there'll be hell to pay for the rest of our lives. No, we'll have to leave it be, get over it, carry on as if it hadn't happened."

"That's ridiculous," he protested. "You've been injured."

"My hair will grow back in, Jon. My lips'll mend." She managed a bruised and painful smile. "You'll be wanting to kiss them again in a few days."

"I want to kiss them now!"

He got to his feet and came to her chair and hugged her fiercely.

"Mind it does hurt a bit this morning," she laughed faintly. "No, no, we have to carry on; not run away, but not do anything to make it worse for us either. I've got to work in that place, Jon."

"You don't have to, you know. We could go away."

"No. How many times do I have to tell you, man? I have to work there like you have to work at Parsons'. Let's not fight each about this Jon, let's fight together on the same side, to get over this and make our lives better. D'you not realise this Christmas is going to be our first one together in the same house? It's going to be this house, the one you found for us, the one we've already made into a home. Then next year there'll be the launch. That'll be a big day on the river, the biggest we've ever seen; a big day for you and your family, a big day for us. We'll keep working for it until the ship goes down the slipway, and after that while she's fitting-out, and after that when she sails down the Tyne, and after that too, when there'll be other jobs for you and me and our children."

She looked up at him, bruised but smiling as best she could; clear-eyed, more lovable than ever, and waves of love for her went through Jon. He saw her on that very first day in the drawing-loft, demurely presenting her drawings. He saw her barefoot on the beach, drenched with blue and golden sunlight, declaring her love from the sea's edge. He saw her dancing like a spirit in dazzling moonlight. He saw her hurt and tearful and vulnerable as he washed her in the hot bath, then saw her rising from her misery into glorious new strength. Her love for him was the best thing that had happened to him in his life, and he told her so again, there in the warm kitchen of the little house near the mouth of the river that had so directed their lives. In the house with the sea that was always there beyond the end of the street, he told her so again and again as their momentous year turned towards its close and a new one loomed over a wintry horizon. Somehow, it was the same divine resolution that came after a storm, as if evening clouds were burning richly beneath a blue-green sky and floated like Aegean islands in a placid sea. Then there would be the joys of Christmas, this year made simple and homely. After brief darkness would come an even more spectacular dawn. It could be, would be, must be theirs. It would come as easily as vanishing tears might wash a harsh Winter into another Spring.

"Our children, Jon," she was saying. "We'll have them when the time is right. They'll need us, like we need each other."

CHAPTER EIGHTEEN
Many Plans

In the new year of 1906 plans for *Mauretania's* launch were already underway, with a date set for September. While construction work on the hull continued, it was essential to brace the steel against the tremendous and rapidly changing stresses it would undergo during the launch. That unstoppable race of her huge weight down the greasy ways would, in rapid succession, place metal-stretching stresses on the stern, the midships section, and the bow. The fore-poppet on which Matthew and the carpenters had worked so carefully was now deliberately weakened so it would partially collapse and cushion the downward thrust of the bow as the stern rose up in taking to the water. In her first moments afloat, the empty hull would be prone to capsize, so ballast was laid above the keel and the internal wooden honeycomb had to be balanced with equal weight on either side. Matthew Watson and gangs of carpenters were engaged in this work. Vladimir Druginin and Anatoly Melnikov also found themselves grappling with large timbers.

"It is heavy work." Melnikov grumbled into his beer. He and his companion had known far colder Winters in their homeland, but the sunless drizzle of a Tyneside February seemed more depressing as they sat in their gaslit room. "I want to get carving."

"When the ship is launched," smiled Druginin, "when she is fitting-out, then we can begin to create the panelling. Then you can be an artist again, old friend—in the

First Class Dining Room, if you are lucky. I know this is peasant's work beneath our skills, but all kinds of good fortune has come our way. For example, it is fortunate that our Comrade Engineeer has moved into a small house in Tynemouth with his fiancée. It will make it easier to steal the plans."

"I do not like this idea," grunted Melnikov. "How do you know the plans can be stolen? How do you know they even exist?"

"I have made it my business to know," stated Druginin. "I have encountered our young friend several times. He has told me all kinds of things about himself. I have appeared to be his friend at a time when it seems he needed one. If his plans for the air-engine have not been drawn already, they soon will be. We know the launch of *Mauretania* will come later this year, after which the turbine engines will be lowered into the hull. Our young friend is likely to be very busy and will be keen to commit his brilliant idea to paper before other duties distract him. It seems he must also face a divorce; he intends to marry this new woman. Divorce in England is a very disturbing business, especially for members of his class. It can cause a kind of social ruin which he will be keen to avoid. As well as drawing the plans he will certainly make sheets of calculations and specifications which must also be stolen."

"You burden me with more difficult work, Comrade."

"But you are good at it," smiled Druginin. "You have stolen before—and never been caught. You have boasted of this to me yourself."

"Huh! What child has not stolen food and firewood? That was in Russia, where I knew the lie of the land. Here, I

338

can't be sure what I'm looking for."

Druginin gave a reassuring smile.

"I shall tell you what to look for, Comrade. And remember we are looking for something far greater than pieces of paper. Listen to me. A gigantic new English destroyer is to be launched this year: *HMS Dreadnought*. She will be powered by these new turbine engines and carry more armament than any ship in history. I tell you, this one ship will change everything. Do you not realise the Kaiser will be furious? He will want 'Dreadnought' ships for his own navy, for Germany! The whole situation plays into our hands. When we steal the plans of something that could power even more versatile and destructive weapons of war and offer them for sale to the Germans, they should be willing to pay much more than we first imagined. This earns greater sums of money for the Revolution. It is just as I have told you before: bring this war closer and the Revolution itself comes closer."

"You have a passion for this, Valdimir Andreyevich." A disgruntled Melnikov continued to stare at the dripping window. "I admire you for it—but it is I who must risk being caught stealing from a house in a country where we are already suspicious foreigners. It would not be wise for my crime to arouse further suspicion here."

"Indeed not, but if you do as I say your crime will never be detected. Trust me."

"I trust you, but I still have to go through every drawer and closet in a strange house."

"Yes, but you may be as destructive as you wish. The English word is 'ransack'."

"Ransack?" grinned Melnikov. "Good word."

With anxiety still worming in her stomach and the face-of-brass expression she knew she must continue to wear, Maisie thumped her way up the wooden stairs to the drawing-loft. Back to work she had gone, that first day after the attack and every other working day since; and back to work she was going today, she told herself: this day and every day and to Hell with the ignorant, brutal, stupid women who had condemned her morals.

Her policy of ignoring Rosie Sullivan and her gang seemed to have worked. They simply hadn't spoken to her or bothered her again. As for Peggy Dowling, the coarsest and most dangerous of the women, she had spent so much time skiving off work she was hardly the problem Maisie had imagined. Whenever Peggy was in trouble Maisie hoped she might be sacked—but was then actually thankful to see the vulgar girl back in the loft. If Peggy was sacked, the Dowling family might think Maisie had had something to do with it—and that was a risk she didn't wish to run. There must have been gossip in the streets and along the river, but none of it had been said to her face. If it had been said behind her back she hadn't heard it. Her own family had been outraged, but she had begged them to do and say nothing about it, and even her father had seen the sense of that. She was glad that she, not he, had the more fiery disposition. Da's well-known mildness might have had him called a softie now and again, but she was glad he was being soft about this. It was better just to go on the same way. She would ignore the women; they would ignore her. They could think whatever they liked; Maisie told herself she had won. She had survived, they had not ruined her life, her family had accepted her, she was back with the man who loved her and brought her a happiness greater than any of them would ever understand. But the vicious attack and shameful episode of the red paint had left its mark on Maisie: she still felt vulnerable and sometimes horrified, especially when walking home from work. But even that was a challenge she was determined to take and a fear she told herself she must overcome. That's how it was going to be: the women would be ignored but what they had done could never be forgotten. The present might be dangerous but the future would be faced. Each time Maisie came down the steps at the end of a working day she told herself she was getting stronger and her life was getting better.

And Spring did not seem so far away on this Friday night as she hurried home with her wages. Lightness was lasting later into the afternoon sky and the wind off the river seemed to have lost its cutting edge. She was happy to find Jon already in the house. Their kisses of greeting were spiced with surprise.

"You've made supper!" she exclaimed with delight.

"I've done my best with scones and cakes. I had lunch with my father today. He invited me back to Heaton Road and my mother gave us all this." He indicated an array of packets and tins on the kitchen bench. "Betty made the cakes," he added with admiration in his voice. "Good old Betty. She was pleased to see me."

Maisie pulled off her hat and hung up her coat with a sudden anxiety. She wished Jon's talk of his family and servants did not make her feel she might lose him as he was drawn back to his old way of life. At the same time she told herself that such a thing wasn't very likely. Jon was making his home here, with her—but how long would she have to suffer these stabs of insecurity?

"That was nice of your mother. She'll think I'm not feeding you properly."

"Nonsense. I told her you're wonderful."

"She wouldn't expect you to say anything else," Maisie smiled at Jon's innocence, "but I know what a mother must be feeling when her son goes off with a strange woman."

"Honestly, Darling, they don't think you're strange. They understand what's happened and how right it is for us. They're pleased we are happily set up together here."

"I don't quite believe that, Jon. You're their precious son. They're just being nice about what I've done to you." She would change her glum expression, she would fight back tears of annoyance and anxiety…then she heard him say:

"Anyway, they think you're better for me than Philippa ever was."

"Well," she snatched up a plate and began to rearrange the scones at a furious pace, "that's good to know, isn't it? That's put me one rung further up the social ladder, eh?"

"Don't be angry, Darling. They meant it as a compliment."

"Funny how compliments sound like judgements," she snapped, looking away…but she told herself she shouldn't make any more of this; she should face Jon, be pleased he had made supper, be glad they were home together. "Oh, I don't mean anything against your family, love. I know they're nice people. But it's only what I've said before. Your mother will judge me; everyone will judge me, judge both of us. It's like we've committed a crime and put ourselves in the dock."

342

She saw Jon wince at that and she wished she hadn't said it. She saw him try to carry on.

"Actually, I had some good news. I didn't want you to be unhappy."

"I'm not unhappy. I'm just being realistic. There are going to be moments like this, it cannot be avoided." She sat at the table and took his hands with a smile. "The happiness is real, too, you know, and that cannot be avoided either. Now, what's the news?"

"I put your funnels idea to my father: you know, driving cars through the funnels on the day of the launch."

"You mean *your* idea."

"I said it was your idea—because it did come from you. Anyway, let's call it *our* idea. I've asked him to put it to the Board of Directors and he will. He thinks it's a marvellous idea."

They sat down to their supper and talked while they ate, Jon explaining he had also told his father about the air-engine.

"He threw all kinds of problems at me, engineering problems. I'd thought of some of them myself, but he came up with even more. However, he agreed it was a fascinating idea. I saw he was fascinated by it himself. He said it was a young man's job and that I should go ahead and draw the plans properly."

"He gave you his blessing, then."

"In a way, yes. I didn't need it; I'd have gone ahead with the plans anyway, but it was reassuring to have his acceptance of the idea. He can be quite formidable, but when he's on your side you feel you've got real power behind you."

While Maisie poured more tea she heard Jon announce what he called the best news of all.

"Philippa has agreed to the divorce. Eventually, it will be made absolute and we'll be able to marry."

She felt like jumping up into his arms, but here she was, holding the heavy teapot, everything so ordinary…yet that very ordinariness, their quiet sitting together for supper in this house, the simple words that were used to convey such enormous meaning: these everyday things of their new life were the best celebration that could be.

"It won't be until well after the ship is ready," she heard him say.

She put down the teapot, took Jon's hand in hers, and smiled.

"That is wonderful news," she said as Jon rose to hug her shoulders, placing gentle kisses on her hair. She did feel calm and secure, and knew a great weight had been lifted from Jon's mind. "She's putting you through it though, as usual. Why the long wait? Why couldn't you have just divorced her?"

"It's not done that way, Darling. It's usual for the man to let the lady accuse him of adultery and, technically, she divorces him "

"Lady?" Maisie didn't want to sour the mood, but couldn't keep annoyance out of her voice. "I can think of other words for her. And adultery…"

"Well," Jon was quick to declare with a smile, "you

must have noticed. I *have* committed it."

"She probably has, too."

"Probably, and God knows with whom—not that I really care. Even so, I'll play the gentleman in this little drama. It's the done thing. I have committed adultery for the best reason in the world: to show you how much I love you and to prove that we must be together. I'm delighted to have done so. She can accuse me all she likes. I'll admit the truth and we'll be free."

"Fighting talk from my man!" grinned Maisie. "More tea?"

"It should be Champagne," said Jon, "and it will be shortly. The divorce should be made absolute in time for the maiden voyage. I think we should marry just before *Mauretania* sails and have our honeymoon on the ship."

"What," Maisie sprang to her feet, "go to America for the honeymoon?"

"Why not?"

"You can afford it? You can get us tickets?"

"I'd sell my grandmother for tickets for our honeymoon."

They scurried round the table and into each other's arms.

"I think you're the most romantic person that ever was!" she squealed.

"Apart from you."

"No, I'm practical. I'll be in charge of the packing."

"You'd better be. Your trousseau will fill a suite in First Class."

"Oh no, not First Class."

"Oh yes, nothing less will do."

"Eee, I don't know why I'm crying. It's marvellous! It's marvellous!"

She felt his strong hands round her waist as he lifted her feet from the floor and swung her round the kitchen.

"It's more than marvellous," he was laughing, "it's *bloody* marvellous!"

* * *

Dredgers were working on the Tyne, to deepen the channel for *Mauretania's* launch. At each ebb tide a great brown stain of muddied water was pushed out between the piers and swept up the Northumbrian coast by Northward currents. Back upstream, there was excitement when the yard manager Stevenson made an announcement.

"The stern anchor's arriving," he told a group of men who had gathered to watch a steam locomotive haul its flatcars into the slipway. The men knew this anchor would be dropped into the river before launch day, and a strong cable would be run from it to *Mauretania's* stern as a brake when she rushed into the water. Its appearance in the yard marked another significant moment in the progress of this huge

346

undertaking. The enormous black anchor was accompanied by a vast chain of gigantic proportions. "The largest anchor chain ever made," said Stevenson with pride. "It's come up on the train from a foundry in Wales."

Other chains were beginning to be hauled into heaps on the floor of the slipway along each side of the ship.

"Drag chains," explained Jon to Druginin and Melnikov on a day they met under the towering hull. "Have you two ever seen a launch?"

"Never, Comrade. This will be our first."

"Most exciting; you will never forget the speed and power of it. We have to let her go but we have to stop her as well," Jon smiled. "Even the stern anchor and the tugs won't be enough without the arresting force of drag chains. She's so big and heavy she'll make these chains a giant couldn't lift leap and dance along the slipway here like so many babies' rattles, but their weight will help to slow the ship as she goes into the water."

"You will be proud that day I think, Comrade."

"We all will. You'll feel it, too."

* * *

A few days later Jon told Maisie they had been invited by his parents to dinner at Heaton Road.

"Isn't that a lovely idea?" she heard him say. "It's an Engagement Dinner—for us!"

"I'll never get away with going there," she muttered.

"It's nothing to worry about—just dinner."

"I know very well it isn't just dinner," she protested. She had worried about this since they first met and at last it was to happen; she would have to face Jon's family. She knew Jon had been very slow to introduce her to his parents. She knew he would normally have done so when he had given her the ring, indeed possibly before that. But nothing was normal about any of this. Now his parents had taken the matter into their own hands with an invitation that couldn't be refused. What did his family really think of her, and of him for taking up with a strange girl in a new home while he was still married to his first wife? Yes, that marriage was in ruins and would be dissolved, but Maisie knew that every convention had been flouted. Deep in the middle of her being she didn't care—but knew that Jon did. If she knew the love they shared was full of wonders, she also knew it was love across the barriers of class and upbringing. And if she hadn't known it, it had been shown to her with scorn, violence, and the degradation of red paint.

"It's not just dinner, Jon," she continued. "It's to get a look at me and the sort of woman you've ended up with. They'll be staring at me like something from the gutter and I'll be too common to be accepted by your family. I come from a different class."

"I promise you," Jon took her shoulders in a loving hold, "my mother and father are better than that. I've had my disagreements with them, and from time to time I've disappointed them, but they have always remained loving and understanding. They're sensible people. You'll like them—and they will certainly like you. They'll love you for your freshness and honesty and beauty."

"Get away, man," she interrupted. "That's you talking, not them."

"It's all of us. You'll see I'm right. But even if they didn't understand, they would have to accept what has happened. And this class business: it's over. You have left your class. I've left mine. We've become something new. Both classes will have to accept that."

"My class didn't accept it, did they?" she looked at the floor and turned away. "They threw red paint over me."

"All right, if you have to put it that way; but my class will be different."

"They'd better be, Jon, but they'll want to know the far end of what happened to me with the red paint—and I just don't want to talk about that any more." She faced Jon again. "I know it's there all the time in my mind, but I want to start to think about other things as well. I just want to get on with our own life."

"We are getting on with it, Darling." Jon hugged her once more. "Don't you see that going to this dinner is part of getting on with it? It won't exactly be easy for me either, you know—but we actually might enjoy it when we get there."

She nodded and smiled up at him.

"You're right. You're very sensible."

"You're the sensible one," he replied. "I need your good sense."

"Aye well, thank God my hair looks all right." She left his arms and looked at herself in the mirror above the fireplace. "It does look all right, doesn't it, if I keep it up this way?"

"Yes, of course. Anyway, they won't mention the business of the red paint."

"They'll think it's bad manners to mention it."

She saw Jon look embarrassed.

"Well, yes."

"You see? I do know what they're like."

"I assure you, my parents are nothing to worry about."

"I'm not worried about them; you've managed to put my mind at rest—a bit, anyway." She gave him a faint smile. "No, it's me I'm worried about, letting you down with my common ways in front of your family."

"Come on now, don't be so silly." He thought this was over but it wasn't. Yet again he would have to talk sense and show love, and as moments like this went on he felt short of good sense and at risk of not showing love—and he loved her so much, so fully, so honestly, that what he really wanted to do was to match the glorious honesty she always gave him and to bouy her up in these troubled waters. He took her hands once more. "You've never let me down and you never will. You've faced everything: that terrible attack, your own family, the misunderstandings and ignorance of other people. You've gone bravely on, holding your head high, and rightly too. Now you have to face this—and not alone. I'll be there to love you." He brushed her nose with his lips, hoping a playful kiss might help her. "It's only dinner at my old house with people who will undersatnd you and like you."

"I've told you I know it's more than that—but you're right, I'll face it." She slid into his arms. "We face all sorts of things together, don't we?"

"We do indeed." He felt the delicate curve of her back and shoulders, her slender arms round his waist. She was beautiful as well as brave. "By the way," he added, "they're sending Hogett with the motor-car for us."

"The chauffeur?"

"That's right."

"Oh no. What'll he think of me? Everyone knows the worst snobs are the servants."

Jon laughed out loud.

"You're right." Still smiling, he kissed the tip of her nose once more, then her lips. "But I promise, they'll love you as much as I do."

"I wish I could be sure of that."

CHAPTER NINETEEN
Dinner at Heaton Road

"What should I wear for this dinner, Jon?" Maisie stood in front of the bedroom mirror and wrung the sleeves of her blouse. "I cannot go just looking ordinary."

"You never look ordinary, Darling. Just go in what you feel is best. Go as yourself; don't dress up as somebody else."

"Haway man, that's no help! Even my best dress isn't good enough for this and you know it."

"All right then. We'll have new dress made for you."

"Oh no," she shook her head at Jon through the mirror. "If you want me to go as myself there'll be no special dressmaker. Some snooty woman in Heaton charging the Earth? Not for me. I'm a working lass who's done well for herself. I'll go to Fenwick's in town. It's a lucky shop for me; that's where you got me that hat. Fenwick's," she flashed him a smile, "I'd call that doing well."

"Just as you wish, Darling; the best dress from the best shop in Newcastle—but only if you let me buy it for you. I'd call *that* doing well."

* * *

It was a Sunday. Maisie had spent the whole afternoon getting ready: laying out her clothes, polishing her shoes, having a bath. Jon had helped her wash her hair, as she especially liked him to do, and she had dried and brushed it in front of the bedroom fire. They had eaten nothing at tea-time. She was wearing the new dress for the first time. It was pale blue, of fine woollen cloth, trimmed with purple velvet at the collar and cuffs. Her shiny black shoes peeped from beneath the narrow hem. Now the sky was darkening to an evening blue, she had rolled and pinned up her hair more carefully than she had ever done, and Jon was standing at the window in his smart grey suit, looking down into the street.

"Lucky it's a dry night," she heard him say. "Hoggett should have a good run with us in the motor-car. It's a new one, by the way. I haven't seen it yet. Their first motor-car, the de Dion-Bouton, was open; I never saw it with a hood up, anyway." With a stab of poignancy he remembered the open-air drive with Philippa that fine Summer day through Heaton to their new house in Jesmond; he remembered Philippa's hat, her bright smile, her confident banter with his parents. Now he would be driving with this tender girl who would not be confident in banter with his parents, but a girl he loved a thousand times more deeply than he had loved his wife. That wife was still his wife. He felt the fact like a curse—and pushed it away. "This new machine's another French one, a Renault," he went on. "It does have a hood; should be quite cosy inside when it's up. Of course we'll still need our coats and scarves. You look lovely in yours," he added. "Come on, give me a kiss."

He looked wonderfully handsome, she thought as she buttoned his coat and kissed his cheeks, but she felt too nervous to abandon herself to his lips…and before she could decide exactly how to cope with her feelings, a motor-car was rattling to a halt below their window and they were going downstairs and out through the door, the neighbours twitching their humble curtains to look at the rich and exotic vehicle in a street never before visited by such things.

"Good evening, Mister Jonathan." Hoggett saluted smartly and held open the car's rear door. "Miss."

"My goodness, Hoggett," Jon looked over the car, "exotic stuff this one, eh? Had a good run down to the coast, have you?"

"There's new oil in her, sir, and not a whisper of smoke out the back end."

"The way you keep her she'll outlast you and me and all of us—and it's magnificent paintwork." He turned to Maisie. "Isn't that lovely?"

"French Blue," she said quietly, stroking the high gloss.

"Quite right, Miss. The Frenchies are good at making these."

"Everything French is fashionable these days," remarked Jon, "thanks to the King."

"The King has one of these Renaults, now you mention it, sir, painted claret colour. I'd like to see that'un."

"Not thinking of deserting us for Royal service, are you?"

"I understand His Majesty likes to drive it himself, sir."

"So you'd be out of a job. Better stick with us then."

"It's an honour, Mister Jonathan…and to drive you, Miss." Hoggett's red face beamed her a smile. "Now you get aboard, Miss, and mind your skirt."

Here she was, about to climb into a motor-car with Jon chatting away to one of his family servants, talking about the King as if he'd been a next-door neighbour. Not so long ago she'd been scrimping pennies to pay for a ticket on the Shields Ferry; now she was surrounded by luxury and wealth beyond anything she had imagined. It was truly life in a different class. It might be daunting, but it could be exciting.

"I'm not used to being called Miss," she whispered into Jon's ear.

"When we're married he'll have to call you Madam."

"That'll be the day," she giggled.

New thrills ran through Maisie. She had never been in a motor-car before. It sat her higher above the road than she had imagined and she felt like a queen on a throne. She didn't care what the neighbours might be thinking. Let them watch and be amazed. She settled with Jon while Hoggett presented them with thick tartan rugs. The engine ticked over quietly but a gentle shake was transmitted through her body. It was both comforting and exciting. As she had felt so many times with Jon, she imagined she was being transported into a new life. She would try to relax and let it happen around her, accept and be accepted…if only that could be as simple and joyous as being tucked up in a cosy rug in an exciting new machine.

"All right, Darling?"

"Yes, Jon, I'm all right." She sat very quietly while the Renault set off, rattled over the cobbles of Percy Street, under the gaslights of Tynemouth, and then ran more smoothly on to the main road leading to Newcastle. Hoggett accellerated the engine and a wind blew in under the hood. She took Jon's hand under the rug. "I am all right, better than all right. I know I'm lucky to be going to your big family house. I know it means we can get married with your family's approval. That's quite something after what I've been through." She stopped watching the lights and houses floating past in the windy growl of their journey and turned to face Jon. "But like you wanted, I'm going to be myself tonight, not pretend to be anything I'm not."

"That's the way to do it."

"How many servants have they got?"

"Only Betty. They used to have a cook and a little maid too, but they've both gone. I'm not sure why; changing times, I suppose. They're left with Betty as cook and housekeeper."

"What do I call her?"

"Just Betty," Jon chuckled. "She's really one of the family. In a more exalted household she'd be dignified by the title 'Mrs. Bailes', but I'm afraid with us she's just Betty. Betty Bailes: sounds like a music-hall dancer; alas she doesn't look like one. But she's a treasure of a cook, you'll see." He hugged her arm. "It's going to be all right, you know. There aren't any butlers or footmen, it's nothing like that. Betty will bring the dishes in but we'll serve ourselves. It's all very friendly. They'll want you to have a good time."

"I'm sure they will. It's just me being nervous. I'll have to remember what to say and do."

"You won't have to remember anything. Just be like you are at home."

"Oho," she gave a laugh. "They'd like to see that, I bet they would!"

Windblown and rather chilled from the journey yet somehow hot with expectancy, Maisie felt small having climbed down from the motor-car at the towering front door of the house in Heaton Road. Before she could properly compose herself the door opened, Betty was there, smelling of cooking and bobbing a curtsey, and she saw Jon's parents. They looked slightly older than she had imagined; his mother expensively swathed in grey and mauve silk with a heavy necklace of pearls; his father's longer-than-fashionable grey hair giving him an air of adventurous distinction. They were smiling their greetings and extending their hands. As Jon had told her, it all seemed much less formal than she had feared, yet she could not help but be wary of every moment.

"Good of Mother and yourself to ask us over," Jon was saying to his father.

"Not at all. We're at the age when most of our social engagements are funerals; a jolly occasion is somewhat refreshing."

Julia smiled at Maisie.

"Would you like to go upstairs…"

Maisie looked blank.

"…and take off your hat?"

What was this about? Wouldn't she just take it off with her coat in the hall here? Jon put his lips to her ear.

"You're sure you don't want to, er, go upstairs?"

"Why? Are we having a look round, like?"

"No. Perhaps you might want to, you know, go…later."

"I'll take your hat, Miss." Betty stepped in to relieve the situation. "And your coat."

"Well now," William smiled at Maisie, "we hope you're hungry after your drive. What do think of the motor-car?"

"It's lovely. I've never moved so fast." There was a general laugh—and suddenly, here in the panelled hall with its stained glass and great vases of flowers, she felt free and able to say what she wanted. "Now I know why you men can fall in love with engines, not that I didn't know it before." She found herself hugging Jon's arm, felt for a moment that might not be the right thing to do here, then found herself keeping hold of him anyway.

"Engines as our iron mistresses, eh?" William's eyes twinkled. "There's a thought."

"I think if ships have souls, so do motor-cars." Maisie would say what she thought; they would like to hear it anyway. "I felt the motor-car was taking care of me. I felt all safe and cosy as if I was wrapped up in bed."

"Thanks to Hoggett's rugs and blankets," suggested Jon.

"No, not just them, something about the motion and the sound of the engine and the wheels on the road. It was wonderful. I could ride around like that for ever."

"We have a sensational return journey to look

forward to then," said Jon.

"Dinner first," stated William.

"You look very elegant, Maisie," Julia smiled, "and what a pretty dress. The new narrower cut shows off your figure beautifully."

"Thank you, Mrs. Ferris. I hoped it would look all right for dinner."

"It's most suitable. I wish I were of an age to carry off these new fashions so well. And you must call me Julia, my dear," she added with a pointed look beyond Maisie's shoulder to Jon, "now you've been brought into the family." Maisie received a silent hand-clasp from Jon. She knew it was meant to reassure her. If she needed further refuge she would take it in the dress; she had known it would look good and now she had been told. "And *do* let me see your ring...my oh my, that *is* a stone."

"Anyone can see you've honoured her properly, my boy." William was ushering them towards the dining-room.

"I think it's the most beautiful thing I've ever seen." Maisie would confess her truths to Jon's mother. She felt able to say anything now. "I hardly dared wear it at first; now I don't feel right if it's not on my finger. Mind I don't do the housework in it."

"I should hope not, my dear." Julia shot her son a glance. "No maid in that new place of yours?"

"Maisie won't have one. She runs the house herself."

"Goodness me, how primitive."

"On the contrary, Mother, it's very modern. Wives of the future will manage their own housework, you'll see."

"I hope I shall not live that long. It doesn't sound a very attractive future to me, but…if that's the way you young people want it."

"I've always worked," stated Maisie, feeling her confidence totter again.

"Well tonight's a night off, Darling." Jon took her arm. "We'll not talk about housework. Let's go in."

It was an enormous round table, gleaming beneath electric lights. To Maisie it seemed like being in a dream where she was looking down on some magical ocean with an fairytale iceberg at its centre: the great silver bucket from which peeped the golden-foiled tops of two Champagne bottles. Beneath it were islands of shining porcelain, archepelagos of twinkling glasses, capes and promontories of silver cutlery, coral reefs of many coloured flowers and white napkins, all floating on the dazzling sea of white tablecloth.

"The table's new, Jon," Julia was saying, "d'you notice?"

"Yes, Mother, very nice."

They sat down and Betty began to deliver hot dishes and steaming tureens.

"We used to have a long table," explained Julia, "but I like this round one better. Everyone can see everyone else and talk properly."

"Usually with their mouths full," added William.

"We'll try not to do that, Father," said Jon.

"You can say what you like here, both of you, mouths full or not." William took up his napkin and set a benevolent gaze on Maisie. "It's not what you were expecting, is it, Miss. Watson? And don't worry, I'll call you Maisie from now on. I suppose you were frankly terrified—and who wouldn't be, in your position? But whatever your position was, you're in a new one now. You're engaged to my son, who has made some appalling errors of judgement in his short life and been wretchedly unhappy with another woman, but now at last he appears to have seen sense and is going to marry the charming, capable and attractive young lady we see before us. Don't interrupt, Jon—and your blush, my dear, had better wear off pretty quickly with us. A lady who works in our own industry, with us not against us; not like someone I can think of but shan't mention again. A brave lady who has not always had an easy time but who rises above her troubles, a lady who wants to do well and can carry herself in the world, a fine young lady all set to be a good wife and, we trust—when the time is right—a mother. We like that, we like what you have done for Jon, and we like you. And now I've said what I've been wanting to say, we'll drink to it, and drink to you—if Jon will open the bottles."

Maisie, scarcely able to believe what she had just heard, felt herself close to tears, but knew they would not be welcome at this moment. She felt Jon's hand clasp her knee under the table and she herself held on tightly to the edge of her chair. Jon was grappling with the bottles; she knew she had to speak.

"Thank you, Mister Ferris. That's very very kind of you to say those things. I won't forget them. I don't know what to say myself except I love Jon and I promise I'll do my best for him."

361

"That's it then. Jolly good. Can't you get that cork out, boy?"

At that very moment the cork popped and frothy Champagne was poured into their glasses.

"To Maisie and Jon! To Maisie and Jon!"

The bubbles tickled Maisie's nose and filled her mouth with freshness. This was her first Champagne. She remembered Jon had promised Champagne with which to 'launch' their new home but they had been so busy and so distracted by events that the bottle had yet to materialize. She liked the taste and sensation immediately, but thought she had better not drink very much tonight. Even though she felt happy and amazed by her sudden acceptance into this family, she knew the faintest hint of drunkenness or silly words from a loosened tongue would do her no favours.

"You like it?" Julia was smiling over her glass. "I'm so glad. It's our favourite Heidseick. When Jon was a boy he used to call it 'hide-and-seek'."

"Oh I see. That's funny."

"It's not," Jon grumbled into her ear. "It's my parents *trying* to be funny; and being my parents, they have a thousand ways to embarrass me."

Betty brought in the final and most spectacular dish: a dark-looking roast issuing steam and the delicious fragrance of hot meat and herbs.

"No *hors d'oeuvres*," William announced boldly. "Frenchified nonsense. We'll get straight on with a decent dinner; two lamb shanks; hope that's all right for you."

"It certainly is, Father. But I notice you don't mind being Frenchified with your Champagne or motor-cars," observed Jon wryly.

"Two things the French are good at," answered William, handing round the mint sauce, "but they can't roast a joint; they don't have the guts to turn up the heat. Now this is properly hot, you see? Betty could run a blast-furnace."

There was general laughter; they set about the meal and conversation ceased—until William refilled all their glasses.

"You know what I especially like about tonight is that it's not only a celebration of your Engagement—which you must understand we're every happy about—it's also a celebration of us working together on *Mauretania*. We've all been involved in our different ways, haven't we?"

"I know I've been involved, yes," Julia looked with amusement over the rim of her glass, "running this house while you've all been playing with your big ship."

"Your lovely house is like a big ship," said Maisie when the laughter had subsided. "All this beautiful woodwork. I know what our ship's going to look like inside, I'm drawing it—in little bits."

"Yes, of course," said Julia with genuine admiration. "That must be enormously exacting work. You're obviously very clever."

"I was just lucky to get the job—that's when I met Jon," she added shyly.

"Yes. We know that story; very romantic, too."

The dinner progressed with more Champagne and second helpings of the lamb and its attendant vegetables. Maisie began to feel very hot and very full, but she was more relaxed than she had expected. Jon looked more handsome than ever, lounging at the table between courses with the electric light gleaming on his hair. She wanted to take him home and cuddle him up—but there was more food to face first. Dishes were brought in bearing slices of roast goose heaped around with spiced onion stuffing and served with bacon, sausages and more potatoes, cauliflower and peas. Bottles of different wine appeared; Jon and Maisie held to their Champagne.

"And now, my dear," crooned Julia, "you must have some pudding. It's fruit pudding. Betty likes to think it's her recipe but I preserved the plums and peaches myself last Autumn. We have a rather fine plum tree in the garden; it does remarkably well here." She ladled out the rich pudding into gold-rimmed dishes. "Just think, when fruit like this is ripe again this coming year, your big ship will be launched and floating, and you will have been part of it all, so romantic."

"They may be romantic," William stated over the creamy plums, "but they also have solid business ideas, quite brilliant ideas, it must be said. Did I tell you about the funnels idea?"

"You did," said Julia. "You went on about it at great length."

"And I shall go on about at greater length. The idea has been accepted by the Board. The Dowager Duchess of Roxburghe, who is to launch the ship, and all the other dignitaries arriving by motor-car, will actually be driven through the funnels lying on their sides. They should be amazed at their size. A truly brilliant idea; one might call it awesome. The press will love it, and the photographers of course. I can also tell you, Jon, that a luncheon reception will be held in the Engine Works. I imagine you will have to be there. A turbine will be put on view; splendid idea—but don't use it as a model to advertise your air-engine idea."

"I'm not likely to, Father."

Julia gave a light laugh.

"He gets so excited about his ideas…"

"Really, Mother." Jon took another drink.

"…he'd tell them to anyone."

"I know," said Maisie. "Keep your secrets until they're ready, that's what I've told him."

"You listen to her, Jon. There's a wise head behind that pretty face." William brought another bottle from a sideboard and poured a glass for Maisie. "Some Marsala to go with your pudding."

"It's very sweet," Jon told her. "All the way from sunny Sicily. You'll love it."

"It might send me to sleep," admitted Maisie. "I've never had such a big dinner."

"We're very glad you have enjoyed it," said Julia. "We have certainly enjoyed the evening."

"It's been very special for us," said Jon, holding Maisie's hand once again. "We can hardly thank you enough—but please, Father, no port," he added. "We're whacked."

"Hoggett will take you home, then."

"He'll be back late," observed Jon.

"He'll manage," said William. "Can't have you two walking about in the dark."

The phrase suddenly reminded Maisie of walking home in the dark and the terrible shock of the women grabbing her and the horrible insult of the red paint, but she felt protected from those horrors now. She knew she had entered Jon's family and been accepted and that she would be cherished in ways she had never known. Her own family was warm and loving and she had always been happy with them until her father's distress and anger over her love for Jon, but this was the new protection of wealth and influence she had never had but which she understood well enough. If only her Mam had had this kind of money to spend on this kind of food, and the house warm all the time and full of flowers! Well, she told herself, some of this would be hers now and she would grow to understand it and appreciate it even more and her own family would benefit, she would see to that however she could. She loved Jon for himself and would have loved him if he'd been a pauper, but she wouldn't be so daft as to pretend the money and influence of his family didn't matter. She would drink the wine, she would learn to be the lady Jon deserved as a wife, she would be true to herself and her roots but she would grow into this new life and make the most of it for both of them.

"Yes," she said, "I will have this wine. It's my turn to drink to you: you good people who have accepted me and my love for your son. So thank you." She drank off the sweet wine and would try to say something else when she had finished it, but Julia put a kindly hand on her arm.

"You don't need to make a speech, my dear. Just go home knowing we are delighted for both of you."

"Thank you Betty," smiled Jon as the coats, hats and scarves were handed round. We're glad to see you haven't lost your expert touch in the kitchen."

"Go on with you Mister Jonathan, you are a one! And good night and good wishes to you, Miss."

* * *

"Had a good time, then?"

The motor-car was rolling comfortably back to the coast. Jon held Maisie gently under the rugs.

"Oh yes. That speech from your father was wonderful. I never expected anything like that."

"Frankly, neither did I. He's quite a fellow when he gets going, isn't he? You certainly put him in a cracking good mood. I've never seen him so jovial. And that was a bold thing you said at the end, you looked magnificent holding your glass."

"I just told them the truth."

"Well, I love you for that and so do they."

"I think I'm happy at last about all this." She snuggled into his shoulder as the car hummed onwards. If her ride to Heaton had been fraught with anxiety and she had sat rather stiffly in the leather seat, on this homeward drive she could relax and cuddle happily into Jon under their tartan rugs.

"Oh. Took my father to charm you properly, eh?"

She knew he was making fun of her, but she liked it. "The son must try harder."

Maisie snuggled into Jon's shoulder and smiled up at him.

"I think I'm drunk," she said slowly. "That Champagne's wicked stuff—or was it the Marsala? I didn't say anything daft, did I?"

"You were marvellous, Darling. You made the evening go beautifully. And here we are, going home happily together."

"I know where I'll have to go as soon as we do get home."

Jon smiled mischievously.

"Upstairs to take off your hat, eh?"

"I'll be doing it with my hat *on* at this rate! Can the motor-car go any faster?"

At last they were set down in benighted Tynemouth; the street deserted, the sea motionless. Hoggett turned the Renault back towards Newcastle and a starry-skied silence folded around them. Holding hands, they opened their front door...to the sight of overturned furniture, emptied drawers, strewn clothes and scattered papers. Nothing stirred the shocking scene of violation. The only sound was of Maisie's sobs.

CHAPTER TWENTY
The Launch

"Not more business with policemen, Jon, please."

…but he had insisted. The following day a constable came to examine the broken lock on the back door, to walk through the disturbed rooms deliberately left in disarray for his inspection, and to make notes for a report. Later, a plain-clothes detective arrived to hear Jon and Maisie repeat their story. He declared there were no clues to the identity of the intruder and that further investigation would be a waste of police time. It looked like a routine burglary prompted by the arrival of new and unusually wealthy residents in the street. The only peculiarity was that almost nothing had been stolen, as if the thief or thieves had been looking in vain for something particular and left without it.

"They were looking for money," stated Maisie angrily, "and they got my housekeeping box from the kitchen."

The detective raised his hat to them, advised more and stronger locks on the back door, and left.

"Not much use, was he?" Maisie grumbled.

Her consolation was that nothing other than the housekeeping money had been stolen. What Maisie called her 'wedding purse' had not been disturbed from the back of its bedroom drawer.

"I didn't know you had a 'wedding purse.'" Amid the anxiety and depression the burglary had caused, Jon felt a warm glow to learn that she had been saving money for their wedding. "You've kept that well hidden."

"It was supposed to be a secret," she confessed miserably.

"Well, I'm glad it still is a secret—and I'll see that your housekeeping box is refilled tomorrow. They made a mess, but really we've been very lucky. There's no damage to your lovely paintwork in the bathroom. They could have taken clothes, food, ornaments, anything."

"No," said Maisie heavily, "just money. That's all anybody wants out there." She took Jon in an embrace, feeling cheered and safe in his arms. "I'm glad we want other things as well."

"We have them, Darling—and we have each other."

* * *

As *Mauretania's* launch approached, there was much discussion between Maisie and Jon about where they would be to view the event that now loomed almost as large as the ship herself in every calendar on Tyneside. With considerable annoyance, Jon explained that he and his parents were invited to the luncheon and would proceed with the dignitaries to the launch platform itself. This was an honour and an excitement, and no doubt he would see what they now called 'the funnels idea' brought to its sensational climax, but it would mean he could not be with Maisie at the moment the ship went down the slipway, a moment of drama and romance they had both imagined and talked about so much. Jon's disappointment was keen; then he discovered that Maisie had launch-day commitments of her own. A party of drawing-loft girls had arranged a crossing to the South bank of the Tyne and a picnic on the Ballast Hills at Hebburn to gain what would undoubtedly be the best view. Maisie didn't especially wish to witness the launch in this company but felt unable to manufacture any excuses and would have to go. At the same time she had to admit, with some excitement, that she should be given a spectacular and uninterrupted panorama of the Wallsend shipyards and the action of the launch. Some of the girls had been across already to determine the best position and had returned to the loft with tales of how splendid *Mauretania's* freshly painted stern looked, pointing directly at them from her enormous shed. Maisie told Jon that her father was likely to be down at the hull with the other carpenters for the 'setting-up', breaking out the supporting timbers and knocking in the long rows of oak wedges that would raise the ship off her keel blocks until she hung only on the hydraulic launching triggers. To Jon this seemed an awesome engineering drama, a great feat of human endeavour and a romantic beginning of the ship's release to her new waterborne life. He had visualised this when he had first stood on the vast decking of the berth before the keel was laid. If he couldn't be with Maisie, he would wish to be working on the hull, just as he had imagined so long ago. Now it was an experience that would be denied him.

"But you'll have one of your turbines on view," she tried to console him. "You can stand proudly beside that on the day; everyone will be amazed when they see how those delicate vanes can make such power."

Delicacy, power. Had not all his life been a curious juggling of those two principles? And here he was again, having to juggle his desires and his responsibilities and his anxieties and his love.

"And I'll be on the other side of the river, Jon. Don't worry, I'll be looking right at you when they wave her down."

"I'll still want you closer. There's an old Hexhamshire song, *Water of Tyne*. D'you know the words? *I canna get to my love though I should dee, water of Tyne runs between her and me*."

"Of course I know it, man. We sang it at school."

"It'll be like that. I'll be pining for you."

"All right then, but don't be too upset. In a way I rather like having the river running between us. D'you not see? It's what brought us together, it's only keeping us apart for a day—and just think, there'll be a moment when the ship's floating exactly halfway between us, as if she's run out from you to me, and if I hold out my hands it'll be like catching her for you, with all the hooters going and people shouting and cheering. Nobody'll know it, but I'll be cheering for you."

Not for the first time, Jon felt his heart might burst with love for this girl.

"You're just wonderful," he told her.

* * *

September 20th, 1906 dawned chill and rainy over the Tyne, but nothing could dampen the sense of holiday. Shops were closed and almost every worker on both sides of the river had been given the day off. Although the launch would not occur until the afternoon flood tide was at its highest, crowds had been gathering from early morning to secure the best views. Swan Hunter's shipyard and the neighbouring engineering works wore the unfamiliar atmosphere of a fairground decorated with flags, banners and bunting. Large areas of the yard and slipway had been cleared and swept to create a processional route for the motorcade of visiting dignitaries: past the enormous boilers, up and down the wooden-ramped way through an awesome tunnel created by sections of three funnels lying on their sides, and into the berth with its launch platform under the towering expectancy of *Mauretania's* bow.

The normally raucous works building now affected airs of gentility as it played host to the official launch-day luncheon. Jon sat with his father and mother in the beflagged room and listened to Lord Inverclyde, the Chairman of Cunard, making laboured jokes about the costs that had been involved in this huge project. Jon could not entirely escape his moods of mixed feelings, both privileged and frustrated. It had felt like a huge honour to stand beside the glistening turbine that had been put on display and to answer questions about it from guests who—exactly as Maisie had predicted—never imagined such delicate vanes could produce such power. Would he one day explain his own air-engine to astonished admirers? It was quite possible, and all the possibilities were thanks to his father securing this position for him, thanks to Maisie for giving him the hot-air idea, thanks to the amazing circumstances that had made up his recent life. It was also an honour to be among these dignified and important people; yet greater loveliness might be had standing in a common crowd with an arm around Maisie's waist. Now came a toast to the Dowager Duchess of Roxburghe who had arrived in a huge motor-car to name the ship. There were enjoyable moments in all this, but the things that mattered most to Jon lay outside the decorated wooden walls and open windows, beyond the excited talk and the formal speeches. They were the turbine with its glittering vanes and the secret excitement of his idea for the air-engine; the enormous ship poised on its slippery ways, and most vital of all, the slender, gentle, yet vivacious woman so full of warmth and life and love. Somewhere in the crowds on the opposite bank of the river, Maisie would be standing quietly excited and proud. He had wanted to be with her, but since that was not possible he would have preferred to be down under the hull with the hammer gangs. Their relentless beating, audible below the genteel chatter, formed a restless counterpoint to the martial or jovial music still coming from the Artillery band outside and was an insistent reminder of his hopes and dreams.

Over the river, on the Ballast Hills at Hebburn, Maisie and the drawing-loft girls had made a space for themselves among expectant crowds determined to enjoy what would undoubtedly be the finest view of the launch. Boots, raincoats and umbrellas were the order of the day, since it had been raining from the early hours, but spirits were high and the sky was lightening to a drier afternoon. There were even a few rays of sunhine poking through parting clouds as the girls set out their simple picnic on a waterproof sheet. Maisie had been hugely relieved to find that Rosie Sullivan and Peggy Dowling were not in their company. Those raucous girls and a few others had not wished to cross the Tyne and would be witnessing the launch from another viewpoint. 'Let them be wherever they like,' she thought to herself, 'as long as they're not here to spoil the fun.' Amazingly, the terrible incident of the red paint had not been mentioned, although Maisie was convinced the other girls must know about it. If she had to be with them here she didn't want that horror to splash her day with shame and insult. She pushed the thought away and looked across the river. There was the ship, directly opposite, poking backwards out of the glass-roofed building-shed, with black-coated spectators crowding every possible vantage point around her. Her name

Mauretania was painted proudly on that elegantly curved stern, together with her port of registry, *Liverpool*. Maisie thought it was a pity *Wallsend* couldn't have been painted on instead, since that was the place of her birth—but she knew they didn't do that with ships. Anyway, she smiled to herself, she was a lovely sight. Maisie would have liked to draw her from this angle, but had not thought to bring any artist's materials today. The most noticeable feature, upon which everyone was remarking, was that her four screws had been painted white for the occasion. From this distance were they like flowers, earrings, or brooches? Maisie decided they were like clover leaves set as delicate ornaments beneath that beautiful stern. She could not help thinking, with yet another surge of pride, that those screws would one day be turned by the engines on which Jon had worked. Where was he now? Somewhere at the bow, no doubt, with his father and mother and Sir Charles Parsons and the other dignitaries. He was a lucky young man; yet she knew he thought himself cheated of his true desire to be with her. It just wasn't possible today, she told herself. They would be together tonight and celebrate the launch their own way, celebrate each other, celebrate their love.

With the luncheon over, Jon found himself in Sir Charles Parsons' smoothly ticking motor-car, chatting to the great man himself about his boyhood ride in *Turbinia* and how this ship would turn out to be almost exactly a thousand times heavier. Chuckling about tight squeezes, Jon's father and mother joined them and the car took its place in the slow-moving motorcade, led by the Dowager Duchess of Roxburghe's stately vehicle and cheered on by crowds of shipyard and engine-shop workers. Jon's heart beat faster as they came to the spectacular row of funnels and the cars chugged through, two abreast. The effect was as amazing as he, Maisie, or anyone could have wished. "Clever lad," Parsons muttered to Jon as they creaked through the strangely echoing vaults of the funnels, their top sections towering alongside like a gigantic guard-of-honour holding steam whistles aloft instead of swords. It was like being in the middle of a fantastic dream. "This was a capital idea of yours," added the famous engineer as the cars stopped for photographers to capture a scene as bizarre as anything from Wonderland.

The cars were cheered to a halt at *Mauretania's* bow. While the Dowager Duchess made her way to join the well-dressed and highly polished party on the launch platform, Jon excused himself.

"Thank you for the ride, Sir Charles. I shan't forget going through the funnels like that."

"Nobody will," smiled Parsons.

"I'll join you later, Mother. I'm going down to the ways, Father. I really want to see her move from down there."

"Very well, my boy. Mind your head and for Heaven's sake keep clear of the drag-chains. And come straight back up when she's off, will you? Sir Charles will be expecting us."

Jon forced his way through crowds of shipyard employees and their families. He remembered that Maisie had told him her father would be down here with the other carpenters, knocking away the supporting timbers. Jon looked for Matthew and was prepared to greet him, but was somewhat relieved to meet no-one he recognised, each figure dwarfed by the massive walls of the ship that rose above them.

Now the flood tide was at its height. Up at the bow, the Dowager Duchess was ready with her bottle of Champagne, her hand on the little capstan that would signal the ship's release. An expectant silence enveloped the riverbank, but down by the greased ways, in awesome proximity to the hull, Jon became aware of alarming groans and squeals as the wooden cradles took the strain of thousands of tons of steel. Like a tortured giant in an agony of pressing metal and stressed timber, *Mauretania* was hanging on her triggers. Jon looked up towards the beflagged platform with its top-hatted crowd. Why were they waiting? What was the delay? Then came a tremendous, shocking crash of heavy metal. The triggers had fallen, there was yet another moment's delay, then with a new sense of shock Jon saw the enormous bow begin to move. Everyone was here to see her move, but now she was moving it was almost unbelievable. The great ship slid down with surprising silence, revealing crowds of workers suddenly facing one other rather than impenetrable walls of riveted steel. It seemed a movement almost without effort, a dreamlike gliding-away on a magic carpet—then came wild cheering from both sides of the river, a great shout of glee and triumph. As the voices swelled, the steel hawsers that ran from the hull snapped tight and a thousand tons of drag chains roared and danced down the slipway, throwing up clouds of dust and tossing stray pieces of timber into the air as they began to slow the ship. But she was still sliding beautifully to meet the water: the stern with its rudder and screws submerging and sending a great wave to rage up the opposite bank; then she was half afloat, actually bouyed up for the first time. Matthew, his tiresome hammering done and his view no longer obscured by the hull itself, could watch the woodwork of the fore-poppet on which he had worked collapse precisely as expected. Over the river, Maisie and the drawing-loft girls, deep in the crowd of exultant watchers, were deafened as all the factories along the banks and all the steamers in the Tyne seemed to be hooting their sirens and whistles at once. She thought it an amazing sound, a strangely barbaric acknowledgement by industry of industry itself. She had only moments to reflect on this, for suddenly *Mauretania's* bow made its dramatic drop from the slipway and the ship was completely afloat, an amazing consummation captured in yet another magical sight as the hull rode shockingly high, somehow utterly majestic and calm above the flooding, swirling, debris-laden water. Then Maisie's view was obscured by clouds of steam from ships' whistles and the funnels of the tugs surging frantically to shepherd their huge new sister to safety. Down at the slipway, Jon suddenly saw the biggest ship in the world was afloat right in front of him...and he was being distracted by familiar voices.

"Comrade Engineer!" Vladimir Druginin and his friend were suddenly beside him. "How does it feel to make history? The biggest ship in the world! You are part of it, part of history!"

"Indeed. Remarkable you should say so. That's just what I was thinking. And remarkable to meet you here. Nobody seems quite sure where anyone else might be today."

"Drink with us, Comrade?"

Melnikov had produced a bottle of colourless spirits from his coat.

"We toast her in vodka, of course," smiled Druginin.

"Of course—but thank you, no. I must go back to the Engine Works at once. I really just sneaked down here for a more exciting view. Anyway, I must go. I've been with the launch-party. It's a big day for my family."

"Certainly," said Druginin, his smile still wide.

"You chaps enjoy the rest of today. I look forward to seeing your woodcarving when the fitting-out begins."

"So do we! You will like our work, I promise."

"Capitalist pigs," muttered Melnikov as he watched Jon return to the launch platform and saw him greeted by a raising of top-hats.

"No, no, Comrade," Druginin returned the bottle after his swig. "You should broaden your mind. They are quite charming people. They have created a great spectacle for all of us today. We will do well to cultivate their graces—after the Revolution, of course."

"It is the workers who have created this," declared Melnikov, shaking his bottle.

"Yes, but do you not see that English life can offer something more pleasant than just being a worker?"

The tugs were taking *Mauretania* now, fussy little paddle-steamers guiding the vast hull with great care towards her fitting-out berth. Jon knew she was to be moored far enough from the riverbank to prevent her grounding as she grew heavier with her fitting-out, with a temporary bridge from ship to shore over which gangs of craftsmen and labourers would swarm throughout the coming months. *Titan*, the world's largest floating crane which had been the cause of much admiration and comment on the river, would come alongside to lower *Mauretania's* boilers, engines, and every other heavy piece of machinery and superstructure into the hull. She would be surrounded by booms and hawsers, hammered and riveted by hundreds of hands, her metalwork beaten and her woodwork sawn, her interiors dressed and her topsides painted before she would move again…but for this glorious moment Jon saw she was free on the river of her birth.

She was swinging now, to point downstream as if in tantalizing readiness for her eventual departure. Suddenly, and only for a slow moment, Jon and the other spectators were granted a sublime bow-view of her graceful lines. Jon felt a pang of her exquisite beauty as the razor sharp stem came to face him, its anchor-holes like the eyes of some gigantic but elegant racehorse. She was a dream-ship come true at last, in proportions so noble and perfect that tears of joy might be prompted with the still-resounding cheers of glee. She rode proudly between the tugs, towering over everything in the river. She would never ride this high again, her hull would be painted Cunard black and never gleam with such whiteness, but for this moment she was like a naked goddess released from her temple.

* * *

After her long wait to join a ferry heading North over the crowded Tyne, Maisie faced a hectic journey from Wallsend to Tynemouth along streets that still wore the atmosphere of a gaslit carnival, jostling through crowds still waving flags and chattering excitedly about the launch. After all that, she was pleased to be home before Jon. She knew he would be much later. He was dining, unavoidably, with his father and Sir Charles Parsons. To Maisie's dismay, women had not been invited. A day would come, she told herself, when women would no longer accept exclusion from such celebrations, especially women who had worked alongside men on the same big job, but this was hardly the time to raise the issue. It was just another annoyance she and Jon would have to tolerate on this day which had seen a great moment in their joint endeavours on the ship yet had contrived to keep them apart.

She took off her hat, coat and gloves with relief. She had felt 'bundled up' in outdoor clothes all day. In her progress through the house she pulled off her boots and felt happier without them. Later tonight, she smiled to herself, Jon would take off *all* her clothes. She lit the fire in the bedroom and plumped up the pillows, wanting Jon's golden head next to her dark one on the white linen. She smiled again. They were lovers! It was wonderful! Perhaps more wonderful still, she thought as she went busily through the rooms, they were true friends. On quiet evenings throughout this Summer they had sat happily together in the kitchen or lain together in bed and talked late into the dusk as darkness had settled over the sea and over the great river on which *Mauretania* now floated and over the towns and city that clung to its banks. Such talk! They had told their stories over and over again, learned each other's histories, shared each other's ideas. And they had made a home in a place where they could both be happy. Everything that had brought them together had happened here; here they were still, in the places they knew and loved. The great upheavals which their love had brought might have moved them into new and drastic situations but had not wrenched them from their homeland. They had not even been wrenched from their families; their families had begun to understand and accept. In spite of every problem and crisis that had come their way, every objection that had been raised, every cruel stroke of Fate or situation that had conspired against them, they were safely at home. It seemed to Maisie that they enjoyed a great freedom of spirit, that a lasting peace was enveloping them, sweeping gently over their troubles like an incoming tide, making those troubles smaller beneath the swelling wonder of this great joy.

She would make this a special night. Back downstairs, she stoked up the kitchen range. It had certainly been a special day, and it was going on late into the evening. Of course Jon would have dined well but she would still lay out a light supper, something warming before they went to bed. He would be tired, must be, even more than she was. He had had to deal with so many important people and be 'on parade' all day. They could be cosily together at home now, though.

At last there was a knock on the door. Of course, Jon wouldn't bother to find his key in his waistcoat pocket, he would know she would let him in. She ran gleefully to open the door. Surprise leapt through her. Against the darkness of the street stood the slender figure of a woman…and brought to startling life a photograph Maisie had once been shown. She recognised the expensive clothes, the stylish umbrella, the proud tilt of the head, the sweep of bright hair under the latest hat. It was Philippa.

CHAPTER TWENTY-ONE
Confronted

"May I come in?" Philippa asked pointlessly as she stepped over the threshold. "I should like to see Mister Ferris."

"He's not in," stated Maisie shakily.

"But you are, and you'll do." She pointed at Maisie with the umbrella. Its elegance was utterly unlike the Summer frivolity of the parasol Maisie treasured from that wonderful day on the Long Sands; this was wielded with an imperious cruelty. She hated the sight of it and the woman who had trespassed upon her happiness with such shocking speed and who was now closing the door with grim force behind her. "Yes," Maisie suffered the visitor's sharp scrutiny, "I think you'll do very nicely. Pity about the house, but I can see immediately what he likes in you."

"I know who you are," Maisie found a stronger voice, "but not what you want. Whatever it is, you should leave this minute. There's nothing for you here."

"No," Philippa's features softened into a slight smile, "I don't imagine there is. Still, I wanted to see...to see you both, actually."

She had led the way into the front parlour; fury rose in Maisie.

"You're not welcome here, Mrs. Ferris. I want you to get out—now."

"Calm yourself," Philippa gave Maisie something like a grin, "and remember your manners, if you have any. The lady of the house does not tell visitors to 'get out'. I shall leave, as you ask, but not until I've had a look around and a little chat. You realise of course that I shall not be 'Mrs. Ferris' for very much longer; that is a title under which *you* can labour for the next few years…and by God," she cast another glance around the room, "you'll be labouring in this little slum."

"I think you need to remember *your* manners," retorted Maisie, "if *you* have any."

A laugh escaped Philippa's lips.

"The woman has spirit! I like it. I'm sure Mister Ferris likes it, too. Is he teaching you manners, by the way? He could, you know. He could improve the prospects of any shop-girl."

"If you've come here to insult us both, you can leave now. I've told you, I want you to go."

Philippa's aspect softened slightly.

"I'm sure you do. I haven't come here to insult either of you, although I can understand that my very presence must seem insulting to you. But how about yours to me? Never mind, we'll not pursue that. No, I'm here for something quite different: to declare some truths."

"I don't want to hear them."

"In this life we must hear all kinds of things we should prefer not to. Surely the truth is worth listening to?"

Maisie faced Philippa savagely...

"When Jon gets back, and he shouldn't be long, he'll run you out of our house!"

…and was given an acid look in return.

"Plainly, you don't know your lover. He is far too well-bred to even imagine such things. You're not coarsening him, are you? I suppose you are, and I suppose he thinks he likes it. Men are such fools. No matter." Philippa took a haughty stance in front of the fireplace. "Since you have failed to invite me to sit down, why don't *you* occupy that hideous little chair and listen to the truths I promised you?"

She was rattling on, giving no chance of reply. Maisie realised she could do nothing but sit on the chair. She wouldn't sink to hitting this woman, kicking her shins and dragging her out on to the street by her hair. She wanted to, but starting a fight didn't seem the safest way to be rid of her, and a horror of violence flooded back from the red paint attack. No, she would sit and play this game of words and hope that Jon would come in at any moment…then she hoped Jon wouldn't come and that this cruel and sarcastic woman he had been so right to leave would be gone before he had to suffer another dose of her venom.

"And the first truth is that I'm not really here to meet you at all. I was here for the launch. I suppose you saw it? An exhausting day, but quite a spectacle. Cunard bought my painting of the *Mauretania* and invited me here to deliver it to some of the company Directors. That's sweet poetic justice, isn't it? I'm married to one of the engineers, produce an extraordinary work of art based on his ship, sell it to the owners, and come to the launch as their special guest—without telling my husband or meeting him on one of the biggest days in either of our careers. That's either sad or funny depending on one's point-of-view. I think I would have attended the launch anyway, to see my painting 'come to life' as it were. Is that sentimentality? I suppose it is. In any event, I wouldn't have told Jon I was up here. That's part of my acceptance that our past is over." Suddenly, Maisie saw a tenderness flash into the hard, bright face. "I have not always accepted that, you know. For some time I wanted to stay married to him. I loved him…in my own way. So you see," she turned another faint smile to Maisie, "I've decided to make some confessions as well as tell some truths."

"I'm sorry you're such an unhappy person," said Maisie, "but you shouldn't have brought your unhappiness here. It'll do you no good."

"Perhaps not, but it will do *you* some good to listen to me. Some time ago, when Jon made me angry, I warned him I would come back into his life and cause him hurt and harm. I confess that was one of my intentions today, but now I discover I've changed my mind. It's not altogether a sudden rush of finer feelings, it's that I can't actually be bothered. His life will drag on its own way, presumably with you. I have more important things to do now than spend time interfering with it—but I did want a look round. Dear me," she glanced at the curtains and up at the ceiling with its faintly cracked plaster, "the very love-nest itself. And is there any woman in the world who wouldn't want to see her rival in the flesh? Her successful rival." She stared at Maisie as if expecting some response but received only silence. "Well, he's with you and not me, isn't he? You must have *something* he likes. Quite obviously it's not witty conversation. I also came to let my husband know that his small part in my success has not been forgotten. I thought how pathetic it would be to come all this way, attend the launch in secret, and not tell Jon the painting he inspired has done well for me."

"I understand that." Almost against her will, Maisie

found she had to speak. "I'm an artist, too."

"Is that what you think you are? I understand you draw plans for a living. You're not an artist, you're a drudge of a housewife-to-be—in a house that would kill the soul of any artist. You have discovered what you call love, but you will never discover that love and Art destroy each other. And here is another truth you should know: there is a myth that Jon rescued me from loneliness and abject misery and that my life couldn't be complete without him, but it simply isn't true. I discovered I was quite happy on my own, going about my own business my own way. I suspect many people are, which is perhaps why so many marriages are wretchedly unhappy. Jon was an interference in almost everything I wanted to do, although he believed he was helping me. Oh, it's true he inspired the *Mauretania* painting. It wouldn't have been created without my marrying into his family and his career, but he could never inspire another of my works of art. As I said, love and Art destroy each other—or at least marriage and Art do. I must certainly never marry again. I need solitude; it's not lonely, it's very satisfying, just doing my own work my own way. I love that. I can't love another person; not that I don't need a man from time to time, of course, provided he's entertaining, does what is required of him, and goes away again when I'm bored. This suits me, but it wouldn't suit you. If you have no idea what I'm talking about you may consider yourself fortunate."

"I understand you well enough," replied Maisie evenly, "but I think you should say no more and go."

"I think I should stay," smiled Philippa, "and await the return of your lover—or shall we call him my husband? He still is, you know. I could see how he is these days, satisfy my curiosity on that score. Meanwhile," she added with affected weariness, "we could chat about how well or how badly he treats you." She looked witheringly at Maisie's grey stockings. "Can he not afford shoes for you?"

"If you must know, I don't like wearing shoes. I feel freer without them."

"Freer still without those ghastly stockings, I imagine. They are decidedly unflattering. Is not the spirit of the Age symbolised by a woman dancing barefoot? Usually in a filmy gown falling off the shoulders. D'you have such a dress? I've used the image for advertisements; it can sell almost anything from soap to railway tickets. You could hardly model for the posters, but I applaud your sensuality. We may have something in common. Did you know I sometimes work naked in my studio? The occasional spatter of cold paint over my hot skin can be very erotic; at least some men tell me so."

Maisie looked down.

"The idea offends you. Your embarrassment is very provincial…but in your search for sensuality and freedom I suppose discarding your shoes is a commendable start. Of course you could live as barefoot as a Spanish nun or throw away every rag of your clothing like an Indian mystic, you would still find no true freedom in marriage. Perhaps you don't need it. You've already decided you prefer love to Art, and I suppose whatever drawings you do are fulfilling and fun, aren't they? A nice little hobby for the next Mrs. Ferris; you may have talent, perhaps you can paint prettily…"

Maisie stood up, enraged. She could hardly keep her hands off this woman

"I've heard enough from you," she said darkly. "Just go."

It had some effect. Maisie sensed a weakening of resolve as she saw Philippa fiddle with her umbrella.

"He is late home," she said, a new tiredness in her voice, "leaving you for the glory of his work."

"He has a dinner invitation he could not decline."

"Of course. Launch day. Perhaps it's been too long for all of us. His career is very important to him. Be wise enough to let him have it, don't suffocate him with your devotion."

"Just go!"

"I shall go." With great relief, Maisie saw her turn for the door. "Tell Jon the painting has brought me considerable fame and fortune, which he knows I greatly enjoy. Tell him I came to have a look at you and—amazingly—quite liked what I saw. Tell him I understand perfectly why he might be happy with you. Of course none of that changes what you are." She turned to face Maisie again. "You remain a common slut."

Maisie's hand flashed up. She knew she was going to slap the woman's face but was unprepared for the loud noise it made. The silence that followed was almost as shocking. She filled it with a second blow from her other hand.

"Shouldn't I be doing that to you?" The infuriating voice emerged again. "It wouldn't improve the situation. I abhor physical violence. I suppose it's quite natural to a degraded woman of your class. You probably enjoy it…"

Maisie rushed to the door and pulled it open.

"Get out!"

Philippa strode into the darkness and turned to face Maisie again.

"I predict some kind of tragedy for you," she declared, "when Jon's innocence and weakness get him into another scrape and his parents aren't there to buy him out of it. You'll suffer, unless someone stronger than you comes to help him. I wonder who that could be, and if they will?"

Maisie slammed the door, held her back against it, and at last allowed hot tears to rush down her face.

* * *

"So you failed," Vladimir Druginin rebuked his companion, then flashed him an unexpected smile, "but you may blame me for your troubles, old friend. The plans were not there. You searched, but found nothing."

"I told you," protested Melnikov, "I found some technical papers; some drawings of machine parts that may or may not have been something to do with this engine, but I deliberately left them so as not to arouse suspicion that the plans were our target. I stole some money instead to make it look like the work of a commonplace thief."

"Indeed. Excellent. You did nothing wrong. The failure is all mine. I miscalculated and sent you on your daring mission too soon. The plans are simply not ready; but one day they will be, and we will have them. You will not be asked again to steal them. In fact our young English friend will—in a manner of speaking—*give* them to us."

"Give them? Are you mad?"

"Let me explain. He has been foolish enough to let

me know he intends to go on *Mauretania's* maiden voyage and have these plans developed by sympathetic financiers in America: an idea that proves he is as wise as he is foolish. No matter; he also has the romantic notion of taking the woman who will by then be his new wife. It is to be their honeymoon. It *is* a romantic notion, don't you think? Does it not appeal to your sentimentality? We Russians, the Germans and the English do have this in common. It is what the English might call 'a very sweet idea'. Very sweet indeed, for it means we may never have to steal or even handle the plans at all."

"What?" Melnikov's mood darkened to a kind of anger. "Explain yourself. The plans must be stolen!"

"And they will be stolen," continued Druginin calmly. "They will be stolen on the voyage, but—rather neatly, I think—not by us. We, or rather you, my old woodcarver friend, will construct a secret compartment in the ship. It will be with the engineer's full knowledge. It will be our wedding-present to him. We will tell him it will be a completely safe place in which to hide the plans during the voyage. We will already have warned him, if he is innocent enough not to have thought of it himself, that foreign agents are aboard and have heard a rumour that he is carrying plans of a secret weapon."

Melnikov gave Druginin a doubtful stare.

"Yes, I know it sounds dramatic, but he will believe it. Why should he not? In any case, it will be largely true. We will have told a German agent, with whom I am already in contact and who is ordered by the Kaiser to secure German victory in the coming war by any means, that plans for a revolutionary engine are in this young man's possession. The agent may search for the plans as much as he likes; he will find nothing and will have to be told where they are…only after we have been paid, of course. The theft may even be accomplished before the ship leaves Liverpool, thereby saving the German government the cost of a ticket to bring their agent and his little package all the way back from America." Druginin beamed at his companion and threw up his arms. "You like this?"

"This secret compartment." Melnikov, now also smiling, walked softly about the room, stroking his chin. "It would be better not to construct it in the panelling of a private cabin—which would be my first idea—but in some area of the ship so public that anything like a secret compartment would never be suspected."

"Good thinking, Comrade." Druginin was gleeful. "If you practice really hard, you could be almost as devious as myself!"

CHAPTER TWENTY-TWO
Fitting-Out

When Maisie told Jon of Philippa's visit she saw him fill with rage—mostly against himself for not having been there to protect her, but also against Philippa for her invasion of their hard-won and precariously established happiness in their new home. He told Maisie he thought she was playing down the incident; he wanted to know everything about it and was full of obvious but difficult questions. How had Philippa found her way to the house? Where had she been during the launch? What was the story of Cunard's purchase of the painting? What, exactly, were her threats? What could be made of her curiously calm reaction to having her face slapped?

Maisie was slow to offer answers; she simply didn't have them. Every time Philippa's unexpected violation of her privacy was talked about, she found it even more disturbing than the attack with the paint. She knew where that had come from, understood the mentality of the women who had wanted to degrade her, and—once the shock was over—knew how to deal with it. This was more subtle. The threat had come from Jon's own past, a past she knew he had no wish to inflict upon her, but which was inescapably in their lives and filled with this devious and dangerous woman. The divorce appeared to be going ahead, but did Philippa still have Jon in some wicked, impenetrable power? Would it be best to confront her again or ignore her? What would she do next? How would this strange experience haunt their future?

These were the questions that stung Maisie's mind and would not go away, however loving and calming Jon tried to be when his temper had cooled. Philippa had been right about one thing, she realised: Jon was certainly an innocent. She knew that already, of course. It was what made him so endearing, so lovable, so good a man. But, she thought, he must have been like putty in this woman's hands, for a while anyway, until he'd fallen out of love with her. That wouldn't have been difficult: she had no warmth, no honesty, was anything but lovable. She would know how to trap a man and beguile him with her body and her wheedling ways; her glamour, too: the excitements of her talent and the promises of her career. But if Philippa ever truly loved anybody it would only be herself. She had huge ambitions and a will of iron. Would she use it to reclaim Jon and destroy his new happiness? And whether or not anything like that might happen, right now, in her own home, Maisie had the feeling that Jon's innocence would prevent him from ever understanding what had passed between Philippa and herself. Faced with inexplicable things, he might imagine a strange conspiracy of the two women he had loved, coming together behind his back to dice with his future.

Reflecting on all this, there were moments when Maisie felt very plain and awkward and she was shot through once more with insecurity. How could she ever really compete with this glamorous, educated, talented woman who might have been a rebellious outcast from her own family but was closer to Jon's class and inventive spirit than she would ever be? Had her own recent life been nothing more than a fantastic piece of luck, luck that would run out when Jon saw everything Philippa was and everything Maisie could never be? Jon was telling her not to worry, covering her with kisses, reminding her of the warm acceptance his parents had shown her, asking her to think of the future and make plans for the wedding and honeymoon. Yes, it would be an exciting escape to America on the wonderful new ship with Jon's designs for the air-engine in their luggage and all kinds of possibilities ahead, but when he told her once again they could overcome every bad influence from the past, she did not feel so sure.

* * *

The gigantic floating crane *Titan* was alongside *Mauretania* now; every day it swung loads of steel, wood and fittings into the hull as workers swarmed over the temporary bridge to labour in a vast cavern of reverberating noise. Riveters continued their thunderous work on decks and bulkheads while carpenters—Matthew Watson, Druginin and Melnikov among them—began sawing and hammering to distinguish the interiors of the largest liner in the world. Engineering work, however, took precedence over decoration, and *Titan* was employed to lower the enormous boilers and other heavy engine parts down to their places near the keel. It was both strenuous and exacting work, with huge weights and vulnerable machinery to be guided down long shafts past the edges of the seven decks and many other fittings, each yard of descent fraught with potential snags and collisions. The greatest delicacy of all would be excercised in lowering the six turbines. It was essential that they should travel down through the ship without the slightest damage to their delicate vanes, and they would be handled like porcelain.

As part of the turbine team, Jon was involved in this last crucial journey of the engines from workshop to ship. Once the lower turbine casings were in place far below *Mauretania's* waterline and left open to receive the massed rotors on their shafts, it was necessary to wait for a calm day: no swell in the river, no wind in the sky to rock the crane and its precious cargo. So it was, on a still and sunny morning on the banks of the Tyne, that Jon witnessed the lift of the first turbines.

Crowds of workers had gathered along the great ship's fitting-out berth and were watching the turbines' stately progress from the engine shed, drawn by steam traction-engines at a careful, trundling pace. Out here, under full sunshine, the exposed vanes glittered with a ravishing sparkle, as if enormous Christmas decorations gifted from some gigantic fairyland were being paraded before a fascinated public. Jon and the other engineers walked alongside, escorting the turbines to their new workplace with a reverence that sometimes looked solemn, as if the body of a hero was on a gun-carriage, and sometimes joyous, as if proud fathers were presenting a brood of talented children. As the first turbine was hauled into position beneath the towering jib of the crane and workmen began to attach carefully-lowered chains, a motor-car pulled up on the berth. First out was Jon's father, looking elegant in an immaculate coat. He was followed by Sir Charles Parsons, who raised his hat to acknowledge the doffed caps of the workers and raised bowlers of the managers. Jon moved over to greet them.

"Good morning, Father...and to you, Sir Charles. You both look well."

"You too, my boy." William surveyed the busy scene with satisfaction. "Proud day for you and all of us."

"Lucky with the weather," remarked Parsons. "Not a breath of wind."

"That's what we wanted, Sir Charles," replied Jon. "We'll get these two in today, then see how we go with the other four."

"Six of your best," smiled William at the great

inventor, "all polished up and ready to drive her to America—at a record speed, too."

"Steady on, Ferris. You haven't got her funnels on yet." There was good-natured laughter. "Last time I saw those I was driving through them. What a bizarre idea that was," Parson's turned his smile on Jon, "but I shan't forget it."

"Nor will the public," answered Jon happily, remembering his day in Newcastle when Maisie saw the tram and wondered if it could pass inside the funnel. "Now they'll be queueing up to ride in the ship with the biggest funnels in the world—and the best turbines."

"We must allow our young men their bursts of pride," said William aimiably.

"And our old men," Parsons reminded William with a gleam in his eye. "Our generation invented these things; now we see our children playing with them. It's not a bad arrangement."

"Not bad indeed," declared William.

"Look, Father!" Jon took William's arm as bursts of steam issued from *Titan* and a hooter was sounded above a clatter of machinery. "She's going up."

The gigantic crane, looming over the ship it served, lifted the first turbine in a seemingly effortless arc. Higher and higher it went, swinging into position over the ship…and hung there for long minutes while men aboard took hold of guide ropes to settle its position. The glittering vanes flashed silver against the blue sky. They would not see the sun again, mused Jon, as their descent began.

"Three cheers for Sir Charles Parsons!" somebody

yelled, and the cheers were given and hats were raised.

Now, thought Jon, the marvellous machine he had helped to build was on its slow journey to its hot, dark bed in the engine-room. Its upper casing would be fitted and soon, instead of sunlight and blue air, it would know superheated steam roaring against its vanes. Then it would be alive, and give life to the ship, and enrich the lives of all who travelled on her: all this, from delicate vanes of polished metal created in his home town. He was proud indeed. His father's voice interrupted his thoughts.

"When you go home tonight, my boy, you'll find a little present from your mother and myself. We thought you'd like to share something with Maisie to mark this special day. How is she, by the way?"

"She is well, Father. We are very happy."

* * *

"The Champagne was a lovely idea." Maisie was curled up in front of the fire, holding her glass to catch rosy light from the flames. "It was delivered just after I got home; a real surprise."

"More welcome than our last surprise at the door." Jon's voice contrasted darkly with the sweet gurgle of the bottle as he poured the last of the Champagne.

"Don't let that woman ruin our happiness, Jon. She's gone, and she'd better not come back."

398

"I don't think she will. What she calls her 'fame and fortune' should keep her busy and well away from us. I do wish I'd been in so we could have faced her together. Anyway, you dealt with her bravely."

"And you're getting your engines in," said Maisie brightly, as if eager to dispel fears about Philippa with enthusiasm for *Mauretania's* progress.

"Well, two turbines. It's a start."

"Yes," Maisie rolled on to her back on the fireside rug and watched the bubbles rising in her glass. "You get the idea she'll be leaving the river soon. That'll be a grand day—and a sad one. Men will be laid off. I'm still drawing parts for the superstructure, but I'll be laid off too when the job's finished." She smiled up at Jon wistfully. "I'll have time to learn to be a housewife."

"There'll be other ships."

"You mean you'd want us to go back to the yard?"

"You've done well there, you're experienced now." Jon sat beside her on the rug. "I know you like the work."

"I like the respect of being in work," Maisie studied her Champagne as she spoke quietly, "but I suppose that's part of my life that's gone now, or should go. I suppose the new Mrs. Ferris doesn't go out to work in a shipyard. That's what you and the family would expect, isn't it?"

"My wife doesn't need to have a job, if that's what you mean."

"You know what I mean. People of your class don't respect working women."

"That's not entirely true, but I don't necessarily agree with it anyway. Why shouldn't a wife have a job of her own and the respect that goes with it? My first wife had a job, a whole career."

"You don't want me to be like her, do you?" Maisie took another drink. "Anyway, what I'm talking about is working-class respect, respect for a lass in work. Your class respects wives who *don't* work."

"Perhaps, but I don't want you to feel tied to a domestic life just doing housework," he wagged his finger jovially at her, "since you won't allow a maid in this place. But the point is, we don't have to stick to the old conventions."

"We haven't done much of that," she giggled.

"No—and a good thing, too. You keep working at the yard if you want to, but know that you don't have to."

"I'll not work there for ever," she looked teasingly at Jon, "not when there are children."

"Good." Jon drained his glass. "They'll need their mother at home. We're just being careful about children at the moment."

"I know we are. I know what to do; I know when it's safe for us. We want our child to have the Ferris name, be born to properly married parents. We don't want a bastard."

"That's not a nice word."

"It's not a nice idea. There've been more than a few bastards born in Union Street and their lives have been made a misery by narrow-minded folk."

"Quite." Jon kissed her forehead. "We'll make a fine family when the children come. We make a fine family already."

"I see now," said Maisie, rolling on to her elbows to take a final drink, "that between us we can deal with anything: you at the yard, me in the drawing-loft, both of us here at home. I love it here, you know. It's like we're married already, isn't it?"

"Yes, it is. And in this modern marriage the husband will do the washing-up." Jon got to his feet and carried out the empty glasses. "Off I go to the damp scullery with only the rats and cockroaches for company while Madame disports herself on the boudoir rug."

"You're daft, you are," she giggled, " but I love you."

* * *

With her engines in place the ship seemed suddenly potent. When they were connected to her shafts and screws she would no longer be merely a hull but a real ship enlivened with awesome power to amaze mankind and taunt the gods of speed and distance. She might still be awaiting funnels, superstructure, fittings and dressings, but she had become a live machine. Like a racehorse under starter's orders, like a sleek greyhound straining at heel, she required only the touch of humans to set the spur or slip the leash. And, thought Jon with a smile, those engines, revolutionary in every sense, were already the inspiration for another yet to be built. Whenever he saw the great ship at her moorings, pointing downstream towards the destinations of her new life, he told himself he must strive to build the rest of his own new life, labour at his calculations, complete his designs, and draw the full plans as carefully and as quickly as possible.

Determined that their new liner should feature luxury to match her sensational speed, Cunard had ordered a lavish scheme for her interior. Jon and Maisie joined excited talk along the river as they and their fellow workers witnessed extravagant-looking deliveries to the ship. Of course there was to be a grand staircase connecting the First Class accommodation through five decks, with the excitingly modern addition of two electric lifts. A magnificent glass dome was being constructed over the two-tier First Class dining-room. They longed to go aboard to see these wonders for themselves, but Maisie's position in the drawing-loft carried no automatic right of access to the ship. Even Jon's influence, connections and direct involvement with the turbines had yet to earn him passage over that tantalizing temporary bridge into the busy hive of developing decks. One day they thought they might sneak aboard with some delivery men; another that they might have to wait for the ship's public viewing-day and go over her like tourists. Neither escapade seemed likely or appealing and they told each other they might only see the ship properly when they went aboard as passengers at Liverpool.

"For our honeymoon!" Maisie would say, adding "we're not even married yet" in a gloomier tone.

"We will be, as soon as possible," Jon would reassure her with a kiss—while he himself had little idea what Philippa was doing to initiate the petition for divorce he would so eagerly accept. While the ship was being worked upon to completion, there were days when Jon and Maisie felt their own lives were still in need of sympathetic craftsmen and skilled joiners.

Inside *Mauretania*, complex plasterwork was being applied in Renaissance and Eighteenth-Century French style, rich carpets were appearing in breathtaking hues of pink, green and red, and extensive and varied panelling was to be fitted throughout First Class. It was in carving the choicest woods that Druginin and Melnikov had been employed in the joinery shop along with the Palestinian craftsmen Maisie had noticed at the yard. Their work was painstaking and superb, and magnificently carved panels of oak, mahogany, walnut, maple and sycamore could be seen leaving the shop. It was while these exquisite pieces of carpentry were being taken aboard for fitting and finishing that Vladimir Druginin invited Jon and Maisie to the Low Lights Tavern on North Shields Fish Quay.

"I'm not going there," protested Maisie hotly. "You know as well as me the place has a bad reputation. It's the worst pub on the river."

"Our Russian friends drink there," explained Jon.

"*Your* Russian friends. I don't want to meet them. I've had enough rough treatment from odd folk on the Fish Quay."

"I know, Darling, but these two are good enough fellows. You'll come to no harm with them. They are interesting men. Their work is on a level with what you or I do in our different ways. Since they go aboard every day, they might get us a look over the ship. You'd like that, wouldn't you?"

Maisie was eventually persuaded to accompany Jon to the rendezvous.

"But I'm not coming along because I'm interested in these foreigners," she explained, putting on her oldest coat and dowdiest hat; "I'm coming along to keep you out of trouble. And hide your wallet while we're in there."

As Jon and Maisie made their way to the tavern, smells from the reeking smokehouses mingled with the stench of piled herring boxes and fumes from the oily river. They squeezed through a raucous crowd of drinkers to find Druginin and Melnikov occupying a corner table in the wooden-floored, smoke-filled room, as far from the noisy bar as they could contrive. Still wearing their long coats, they sprang to their feet and snatched off their caps to greet Maisie in good English and shake hands, but polite exchanges were short and the smaller, more voluble Russian seemed eager to get down to whatever his business was. Maisie remained suspicious of it and of the men themselves. She did not want Jon involved in anything that might harm him or become yet another threat to their fragile happiness, but as she listened to Druginin she began to understand how these strangers might be helpful.

"You have our sympathy about the robbery," he was saying. "It seems to me it must have been an act of revenge by members of either class you have enraged by your liaison."

Maisie reddened and looked at the floor.

"Do not fear this truth," Druginin told her. "We understand your love, we salute it," he smiled. "We also know you have outraged the class to which you have belonged. Their disdain for you, their violent attack, this robbery: symptoms of tensions the Revolution will eradicate forever. But for the moment they exist. You have been assaulted by your fellow workers; your house has been invaded: acts of war in the great struggle between the classes."

"That's all very well," said Jon, eager to move from a subject he knew was distressing Maisie, "but we're not really interested in politics. Anyway, our own families have begun to accept us as a couple and our plans to marry."

"Your own families, but not yet the world, eh?" Druginin smiled bitterly. "And I know you *are* interested in politics," he stared at Jon, "if only because circumstances force you to be—but enough of that for the moment. You must see that the robbery shows how vulnerable your possessions can be. Imagine if the plans for your air-engine had been stolen. Have you thought of that?"

"Of course," replied Jon. "But fortunately the plans are not finished and not in a state to mean anything if they *were* stolen."

"For the moment, then, you are lucky. But do you not see that when the plans are complete they will be of international importance? How can you say you are not interested in politics when everything today is political? And what could be more political than an invention that could be used as a weapon in the coming war? You have invented a great and powerful machine."

"Not yet," replied Jon steadily, "I've only imagined it."

"I saw it with my own eyes," Druginin was vehement, "that night on the polished table! I saw what could be a new wonder of the world. So did you. Complete the plans, make it a real possibility, then those plans will be political documents of the highest and most dangerous importance. Think of how Germany is building up her armaments. Are you blind? These plans would be food to the German appetite for machines of war. If some common thief could steal money from your house, some German agent could steal the plans."

"Are there German agents in Tynemouth?" asked

Maisie with a doubtful look.

"Who knows? Would they tell you if they were here? The shipyards, the factories, the chemical works: any place with industry could be of interest to the Germans. They have spies everywhere. We know this."

"It's far-fetched, man. You just want to involve us in your revolution."

"All right!" Druginin bristled. "Why d'you think we came to England? To carve wood on a boat? We came to further the greatest revolution history will ever know!"

"And that's what you want us to do, isn't it?"

Druginin steadied himself, looked at the silent Melnikov, and drew a calmer breath.

"We want you to keep these plans for the English. Germany will be your enemy and your husband's enemy, if perhaps not next year, then soon enough. You will be helping your own country, not a workers' revolution—although millions of Russian workers might come to thank you if this machine is kept out of German hands. Think about it…comrades."

Maisie gave Jon a stern look.

"Are you going to be involved in this?"

"He is involved," Druginin spoke firmly, "and so are you. Now listen. You must understand that when the plans are completed they must be kept not in your own house but in a place of complete security and secrecy. We offer you such a place."

"It is built already," said Melnikov unexpectedly.

"What?"

"It is built already," Melnikov repeated. "I have built it. It is on the ship."

Jon and Maisie listened with growing amazement as the two Russians, with much animation but many furtive glances around the room, began to describe a small secret door that would open in a panel near the foot of *Mauretania's* grand staircase. The door was undetectable among the decorative woodcarvings of the French walnut. There was no keyhole and no key. Its silent mechanism was worked remotely by pressing a particular bunch of grapes carved on another panel. Behind the door, Melnikov had constructed a safe lined with metal and sealed with cork to make it waterproof and fireproof. When it was convenient to do so, they would take Jon aboard and show him. Then all he had to do was deposit the plans there and, when the maiden voyage took place, sail to America.

"Perhaps I should say 'steam to America,'" Druginin concluded, flashing a big smile at Maisie. "I know how important steam is to your man."

"But on the staircase," protested Jon. "There couldn't be a more public place on the whole ship!"

"Precisely. Who would suspect such a thing in such a place?"

"But do not worry," Melnikov spoke with timely reassurance from the shadows of his corner. "I have built other secret door to work same way. It is in children's playroom."

There were long moments of silence, the dawning of possibilities, quietly spreading smiles.

"Another drink?" offered Druginin.

Maisie refused it and asked "Why are you doing this for us?"

"Because we admire you. We believe in this man's idea."

"You're doing it for your revolution."

"That also, but it is not only our revolution. The whole world will benefit."

"Perhaps," said Maisie. "We're not keen on revolutions in England."

"This we have noticed," smiled Druginin. "But what should you care? You are leaving England for America, and America has already had her revolutionary war...the war you lost," he reminded them with a grin, then became serious again. "Think of this as our wedding present to a man and a woman we admire. He took me into his trust, showed me his great work. Accept ours. You do not have to use it if you do not wish to—but I think you will come to realise that you must." A new hardness came into Druginin's voice. "Now go home to your safe little house that might not be so safe. Go home and lie together in your sweet love that might not be so sweet when there is war with Germany. Go home and be English," he turned to Jon, "and do what good Englishmen are supposed to do: safeguard your home, your wife, and your country."

Jon and Maisie walked back to Tynemouth in a darkness filled with new thoughts and very few words, but as they approached their front door, Jon did speak.

"The plans are nearly finished. I'm not showing them to anyone here. I *will* take them to America. You see how our Russians have struggled to warn me of their political importance? Well, let those men take me for an innocent fool; they're only telling me what I know already. Of course I realise this engine could be used to power some weapon of war. Of course it will have military value. In these dangerous times, the plans have acquired a huge political significance. They mustn't fall into the wrong hands. The Kaiser is building up his navy to match ours. As soon as our *Dreadnought* was launched he wanted big battleships of his own. The Germans would want an air-engine if one could be built. It's an idea they might have had already. If I could imagine it, so could some clever German engineers. But the fact remains I *have* imagined it, and I do believe it could be built. So I'm taking the plans to America—for potentially generous funding, but also for the sake of our national security."

"They'll come with us on our honeymoon, just as you explained before?"

"That's right, but now they won't have to take up any space in your trousseau, Darling. They'll travel in their own special accommodation, won't they? I can't wait to show you this door once I've been told where it is."

"Calm down, patriotic English lad." Maisie hugged his arm. "Remember it's supposed to be a secret."

Jon stopped them outside the door, kissed her, and said "I'll have no secrets from my wife."

* * *

"Could you wish for a more pleasing English couple?" Druginin asked Melnikov as they trudged long, benighted roads back to their lodgings.

"Their speaking was difficult for me," came the grumbled reply. "I could wish for better English words."

"Oh, the English words you spoke were perfectly convincing," Druginin smiled with satisfaction at the firm ring of their boots on the cobbles, a smile that became a gleeful laugh. "And we have what we came for: a perfectly convinced Mister Ferris!"

CHAPTER
TWENTY-THREE
Trials

As *Mauretania* neared completion in the Tyne, Philippa left London for Paris. Commissioned again by Robert Gough, she had to create posters advertising lemonade and mineral waters. Lemonade sold well enough, but she reminded Gough that mineral waters were not especially popular in England. The advertising imagery would be a challenge; she would seek inspiration from the French, who drank bottle after bottle of mineral waters. She would go to Paris, and he would provide first-class travel on the trains and ferries, wouldn't he? She gave him the sly smile that signalled she would keep his unsavoury secret only so long as she was given whatever she wanted out of their business arrangement. Further publicity about the sale of her *Mauretania* painting to Cunard would be appropriate, would it not? After all, it was he who had arranged to exhibit it first—and to such great effect. All Robert's customers should be told once more about the sensational woman artist who created their posters; how her fine art was now to adorn the Boardroom of the world's principal steamship company while her commercial art was available at competitive rates. Of course the competitive rates Robert might charge his customers would have no effect upon her fee. Indeed she wanted a larger one for this venture. She would approve the brochure with its full-colour reproduction of the painting when she returned. He was such an astute businessman, she reminded him with her jaunty *au revoir*: he could always be relied upon to advance her reputation—and protect his own.

Marcel, too, was astute—but as a lover, not a businessman. He could always be relied upon to please her. She had discovered, somewhat to her surprise, that his idea of love-making was essentially simple. He was romantic about it in the same way that Jon had been, and always careful to satisfy her before satisfying himself. He considered himself an artist both within and beyond the *boudoir* but scarcely discussed what he appeared to regard as his rather lowly work as a printer. He believed, as lovers, that Philippa and he should inhabit a world beyond the mundane; so they established and maintained a routine of assignations in parks and restaurants, alive to the chestnut trees and horses-and-carriages and motor-cars in the Bois de Boulogne, to the aromas of rich food and wine, and to sensual adventures in her hotel bedroom. But the reality of this itself became mundane. Philippa began to feel almost motherly towards Marcel, buying him new shirts and ensuring his coffee was served at the right strength in his favourite café. And Philippa had no aspirations to motherhood. She left Paris, taking definite ideas for her posters and leaving Marcel with cloudy ideas of his romantic entanglement with an Englishwoman.

Robert Gough's clients were delighted by the designs his celebrated woman artist had produced and the 'Paris in a bottle' posters appeared all over London. Their success brought Philippa further lucrative commissions and her rooms in Chelsea were lively with visiting businessmen and advertising agents. She also established a programme of *soirées*, attended by the circle of printmakers, photographers, writers, fashion-designers and other artists which revolved around the young and slender woman who had become the toast of London's creative community. It was in this way she met her next lover—older, more sophisticated and unquestionably more fascinating than Marcel—and paraded him arrogantly at a reception in Robert Gough's printing works.

"Styford Bywell?" Gough was appalled, and took Philippa aside to voice his disapproval. "He's the most vicious rake in London."

"You can talk." She eyed him with malevolent sarcasm. "You're just the man to warn me against vice."

"My vices are nursery pleasures compared to Bywell's. He was expelled from Harrow, sent down from Oxford, drummed out of his Regiment and blackballed from his Club."

"Good Heavens," Philippa grinned, "a perfect record. Irresistible!"

"I tell you, he is utterly depraved."

"Utter depravity?" Philippa's eyes gleamed with mocking laughter. "Now that's right up my street. What exactly does he do?"

"Only the Devil knows what evil he practices, but he mixes with the scum of humanity and takes their filth into the upper reaches of Society. He is a devotee of the Occult, whatever that entails—and I'm disinclined to find out. But it's well known he has entry to some of the most powerful circles in England: the great houses, Parliament, the Army…"

"No doubt the Church and the Judiciary as well," Philippa smiled over her wineglass, "corrupting them all as he goes, eh? Well, he's definitely the man to know, isn't he? Oddly enough," she added with a piercing stare, "he's perfectly normal in bed—not that *you'd* have any idea of normality."

Their conversation was stopped by the appearance of Styford Bywell himself, holding Philippa's coat.

"We're off," he announced in the husky voice of a man who seemed older than his years, the effect heightened by bony features and prematurely grey hair. Yet he was handsome, with a timeless quality, as if he might have looked like this as a youth and would retain his distinctively erect bearing into old age. The humourless gaze of his cold blue eyes fell upon Gough. "Had enough of your party; leaving you to your queer friends."

"We're week-ending in the country," chirped Philippa. "Lord Whittledean's place. We're going down in Styfie's motor-car tonight. Herons, isn't it, in Hampshire?"

"I know of it," said Gough evenly, ignoring Bywell. "You'd be better off going home to Chelsea on your own. You'll have a long drive with only regrets at the end of it. I know what goes on at Whittledean's place."

"I challenge that, Gough." Bywell spoke calmly. "You may have heard malicious gossip spread by the uncultured, but your mind can scarcely conceive what goes on there. The very talented Mrs. Ferris, however, has opened herself to new possibilities. Her life is not standing still. One day she persuades the public to buy Burton's mineral-waters by suggesting that all the delights of Paris might pour from a bottle (what a preposterously silly drawing that is, but it works, doesn't it?); the next she will explore the very boundaries of awareness, perception and sensation. Since young Whittledean inherited, he's made Herons a temple to knowledge and experience far beyond the commonplace. Philippa is growing into a remarkable woman, you, Gough, remain a baby in these matters."

"And I think baby is past his bedtime." Philippa tapped Robert's cheek with her glove. "And that 'Mrs' business reminds me," she turned to Bywell with a breezy manner, "my petition for divorce has gone through. I put it off far too long, now I must be rid of that part of my past—or does that part of my past want to be rid of me? It hardly matters," she gave an insincere laugh, brushing her hand round Styford Bywell's collar, "let it go. The petition will certainly not be contested, and my silly ex-husband will get what he's wanted for so long: freedom, or what he thinks is freedom. You do know he's taken up with some dreadful girl from the slums, don't you? Not much of a future there, but he's welcome to it. It's *my* future that I'm interested in."

"So," Bywell continued to Gough, "the future beckons. Join us." There was no warmth in his smoothly-voiced offer. "Broaden your experience."

"Oh no, Styfie," Philippa swished into her coat and gave Bywell an imploring look, "Robert's a terrible spoilsport. He mustn't come along; he'll play by the rules." A giggle burst into her voice. "There are no rules at Herons are there?"

"There *are* rules at Herons," Bywell stated coldly, ignoring Gough and leading Philippa out to the motor-car, "but you'll learn them soon enough."

* * *

At last, *Mauretania's* building was complete. Final work was accomplished unobtrusively on her rigging and interiors, but any sense of anticlimax was dispelled on the day she was to be taken out to sea for her first trials. Thousands of spectators gathered on the banks of the Tyne to witness the gigantic ship's first move under her own power. It was a moment of huge importance on the river. The sense of holiday which had attended her launch was replaced by a frantic excitement as the enormous ocean liner—awesome four-funnelled product of years of brilliant invention and intensive labour—was suddenly being edged towards the open sea. Tugs were guiding her down the river but soon she would be free of them to breast the waves beyond the piers and take to her natural element. Everyone involved in the design and construction of every component from her engines to her ornament was both thrilled and made anxious by the prospect of the tests that lay before her in the grey North Sea.

Jon took Maisie to watch from Collingwood's Monument overlooking the mouth of the Tyne. It was a superb vantage point, and standing on the flight of wide stone steps leading up to the famous old Admiral's gigantic pedestal overcame any problems of trying to see above the heads of a crowd. Jon had hoped his position on the engine team might have earned him a place aboard for these first trials, but that privilege had gone to more experienced colleagues. Any disappointment he felt was cancelled by the joy of being able to hold hands with Maisie on this important occasion. He would not have liked to be parted from her or to think of her alone in the crowd—and he had good news to share.

"Oh, look, look! Here she comes!" Maisie jumped up and down with girlish glee as all heads turned to face upstream…and saw the four tall funnels in Cunard red-and-black and the vast white superstructure of the new ship sliding round the bend in the Tyne beyond the Fish Quay. It was a curiously unsettling vision, as if the buildings of a town were miraculously on the move. "She's so big! She's so big!" Maisie was squeezing Jon's hand in excitement. "It's like she's filling the river!"

Mauretania's parade downstream was indeed an awesome sight. The biggest ship in the world did seem to fill the river from bank to bank. The flotilla of little boats steaming and paddling around her massive hull was steadily parted by the inexorable progress of her gigantic but elegant prow, and her stately progress was accompanied by the sound of cheers that floated downstream on a gentle Westerly breeze. Maisie found every memory and emotion was stirred. She saw the new liner was passing the old *Wellesley* training ship and the white towers of the High and Low Lights above the Fish Quay where they had shared the scalding fish and chips and Jon had given her the ring and she had given him the 'hot air' idea; she remembered getting her job in the drawing-loft and her mother defending her against her father's anger about Jon and moving to her new home at the mouth of this same river and all the other amazing things that had happened to her, each one somehow embodied in this beautiful ship her lover had helped to power. She wiped tears from her face and grasped Jon's arm.

"What are you thinking? Are you worried about your engines in there?"

"No. I'm remembering being down by the river as a little boy, watching other ships go out. I'm remembering everything that's happened."

"Me too." Maisie's hug grew tighter. "We've seen and done some things, us two, eh?"

"We certainly have. I never thought I'd see a ship as big as this, or that I'd have anything to do with her."

"It's your engines that are making her go."

The tugs were guiding *Mauretania* but her turbines were spinning. Black smoke poured from her three after funnels as her razor-sharp bow came to Lloyd's Hailing Station; from her forward stack came a sudden flutter of white steam…and moments later the exquisite thunder of

Mauretania's great whistle: a sound both lustful and poignant, to be remembered down a lifetime. It surged through the crowds, who responded with a faintly audible sigh, as if arrows of ecstacy and longing had been sent through their hearts. It seemed the deepest, saddest, proudest, most tearful and glorious sound in the world and everyone wanted to hear it again…and here it came once more: another blast saluting well-wishers on the Southern bank. It was glorious, it was beautiful, it was awesome. 'Leave, leave, leave,' it seemed to roar and whisper, 'leave the old and face the new.' Now she was passing directly below the Monument with another blast for Lord Collingwood, his statue staring out towards Trafalgar. 'Victory! Victory!' the whistle seemed to roar. Jon and Maisie could see down on to her decks, imagine themselves behind the port-holes; so many port-holes, nobody could count them as the great hull slid past. There would be new victories in this ship with speed records broken on the Atlantic in a new age of steam the old Admiral would have welcomed. She was at the river's mouth now, giving more blasts in salute to the black-coated crowds that lined both piers and strung around the lighthouses. She was free of her tugs and breaking the slight waves of the bar between the piers—then she was alone on the open sea: huge, powerful, but already looking smaller as she stood away from the shore of her birth.

"When will we see her again?" asked Maisie as the people began to disperse, a sense of loss in many hearts.

"She has five days in the North Sea," Jon reminded her. "She'll be back for final adjustments before she goes to Liverpool for the main trials with Cunard. We should see her go out again that day; that's when she really leaves the Tyne. Then we'll see her again in Liverpool—for our honeymoon."

"Then we'll be on her, as passengers to America! I can hardly believe it, Jon."

They walked back to Tynemouth, *Mauretania's* diminishing smoke still visible in glimpses out to sea. It seemed to Jon it was the right time to tell Maisie his news of the divorce. He had heard from his father's solicitor that Philippa had filed her petition, now being allowed after three years of marriage. The *decree nisi* should be made absolute in time for them to marry in November, so *Mauretania's* maiden voyage could indeed become their honeymoon.

"I never know what to say after these bits of news, to be honest." Maisie was walking steadily beside Jon, but grasped his arm with a new fervour. "Except to say 'thank you' and kiss you."

"That'll do," Jon laughed as they nuzzled lips and noses. "Kissing in the street," he added. "Unheard-of!"

"You'll hear more," Maisie giggled as they neared their front door. "When we get in we're going straight upstairs. Then I want to talk about some ideas for the wedding."

* * *

Styford Bywell drove his Daimler-Benz through the night; Philippa, wrapped up in her motoring clothes, dozing as best she could as they rattled across Surrey. She was dreamily drunk and thought how luxurious it felt to loll her head against the rich leather seats of this motor-car. Before her lay the forests of Hampshire, the great house of Herons, and whatever excitements Lord Whittledean might lay on for her. It was rumoured to be a constant party at Herons with guests arriving at all hours and staying as long as they wished.

Hampshire before the sunrise and some refreshing Champagne! She smiled to herself at the promise of delights to come and dozed again.

In the last, receding darkness of the night she was prodded awake as the cogs of Bywell's car were ground into its lower gear and they turned into the long, rhododendron-lined drive that led to Herons. Ahead, the tall gables and gothic windows of the house made a severe contrast with the lush and richly planted gardens just becoming visible in the first light of dawn. They drove to the steps of the imposing front door; the engine, whose beat had accompanied Philippa's sleepy imaginings all the way from London, ticked down to a silence that seemed to rush across the lawns and caress her tired soul. Then the silence was filled with a dawn chorus of birdsong as new light flooded the sky.

"Oh, how lovely," she remarked, climbing down to the gravel. "D'you hear that, Styfie? What a perfect welcome from the Blackbirds. More than you can say for the servants. There's nobody about at all. We are rather late of course," she added with a smile, "or should I say rather early?"

"The arrangement is that we let ourselves in," explained Bywell curtly. "I know the drill here."

"I should hope you do. If this is one of Lord Whittledean's famous party nights, it looks as if we've missed the fun."

"I think the fun is actually just beginning."

Styford Bywell opened the massive oaken door and crossed the threshold as if it had been his own. Inside, it became apparent that Herons had not been modernised: the darkly panelled hall was hung with dull Victorian paintings and animal trophies.

"Old Whittledean, George's father, did a lot of shooting in India," explained Bywell. "He spent a fortune building this place; for all that, it still has the feeling of a tradesman's mansion. He was a dull old buffer really; you'll find the son much jollier."

"Whenever we meet him," remarked Philippa drily.

She was relieved to find the gloomy aspect of the house dispelled by a welcoming warmth and an unexpected fragrance. Was it the scent of flowers, expensive perfumes of as yet unseen guests, French soaps and cosmetics, or spices of exotic food? She could not be sure. At last a servant entered the hall, introduced himself as Lord Whittledean's butler, and welcomed them. A footman appeared, took their coats, and offered a tray set for coffee.

"Ah yes," Bywell took cups for himself and Philippa, "Whittledean's famous coffee. I remember this stuff, comes from Turkey or somewhere like that. Just what you need to start the day. Cheers."

The coffee was hot and fragrant and Philippa drained her cup thankfully

"Lord Whittledean's party is in the Garden Room," explained the butler before he and the footman left silently.

"Another cup before we go in?" Philippa poured herself more coffee. "That was a long, chilly drive but I'm warming up nicely now. Right." She set down the empty cup, adjusted her dress, and took Bywell's arm as they went through the house towards a rosy glow beginning to light long windows ahead of them. "A party at dawn; just the sort of difference I like, Styfie. You know all the right people. Oh, look," she stopped in surprise as they entered the Garden Room, "they're holding a séance. What fun!"

421

The Garden Room was a confusion of ferns and gigantic fuchsias, some in enormous classically-styled urns, some growing from beds of soil in the tiled floor. A mature vine trailed under the glass roof, laden with darkening grapes. Beneath them, six women and three men sat at a large, round, marble table, lit by candles and by a strengthening pink light from the windows. The men were clad in jewel-coloured dressing-gowns of richly embroidered silk. The women wore simple linen nightgowns, some white, some grey; all had their hair unpinned to fall untidily about their necks.

"They're still in their nighties," Philippa giggled into Bywell's shoulder. She was suddenly very tired, but the extraordinary sight surprised her into laughter. "And what messes they look." It seemed funnier still that none of these people bothered to rise from the table or offer any greeting. "Are they all so absoloutely sloshed they haven't seen us," she whispered, failing to fight down her giggles, "or is it just a particularly dull kind of séance?"

At this, all heads turned to face the newcomers and one of the women stood up. She seemed older than the others, who were all about Philippa's age, and streaks of grey were visible in her ragged hair.

"This is not a séance, you stupid girl," she declared in a loud but cultured voice. It rang oddly in Philippa's ears. Was there a strange echo in this room, or was she beginning to fall asleep standing up? She clung to Bywell's arm and tried to focus on the strange scene. "We are here to commune with Rex Mundi, King of the Earth," continued the woman. She fixed Philippa with a piercing gaze, but, receiving no response, sat down with a dismissive wave to Bywell. "Oh, she's going. Take her to the garden. She will wake to meet her god."

In a pigeon-loft in Wallsend, workmen with rough hands but tender fingers awaited the return of three birds. First home was Princess. Her tired wings were held and her head stroked while a message tube was removed carefully from her leg. The paper was unravelled and at last there was news from *Mauretania*: 'Off St. Abb's Head, making good speed, Southerly run tomorrow, all well."

The next day, the second pigeon Rudolf fluttered in from the East. His message told of a fast run down the coast to Yorkshire, averaging over twenty-six knots. There were smiles in the Boardroom at Swans and cheers throughout the shipyard when this news was read out to the assembled workers. On the fourth day of the trials, the third pigeon Betty flew over many miles of sea and safely home to Wallsend, but her message was not met with smiles. The ship had steamed with its expected speed and safety, but even before her engines were run up to full power, severe vibration was being transmitted from the stern. It could be felt throughout First Class and even as far forward as the bridge.

"It's not the turbines," Jon insisted to his father when they discussed the trial results over another family dinner at Heaton Road, "it's the screws."

Maisie smiled to hear him defending his engines, but it was easy to smile over this talk about the ship. She wondered how easy it would be when they came to the wedding plans.

"Of course it's the screws," William was saying, "four of them thrashing around under the stern. They'll have to be changed to a better design to cope with high speeds, but that won't happen for some time. For the moment, Swans will have to strengthen the after-sections—and they'd better do it before she goes for her acceptance trials. Cunard won't want their precious passengers shaken to pieces over dinner. Anyway, keep First Class well oiled with Champagne and brandy and they won't feel a thing. Now then, when are you two getting married?"

"As soon as we can," Jon answered firmly, "once the decree of divorce is made absolute. Maisie has some strong ideas about the wedding."

"Quite right," said Julia. "Bride's choice."

The bride's choice was revealed over pudding—and the pudding was scarcely touched while the wedding plans were debated. Maisie was secure and confident with her new family as she explained her first idea had been to postpone the wedding until they arrived for a glamorous ceremony in New York, but she had accepted Jon's objections and realised that if they were going to occupy a First Class cabin on *Mauretania* it would be better to travel as man and wife. Relief was visible in Julia's face. The idea of being married on the ship itself had occurred to Maisie but she knew that Cunard captains were discouraged from performing shipboard weddings and this notion was consigned to the world of romantic novels, where William thought it belonged. So Maisie had agreed with Jon that they should marry in England as soon as possible and make *Mauretania's* maiden voyage their honeymoon while Jon took his schemes for the air-engine to America. This was applauded. The plan to be married by Jon's Uncle Simon, who was vicar of a remote and ancient church on the moors in one of the emptiest parts of Northumberland, was met with silence. Maisie wondered if the silence was amused or horrified, then William broke it.

"Thockrington? You couldn't have chosen a more

out-of-the-way place, apart perhaps from Timbuctoo. You'll be thin on guests; a few sheep if they're feeling sociable. It's in the middle of rough country, miles up from Belsay. Nobody will be able to get out there!"

"I know where it is, Father. We went up there with Sir Charles on that day out from Wallington Hall."

"Yes, and it took all day in the ponies-and-traps. It's like something from *Wuthering Heights*."

"As long as it's not like the wedding in *Jane Eyre*," offered Julia, "where someone turns up with unwelcome news."

She received a disapproving look from William.

"That remark is in poor taste, my dear."

"There's a flavour of poor taste in *all* this," continued Julia. "They've chosen somewhere so awkward and peculiar, perhaps they don't want us at their wedding."

Jon looked pleadingly over the table.

"We didn't say that, Mother."

"You didn't have to."

"I loved the idea of that little church when Jon told me about it," explained Maisie quietly. "He didn't tell me about it as somewhere to get married. That was my idea. He was just talking about odd places he knew in the countryside. It's true, we don't want a lot of people." She dropped her eyes to the unfinished meal. "To be honest we don't want anybody. Just us."

"What," bristled Julia, "your own mother not see you

married? That's outrageous."

"It's my father...he doesn't...'

"I don't know about your father, but I'm ready to swear your mother will want to see her beautiful daughter happily married. And," Julia silenced any interruption with a stern look around the table, "if you don't want us—well, I can actually understand you two young romantics wanting to run off over the moors and get married by dithery old Uncle Simon with nothing there but the wind and the curlews. You see I'm a romantic, too. Now I come to think of it," she turned to William with a peculiar smile, "I shouldn't have minded at all if you'd had the idea of marrying *me* in Thockrington Church. I should have felt thoroughly swept off my feet. Anyway," she turned back to Maisie, "I'm not insulted, but your own family might be. I'm sure they are not as unconventional as we are—as we've *had* to be, coping with you two. Don't interrupt, it's a time for plain speaking. I'd speak plainly to your mother again and invite her."

"You might invite your own mother as well," William told Jon sharply.

"They're right, Jon." Maisie was eager to make peace. "We should all go. It was a silly idea of mine just to run away together."

"Haven't you done that already...so to speak...to Tynemouth?" Julia had a wicked twinkle in her eye. "At least this time you'll be running away to get married."

"I will talk to my mother," said Maisie.

"And have you thought of your dress?" added Julia.

"What woman hasn't thought of her wedding dress?"

426

William gave his wife a stern look, then stood up and raised his glass to Maisie. "Bravo! I like this idea now; I really do. Just the five of us, six if you can persuade your father, seven if you count old Simon. When did he last do a wedding service, eh? He'll have to rehearse; he'll be lucky to get through the Lord's Prayer at his age. Better book him for the job before he's booked at his own funeral."

"Really," tutted Julia, "now who's in bad taste?"

"Well," smiled William, "the antics of these two put me in a good mood, a mood to tell the truth and be happy about it. I think this idea is rather wonderful; come on, I know you do, too. Think of it: they marry in that tiny church out there on the moors in the land we all love, then they're off to America on the maiden voyage of the biggest ship in the world. You and I are getting on, my dear, but we're still witnessing great events in great times. Let's be happy about them, and make the most of them, and create wonderful memories for ourselves and stories for the grandchildren nobody else will quite believe. I say cheers to all of us, good health, and love and happiness!"

CHAPTER
TWENTY-FOUR

In a Strange Garden

Slowly, Philippa stirred to a comforting warmth on her face and body. At the same time she began to hear music…no, it was singing…no, it was a bird. She opened her eyes to a dazzle of green and yellow light as bright sunshine dappled down through a canopy of leaves. She was lying on her back under great trees, without the strength or will to move, still tired in a way she had never known before yet suddenly wide awake. She felt dry grass with the palms of her hands, felt the weight of her body pressing into the grass, a rustle of leaves under her hair when she moved her head. She saw she was in a garden, bathed in Autumn sunlight, still as warm as Summer but tinted with gold amid the lingering green. Her muscles felt liquid, useless. She could hardly lift her hand. She was trying to remember how and why she was lying on her back, unable to move in a strange garden, when a shadow flickered across her face and she started up in alarm—only to find her head still swimming with this curious tiredness and her arms scarcely able to support her weight.

"It's all right," said a voice: young, female, eager, right behind her. She made an effort to sit up, then sank on to an elbow. "You've woken up." The voice became a face, swivelling round to smile at her. "Hello." It was a girl with bright dark eyes in a sharp young face. She was wearing what must once have been a linen nightgown, now with the sleeves cut out and the hem cut short to form a ragged tunic. Her brown hair had been cropped off roughly like a boy's. The whole effect was startling, unexpected and disturbing. Philippa struggled to come to fuller consciousness and make sense of it. "It's all right," continued the girl, kneeling beside Philippa with sunlight on thin, bare arms, "really it is. I'm Kitty. I'll be your friend."

Philippa was awake now—still strangely drunk, she thought—but able to sit up.

"What in Heaven's name…?"

"Oh, that sounds funny!" The girl laughed with very white teeth in a face that might have been suntanned or dirty or both. "Don't you know there's no such thing as Heaven? There's only the Earth and the pleasures of it. That's why we are here, in this lovely garden."

Philippa sank back on to her elbows.

"I feel terrible. I have to get up and leave—but I can hardly move. I need a drink."

"You need more Honeydew."

"What?"

"Honeydew. It's the special wine Lord Whittledean gives us. It doesn't make you drunk like other wine, it makes you sleepy then wide awake, then completely happy, then sleepy again, then you wake up very slowly and you see things more clearly and understand everything, and the whole world looks better. You see more colours and hear more music and everything is better than it's ever been before." She looked down at Philippa with a broad, childish grin. "You must have had too much all at once last night. You're still very sleepy."

"I only had that damned coffee." Philippa rolled in annoyance and frustration, still unable to stand up.

"Oh, the coffee," Kitty smiled again. "I don't think that's Honeydew. They put something else in the coffee when you arrive."

"It's a drug, you little fool! It's knocked me flat, and look what it's made of you: dressed in rags and talking pretentious nonsense. I'll drag Styfie through the courts for this; he's had me kidnapped...as far as I can see by opium-takers and lunatics!"

"Don't be angry," Kitty said gently. "Honeydew and other things like that are gifts of Nature, for us all to enjoy. Lord Whittledean has them brought from France, but I think they really come from Arabia. Oh look," she pulled suddenly at Philippa's stole, "you've still got your old clothes on."

"Get away from me! Oh my bag, my jewellery! I've been robbed! Even my rings!"

"It's all right," crooned the girl, "they'll be in the house somewhere. You don't need them out here; you don't need them anywhere, really. Jewellery just spoils your body, and you won't want your old clothes after a while. They'll get all damp and dirty and come to pieces, and they're hiding the beautiful person you are. You should throw them away. Look, there's a tear in your dress already and a hole in that stocking. I burned my clothes. We had a big bonfire in the garden and we danced with the light of the flames on our skin. It was lovely. Now I only have this," she indicated her ragged gown, "and I only wear this sometimes. I like to be naked. When the moon comes up I'll be naked in the garden, bathed in moonlight, and my lover will come to me." She plucked at the torn hem of Philippa's dress and let it drop to the grass, rattling on in her childish voice, gushing and enthusiastic, both compelling and infuriating to Philippa. "I could help you out of that dress and pull off your stockings. Once you've thrown them away, you'll never want to wear clothes again. Just think, I used to live in a London street, now I live in a beautiful garden with lords and ladies. Of course I do go into the house sometimes," she explained to Philippa's stare, "when it's very cold. I sometimes sleep inside, but I like to sleep on the ivy under the trees if it's warm enough. I'm always warm when I drink the Honeydew. I used to sleep under gloomy blankets; I used to wear clothes—worse than yours. How did I ever bear to have ugly stockings on my legs and wear a corset? A corset! I did. But now I can have the sunshine on my skin and the grass under my toes. Now I'm as free as a fairy. One of my lovers calls me his fairy—says I look like one."

"It's your wild hair, I suppose, what there is of it." For a moment Philippa stroked the small head, then recoiled.

"It's all right, you can touch me. We all touch one another." Kitty's little hand was at Philippa's neck. "Your hair is still pinned up—in places. Most of it's coming down. No woman should have pins in her hair. I'll help you take them out."

"Leave me alone, you stupid girl!"

The hand was withdrawn, apparently without offence. It seemed Philippa could say anything to this young woman and it wouldn't hurt her. All her words had a faraway wistfulness.

"After I'd been here for a while I cut my hair off. It's easier without long hair when you're living in a garden. I could cut yours off for you if you like."

"No! I told you, leave me alone." Fear soaked into

431

Philippa as she felt her limbs still heavy and useless. She had been drugged and flung under the trees; she would be stripped and shorn by this mad girl and her companions; she would be taken back into the house and raped; she would never escape the vicious captivity of Whittledean, Bywell, and his corrupt associates. She told herself what a fool she had been to go with Bywell, willingly, into this place of evil. At the same time, to make sense of it all, she realised she would have to play along with this unfathomable creature: some silly girl from London who imagined herself as a wood-sprite and seemed to have lost her reason in living out the fantasy. To extricate herself safely from this sinister garden, Philippa would need to know more.

"How long *have* you been here, Kitty?"

"All Summer."

"Really? And how old are you?"

"I'm nineteen."

"You're nicely-spoken, you seem well-educated…"

"So do you."

"…so what are you doing here? How can you allow yourself to believe such wicked nonsense?"

"How can you live in a world that *thinks* it's wicked nonsense? Don't you want to leave that world and have this instead? If I were you I wouldn't be angry with your friend. He's brought you to Paradise."

"It's not Paradise," shouted Philippa—then found the effort gave her a new headache and she fell back again in to her elbows, "it's slavery! You are the slave of some terrible drug and some wicked men. You're living in rags in the mud of this garden and your own filth."

"The rain washes me. I like that. Look," Kitty stroked her brown arms and legs down to the muddied soles of her feet, "my legs are earthy brown, and I suppose my back is too, where I lie on the Earth. My lover last night said I was quite deliciously dirty!" Kitty looked down with a teasing smile. "Are you afraid of men touching you?"

"Of course not." Philippa gave the girl as hard a look as her stupified face could manage. "Young woman, I am not exactly what you would call a shrinking violet in these matters—but I don't propose to prove it to you by running through a catalogue of my men."

"You don't have to have men lovers here. You could have a woman lover. My friend Julia is one. Sometimes it's nice: she strokes my skin differently from a man."

Disgusted as she felt, Philippa realised objections would be no help. She tried reason. "So, your lovers—both men and women—come to you in this garden. That is what happens to you wretches here, every night?"

"Yes, and sometimes in the afternoons, like today, when it's still and warm and lovely. But you mustn't think we are wretched, and you mustn't think there are only women here for the pleasure of men. Oh no, there are men here for the pleasure of women. You may go into the house and choose one, when you feel well enough. Don't look like that. It's lovely."

"Lovely might be your favourite word, you silly child, but none of this really is lovely, you know. It's dreadful. Are you not free to go?"

433

"I don't want to go."

"Are you not concerned about becoming pregnant," Philippa stared harshly into the impassive, elfin face, "having babies?"

"Oh no, we don't have babies here. There is a doctor who can stop them growing before they are born and he takes them away. It does't hurt—then we can have our lovers again."

"Good God, is that what becomes of you?"

"Don't say god. There isn't a god, not your god anyway. There is a great natural power that runs through everything. We feel it, we know it, we are part of it."

"Well," stated Philippa as firmly as she could, "I do not wish to be part of it. I wish to leave, and I shall," she struggled into a sitting position against the tree, "when I can."

"Don't go." Kitty sprang up. "You're special. I'll find you another drink of Honeydew."

She scampered away on her soil-stained feet, waving her arms childishly in the sunlight. Philippa saw shreds of the charming and the beautiful in the sight, but they were overcome by disgust and fear and her increasing remorse. This was all her own fault. How foolish she had been, through her own wilfulness and lust for sensation, to allow herself to be seduced by Styford Bywell and to sink to this degradation. She forced herself to admit that her folly went further back, right back to her behaviour in her marriage to Jon. How foolish she had been to abandon his goodness. Yes he had been weak, but he had loved her. She should have forgiven his new love for Maisie, or at least tried to understand it better. Damn this drug she had been given! She could still hardly move, but told herself she must. She must go back into the house, retrieve her bag and coat if not her jewels, and escape. Suddenly, she heard music. It was coming from the distant terrace of the house. Someone was singing *Where ere You Walk*: Handel's fine melody, a light tenor voice, piano accompaniment. Its unexpected, extraordinary beauty made her feel worse. She remembered the lost happiness of simple things: her honeymoon, making jokes with Jon about the other people in the hotel, riding in his father's motor-car to her new home in sunny Newcastle, her warm studio at the Jesmond house, the silly fun of playing golf, the fresh wind in her face on the Northumberland coast; things she spoiled and spurned to follow her own path—to this. She looked at her torn dress, felt her hair coming down around her tear-streaked face, and wept at the order and beauty of Handel which could no longer be hers. It was all her own fault. She had not been captured and forced into this slavery; she had associated herself with these people, come here of her own free will. And now she had no free will. She compared her shabby work of seduction on a dozen men to the nobility of Jon's work on his ship and the purity of her own work in the attic studio and the beauty of faithful love. She had thrown it all away, to have it sung back to her in her degradation.

"May I help you?" A man in stylish day clothes was standing over her, tall against the dappled sunlight.

"Yes, yes, for God's sake help me out of here!" She would not care who he was, whether she could trust him or not; she would pour out everything to him, say anything if it was a chance to be taken from this ghastly place into freedom and safety. She wiped her face. "I've been drugged with something, something in coffee or wine, I can't move properly. They're going to take my clothes and cut my hair off. I've already been robbed. I don't want to stay here a moment longer. Please, please help me!"

"If you really wish me to," The man was infuriatingly calm and infuriatingly slow to act, "and if you really are not one of the party girls."

"For God's sake!" Her tears dried to fury. "I am not one of the stupid party girls. I should never have come here!"

"Indeed not. You're not a particular friend of Lord Whittledean, then? It is he who is singing, by the way. Good voice. Talents are not always given to those who would use them best."

"I haven't even met Whittledean," Philippa ran on, wishing only that this man would do something more useful than stand still and question her. "I was deceived. I was brought here…by a friend, a wicked friend. I had no idea I was coming to such a place. I'm a commercial artist. I have a studio in Chelsea. I'd give anything to be back there. I am a married woman but my rings have been stolen—also a rather valuable necklace and my bag."

"Very well." The man snapped into sudden action, bending down to look at Philippa directly. She saw a youthful, athletic figure and a mature face. He was fair-haired and clean-shaven, handsome, but with rather cold blue eyes and a stern expression of disapproval. The eyes had a hardness similar to something she had known in Styford Bywell's penetrating gaze, but she didn't care. At last this man was being businesslike, flooding her with relief and hope. "Have you a coat, any money?"

"Well, yes, I had, but I told you. I've been robbed."

"Your belongings will be somewhere in the house. I shall find them and return them to you eventually. You must not go back in there. Take this money and walk across the garden that way, though the wood, and down the lane to the station."

"What, in these shoes? And I can scarcely stand up."

In an instant he had lifted her to her feet with a defiant expression.

"Yes you can. You'll be a little shaky for a moment or two but you'll manage. The effects should wear off quite soon."

"My God," Philippa brushed her clothes with her hands and attempted to restore the pins in her hair, "was it opium?"

"I don't think so. Another narcotic…and probably a muscle-relaxant."

"How do you know? Are you a doctor?"

"No." He looked around, saw no-one, and helped Philippa step forward. The singing had stopped. The garden was silent. "I'll explain later."

"You'll explain now. I shan't be deceived twice."

"Ah, choosing your male companions more carefully from now on, eh?" There was a hint of humour in the blue eyes. "But your taste is improving already. You made a lucky choice in calling out to me."

"I'm sorry," said Philippa, "I should be thankful. I am thankful. You have every right to despise me."

"I don't despise you. I imagine you despise yourself, but there's no time for that now."

"You're really not one of…one of…these people?"

"Most certainly not."

"Then what are you doing here?"

"I'll explain later. You must trust me. My name is Oliver Gaine. I am an Officer in the Grenadier Guards."

"A soldier!" Philippa felt she was regaining her senses and her balance. "How dashing…but clean-shaven in an age of military moustaches?" She gave him a questioning look.

"You've had a shock, but I see your ability to question things has returned. You should develop it further—later."

"But you can't expect me to go walking about the countryside in a ragged dress and stockings without a hat or coat and looking like a scarecrow. I shall attract unwelcome attention. These are evening clothes, Mister Gaine, or they were. A Guards Officer would have known that. He would also not allow a lady to walk through woods unescorted."

"You're lucky you are able to walk and that you have any clothes at all. And it's Major Gaine. Now stop doubting my credentials and do as I say. It's not far beyond the garden and the through the wood, that way. The station is called Herons Halt. Whittledean had it built for his own use. Speak to no-one. Take whatever train that comes and change when you can for London. I cannot accompany you; I have to go the other way, to Netley."

"The military hospital? You *are* a doctor."

"No, but I must report there." He produced a card from his pocket in a manner to silence objections and command obedience. "Contact me by telegram at this address tomorrow. We will meet for dinner in London."

"Thank you." Philippa's manner softened. "Thank you a thousand times. Dinner in London will be wonderfully civilised after these horrors. You've helped me escape."

Her rescuer continued in brusque mode.

"You'll only manage it if you do exactly as I say. You must promise you will speak of this to no-one until we have met again."

"I promise."

"In particular, you must not take any complaint to the Police."

"Why not? These men should be arrested."

"Indeed, and they will be, but if you or anyone goes to the Police now they will clump their noisy way in here and make inappropriate arrests. Evidence will be destroyed, ranks will close, and the same evil will spring up somewhere else. Now I really can't say more. Please go."

"I shall. Thank you."

"Can you walk safely?"

"Yes." She began to step unsteadily through the leaves. "My head is clearing and my legs are stronger."

"Good. Remember, you may be in great danger—mortal danger—if you make this public or have any further dealings with these people. They already murder unborn children."

Philippa stopped and turned.

"You know about that?"

"Yes."

"I discovered that, too. It's truly appalling. Can you help the other women here?"

"I shall try, but you must go now."

"Goodbye then—and thank you."

* * *

"Are they Pagans?" Philippa asked Oliver Gaine across their table at the Café Royal.

"Of a sort. I could give you the official lecture on their beliefs but it would take all day and we'd both get lost in it. Let's just say they worship Rex Mundi, a deity akin to Pan, the Green Man and gods of the Earth. He inhabits woods and gardens and all natural things. He represents the forces of Nature; also human instinct unbridled by law, convention or other rules of behaviour. He is an anti-Christ in that he is earthly not Heavenly, bodily not spiritual, so some people equate him with the Devil—but he's not the Devil of the Bible or the Church. He is not necessarily a force of evil."

"But these people are evil."

"Oh yes."

"Yet you seem to approve of their mad religion."

"Not entirely, but I hope I understand it. The beliefs themselves are innocent enough, or should be. Whittledean and his crowd abuse them for their own gain and pleasure.

440

That's the evil. My own opinion—which I should probably not parade before my colleagues and superior officers but which I somehow feel able to share with you—is that there's nothing wrong with worshipping something called Rex Mundi if it represents all that is good in the natural world. The original concept is probably laudable; we've spent most of the last century getting away from Nature, perhaps there's a need to get back to it—but, as you have discovered, these people have corrupted the ideal. They use it first as an excuse for lascivious, licentious behaviour, and ultimately to condone appalling crimes against these women and against society as a whole. I suspect that true Pagans—who I'm sure exist, though I've never met any—would despise and denounce them. Certainly no decent person should have anything to do with them."

"Quite."

"Are you really all right?" Oliver spoke with sudden tenderness. "Did you sleep properly last night?"

"Yes, thank you," answered Philippa. "I was decidedly wobbly on that walk to the little station, but once I came home I recovered well. The effects of the drug, whatever it was, wore off pretty quickly, as you said. A hot bath and a change of clothes and some restorative hairdressing work wonders for a girl. However, I can't say I wasn't shaken by the whole business. I think it's had a profound effect upon me. I feel as if I've seen into a dark pit."

"In a sense, you have. It remains for you to decide what to do about it."

Philippa was determined to lighten the mood.

"I intend to enjoy today, first of all," she smiled. "You have been enormously kind and helpful."

She sipped her Mosel. She was relaxing into the company of her fascinating and extraordinary saviour. Perhaps, alongside his dashing dress and manner, Oliver Gaine could be annoyingly pedantic in explaining things, perhaps even a little pompous, but this could not prevent Philippa from smiling at him over her wineglass. He was, after all, the almost unbelievably handsome, upright and honourable man who had found her, rescued her, and restored her to one of the experiences she most enjoyed: a sophisticated and expensive dinner in London. It had begun with sole, each delicate fish smothered in a creamy sauce. Then had come roast pheasant—which Philppa amusingly hoped had not been shot on Whittledean's estate. Oliver had replied that he would take the risk, but that roast heron would be out of the question. Perhaps this was more contrived than it was funny, but she laughed merrily at it. Only the day before she had feared never to be merry again. And now came the pudding, delicately crowned with pretty waves of sugar, and an even sweeter wine to go with it, and brandy to follow if she wanted it, and she did. She was bathed in a glow of contentment and a belief that all could be right with her and with the world. She felt she could relax, perhaps in ways she had not found for years. There seemed no need to say clever things, no need to pretend to be anyone other than herself. She had even stopped flirting with him—overtly, anyway. She would really never stop flirting with an attractive man, or any man who bought her dinner, and this made her smile happily to herself. She was content: not a state she inhabited too often, she told herself with a rather sadder smile, but it was lovely. She could even admit and say things she would have found unthinkable before her rescue.

"That girl Kitty. I was actually frightened of her, when I got over my surprise at seeing such a creature, but now I feel acutely sorry for her. She had been completely deceived. Really, she was quite sweet and innocent."

"Sweet perhaps," replied Oliver, "but I doubt her innocence. She would have known what she was doing. The drugs do not completely rob the taker of reason. They remove the bonds of conventional behaviour. She would think what she was doing was fun or clever or exciting. In later life she will regret it of course—and the narcotics are addictive. As I told you, it's not opium, it's mostly hashish, the stuff of lotos-eating, but they use other far more sinister drugs. There's something derived from poisons used by Indians of the Amazon forest. I suspect you had been given a little, which made you unable to walk. Too much can be deadly. Whatever the poor girl takes, she will find it very difficult to stop. She is to be pitied, not censured."

"I do pity her. I'm sad that something so evil should come out of something so beautiful: Nature, the human body, our natural desires. All beautiful things, corrupted. The sense of waste, the dreadful abortions. Could she and the others be rescued?"

"Perhaps." Oliver took a drink. "I can make no promises, only that the men behind all this will eventually be brought to justice: for rape, false imprisonment, all kinds of offences. Bywell and the others who procure the girls for Whittledean's 'parties' will certainly go to prison. It will be more difficult to convict Whittledean himself. There will be a tremendous scandal and tremendous resistance from the highest places, but eventually, he and his kind will go down."

"So," Philippa sank back in her chair with her glass of wine, "enough of them. You promised to explain about yourself over dinner. It has been a splendid dinner, thank you, but the explanation has yet to appear."

Oliver put on a matter-of-fact voice.

"I am a soldier attached to a special department of

443

His Majesty's Government. That's all I can say."

"A secret agent!" Philippa grinned broadly. "Well, I never expected to meet one."

Oliver tutted.

"An agent in that I have been lent from the military to the civil service, secret in that most people, including yourself, shouldn't know…but really you must get any romantic ideas from fiction or the newspapers out of your head—and certainly out of your speech," he added with a fierce look. "Put it this way: I'm doing detective work the Police can't manage. I am deemed able to mix with certain suspects. I truly wish I didn't have to, but I must do my duty."

"You have done it splendidly, Major Gaine," declaimed Philippa, raising her brandy, "and I shall keep your secrets. I shall relish my moments with the honourable Officer who puts King and Country before his own pleasures, and I'll toast him." She drained her glass. "You know," she went on with a widening smile, "I don't think I've ever had a more peculiar conversation. One moment I'm talking to a half-naked girl who may be mad or bad or both; the next I'm being given orders by a government spy."

"Your words, not mine."

"Well, you are, aren't you?"

Oliver Gaine remained impassive.

"You cannot possibly draw me on this. Just be thankful I came along and was there to do my duty. I must insist you leave it at that."

"Yes, I suppose I must," she said with a sigh, "and

leave you…to do your duty."

"It's been a very pleasant duty, I can assure you."

"And apart from that," Philippa went on a little wearily, "I must thank you again for retrieving my jewellery, my wedding ring especially. It must have been difficult for you, even dangerous, searching for it in that house and bringing it all out. A wedding ring can be useful to a woman in this world, even if a husband isn't."

"You are estranged from him?"

"Divorced—just now, in fact, but we have been apart for some time." Now it seemed easy for Philippa to talk about Jon, to explain herself to this beautiful but ultimately cold man in the light of the understanding they shared and the decisions she had made. "I met him at a critical part of my life. The love and the marriage he offered were the answers to many problems, or appeared to be. We tried to be happy. I gave myself to him as best I could…but the truth is, I am not a very 'giving' person. Then I was infuriated when I discovered he had betrayed me with another woman. But the fault was mine really, not his. I shouldn't have let him marry me. I shouldn't have married anybody. I know there are benefits in marriage but I need the single life now. I have had a number of lovers, but I shouldn't have associated myself with men like Styford Bywell. Unfortunately, men like Styford Bywell are devilishly attractive."

"Devilish is the word."

He was dry, cool, unpeturbed by her confessions.

"Very witty, yes. So it's the single life for me."

"Not thinking of becoming a nun, are you?"

His wry smile deserved an even answer.

"Now be realistic, Major Gaine. No Mother Superior worth her veil would have me in her convent."

"Good." He brightened and gave her a smile. "That means you will be able to carry on your quest for innocence in the real world, in everyday life."

"Do I have a quest for innocence?"

"I believe you have found one—after what you have experienced. It has actually been good for you. Decency, purity, innocence. Those are the things you really want to find again."

"Yes, but I might not deserve them."

"But you'll go looking for them."

"Yes, you're quite right, very perceptive."

She felt secure. The warm plush of the Café Royal had her in its spell: the silent waiters, the delicious food, the atmosphere of seclusion and expense. If she was not yet entirely happy, she knew she could be. She would not step beyond this sudden contentment.

"So," he said quietly, "you will not be taking me into your bed."

"Nor shall I be going into yours," replied Philippa evenly, "despite your being one of the best and most attractive men I have ever met. Perhaps because of that." She read no hurt in his eyes. They were equals in this. Again, she felt secure. "I want to do something good for a change," she continued. "I want to reclaim a decent life. Perhaps I haven't deserved one, but I do want a decent life, decent on my terms. You have no idea how unlikely that sounds, coming from me, but I mean it." She relaxed again over her wine and watched him watching her. "What extraordinary things we say to each other, and how easy it is to say them. Quite extraordinary."

"*You* are extraordinary," said Oliver, raising his glass to her.

"You also. But we must not become lovers. I mean to do something good one day."

"Something good, eh?" There was that hint of teasing she had known in his voice before. "Am I not good?"

"Far too good. That is why my behaviour must change. You are a remarkable man. You've made me want to do something better with my life and perhaps some   good of my own in the world."

Oliver looked into his brandy, then up at Philippa.

"Then you should go away for a while. Not simply to remove yourself from temptation, but for your own safety."

"Away?"

"Yes—beyond the reach of Whittledean and his associates. You have escaped their clutches with information about what they do. You are at large. As I said when you were leaving Herons, you may be in great danger."

"You can't really think Styfie and his friends would hunt me down. They just want to get on with their orgies, don't they?"

"They do, yes, but you have information that could

447

stop them. They will realise you left with my assistance and that we must betray them to the authorities."

"So you are in danger, too."

"It's a soldier's life. But I have the protection of the Army and I'll be posted elsewhere. If you stay in London you will be at severe risk. They would want to eliminate you."

"Eliminate? You mean murder? You can't be serious."

"I fear I have to be; so must you. We have already acknowledged that they murder unborn children. They will want to silence you. The women who succumb or collude with them are no threat—but you left Herons very much without their permission and were assisted by a man they now know had been set to watch them." He gave her a harsh look. "You don't honestly see yourself as a campaigner against these people, do you?"

"I could try."

"It's too early to bring effective prosecutions—even if you gave evidence, which you certainly must not do. Try good works in another direction, in your own life, if that is what you intend. Have nothing more to do with Bywell, any of his friends, or anything that happens at Herons."

"Isn't that the coward's way out?"

"It's the sensible way out. You have already seen how dangerous these men can be. While you *are* here," he continued his instructions, "accept no invitations from anyone you don't trust absolutely. Try not to answer your door to strangers. A stabbed injection of that Amazon drug would be lethal."

"My God, yes, when I think about it, I see what you mean. Go away...I suppose I shall have to. Well, I could go to Paris. I have work there."

"Paris is no good." Oliver Gaine resumed his cold reasoning, issuing orders. "We know Whittledean has many contacts in France. You must go further afield, perhaps to America. There will surely be openings for a commercial artist in New York, Chicago, or San Francisco. Think of it as a great opportunity, beginning with an exciting voyage on a big ship."

A dreaminess entered Philippa's eyes. Despite all their extraordinary talk of evil and danger and their own relationship, she still felt relaxed and happy, safe and secure; but, thrusting through her contentment, came a stream of memories and associations to provoke an oddly powerful excitement, and she knew what she was going to do.

"I have known a big ship," she said slowly. "She became part of my life. I imagined her before she was built, imagined her rather nicely for a painting that has done rather well—but that's another story, at least one I shan't burden you with. I believe the real ship has turned out rather well, too." She shook hands with Oliver Gaine in an appreciative farewell, and allowed him to kiss her hand. "I'll just be in time for her maiden voyage."

CHAPTER
TWENTY-FIVE
Acceptance

Once again, thousands of people crowded the banks of the Tyne to watch *Mauretania* make her final departure from the river of her birth. She was bound for her new home port of Liverpool, then for her acceptance trials in the Irish Sea. There was a sense of pride and a sense of loss. There would be other ships and other work along the Tyne, but perhaps never a ship so great as this nor work so glorious. The gigantic liner, now painted and dressed to perfection, was escorted to the sea by the busiest flotilla of tugs and sightseer's boats in living memory. They wreathed her in steam and smoke and hooted and cheered her on this proud but poignant progress to her new life. When she slid away between the piers and gave her long, magnificent, soul-stirring, final blast, the river—and many lives—seemed empty.

Jon and Maisie waved her away from their spectacular vantage point on the North Pier. It had only been a short walk from their house in Tynemouth, but every step through the crowds and every moment waiting in the chilly Autumn afternoon had seemed laden with significance. The ship that had brought them together was completed and leaving the Tyne—but she was not leaving their lives. With excitement scarcely contained by their clasping hands and beating hearts, they imagined themselves aboard on their honeymoon to America.

Matthew Watson—with his wife, his other daughter and his son—squeezed between the hats and coats of onlookers gathered on the scrap of dirty beach just downstream from North Shields Fish Quay. Little George, now a boistrous schoolboy considerably bigger than when his father left him for that first day's toil on the ship, was excited to be lifted up to see the great liner slide past. Matthew felt unable to share the boy's innocent happiness. The ship had brought him work but cost him a daughter, strained his relations with his wife, and left him a family marked by scandal and shame. Perhaps life would be better with the ship gone, but how could he accept Maisie's insistence on marriage with the engineer—a man from another class, from another life—with anything but bitterness? As *Mauretania* hooted and the crowds cheered, he wanted to accept the marriage, but admitted to himself it was just beyond him. The man was divorced at last, Maisie was of age, her mother was more than happy now and busy with plans for the wedding, and thirteen-year-old Ellen had become consumed by enthusiasm for being a bridesmaid. It was all she could talk about. The prospect of walking down the aisle with her big sister was obviously more exciting to the girl than standing on a cold beach watching a ship. This outing was supposed to be a treat, but she was giving her father sullen looks. Had he been doomed, thought Matthew, to breed wayward daughters? Perhaps all fathers felt the same; perhaps it was his own fault; perhaps no-one was to blame; perhaps he should simply let it all happen and give up the struggle for obedience and decency. The rest of the world seemed to have done just that. In a way, it would be relaxing to accept the marriage and have his girls smile at him once again—but it still didn't seem right.

"He won't give me away you know," Maisie reminded Jon on their walk through thinning crowds back to Percy Street, "he's said so again."

"You father's way of making a point, eh?"

"That's all right, though. I don't think I want to be 'given away'. I'll give myself to you on our wedding day—already have."

"The greatest gift I have ever received," Jon told her, taking her arm.

"I don't think he'll even come to the wedding," she added sadly.

"That's wrong. Perhaps I should speak to him again."

"No. Don't go stirring it up."

"What does your mother think about that?"

"Mam's mad about it, but she's keeping it to herself She just wants to keep the peace."

"Perhaps your father will accept us properly one day," said Jon, walking on uncomfortably, "when he sees how right we are for each other and how happy you are. Surely he wants you to be happy."

"He wants me to be decent, he wants me to be respectable."

"You're going to be. A woman in a happy marriage *is* those things."

"Aye well, he still thinks it's disgraceful I went to live with you before we were married. I had red paint slapped over me. He hasn't said so, but I know he thinks I deserved it."

"That's monstrous," said Jon with rising anger. "He should understand that falling in love is not immoral if it's mutual and leads to marriage. The modern world is changing, it's all different."

"You'll never get that one into his head," Maisie chuckled. "You'd have more luck explaining your air-engine to schoolkids," she giggled.

Jon stopped their walk.

"You can't be happy about this. You can't think it's funny."

"It isn't funny and I'm not happy—but I do accept it, because I have to. You have to and all. Look," she started their homeward walk again, "we'll have a grand wedding out there in that lonely country place you've told me about, with only those people who really want to be there. If you want to be modern, that's a modern way: just us and anyone from the families who wants to be there, and we won't hold it against anyone who doesn't. That's the modern way, Jon, not forcing someone to do things they can't do."

"I love your idea of our wedding for just us," Jon smiled at Maisie's bright face under her hat and felt a great glow of love for her. "I couldn't think of anything more romantic…but surely your mother has to be there."

"Oh yes, she will be."

"And your sister Ellen—doesn't she want to be your Bridesmaid?"

"You bet she does," smiled Maisie, hugging Jon's arm again. "She's going daft with excitement. She wanted to try my dress on the other night but Mam wouldn't allow it; said it would be bad luck."

"What's your dress like, by the way? My mother's keen to know about it and so am I."

"You won't get me telling you that," said Maisie laughingly, poking Jon in the ribs with a finger. "Now that *would* be bad luck."

"Well, how about your little brother George as Page Boy?"

"Oh no, you'd never get him into that sort of outfit. He thinks it's silly. You can see him trying to keep out of the way. You can tell he doesn't fancy a whole day with the girls."

"He'll fancy days with girls soon enough," answered Jon. "Anyway, I'm sure he'll like the ride in the motor-car. It will truly be a great day for us all," he added more seriously. "I just wish your father would accept our marriage properly."

"Could you accept it if a man took me away into a world you could never reach?"

"Of course not."

"Well, it's the same for him."

"But it's not a world he can't reach. We're all in the same world. You and I have crossed the old barriers. We've torn them down. I know your father is a good man and I accept him as my father-in-law. Why doesn't he accept me?"

"Because he just can't."

* * *

"Tell me, Dear," Julia Ferris gave her husband a searching look, "since it has fallen to us to organise this wedding instead of Maisie's father doing his duty…"

"We can't push for that," said William curtly. "You know he's decided not to be involved."

"Which makes it terribly awkward, don't you think? However," she continued, resigned but still anxious, "how do you propose to get everyone out to Thockrington Church?" She threw up her hands into the stained-glass sunlight of the big house in Heaton Road. "It'll be like a like an expedition to the North Pole!"

"We will hire two motor-cars with chauffeurs," explained William. "Maisie's family will go in one; you and I will go with Jon in the other. Maisie can have pride of place in our own car with Hoggett driving. He'll collect her from Wallsend. She and Jon have agreed she should spend the night before her wedding in her parents' house. Jon will be here with us."

"Well, there's a nod towards tradition and respectability I suppose." Julia straightened flowers in a vase. "Everything else is wildly outrageous. Can you imagine the awkwardness in that house with her father there?"

"Yes, unfortunately I can. But Jon assures me she wants to be with her mother and sister on the night before, getting the dress and other things ready I suppose. You know what women are like about weddings."

"Yes, William, I do." Julia took a flower and made a buttonhole for her husband. "I went through one with you and I was happy to start our married life on solid ground, not with half-baked plans for a motoring expedition around Northumberland, having already broken moral codes and outraged Society."

"Wouldn't you have liked to have outraged Society, told it what you thought of it, just for once?"

"Not on my wedding day…oh, I know you're making fun of me."

They smiled and held hands in the big bay window, watching motor-cars pass their brick-walled garden on Heaton Road.

"Only a little. I know you want our boy to be happy."

"He's given us some heartache down the years."

"And much joy," put in William, determined to cheer his wife. "He's had his lazy moments, he's made his mistakes, but he's a first-rate engineer and a fine son. I'm proud of him. You should be proud of him, too. I'm especially proud of his behaviour with this girl. He's done the right thing, or tried to, and she's very good for him. She'll make a wonderful wife."

"Better than the first one, I hope."

"I don't think that would be difficult. Come on, my dear, you know you never particularly liked Philippa; nor did I, if I tell the truth. I now doubt that Jon actually liked her. He was bowled over by her vivacity or whatever you want to call it. But this girl is good and honest, completely honest. That's what can be unsettling about her, but it's also what is beautiful about her."

"Yes, I see that beauty in her. And I know she's made big efforts to fit in with us and a new way of life; it can't have been easy for her. It's been rather tiring for all of us." Julia rested her head against William's shoulder. "She's a brave girl in all kinds of ways, isn't she? That must be part of what Jon loves in her. I hope she makes a lovely bride. She'll have a long, windy drive up to Thockrington."

"Yes, we'll all be leaving at the crack of dawn. The cars from Wallsend will have to leave first: they have an extra ten miles to do. No doubt Hoggett will go flat out on the Military Road while he can; it's mostly farm tracks once they turn North from there."

"The poor girl will be blown to pieces with her veil all over the place. Wouldn't she like to be with her mother and sister and little brother in *their* car?"

"Apparently not. She seemed especially delighted at the idea of going up alone with Hoggett driving. She likes motoring."

"It's a good job she does. Three motor-cars involved, going all that way into that wild part of the country. It sounds terribly difficult and expensive."

"It's what they want. We can do it for them, and we should. Old Simon is looking forward to officiating." William chuckled at the thought of his elderly clergyman brother and his wife Constance making fussy preparations for a family wedding that would seem almost exotic in their remote parish. "It will be quite an event for him. You can imagine him chasing mice out of the vestry and ironing his surplice."

"Yes, he is rather sweet—but," anxious tones returned to Julia's voice, "then there's this business of the Wedding Breakfast…"

"It'll be more like tea-time before we get round to that," William stated quickly.

"Indeed, with all that travelling to do, and then coming home in the dark; oh, I don't know, never mind; but

I'm concerned about Simon's offer to hold the Reception in that little Vicarage at Bavington. Is that really suitable? I was only there once with you and it struck me as nothing more than a farmhouse kitchen. Rather small, wouldn't you say?"

"I'd say it's a rather small wedding. Think who will be there."

"I'm still thinking of who will *not* be there."

"We've been through all that. We must accept it's going to be a very small affair, and very different from Jon's first wedding. And I don't think that's a bad thing."

"Perhaps—but then there's the food. Do Simon and Constance have a maid? Can Constance cook? Shouldn't we send Betty ahead to make sure at least we all get a decent meal?"

"You know we can't do that; they'd be terribly insulted. Constance is a vicar's wife; vicar's wives are famously capable, especially in country places. I'm sure she's looking forward to it as much as old Simon; it should be rather exciting for them. No, no, we can't send Betty. Apart from anything else, we'll need her here for when we come home at night."

Julia wrung her hands.

"It's all so, so…utterly unconventional!"

"It is—and what else would you expect from our boy? I prefer to call it spontaneous. That's the most difficult thing to be in this life, and these two have managed it. You're worried because you're his mother and I love you for that; he does too, but you must realise he's happy with Maisie; you've seen them together, you can tell."

"Yes," sighed Julia, "there's no doubt of that. They twinkle at each other like stars."

"That's a good way of putting it. I'd tell them that, if I were you."

* * *

Mauretania steamed around the North of Scotland through calm seas; delegations from Swan Hunter and Cunard enjoying the great ship's first cruise, luxuriating in her vast spaces and pleased by her brisk turn-of-speed. A few days later, Jon called at the house in Heaton Road, waving a telegram.

"This should interest you, Father. She's done over twenty-six knots on the Skelmorlie, and the crash turns were better than expected."

"I wish you two would speak English." Julia bustled into the room. "You have a language of your own. What on Earth is the Skelmorlie?"

"The Skelmorlie Mile, Mother, off the Ayrshire coast. The big ships are tested over the measured mile there. *Mauretania* has put all the others to shame."

"As we knew she would," smiled William. He turned to Jon. "Your engines work nicely, then?"

"Nicely isn't the word. Spectacularly, I'd say. She made two runs up and down the Irish Sea at constant high speed; no problems at all, it seems."

"What is a crash turn?" persisted Julia.

"Not something you'd like to experience," explained William. "They put the ship hard to port then hard to starboard at full ahead. Wash and water everywhere, things falling off shelves, lockers springing open, people falling out of bunks. They have to do it at least once, then hopefully never again. But this one is a nimble ship, despite her size. Our favourite ocean liner has survived. Now Cunard will be as proud of her as we are."

"Well," smiled Julia, as if with relief, "you must be very pleased. Now Jon, is Maisie's dress ready? What is she wearing on her head?"

"For Heaven's sake, Mother, you'll have to wait and see—like all of us."

"All? From what you say, there'll be hardly anybody there."

"*You'll* be there, Mother," Jon laughed, "and you must stop worrying. You'll enjoy the whole day. Just wait and see." He turned to his father. "The ship's heading back to Liverpool now; Cunard to be official owners. You know we sail on November the Sixteenth."

"Mmm." William looked at his watch and pocketed it with a broad smile. "Just time to get you married, then."

* * *

It was the day of the wedding; the morning cold, still

and dark before its Autumn dawn. Hoggett had been sent off to Wallsend to follow the first of the hired Renaults in the Ferris's own car; its bonnet dressed with white ribbons and its back seat strewn with white roses. Now the second chauffeur-driven Renault was ticking over steadily outside the house in Heaton Road; the distant town just waking, the little procession of parents, son and housekeeper the only movement in a hushed street, the stars gone out of a suddenly luminous sky.

"Looks as if we'll have a clear day with sunshine," declared William. "And you deserve one, my boy. Now then, see your mother's tucked in properly there."

"Don't fuss, William." Julia adjusted her hat and scarves. "I'm dressed for the Himalayas, not just Northumberland."

"You keep well wrapped up now," said Betty, putting another rug around Julia's legs. Jon gave her a smile.

"Are you not sorry you're missing this adventure, Betty?"

"Aye sir, I'd like to see you wed to your new lass, and I do fancy a ride in the motor-car all the way out to those lovely places in the country up there, but I need to be at home to keep the house warm and have something ready to eat when the family gets back tonight."

"Goodbye then, Betty." Jon bent to kiss her, noticing her moist eyes and trembling lips. "We're counting on you to look after things here—and I'll see you when I come back from America."

"Then I'll wish you and that grand girl every happiness." She shook his hand. "And second time lucky, sir."

The car grumbled into gear and clattered away.

"I am, Betty," shouted Jon, "I am!"

* * *

Maisie's trousseau had been sent by train to Liverpool with Jon's cabin trunk and suitcases. The motor-cars were due to arrive. Now she stood in the parlour of her childhood home with nothing in her possession but the bouquet of pink roses and lily-of-the-valley her mother had made so carefully for her. Everything else had been sent away or remained at her new house in Tynemouth; she was left with this bouquet and a sense of freedom. Even her simple wedding-dress—white, with a cream-coloured waistband embroidered with forget-me-nots—fitted so well it felt like a liberating nakedness, as if she had been stripped of everything and made ready for a new life. It was precisely how she wanted to feel. She had chosen to wear her hair long. It hung girlishly beneath the short veil thrown back to frame her face with white lace beyond the rich curtains of hair.

From the earliest hours, it had been a difficult morning. Maisie's mother Alice had been indefatigable: coping with Ellen's excitement as her middle child clambered into her Bridesmaid's dress, blue to match the embroidery on Maisie's waistband; hustling the sleep out of little George's eyes; helping Maisie to dress; keeping out of her husband's way. Matthew was sullen, consumed by his refusal to give his blessing or attend the wedding—yet here it was, going on around him in his own house, his wife fighting back tears of disappointment, his daughter giving him pleading looks with those eyes of hers. He saw her being dressed for a sacrifice;

462

soon, no doubt, to be undressed by that young man who had already had his way with her, with her own consent, over and over again, time and time again in their own secretive house long before it could be sanctified as a marital home. Then she would be taken into a life she'd never manage, with people she could never cope with, with a family and their friends who would always despise her as common. It was no good. He couldn't bear to watch it another minute. There would be no more shouting, no more arguments with the wayward women in his house. He would put a stop to it all.

"I'm going out!" he cried, grasping the handle of the front door as if he would strangle it. "I'll have no more of this day!"

"No, man!" Alice pleaded. "It's *her* day. At least see her off. Stop upsetting her!"

"Aye, I'll stop. I'll stop it all!"

He vanished into the darkness of the street, slamming the door behind him.

"It's all right now," said Alice as calmly as she could. "He's gone. It's over."

"It's not, you know." Maisie began a sob. "He's right mad, he is!"

Little George came running into the parlour.

"The motor-car is here! The motor-car is here!"

"No more tears now." Alice held her daughter's slender arms. "We're off to that country place. Are you sure you don't want to come with us? D'you really want to travel all that way in the other car with just that chauffeur?"

"Aye, I do." Maisie was recovering. "It's all arranged. Mister Hoggett's a nice man. He wants to drive me. He's proud of me."

"I'm proud of you too, love. Now be a brave lass, don't let the other bairns see you're upset…"

"I'm not upset now. I'm happy. I'm happy."

Her mother kissed her on both cheeks and wiped her eyes.

"Now, here's your Grannie's tartan plaid. You wear it proudly—proud Maisie."

"Aye, I will. Now off you go in that motor-car. I know you've never been in one. You and the bairns will love it." She pecked her mother's cheek. "See you in the church, Mam."

She was suddenly alone, utterly alone in her strange white skin of a dress. She wanted Jon. She wanted Jon so much! She stood in the silent house that could never be her home again. She didn't want it as a home; she had one of her own now, she was a married woman…well, nearly. She found herself on the brink of a giggle. When she'd been growing up she'd never thought life would work out like this! Then she heard the rattle of another motor-car and she was suddenly on the doorstep, knowing perfectly well the neighbours would be nosing behind their curtains, even as early as this. Hoggett stepped down from his car.

"Now now, what's this, Miss? Tears on your wedding day? And I was only saying before how lucky we were the rain's held off!"

"I'm just a bit upset, Mister Hoggett," Maisie sniffed,

trying to control herself for this kind man—and those nosey neighbours she could see were still twitching their curtains. "My Da's not happy about this wedding. He's not coming to see me married and he's stormed out in a temper like I've never seen."

"Oh, divvent worry about him, Pet. He'll see sense when he knows how happy you are. He's obviously decided he doesn't matter today, but you do. Right?"

Maisie nodded.

"Right. Now dry your eyes." Hoggett offered a large handerchief while he made a final inspection of the car's wheels and engine. "It'll all work out. Now, did your Mam and your little brother get away all right in the other car?"

Maisie nodded again.

"We're all set then…and I have to say it, Miss," Hoggett put on a beaming smile, "you do look beautiful, but I didn't know you were from the other side of the Border."

"Aye," Maisie applied Hoggett's handkerchief and felt herself recovering in his jovial company, "the tartan's on me Mam's side."

"Well, I've never seen a finer Scots lassie. In you go now and stop fretting. It's all ganna be fine."

Maisie wore the light plaid over her shoulder, slender enough to preserve the delicacy of her wedding dress, romantic enough to proclaim her Scots descent. The tartan was Dress Gordon, clasped with a silver brooch: the only piece of jewellery she wore. Before they set off she gave her Engagement ring to Hoggett.

"Hang on to this for us, Mister Hoggett. I'll need it back after my wedding ring goes on."

Hoggett held the ring as if it had been a holy relic.

"Why, it's a bobby-dazzler, this one. I noticed it when you first got it. Well," he pocketed it in his waistcoat with a proud smile, "it'll be as safe with me as the Crown Jewels in the Tower, Miss."

Maisie felt her smile returning.

"You won't be calling me that for much longer."

"No, Miss, and I'll be very happy to call you Madam. May I offer you my very best wishes now, in case I don't get a chance later on in all the celebrating?"

"Thank you, but you are part of the celebrations, Mister Hoggett. You have to make sure Jon gets that ring so he can put it back on my finger after the ceremony."

"Well, I'll be proud to, Miss…and now we'd better be off into the wilds. You don't want to be one of them brides who think it's clever being late. That's one old tradition we can nicely do without."

"We're doing without most of the old traditions, Mister Hogget; we're making new ones. And thanks for being so nice to me this morning. So, off we go now: it's the ride of my life!"

A deep laugh bubbled out of Hoggett's round face.

"Mine too, if I'm honest," he confessed with obvious delight.

"Haway then!"

466

The car growled away from the now-lonely door of Maisie's childhood home, but her ordeal in these streets was not over. A dark knot of women unravelled into waving arms and shaking fists as the car turned its first corner.

"A white dress? It should be torn off her back!"

"Slut!"

"And what's she got to hide under that veil? He's seen everything already!"

"Aye, she should go to him in her red paint!"

"She should go to him naked!"

"Slut!"

"He'll have her naked soon enough, then she'll know what she's in for!"

"Slut!

"Slut!"

Hoggett accellerated in defiance; Maisie looked frozenly ahead. She was glad her mother and Ellen and especially little George had missed this; it wasn't something a child should have to see…but the strangest feeling swept over her. The stupid, ignorant insults didn't matter; they couldn't matter, they would never matter again. She had been called a slut by Philippa and had slapped her face for it. She had been called a slut just now from the street corner and had been driven past it on her way to her wedding. She had defeated the forces against her. She would not shrink from them, nor let them make her cry. She would smile at her new good fortune. The car was running swiftly through the streets of Wallsend on the way to Newcastle and her future. The pull of the engine and the sprays of flowers that had been strewn across her seat were proof of her escape…and there were better people to cheer her on her way. Children waved and shouted as they saw the white ribbons flapping across the windscreen and Maisie's veil fluttering from the back seat. Women, carrying baskets or chatting on street corners, stopped to stare. More than one man raised his hat.

"Get used to it now," Hoggett said proudly, "you look like a princess."

Ships hooted from the river, smoke from the factories rose into the still, cold, morning air. The car picked up speed on its broader road, then was snarling through suddenly-crowded streets as they drove into the bustling traffic of Newcastle. Maisie was on the brink of tears once more. This was her own great city, and Jon's. 'Going to town' had been a childhood treat and was still a special occasion; she had never expected to be driven through the long-familiar streets being stared at as a bride in a motor-car, bound for the wildness of open country and the man who adored her, her wedding, her honeymoon, and a voyage to America on a ship she had helped to build. Her Cunard ticket would be almost as sacred as her marriage certificate. If she had thought about this before today, she would have been shy and daunted by the prospect, but she found herself enjoying the shouts and waves of the astonished people she was passing. She found herself smiling. She was a queen riding to her coronation, she was Cinderella going to the Ball—but this was Newcastle, today, in 1907! She began to laugh. Wasn't it every little girl's dream to marry her handsome prince? And wasn't that so often the end of the dream? But this was a beginning: a beginning of something so big and exciting that she couldn't help but laugh out loud.

"Thank you Mister Hoggett," she shouted from her

proud seat, "it's a lovely ride this morning!"

"You hold on to your flowers now, Miss. We'll be gannin along the Military Road faster than ever."

Hoggett—ardent Northumbrian and amateur historian—began to deliver a running commentary as they drove West out of the city along the line of Hadrian's Wall. He was full of tales about the Romans and delighted in getting his tongue round the sonorous names of Corstopitum, Brocolitia and Borcovicium, until Maisie felt they might be marching with helmeted cohorts to defend the Northern outposts of the ancient empire, even though she was in a rattling motor-car and hot-oil smells rushed back from the engine to remind her of Twentieth-Century excitements. As they turned North off the Military Road to follow the line of the Roman Dere Street, she was treated to more tales of Northumbrian history. They crossed rich farmlands of the famous families of Blackett and Swinburne, the ploughed fields glistening in Autumn sunshine; then on to open, tussocky grazing towards the land of the Charltons and the Fenwicks, the Dodds and the Milburns and all the other infamous reiver families who stole sheep from the Scots and from one another and whose bloodstained exploits Hoggett recounted with boyish glee. Beyond those hills was the desperate fight between Corbit Jack and Barty of the Comb; in a dungeon over there, the appalling starvaton of Sir Reginald Carnaby by the Heron family; on that hill lived Katherine Fenwick of Harnham, who was so beautiful that people blocked the streets of Durham just to look at her; of course up here in their own county, Hoggett added, the competition was somewhat stiffer.

A motor-car was still an unusual sight on the farm tracks of Northumberland. This one, dressed with white ribbons, seemed to the lonely shepherd like something from a fairytale. The bride waved back to his wondering stare. Luckily, it had been a long Summer and a dry Autumn. The wheels spun up clouds of dust rather than spatters of mud as they crossed this landscape of faded heather and fox-coloured bracken. Here, Hoggett told Maisie, on frosty mornings to come, the merry hounds would flow like a river of tan and white over hedges and ditches to the horns of pink-coated huntsmen, setting up their wild and haunting music beneath these vast, unclouded skies—just like today, she thought, when floods of golden sunshine had come to make every colour strong and vivid and give the pink roses in her bouquet the bright gleam of Summer, even so late in the year. But what did seasons matter now? She felt her love was timeless.

Thockrington Church, built by the Normans in 1100, remained one of the most isolated in England. It occupied a prominent position on a ridge of the moors and was a landmark in this sparsely populated countryside. Jon's father had said it always reminded him of Noah's Ark aground on Mount Ararat—and indeed the building had a slightly lopsided look, as if it in ancient times it might have come to rest as the Flood subsided. But everything was dry and sunny today. The small stone church stood on its naked hill, looking windblown even on this miraculously still day…and it was the stillness that Maisie felt when the car stopped and Hoggett switched off the engine: a divine hush, falling softly to bless her.

Hoggett opened the car door, held it, and offered his gloved hand. 'Go-back, go-back, go-back' cackled an invisible red grouse. Maisie smiled at the strange omen for a wedding. So many people had wanted her to go back: the sneering workmen at the shipyard, the drawing-loft girls with their ignorance and jealousy, the vicious women with their red paint and street-corner insults, her own father with his sad and angry disapproval—back to a life that would never allow her to rise into the wonder of love and the glorious opportunities of living in a new and exciting world. She did not want to go back, she would not go back, she would never go back. With a simple, light step and a polite 'thank you' to the beaming Hoggett, she put her polished shoe to the dry ground and felt the wide silence of the moors fold around her. There was an unexpected warmth in the still air, and a scent of pines. Ahead, beyond the dry-stone wall and its iron gate, she could see her mother and Ellen and little George standing in the church doorway ready to welcome her; she told herself the man she most wanted to see would already be inside, and that she should not hurry. On the short walk to meet her mother she realised the seemingly-silent moors were not so silent. She could hear the cries of distant sheep, and suddenly the sweet, haunting, liquid song of a curlew. She knew that no organ or harmonium would play in the church and that this magical, tumbling music must be her wedding song.

She was inside a dream. Everything seemed slow and deliberate, yet all was happening so quickly, so effortlessly, it would be over in moments. Her mother kissed her, she bent down to kiss little George, Ellen came up gravely to straighten her dress and veil, stood behind her…and she was ready, walking, holding her bouquet, seeing the church was flooded with candlelight and smelling its warmth. There was Jon, immaculate in his morning dress of grey frock-coat with blue cravat and sapphire pin, standing with the vicar who was old and bald, and behind them, the light coming in through clear windows in the old stonework; her shoes ringing bright and hard up the aisle, although she was trying to step as softly as if she had been barefoot on a beach—and she remembered meeting Jon on Tynemouth Long Sands, illicitly, in hot sunshine, against all the odds; and now they were meeting properly, in cool Autumn, with the blessing of a vicar, and meeting for ever.

"Hello," said Jon quietly, taking her hand.

She had not expected him to use that word, hadn't known what they would say until they had to speak the words of their vows. It was funny.

"Hello," she almost giggled, but very quietly, and when she came to her words she was very slow and steady and thought she could still hear the faint calling of the curlew in the blue air outside, but she couldn't be sure. Her certainties were of Jon's hand, the smiles of his parents, the proud walk of her sister in that blue dress as they came out again into golden sunshine and the completely unexpected sight of a photographer with his cumbersome camera set up beyond the church door, which Jon's family must have organised in secret. Above all, her certainty was of a simple rightness. This was right, it was what she had wanted for Jon and for herself and now it was here she felt neither overwhelmed nor madly excited. She felt the still, soft quietude of happiness.

With her Engagement ring back on her finger beyond her new and gleaming band of gold, she enjoyed the short drive to the Vicarage at Bavington. Maisie and Jon noticed that pears had dropped in the Vicar's garden, cosy in its hamlet, and that the pear tree's leaves were a sudden bright red, as surprising as the late honeysuckle that still bloomed at the end of this extraordinary Autumn. The few guests filled the kitchen and parlour that formed the main rooms of the house and the Wedding Breakfast proceeded happily with hot punch and mince pies.

"Christmas has come early," remarked William to Julia. "I told you the food would be all right, and everyone is perfectly relaxed. Look at Hoggett and Simon. If it's not motor-cars, it's Roman history "

"She is a native of Wallsend, I understand," the Vicar was telling the chauffeur. "Ah, the fort of Segedunum. How you and I should like to go digging around in those ruins. We must imagine it was a hard life. The Wall had to be the worst posting in the Empire—apart from Judaea of course, always a troublesome province. Now, Mrs Watson," he turned to Alice, "did you know we had late-flourishing pears here? Oh yes, even this far North. You must take some home."

"The children were wonderful," said Julia, looking beyond her plate to Jon and Maisie. "They said their words so nicely, and your brother led the service charmingly. But it's all over so quickly; they're properly together now and leaving tomorrow for that tremendous voyage so far from everything here. I feel we're losing them almost before we can enjoy their happiness."

"We shan't lose them, my dear. We have won her into our family and she loves us. I think we all feel privileged. They may be in America for some time while Jon sells his idea of the air-engine, but he'll manage that. Americans like to be sold things; he's made the right decision to take his plans over there. The whole family will benefit from his success—and now it *is* a whole family."

"And do you think, my dear," Julia continued conspiratorially over her wineglass, "we might be grandparents at last?"

"I should jolly well hope so. They've staved off parenthood long enough."

"Well they've *had* to, for decency's sake."

"Let's try and keep decency at bay; there's nothing like it for spoiling a marriage."

"Really," Julia turned her husband by the arm, "this is not quite the conversation to have in a vicar's wife's kitchen."

"Why not? Old Simon can do the Christening—unless he's in that unkempt graveyard by then."

"William, you've had too much punch."

"I certainly have not, for here come the new couple and we must toast them again."

"Wish us well, Mother." Jon held Maisie's hand as they came to say their goodbyes. "You know we must go back to Tynemouth now, then it's the train to Liverpool."

"Bless you, my darling boy," said Julia with a sniffle. "Bless you both."

"You've been wonderful to me," declared Maisie to Julia and William. "You've accepted me, you've made me welcome, and you've made me happy."

"And now that's his job," said William with a twinkling eye and a pat on Jon's shoulder. "Bon voyage!"

On the long drive back to Tynemouth, Maisie was gently but persistently shaken by the motor-car; Jon beside her, holding her hand and pressing his knee against hers. She became acutely aware of her own breasts, swelling and moving behind her dress, wanting to be bare, wanting to be kissed. She wanted the plaid off her shoulders, the dress off her hips, the stockings off her legs; wanted to give her naked body to the man she loved, the man who had married her and given her a new life...and so it was in the little house beside the silent midnight sea, hurrying upstairs from the chill darkness to a quickly-warming bedroom and a bridal bed on which Jon had strewn more roses. He had also left her an unexpected present.

"Look: a new hat for when you're on the new ship."

"No more clothes," she giggled, pulling off her headdress, putting on the hat with a smile, then tossing that away, too. Once more came that feeling of being inside a dream: her own dream come true. As he undressed her and took her into bed with a wild flurry of kisses, the dream rushed up into scorching reality…then sleep overtook them, delicious sleep and a feeling of triumph.

* * *

The early train for Liverpool hissed at its platform in Newcastle Central Station: a bleak cavern of hectic noise and cold wind. Mild Autumn had been howled away in a single night and angry gales blew from a dark sky. Porters heaved trunks and cases, passengers scurried, doors slammed. Jon and Maisie found their compartment and snuggled as best they could into the padded seats.

"Thank Heavens for First Class," said Jon.

"I've never been First Class on a train before," admitted Maisie with a laugh, "and I never would have been, if it hadn't been for you."

"From now on, Darling, First Class all the way. That's what I promised, and that's what you shall have." He stood up and pulled down the window. Cold air rushed in. "Well, it's goodbye Newcastle. Look, you can see the Castle from here. The sun's coming up behind it."

Maisie joined him at the window. Her view obscured by steam and smoke. A solitary figure loomed through it to stand before their carriage door.

"Oh my God," she whispered. "It's my father!"

"You cannot hide!" His voice was hoarse and dark.

Jon gripped Maisie's waist, keeping her beside him at the window.

"We're not hiding, Mister Watson. We're married now and going to America."

"I know you are. That's why I've come." He looked pleadingly up at Maisie. His face seemed to crumple; he began to gabble his words. "I've been wrong, I've been a fool. I couldn't believe it was right for you but I've been awake all night, coming here, walking through the town and now I know different. I had to catch you before you went. I had to tell you I was wrong. You've married a good man; he's done the right thing for you, he and his family. I couldn't see it at first, like, but if you tell me you're happy, really happy, I'll be able to rest."

"I'm happy, Da," sniffed Maisie, "you know I am!"

"Then I have to accept your marriage and your man." He turned to Jon. "I wouldn't shake your hand before, lad, but I will now."

"You don't have to, Mister Watson," Jon spoke firmly. "I shan't force you to that, not if you really don't wish to."

"I do. I must!"

Their hands clasped in the cold air.

"Take care of her. She's been given a rough time by the Wallsend folk—and by me."

Now Maisie grasped her father's hand.

476

"You couldn't help it, Da, I know. Now be sensible and go home. Go back to Mam and tell her what you've told us."

A whistle blew; a sudden burst of steam was whipped by cold wind; the train creaked forward; their hands were jerked apart.

"I'm glad we all worked on the ship together!" shouted Matthew. "I'm glad we did that! At least that worked all right!"

They waved as best they could from the window; smoke and steam hid Matthew from view. Jon pushed up the glass and cuddled Maisie into the swaying   seat.

"We never said goodbye properly," she whimpered.

"He meant to. No need to cry now. He understands. He can be happy."

"I love him…not like I love you…but I love him."

She buried her head in Jon's coat.

"Darling Maisie, I am so proud of you."

CHAPTER TWENTY-SIX
An Enchanted Palace

The train delivered Jon and Maisie to a wet and chilly Liverpool; the station buzzing with activity as transatlantic passengers arrived in heavy coats with piles of luggage. They learned that the boat train from London was late and that *Mauretania's* departure would be delayed. Jon led Maisie to the Adelphi Hotel while mist obscured tall buildings in the great commercial city.

"I planned for us to eat here anyway," he explained, "we'll just have more time. There should be a telegram for us."

Liverpool's Adelphi Hotel was the most luxurious in Britain outside London and was as grand as the great ocean liners whose passengers it served. Its great public rooms were echoes of what might be encountered on the ocean, its attentive service a foretaste of mid-Atlantic pampering. Jon collected the telegram he had expected from his parents, escorted Maisie to the spectacular Grill Room, and ordered a meal.

"They wish us a happy voyage," reported Jon, handing the telegram to Maisie, "and look: they say our house will be properly attended-to while we're away. I suppose they mean they'll send Betty every so often to keep the place aired."

"I tried to give everything a good clean that last day before the wedding," Maisie smiled wistfully. "I didn't like being on my own, you getting ready at Heaton…"

"But it was a good chance to do some housework, eh?" Jon grinned. "While I was away."

"You know what I mean!" she laughed. "But it was the right thing to do, to go separately to the wedding."

"Of course—but when we did meet up in that little church, I've never enjoyed meeting you more."

"Me too", she breathed, taking Jon's hand. "It was wonderful. I know the whole thing took some doing, for both of us, but it was the best thing I've ever done."

"Thank you for saying that, and meaning it." Jon kissed her hand. "And now look where we are: in this amazing place. Did you know this is where winners of the Grand National come to celebrate? Not the horses, the owners and punters. Believe it or not, Uncle Simon used to be a gentleman jockey."

"That must have been a while ago," laughed Maisie. "When he married us he didn't look as if he could get on a horse never mind ride it in a race."

"It was before he was a vicar—or perhaps at the same time, I'm not sure. When he was much younger, anyway. He was full of stories about racing; not that he ever rode in the Grand National, at least I don't think he did. That's how I knew about this hotel, but I never expected to see inside."

Maisie changed the subject.

"Have you got your plans safe?" she asked.

"Yes. They're here in my briefcase. I've kept them separate from the rest of the luggage."

"You're going to find this secret compartment and put them in there," stated Maisie, then looked doubtfully at Jon, "but can you really trust those Russians to make it work?"

"Oh, it'll work all right. They proved it worked. After that night at the Low Lights they were going to take me aboard and show me, but I never had the opportunity to go. You may remember the original idea was to take the plans out of our house and put them aboard as soon as the secret panel was ready. That's what the Russians wanted me to do, but I didn't."

"Because you didn't trust them," interrupted Maisie. "You thought they might go back open the panel and steal the plans themselves."

"No, I didn't think that. I just didn't want the plans out of my sight, lying on the ship, however well concealed. Then she went on her sea-trials, then we were getting married—but I did have a meeting with the Russians. I know I said I'd have no secrets from my wife and I won't, but I didn't tell you because there was so much going on with the wedding and you had enough to worry about with all that business with your father. Anyway, being married to you is much more fun than playing at international intrigue."

"Be serious, man," Maisie whispered as if their fellow diners might be eager to steal plans for an air-engine, "it's a serious business."

"Oh, I'm taking it seriously enough; so seriously I had the Russians draw me a diagram of where the secret panel is and exactly how it works."

"Give us a look, then."

"I can't," Jon smiled blandly. "I deliberately

destroyed it in case it fell into the wrong hands."

Maisie widened her eyes, then narrowed them at Jon.

"Not before you memorised it, of course."

"Of course."

"Well, now who's playing international intrigue? You're a clever lad-and-a-half, eh? I'm proud of you. So all we have to do now is get on the ship, put the plans in the secret compartment, and take them out again when we get to America."

"That would make for a honeymoon with added spice, wouldn't it, but I don't think I'm going to use the secret compartment after all. All this cloak-and-dagger stuff, it's hardly necessary. It's only Druginin's speculation that there'll be a German agent aboard—and even if there is, how could he know me or know where to look?"

"Oh, come on, that's easy. He could find out what cabin we're in and search it," retorted Maisie, hoping to re-kindle Jon's determination. "That's what the Russians were afraid of. Anyway, you can't carry that briefcase with you day and night. We can't go down to dinner in First Class with you humping that great thing around."

"I'll deposit it at the Purser's Office."

"Not good enough," she insisted. "The Purser could be bribed."

"I promise you, Darling, Cunard Pursers are not open to bribery. Ask anyone between here and New York."

Maisie would not give up.

"Your briefcase could still be stolen from the Purser's Office. No, it's got to go in that secret compartment. The Russians called it their wedding present to us; we might as well use it."

"Now who's playing international intrigue?" Jon smiled at her vehemence.

"We have to, my love! You've invented this amazing thing; we can't risk losing it to foreigners. But there's still something to sort out," she continued, pushing her plate aside. "What if somebody sees you opening a door in the ship's woodwork? It's supposed to be in full view at the bottom of the stairs, isn't it?"

"Yes, it is."

"So, I'll be standing in front of it while you open the door. I can be adjusting my hat or something."

"Oh," said Jon with a slowly widening smile, "I *knew* there was a good reason for buying you the new hat."

"I learned a thing or two about being crafty from your Russians," said Maisie pertly. She raised her glass to Jon. "This is going to be a very exciting honeymoon, starting with this very good meal."

"I have to say," Jon admitted, "I don't know if this is a late lunch, an early dinner, or a big tea."

"It's lovely anyway," smiled Maisie. "Thank you."

So they put aside further discussion of their plans to conceal Jon's drawings. They chatted, clinked their glasses, and looked around at the grandeur of their surroundings—but all the time they were distracted by a mounting excitement, a stir of expectation. They knew that beyond the rain drizzling into the Mersey, beyond the ceaseless bustle of the dockland streets, stood the ship of their dreams, the ship of their love, the ship of their lives. They had been part of her creation and she had been part of theirs. She had led them to love and marriage, but her mystical acts of Fate had yet to be completed. She had to take them, as man and wife, into her vast and gilded interiors, let them luxuriate in her splendours, keep their secrets safe, lull them to sleep in their cabin stirred by the sea and the spinning turbines, and keep them as cosy and secure as if in a womb from which they would seem to be born again into a new land on the other side of the world. So they did not spend long over the brandy Jon had ordered to combat the cold of their journey to the waterfront, nor linger over re-reading the telegram. Maisie secured her new hat and they made for the docks. They joined the scurry of embarking passengers, presented their tickets and passports, and—hearts beating faster—were suddenly aboard the most spectacular ocean-liner in the world, thronged with travellers marvelling at their first sight of her magnificent public rooms and finding labyrinthine ways to their cabins. Her ribs and engines, hidden beyond the crowds and the decoration, seemed as vital to Jon and Maisie as their own bodies.

Mauretania was instant excitement and delight. In First Class, she was an enchanted palace of majestic rooms, gleaming pillars and glittering domes, luxurious carpets and gilded panelling, all flooded with a beguiling warmth and the brilliance of electric illumination. Even the scurry of late boarders into the hectic business of a wet and protracted embarkation-day could not tarnish her glamour or weaken the charm of her welcome. Indeed, despite her awesome size and magnificent decoration, she seemed the friendliest of ships. Jon and Maisie, escorted into an electric lift by their steward, felt immediately at home in her elegant yet comfortable interiors.

"But home could never be quite like this," smiled Jon, offering Maisie first entry when they arrived at their cabin. She saw not bunks, but two comfortable beds with pretty pillows and curtains, a rich mahogany wardrobe with mirrors on its doors, a dressing-table in the same wood, and a neat washbasin with gleaming taps. Twin port-holes were smartly curtained. The comfortable carpet was of maroon and cream checks; the glossy metalwork gleamed brilliant white. Fresh smells of new paint, clean carpet, and expensive soap came to entice her in.

"And look at that!" she squealed. "It's a telephone!"

"For ordering things, I suppose," laughed Jon. "I see our luggage hasn't arrived yet. I'm sure they'll send up the right bags."

"Oh, it's wonderful, my love!" She clung to Jon, kissing his neck and face. "All the way to America in this beautiful cabin." She backed off suddenly. "It must be costing a fortune!"

"Only part of a fortune—fortunately." Jon smiled and peeped beyond the port-hole curtains: more rain lashed the gigantic hull. "Anyway, I'll try to make another one in America—which reminds me, we have something to see to before we settle in or do anything else." He patted his briefcase. "If we're going to do it, we'd better do it now."

"What," Maisie was suddenly anxious, "with everyone bustling about?"

"Yes, it's actually the perfect time. Everyone is intent on finding a cabin or going somewhere, nobody will be loitering or looking at us. But before we go I have to give you this."

He took her lips in his, tenderly at first but in moments the kiss was very hot. He crushed her gently her into his arms.

"Which bed d'you want us to have?" she whispered. "Not much choice: they're both a bit narrow, like."

"The one under the port-holes."

"We can put things on the other one."

"We'll christen ours later. Come on, let's take a walk up and down those stairs."

If *Mauretania's* turbines were her masterpiece of engineering, the Grand Staircase was her masterpiece of interior design. It swept through the ship, extravagantly broad, connecting five decks of First Class accommodation with the magnificent public rooms. Its woodwork was of gleaming French walnut, its carvings were rich, its soft green carpet was a tempting stairway down which Maisie stepped as elegantly as she could, feeling proud and privileged on Jon's arm. Again she was visited by the notion that life had recently taken her into a fairytale that had actually come true, and that her fragile happiness and security had been made sweetly solid.

"This is how we'll come down to dinner", she whispered to Jon, scarcely containing her glee.

"It certainly is," he answered with a smile, but at every step she could sense his anxiety. They wouldn't be free of it until the documents from his briefcase were safely inside the secret compartment—but would it be easy to find? Would it open properly? Would anybody see them doing this? At last they came to the sweeping foot of the staircase and sat down on one of the plush-covered seats built into its woodwork.

"Don't look at it now," said Jon quietly, "but the panel is behind you, a little above and to your left." He stared ahead into a grand vista of the ship's central area. "It has a bunch of grapes carved on it...but it's too busy here at the moment," he added, suddenly standing up and leading Maisie through a confusion of passengers still finding their bearings. They went into the First Class Lounge. Only a few passengers were there. A steward bothered them with the offer of an aperitif. Jon waved him away. Distractedly, they glimpsed at the black night beyond the curtained windows, admired the spectacular oval dome high above their heads, and studied the statues of *Columbia* and *Britannia*.

"Britannia rules the waves," commented Maisie, just for something to say in these tense moments, "but Columbia has a prettier face."

"American girls are all supposed to be pretty," said Jon flatly, "but I'll bet you they're not."

"How do you work the panel?" asked Maisie.

"You push one of the carved grapes. It's easy to remember: left, right, left, right."

"What's that supposed to mean?"

"It means look for the bunch of grapes on the left-hand side of the bottom of the stairs; in the right-hand panel above the seat push the grape on the left-hand side of the bunch and the panel to its right slides open. You lock it by sliding it back."

"How d'you manage to remember that?"

"I damn well can't forget it. It's burned into my memory with worry."

The steward reappeared with the suggestion that Sir might care to deposit his bag with the Purser while Madam might enjoy a sherry before dinner. Again he was dismissed, and they felt they had to leave the Lounge—but slowly, arm-in-arm.

"Madam's going to be sick if we don't get rid of that bag," hissed Maisie.

"Sir is already shaking," added Jon, squeezing her arm.

"That was your idea, to put it in the Purser's office."

"Yes it was, but you said we should use the other place and you were right and we're going to—when there are fewer people milling around out there."

They were back at the foot of the staircase.

"We can't wait all night," whispered Maisie. "Perhaps it's better with more people around. If there were only one or two, they'd notice. I've seen the bunch of grapes," she added, looking the other way.

"So have I."

"Haway, then. I'll do something with my hat—over here."

Suddenly she was gone from Jon's arm, stepping well away and dropping her hat on the floor and saying 'Oh!' in a loud voice and looking for the pin and some people were bending down and helping her and he knew he had to move quickly. 'Left.' The panelling was directly in front of his face. 'Right.' The deliciously polished carving of the grapes was under his fingers. 'Left'. It took only the gentlest push. 'Right.'

Amazingly, joyously, incredibly, a panel had slid open, revealing a space far bigger than Jon had imagined. It was a neat cupboard, lined with pale cork. He simply placed his briefcase inside and slid the panel shut. It closed softly, leaving no hint that it had been a door. The business was accomplished in a matter of four or five seconds. Jon looked around. No-one appeared to have noticed. The knot of figures around Maisie was disentangling; she was standing up; a tall, elegantly dressed man was smiling at her.

"Your hatpin, ma'am."

With a few steps, Jon was at her side. His relief was enormous. Her smile told him hers was, too. The man was American, gracious and garrulous at the same time.

"That sure is a pretty hat I nearly walked on there."

"Thanks, yes, it's nice, isn't it?" Maisie was laughing with relief; Jon too, holding her arm, wanting to kiss her, shaking hands with their American saviour while she giggled on. "My husband just bought me it for the voyage. We just got married. We're going on our honeymoon to New York. This is my husband."

"I congratulate you sir, and you ma'am. Chester Bryson. Bryson's Stores, y'know, all over the mid-West. Honeymooners, huh? Wait until I tell my wife. She will be so excited to have Honeymooners at our table—for you surely will dine with us tonight and bring us all luck for this voyage."

"No, no," Jon managed, "we couldn't impose ourselves…"

"Nonsense! Don't be so English. You're going on honeymoon, my wife and I are going home, we're all going to America together—and I reckon I've assembled more money round my special table tonight than has ever been brought together on this ocean. Could be good for your business, young man. What is your business?"

"I'm an engineer."

"Well, I got the van Hoofs dining with me, they run textile mills, and the Dexters, they make automobile parts, and I got Manny Bloomstein, he's going back to his finance-house. You could do some deals, kid."

"It's enormously kind of you, but…"

"The lady would like it." He turned his glowing smile upon Maisie. "Wait 'till you see Mrs. Bloomstein's diamonds. I gotta keep my wife talking to new people or she'd spend this whole voyage telling me her own diamonds are not big enough. I sold twenty per cent of my railroad stock just to kit her out with new stuff so she'd look good on our trip round Europe." He beamed his ebullience at Jon, who was becoming charmed and intrigued by the American's voice. It seemed to contain echoes of an English taken across the Atlantic by the original West Country settlers so long ago, but had not developed into the familiar and much-despised drawl. Energetic, relaxed and fastidious all at the same time, the voice seemed part of his difference, his exclusiveness, his enormous wealth—and money seemed to be its favourite subject. "Being married is an expensive enterprise, as you will discover sir, but there is no greater joy for two people in love—as I can see you most certainly are." His glee flowed back towards Maisie. "You gotta help me, lady. You're bright, you're young, you're beautiful. Please grace my table tonight. You two will be like a breath of fresh air off the ocean. Apart from that, you owe me a favour: I did find your hatpin."

Jon shook Bryson's hand again. He would have shaken anyone's hand, he felt so relieved that the plans were safely hidden. As so often at momentous events in life, he realised it was the tiny detail he would remember. Chester Bryson's silken necktie was the same shade of grey as his heavy moustache. His full lips, their pinkness just visible behind the curtain of grey, already looked primed for the after-dinner cigar.

"How can we possibly refuse, Mister Bryson?"

"We have something to celebrate, anyway." Maisie was still flooded with relief, too. She was radiant. "We helped build the ship."

"You don't say!"

"Yes. I drew the plans and my husband helped build the turbines."

"Well, whaddayouknow? Wait 'til Louella hears this. You're not just Honeymooners, you're part of this fabulous ship! She'll want to know the far end of your story. Get ready to tell us all. We've taken the big table at the far end of the First Class Dining-Room."

"Where else, Mister Bryson?" Jon gave him a wry smile.

"Well, I could've ordered a steak in the cabin, but then who'd've seen Louella's diamonds, huh?" He smiled hugely once again. "We look forward to your company."

"And we to yours. We're going on deck to see the ship leave port. Mustn't miss that."

"See you later."

They felt safe, they felt happy, they felt free—as if

they could really begin their honeymoon now. They hugged each other, walked up and down the Grand Staircase once again just for the fun of doing so, and at half-past seven they stood at *Mauretania's* chilly rail to watch her lines being cast off, her vast black sides edging away from the quay, and tugs easing her into the dark river. There was hooting from other ships, shocking bellows from *Mauretania's* own steam-whistles, and a farewell firework display from New Brighton pier. The great liner, seeming to shake off her tugs with both disdain and pleasure, pointed her sharp bow towards the Irish Sea and a hum of motion could be felt from her turbines far below. Her full power had yet to be unleashed, but in this steady cruise out of Liverpool, her maiden voyage—imagined for so long—was at last in progress. A feeling of new life sparked between the passengers watching from her rails. Everyone aboard seemed to have fallen immediately under the gracious but exciting spell of their new ship.

Jon was visited by a surge of triumph. *Mauretania* was under way to America, powered by the turbines with which he and his family had become so intimately involved. He suddenly felt he could do anything and succeed at everything. He had only felt like this once or twice, and then far back in his boyhood. He remembered his momentary excellence in schoolboy games and skirmishes and how they had taught him to snatch victory from a desperate situation and to bear pain in defeat without humiliation or sense of loss; but even then he had suspected that schoolyard triumphs were not preparing him for the real struggles of a grown-up world where all would be shadowy and uncertain, where the enemies would obey no rules, the defeats would be more cruel, the victories more hollow, and where those who were good and fair and honest and strong would not always win. And so he had found it. As an adult he had been stripped of confidence, troubled by soured relations with his father and his disastrous relationship with Philippa; yet now, on this dramatic night, he felt supremely confident. He had succeeded at his work, re-established himself in his family, earned himself some self-respect, created plans for a new type of engine whose possibilities might be extraordinary, negotiated all kinds of difficulties with Philippa at her most objectionable and the Russians at their most devious, and—against all the odds—married the woman he loved and made her happy: of all these things, the one thing he had most wanted to achieve. And now they were aboard together, the plans were safely stowed, and they could enjoy the secure and luxurious freedom of this beautiful ship, Jon became aware of another feeling: calm. It was as if a tumultuous noise in his head had been silenced and a hectic programme of ordeals cancelled. He sensed an immense quiet would follow, gradually to be filled by the sweet murmurs of serenity. It was happening already. As this voyage took them further into an insouciant mid-Atlantic, he knew he would find the peace he suddenly realised he had been craving since the first days of his marriage to Philippa. At last the ocean would bestow its balm upon his soul, comfortably far from either shore, suspended in the delicious limbo of travel, sheltered by the great ship and blessed by the happiness of this lovely girl who loved him. Yes, he had made her happy. Here she was, cuddled into his side, peering down at the hull whose parts she had begun to draw so shortly after their first fateful, beautiful meeting. Now she was his wife: girlish and gleeful in her happiness, strong and womanly in the true love he knew she had for him. It was a wonderful mixture of feelings. He kissed her cheek and found it chilled by the November night.

"Seen enough out here, Darling? We should get ready for dinner."

"Those Americans—I won't know what to say to them."

"I expect they'll be a little trying," admitted Jon. "What they'll really want to talk about will be money. Trouble is, I was brought up never to talk about money."

"And I've never had any to talk *about*," Maisie added wryly.

"Tell them you enlarged the ship's plans to actual size. Tell them about the funnels and the motor-cars driving through them. They'll be fascinated, and it should keep our talkative friend quiet for while. But I can tell he's a good man. I like him. He seems kind and genuine. Apart from that, I like him because he turned up at exactly the right time."

"I knew just where to drop my hat," smiled Maisie, "but I could still let you down in clever conversation with rich people."

"You'll hold your own with them, Darling—and splendidly. There's nothing you can't manage. You're a wonderful wife."

"I'll try to be," she laughed. "I'm proud to be…and I'm proud of that. Look!" She pointed up to the four towering stacks, hissing sculpted smoke into an ink-black sky. The active funnels made an awesome profile: haughty, powerful, spectacular. "I drew them, and you drove through them with all the posh people in those motor-cars."

"You gave me that idea," Jon reminded her with a smile.

"That seems so long ago," she said, "like something from a different world."

"It *was* in a different world—and now we're off to a new one." He gave her another kiss. "But not until we've had dinner."

They hurried back to their cabin and found their clothes had been unpacked and evening-dress laid out. Their steward departed with a hint they should not linger.

"Doesn't the ship seem huge?" said Maisie. "Even larger somehow now we're aboard. Those wonderful rooms! This wonderful cabin!" She took off her hat and kissed him. "Happy?" She selected the dress and shoes she would wear for dinner.

"To tell you the truth, I feel so tired I could sleep for a week, but I'm happy right enough. I don't think I've ever felt happier. I'm married to you, we both worked on this ship, and now we're together in one of the best cabins. I kept my job: harder than you think, and earned the respect of my father, which I had lost: harder still. I broke fom Philippa and held tight to you. I designed the air-engine and we're taking it to America on our honeymoon. That's quite a story."

"No wonder you're tired."

"But I don't want to go to sleep now. I want to take you down to dinner in First Class." He held her tightly. She was fresh and fragant in her new clothes, youthful and vigorous despite their long and tiring day. "Above all I want to know I've done the right thing—I mean the right thing for you. I've taken you away into a new life, a new home; now we're going to a new country, for a while. I have to know if it's all made you really happy."

"Oh Jon," she kissed him softly, "I couldn't be happier. It's wonderful. You've done the right thing, and so have I. It's all been made special and sacred, and I don't mean just by our wedding service. I'm no great one for reading the Bible. I've hardly read any of it to be honest, but my Da was a great one for the Bible. He taught me bits out of it. One story I'll never forget is the story of Ruth, you know, the

Moabite girl who becomes an Israelite."

"Yes," Jon smiled at the sweetness of her expression, "I know that story."

"I even know the words," she went on. "'Whither thou goest, I will go; and where thou lodgest, I will lodge; thy people shall be my people, and thy God my God.' Well, that's me. That's what I've done; that's what I want to do for the rest of our lives." She gave him an ecstatic smile. "I'm so happy I don't want to die!"

"My God, you're not dying?" He held her away in his sudden shock. "You're not ill, are you?"

"No, no," she laughed, "I didn't mean that! I mean I wouldn't want to die now and miss all this happiness. I just want this to go on for ever. I want us to go on for ever—for as long as we live, anyway. That's what I mean. Now stop worrying—and let's go down for that dinner."

They were dressed and ready just as they heard the bugle-call: once more down the Grand Staircase, Maisie light and graceful on Jon's right arm, passing the secret compartment with a clasp of hands and a gleeful smile, and into the splendours of dinner.

Maisie was wearing a pale blue satin dress, soft grey shoes with silver buckles, and her hair put up with pearl-topped pins. She looked bright and girlish against the severity of Jon's evening-dress. She had been told that First Class diners would not wear their very finest this first night aboard, but the spectacle they made was still entrancing. The superbly coiffed and perfumed women literally shone in their shimmering gowns, draped with silk and laden with jewels. Extravagant displays of diamonds flashed out every colour imaginable. As the diners approached their gilded room, a small string orchestra was playing popular tunes from operetta. The sound was light and delicate, a perfect accompaniment to the froth of jewelled and scented laughter from the privileged passengers and the delightful vision before them. There were gasps of admiration. The dining-room was vast and opulent, yet succeeded in being warm and cosy at the same time. The tables were gleaming with white linen and silver cutlery, sparkling with crystal, and blooming with white and yellow roses. Elegant glasses of Champagne stood ready at each place.

"Over here, my friends!" Chester Bryson had seen Jon and Maisie, and they knew there would be no escape from his relentless good spirits. Bryson's wife Louella was a large and cheerful woman, quite capable of matching her husband's banter. As they had been expecting, Jon and Maisie were confronted with an ostentatious diamond necklace on the powdered, perfumed and very ample bosom. They were introduced to the van Hoofs who were travelling with their pretty daughter Edith: charmingly bare-throated in contrast with her mother's diamond-laden neck.

"Me too," confessed Maise, stroking her own neck, "I don't like heavy things on me, either."

"Young ladies," twinkled the ever-gallant Bryson, "your skin is so beautiful that neither of you need ornament."

The Bloomsteins were older and less fashionably dressed. The financier had little to say; his wife made up for him with a ceaseless commentary of acid gossip.

"See the Dettweilers over there? She's too fat, she's looking older and he looks ill. And Myron T. Curtiz, did you see him coming in? They tell me he's got a new mistress, but I heard he put her in Second Class so Mrs. Curtiz wouldn't find out, but she will of course."

"Second Class, huh?" Bloomstein was studying his menu. "No way to keep a mistress. The marriage may survive."

"No, there'll be a divorce, and Myron will be coming to see you, Manny—for help with the alimony. Now look at Molly O'Sullivan on the table behind us. Her mother came over Steerage from Ireland in rags and now she's in a gown made in Paris."

"So? My mother came over Steerage from Hamburg in rags and I got a suit made in London. Less of the social news, Miriam, and drink your Champagne, it's getting warm already."

"Yes, but have you seen the Bilinski's daughter...?"

Mr. and Mrs. Dexter were the best-dressed and youngest couple among Chester Bryson's American guests. They were affable, and sought to engage Jon and Maisie in conversation about their wedding, their work at the shipyard, and the wonders of the new liner, but were interrupted by the arrival of the hors d'oeuvres.

"Look, Jon," said Maisie, "oysters, and that must be the shrimp butter on toast. What's that black stuff?"

"That's caviar."

"Oh. All funny fishy things," she whispered to Jon. "My Mam always says that kind of fish is better left at the bottom of the sea. I never even liked winkles at home. I'm more of a straight fish-and-chips girl..."

"Don't I know it," smiled Jon, remembering their romantic adventures on the Fish Quay.

"…as long as I get an Engagement ring with it," she giggled. "No, I think I'll wait for the soup."

"We'll wait for the soup," announced Jon.

The dimensions of the ship were discussed and her splendours admired. The soups were brought. The clear soup was a Russian flavoured consommé. Jon and Maisie chose the thick soup, a rich cream of chicken, and found it delicious. Mrs. van Hoof mentioned that tiny ripples were appearing in the millpond of her dish.

"Reckon we're putting on speed down the Irish Sea here," declared Bryson—and Jon made a mental note to cable his father about continuing vibration.

"What if we have to get to the lifeboats?" queried Mrs. van Hoof with sudden anxiety. "I notice we've had no lifeboat drill yet. Well, come on, what if we were sinking? Would any of you know the fastest way out to the boats?"

"Why must people always discuss the sinking of a ship when they're on one?" complained Mrs. Dexter. "It's not quite a nice thing to talk about, is it? I mean, these things do happen. It could happen to us…oh my, I'm doing it myself: talking about sinking."

There was genial laughter.

"I never heard such bunkum." Chester Bryson took up his spoon. "Why, this ship has a double-skinned hull; she's practically unsinkable. And she is the magnificent result of the very finest British engineering. Ask our young friend here. He helped build those smooth turbine engines that only just stir our soup."

There were interjections of 'ooh, ah, really, how

fascinating', and diamond-flashing attention was turned towards Jon. Bryson carried on.

"On second thoughts, don't ask him. The specifications and statistics of the engines alone would boggle your minds. Just accept that a turbine engine at full speed could make crossing miles of ocean seem like stepping over a pond."

"That's all very well, Chester," said his wife, "but we don't want the fun to be over too quickly. I like plenty of time on a big boat. I'm just beginning to enjoy the food and I fancy a few more dinners like this before I have to rough it back in a Manhattan restaurant."

"The day I see you roughing it, Louella, I'll triple your dining allowance."

Merry laughter accompanied the arrival of the fish. It was Dover Sole.

"Traditional English fayre," Bryson smiled at the large fish placed before him, "and plenty of it, huh?"

Jon made conversation from his standing invitation to tour the engine-room with *Mauretania's* Chief Engineer John Currie, who knew of his work at Parsons'.

"I last saw the turbines when they were being lowered into place," he explained. "It should be good to see them settled in."

"Like looking up old friends, I guess." Bryson smiled at Jon. "I admire a man who brings sentiment and passion to his work."

"And I admire you, Mr. Bryson. I am so glad you

were in the right place at a very tricky moment…" Maisie nudged Jon's knee under the table. "…I mean when my wife lost her hatpin."

"Do you know our distinguished Captain Pritchard?" asked Mrs. Dexter.

"I'm afraid not. I don't expect to be touring the bridge, but I'm lucky to be invited below. Chief Engineers can be very jealous of their secret kingdoms, you know."

"Well," said Bryson, "looks like you're in with the right people to get us to New York on time—and if we don't get in on time we'll hold you responsible, young feller."

The fish was followed by the magnificent entrees course: Chicken Lyonnaise, fragrant with its onion sauce, and fillet steaks on beds of potatoes smothered in a buttery brandy sauce, each offering topped ostentatiously with a truffle…and the wineglasses now flushed crimson with the choicest Bordeaux.

"This beats dinner at Heaton Road, eh?" Jon smiled at Maisie.

"You'd better not say that in front of Betty when we get home," she replied between mouthfuls.

The van Hoofs made no secret of the fact that they had trailed their daughter round Europe in seach of a husband and that the trip had failed to produce a fiancé. Nobody seemed to mind, least of all the daughter herself. If she felt embarrassment at having her plight made into table-talk, she covered it with an able brashness.

"Well, Mother, it's just that none of the men you found for me were handsome enough!"

"Or rich enough, I guess." Chester Bryson seized another opportunity to share his opinions. "Most of these old European families just don't have the cash any more. Now maybe it's different in England." He turned to Mrs. van Hoof. "You should have spent more time in London. Plenty handsome young men in England." He turned to Maisie. "This young lady found one." There were chuckles as Maisie looked down at her plate. "Well, I can't deny the truth, even if I have to embarrass you, my dear."

Jon looked him in the eye.

"You're doing a fine job of it, Mister Bryson."

"Speaking of attractive men," said Mrs. Dexter with a gleam in her eye, "we hear the Baron von Telschau is aboard. He was in the papers when some princess or other swooned over him in public. My, is he some good-looker!"

"I don't care," stated Edith van Hoof. "I'm not interested in some German baron with a fierce moustache and sabre-cuts."

"I doubt you'd have those problems, my dear. I understand he's an industrialist, not a military man."

"All Germans are military men," declared Bryson, "which will be why the Baron has not dined with his more civilised fellow travellers. He'll have had sausages and beer in his cabin; now he'll be in the gymnasium, if there's one on this ship, there usually is: a floating torture-chamber dedicated to Teutonic ideals of fitness."

"If he has beer and sausages every night he'll need to spend time in the gym," said Edith. Her pert comment was rewarded with peals of laughter.

"You see why she's still single?" Jon whispered to Maisie. "All wit and no charm."

"Well," smiled Louella Bryson, "even if he is rich, handsome—and fit—I'd beware of marrying him. You'd have to change from a 'van' to a 'von', and you know what they say: 'change the name and not the letter, marry for worse and not for better.'"

"Bunkum," said Bryson. "Edith is pretty enough to charm the entire German aristocracy. But aristocracy's not everything. Like I say, not so much cash these days."

"Well," said Jon as the entrées gave way to the roasts, "our gallant German baron is missing the excellent duckling. I don't think I've seen it done better."

"The lamb smells wonderful," remarked Maisie as steaming dishes were carried past her. "The last time I had lamb with mint sauce was with your folks at the big house. I'd like to have it again."

"If you'd like it you'd better have it, Darling." Jon smiled at her and ordered the steward to pour the next wine, a Beaujolais. "You have anything you want. It's our honeymoon and it's going to be treats all the way."

Conversation flagged as a sorbet was presented after the meat and was in turn replaced by delicately roasted quail on beds of lettuce and celery. Then came Paté de Foie Gras with sweet Sauternes to drink and, after that, the vast confection of a Waldorf Pudding—but Maisie's eye was caught by the enormous French chocolate eclairs with their choice of brown or white icing.

"Where are you putting it all?" smiled Jon, truly delighted that she was enjoying this feast so much.

At last, after desserts of fresh fruit and cheeses and renewed glasses of Champagne, it was time to retire for coffee and cigars.

"Gentlemen," announced Louella Bryson, still beaming with fresh good humour after her mountainous meal, "you may go to the Smoking-Room."

"I am surely on my way," said Bryson, heaving himself to his feet. He turned to Jon. "And you'll come and tell me more about these turbines."

"Thank you," replied Jon, "but no chance of that. Maisie and I are pretty tired. It's been a frantic two days: wonderful, but frantic. We'll take a turn around the deck then we'll be off to our cabin."

"Ooh," cooed Mrs. Dexter, "you two lovebirds!"

"Is it really true you were only married yesterday?" smiled Mrs. Bloomstein.

"Yes," answered Jon, "yesterday. It's amazing; it seems so long ago."

"We've lost track of time," said Maisie.

"My dear," said Mrs. Dexter, "on your honeymoon, on a romantic voyage, you're supposed to!"

"Well," Jon explained, "we mustn't sleep in tomorrow morning. We don't want to miss Queenstown. I've never seen Ireland. I believe it's beautiful."

"Honeymooners," Chester Bryson extended his arms, "I excuse you—and I salute you."

Hands were shaken, cheeks were kissed, and

goodnights were wished.

"Back here for dinner tomorrow," insisted Bryson with a cheeky grin. "You'll have worked up a fresh appetite by then."

At last Jon and Maisie escaped to the shocking freshness of the boat deck. The drizzle had stopped; the night was becoming cold and clear. Stars were visible between parting clouds and there were lights on a distant shore to port. Perhaps it was Anglesey; they could not be sure. *Mauretania* ghosted along. Jon knew she was running well below her full speed, but even here she seemed fast, as if already in pursuit of the Blue Ribband. The funnels hissed purposefully above; beneath their feet was a persistent hum and the slight impression of a curving, slicing, corkscrew motion through the black waters of this calm sea. Maisie, despite all her food and drink, was wide awake and prickled her unease into Jon's tired mind.

"Do you think this German baron could be the secret agent the Russians warned us about?"

"No, of course not. How could he be? A baron? It would be beneath his dignity. All the Russians said was that there might be German agents anywhere these days—which is true enough, I suppose—and that there might be some rumour that an English engineer would be aboard with plans for a secret weapon. That rumour I do *not* believe."

"But," Maisie persisted, "if there was that rumour, how would it get out? From the Russians themselves, of course."

"It's all nonsense, Darling, all improbable stuff, worse than a magazine story. Anyway, the Russians don't want the plans to fall into German hands. They told us that back at

North Shields. That's the whole point of the secret compartment."

"Aye well, I don't trust anyone in this business. You watch out for this German, keep away from him when he shows up."

"Isn't he supposed to spend his time in his cabin eating sausages then working it off in the gynmasium?"

"You shouldn't believe that either. He's a famously handsome womaniser, isn't he? He'll be sniffing round First Class looking for wealthy widows."

"You've been listening to too much of that American dinner-table gossip. The fact is, nobody on board here knows about that compartment but us. This baron and a dozen German agents could walk past it every day and never find it or open it. I'm convinced we're safe."

"Well I'm glad you are. I'm not convinced at all."

"We shouldn't listen to silly gossip or worry about what isn't proven. Let's have a look at the wake before we turn in."

He led Maisie towards the stern. One or two determined after-dinner walkers were striding the boat deck and another couple had braved the chilly night to stand at the opposite rail and look at the distant lights ashore. The man was tall in a long coat, the woman had tied a scarf over her hat in a familiar English way. Their elegance commanded attention, but Jon directed Maisie to look astern and they studied the ship's phosphorescent wake. As he had expected, it had the gentle curve of a much-elongated 'S' being constantly corrected from the bridge—and vibration was far more evident at the stern rails than it had been in the cabin or

Dining-Room.

"It's what I thought," he told Maisie. "There's more work to do on this vibration problem. It's not the engines. When I go down there I should be able to put my hand on a turbine casing and hardly feel a wobble. What she really needs is a set of different screws, but it's so expensive to take a big liner out of service even for a comparatively small job like that, she won't get them for a long time. Are you cold? I am. Let's go in."

They turned, eager to reclaim the glowing warmth of *Mauretania's* interiors and the cosiness of their cabin. The deck-walkers and the other couple seemed to share the idea; they were all leaving the ship's rails together. Then Maisie felt a sudden tightening of Jon's hand. She turned to look at him and saw a strange expression. His lips had actually trembled. It was only for a moment. He was recovering. She took his arm and held him close and fancied she could feel his heart beating madly.

"What is it? What's the matter? Tell me. You've gone white!"

"I…I think I've seen Philippa."

CHAPTER
TWENTY-SEVEN
Into the Ocean

The next morning, in fair weather, *Mauretania* docked at Queenstown for two hours to take on mail and more passengers. The huge liner eased into the wide and beautiful harbour of Cobh, passengers lining the rails and admiring distant views to the mountains of County Cork. Closer to the shore, farms and villages still wore the bright colours of a lush Autumn against a background of brilliant green, all under mild sunshine that made this landfall a warm surprise after a chilly night at sea. Many passengers took advantage of the brief stop to rush ashore, posting letters and sending telegrams.

Jon and Maisie stood on the ship's highest deck and looked down at a dark mass of people embarking for Third Class passage to America. There were women wearing shawls, burdened with numerous children.

"Irish emigrants," explained Jon.

"Just look at them," said Maisie gloomily, "those poor people with nothing but what they stand up in."

"They are the fortunate ones, going to a new life. There's been no luck in Ireland these last fifty years or longer."

Jon privately wished them luck, and luck for himself

and Maisie. He felt in need of some. They had passed a difficult night, much of it uncomfortably awake as they discussed the consequences of Philippa being aboard. Jon could not be absolutely sure that the woman he had glimpsed was she, but the figure at the stern rail with her tall male companion had worn a scarf over her hat in just the same way as Philippa had on that long-ago drive to their new house in Lily Avenue; and when she had turned to go, the erect bearing, the profile, and the profusion of hair glimpsed between scarf and face had been the same. And if that was Philippa, who was the man? It hardly mattered, they told each other. What mattered, insisted Maisie, was not to let her presence ruin their own happiness. She remembered only too well how it had felt to be criticised and insulted by Jon's first wife...but had she not slapped her face and told her to go? And Philippa had gone, accepting the divorce, and if she was travelling to America for business or to make a new life, well, they couldn't stop her. But they could stop feeling threatened. Yes, it was a devilish mischance that she should be on this very ship, spoiling the sweetness of their honeymoon with old woes...but what harm could she really do them now? They were together, married, and on their way to a new chapter in their lives, indeed already in it, making new joys and memories that nobody should be able to sour. If they had to face her they would do so, bravely and secure in their own happiness. Then they would ignore her. All would be well. Look what they had come through together already! This would have to be overcome as just another annoyance. Yes, it might be a cruel trick of Fate, but their own destiny was more powerful.

Jon wished he could share Maisie's strong and simple philosophy. If Philippa really was aboard in First Class, he felt the remainder of this voyage would be a refined torture, a poisoned hell after the delightful success and happy relief of their first day. But at last they had slept, and with no sign of Philippa at breakfast or here on deck, they were beginning to feel easier. Jon tried to convince himself it might not have been Philippa at all.

"Perhaps we'll hear some Irish fiddlers," Maisie's bright enthusiasm cut through Jon's thoughts. "We could go down there later. I love Irish fiddle music. There was an Irish family in Union Street."

Jon shifted uncomfortably.

"We can't really go down there, Darling. It's not the thing to do."

"Oh, I see," she bristled. "'Not done', eh?"

"Well, no, not really. Some First Class passengers visit Third. It's called 'slumming'. It's very rude to embarrass those people…"

"You mean by walking through Steerage in evening-dress and diamond necklaces?"

"Well, yes."

"I don't have a diamond necklace. You could wear an ordinary suit."

"No, really," he said more sharply, "we mustn't do that."

Maisie nudged him with her hip.

"Mustn't go 'slumming'." He found her infuriatingly pert. "I've embarrassed you, haven't I? I'll always know more about slums than you."

"Put it this way," Jon gripped the rail. "You felt rightly sorry for those poor people. Some others don't. Philippa wouldn't. She would go down there, look in at their bunks, and laugh at them."

Maisie hung her head, the mild breeze on her hot face.

"I'm sorry. I'm sorry. You've got enough to worry about without me saying stupid things and doing things she would do."

Jon hugged her waist.

"You're incapable of doing what she would do, and you've never said anything stupid. You're full of good sense. I rely on you to keep me right."

She gave a little laugh in reply, then stared out over the blue water and green fields.

"I'll be glad to get on from here," she said. "Ireland looks beautiful, but it's somehow a sad country."

* * *

Second Class passenger Jakob Schramml settled into his cabin. He had not expected to travel in such style. His was the world of Steerage, of penniless emigrants, of uprooted families, of harsh poverty, of the ghetto, of oppression, of sour disappointments and bleak prospects—but here he was, unpacking good clothes in a floating room better than any he had known on land in the Jewish quarters of Dresden and Berlin. He was a small man with a premature stoop and the slightly shuffling walk of someone who must always be uncertain and insecure, but his eyes were magnificent. They were large and dark, containing and revealing every characteristic from shiftiness to jollity and every emotion from despair to joy. Regarding these eyes in the washbasin mirror, he allowed himself a smile of satisfaction. All was well so far; rather better than he had expected. But if the conditions of his voyage were welcome, they were also unfamiliar, and would surely be full of social pitfalls he must avoid. Indeed he had been ordered to avoid them, to blend in, to arouse no suspicion or even interest. His orders were to do what he had been told to do, do it without being seen, and then to disappear. It would have been easier to do it from the privileged position of a First Class passenger, but his masters had rightly judged he would appear alien in such surroundings—and alien qualities might be noticed. In Third Class he would have been unremarkable, but the access his task demanded might be denied him. Second Class conferred respectability without ostentation. So, Second Class it was, and he would not object. Life in Germany was full of orders, orders had taken him on a cautiously-planned and deliberately circuitous route to Ireland, orders were taking him across the Atlantic, and orders would return him to obscurity somewhere in the middle of Europe. In addition to elements of danger, it was a tedious business, but with his orders came his pay. It was extraordinarily generous: sufficient to buy all his tickets for this journey half-way round the world and back, with enough left over to re-settle him in his old country with comforts he had never been able to afford before. He had only to obey his orders.

While Jakob Schramml washed his face and stowed his belongings, Jon and Maisie watched *Mauretania* leave Ireland and slide into a great expanse of ocean. Their vertiginous gaze down the wall of riveted steel showed her bow knifing through the water and her wake streaming its double track of whiteness astern. An Atlantic swell came to give the first real feelings of a ship breasting significant waves, and the call to lunch was answered on legs that had to adapt to a slight pitching of decks and corridors. Tureens of soup and decanters of wine revealed the motion, but *Mauretania's* vast solidity seemed to settle around the tables and Jon and Maisie were able to enjoy their meal as sedately as if the ship had still been moored in port. To their increasing relief, Philippa did not appear. They began to allow themselves the thought that Jon really had been mistaken. If she was aboard, suggested Maisie, she might be conveniently confined to her cabin by seasickness.

"I'm sorry to say," Jon remarked drily, "she's tougher than that—as you might guess. This little swell won't be bothering her."

"With a bit of luck it'll get worse then, and she can be seasick all the way to New York."

Jon could not help laughing at her naughtiness. They tried to put thoughts of Philippa behind them, finished lunch, and prepared for Jon's visit to the Engine Room. He had sent a message to the Chief Engineer and been told this afternoon would be convenient. He insisted that Maisie should accompany him, and told her that if the Chief Engineer wasn't expecting a woman he would just have to accept that times had changed and that Mr. and Mrs. Ferris had contributed equally to the creation of the ship whose engines he was now lucky enough to command. At the appointed time they went astern and waited in the deserted and windswept Verandah Café, its trellis work and potted plants looking forlorn in the worsening weather.

"Aye, it's a miserable place in the wet and will attract no custom," droned a Scottish voice, and they turned to be greeted by Chief Engineer John Currie, as formidable a figure as a Captain in his brass-buttoned frock-coat and imposing moustache, but with cheerful blue eyes. "We'll be cosier below."

Introductions were made and hands shaken. Currie led them to stairwells and companionways they had imagined but never discovered.

"Despite your duties at the shipyard you'll not have been down to an Engine Room before," he twinkled at Maisie. "No, well, mind how you go and keep one hand for yourself. We're feeling the lumpy seas."

"An Engine Room," Jon told her, "is one of only two places you enter from above and that gets hotter as you go down. The other one is Hell."

"That's an old joke, Mister Ferris, and one we'll not find humorous on this ship."

"That was a daft thing to say." Maisie's whisper was covered by the increasing noise accompanying their descent. "You'll upset him."

"No offence intended, Mister Currie," said Jon hastily.

"None taken, laddie. You'll find the turbines you built at Parsons' sit nicely at home down here and everything is as neat and clean as a front parlour. More Heavenly than Hellish, you'll agree."

"Of course. We're looking forward to seeing it all."

Down and down they went into the convoluted, heaving, metal body of the ship, increasingly warm and noisy with the throb of machinery and roar of vented air. This metallic, white-painted, humming hive beyond doors closed to most passengers seemd more real and in some ways more exciting than the finely-furnished cabins and glittering public rooms they had left. This ship of spartan quarters and relentless toil was as much their creation as the ship of gilded carvings and fine dining. But it was also uncomfortably hot, thronged with busy crewmen, and its strong-smelling mixture of oil, fresh paint and stale odours was becoming nauseous in this rough weather. It was a place without ornament but not without the grandeur of ambitious design; a world without luxury but not without the elegance of efficiently applied engineering. At last came a sense of being below the waterline. They passed near the sides of the hull and fancied they could hear powerful waves beyond the steel plates.

"Well now. The stokehold first, I think."

Currie opened a throbbing steel door and they were plunged into an orgy of heat and noise, assaulted by smells of coal dust and raging fires. There was the shocking spectacle of men stripped to the waist, the glistening sweat of their faces and bodies grimed with ash and coal dust. The range of enormous boilers towered into the roof of the stokehold, filling it with their elephantine, nightmarish presence and almost unimaginable heat.

"See what I mean?" Jon reckoned his words into Maisie's ear would be covered by the din. "Hell!"

On the steel floor, the workers moved at a hurried but ordered pace, back and forth with shovels and wheelbarrows, going with an experienced ease through the rolls and pitches of the ship. Trimmers brought the coal, stokers flung shovelfuls into the furnaces, firemen raked searingly hot beds under the boilers. All were silent and seemed to ignore the clean and finely-dressed visitors to their pungent, scorching inferno, or to regard them with a sullen disdain. Currie explained their relentless routine and how the steam it was required to constantly produce was fed into the turbines. It struck Jon very forcibly that the sleek modern machines that drove the ship were themselves powered by this archaic torment of men hurling coal into furnaces and tending great fires—and how the development of his own invention must forever banish such slavery by using a different fuel in the body of the air-engine itself. Suddenly, a blackened face grinned at them with gleaming teeth and pointed at his equally grimy companion scratching a hurried white circle round Jon's feet. The men nodded briefly at Maisie and went on with their work. She poked Jon in the ribs.

"Money," she told him.

"Aye, you've been chalked," explained Currie with good humour. He knew no visitor would escape without making a donation to the stokers' fund.

Jon groped for some coins and dropped them into the wheelbarrow that had suddenly appeared at his knee.

"I'll send a crate of beer down later," he said loudly.

"That will be much appreciated, sir." Currie had been interested to meet the young engineer from Parsons' and charmed by the unexpected but now very welcome presence of the pretty and intelligent wife, but he would be equally happy to be rid of his guests. The stokehold was a long way from First Class and there was little benefit here to those who crossed the divide. He took them into the Engine Room proper: dramatically cleaner and quieter than the reeking stokehold. With majestic poise, *Mauretania's* six turbines sat inside their massively rounded casings, their drive-shafts running aft to the screws. There was the whine of metal spinning securely on well-oiled bearings. Inside the casings, the unseen vanes of the rotors were working their magic of turning a blast of steam into circular motion.

"They look like giant caterpillars on broom handles," observed Maisie.

"And just as hungry," chuckled Currie. "The beasties need a lot of steam, but you saw us making that nicely enough."

"Wonderfully smooth," said Jon with a sense of awe, "just as I knew they would be."

He approached the nearest turbine, made a protective pad with his handkerchief, and—as he had promised himself and Maisie—laid his hand momentarily against the casing. It was fiercely hot, but only the faintest buzz beneath his fingers suggested the awesome power being generated inside. He felt a surge of pride and intense satisfaction. He had kept that promise to his father not to weaken or fail at this job. He had worked at it, distracted by unimaginable events and tossed by almost unbearable emotions, but he had seen it through. Now it was completed and he was witnessing its spectacular outcome at sea. Maisie sensed his mood and took his hand in a silent gesture that meant more to Jon than he could easily have expressed. The Chief Engineer broke the spell with another announcement.

"I'll not take you into the shaft tunnel; a wee bit wet and splashy in there. We're dealing with a faulty seal."

They still felt an exciting proximity to the four mighty screws churning steadily beyond the stern plates. They could feel the thrashing of the water and the shuddering vibration set up by the blades and the resistance of increasingly heavy seas.

"I'll be glad to get my engines through this weather," admitted Currie as they thanked him and were escorted back up through the ship. "I suspect there'll be more leftovers than usual from First Class tonight," he added wryly.

"The stokers will enjoy that," answered Jon. "I

remember explaining to my wife how well they dined."

"We were having fish-and-chips at North Shields," laughed Maisie.

"I know the Tyne ports," answered Currie. "Well," he continued, steadying himself at a hand-rail, "as you say, the worse for the fine folks' stomachs above, the better for my crew below—but don't let me spoil your dinner now. You enjoy the rest of your time aboard. I trust that you, Mister Ferris, will be telling your father and the people back at Parsons' how sweetly she runs."

"Most certainly, Mister Currie. I shall be proud to."

They returned to the upper decks full of good humour, joking that they needed a good wash, but feeling even more closely involved with the excitement and drama of their magnificent ship's maiden voyage. They knew, with a deep happiness, that it was also their own.

By the time they were dressed for dinner there was light rain from a solidly grey sky as *Mauretania* headed West into a stiffening wind. Spray came over her bows and beat against her Dining-Room windows, but the atmosphere inside remained warm and opulent. Jon and Maisie made another descent of the Grand Staircase, smiling to themselves at their secret knowledge of the plans tucked safely behind its panelling. The string orchestra played tunes from Tchaikovsky ballets, diamond jewellery flashed, sweet flowers bloomed on every table and delicious hints of French perfume drifted among the silken dresses. Through the magnificent doors they could see that Chester Bryson's table was already lively with conversation, and knew their genial host would be fascinated to hear their tales from the Engine Room.

"May I say 'good evening'…"

The voice came from just behind them. It contained the lilt of a smile, perhaps a wry one. It was Philippa's voice.

"...without putting you off your dinner, I hope?"

For a moment they were rigid, remained tightly hand-in-hand, then had to turn. There gleamed the bright hair, the flamboyant dress exposing some seductive throat and shoulder, a glittering necklace, the smooth face looking only a little older than on her wedding day, the direct stare. Suddenly—he could not have said exactly why—Jon remembered how she had looked at Craster, the ecstacy in her face as she stared along the windy Northumbrian coast to the ruins of Dunstanburgh Castle on that very different honeymoon, so long before Maisie had shown him her drawings or *Mauretania* had steamed down the Tyne. He remembered her from what now seemed a time of innocence, an innocence she had corrupted and which Jon himself had allowed to die and which his new marriage to Maisie, delightful though it was, could not contain. He was stabbed with the pain of the loss of this innocence; if he had been alone with time to reflect upon it he might have wept. In the same moment, Maisie remembered slapping this woman's face and what little immediate effect that shocking action had produced. It was a clever face, pretty, even beautiful, but somehow unresponsive, as if it could be beaten and bruised and still wear an impertinent smile. She gathered herself into a kind of pillar of strength to cope with this, felt tight and hard inside and determined that she would allow nothing to destroy what she had just secured. The tall man with whom they had seen Philippa at the rail waited stiffly behind in immaculate evening-dress. Through the frozen tableau Jon found his voice.

"Hello again."

Philippa laughed.

"What you really mean to say is 'fancy meeting you here'—or something like that." She turned a colder stare upon Maisie. "I don't suppose *you* fancy meeting me here."

"Or anywhere," retorted Maisie.

"Touché!" Philippa's smile glittered at Jon again. "The girl has spirit. I told her that in our little meeting in your house. And I sense she has grown even more confident. You: remarkably the same."

"Look, Philippa," Jon held tightly to Maisie, "we are very happy…"

"…and we don't need you to tell us what we're like and we don't want you making us unhappy." Maisie squirmed but spoke forcefully.

"How could I possibly do that? I am divorced from your husband—my, doesn't that sound quaint?—and we're all on a happy ship going to America. *Our* ship, isn't it? Doesn't it feel special being just being aboard her?"

The shock was subsiding but Jon remained wary of her apparent friendliness.

"I might ask what *you* are doing aboard her."

"It's a kind of holiday…and I may have business in New York."

"Plenty of advertising posters over there, eh?"

"I hope so."

She sounded harmless, but Jon couldn't resist a stab.

"Isn't it really that you've been driven out of England

by your own wickedness?"

He felt Maisie wince and wished he had stifled the impulsive comment, but Philippa smiled at it.

"Well, funnily enough, yes, in a way. That's oddly perceptive of you. Let's just say I needed to get away from some people in my past and make a new start in America. Is that what you're doing?"

"Not exactly. It's a honeymoon and a business trip combined."

Would this agonised conversation end? thought Jon. No, she was persistent.

"You know I sold the painting to Cunard?"

"Yes."

"It's in their Head Office. I'd have liked to know it was here on the ship, but never mind," she turned to Maisie, "now I see it did me a lot of good, you know, living in Jesmond with Jon, painting that picture. Pity we couldn't have got on better…but then you two wouldn't have got on so well, would you? Perhaps you wouldn't have got on at all. Perhaps it's all worked out for the best. Part of the agreement about the painting was that Cunard offered me free passage to America on this ship. I have decided to take up that offer, and here I am."

"How very convenient," said Jon flatly.

"It has been—more than you could know. Anyway, I'm not in the mood for recriminations. To be honest, I can barely say 'recriminations' after my three aperitifs."

"We want to go into dinner," stated Maisie, tugging at Jon's arm.

"Oh, no," insisted Philippa, "not until I have introduced my new friend. We only met in the lounge yesterday but we're getting on famously, aren't we, Freddie? Allow me to present the Baron von Telschau."

Her celebrated escort was astonishingly handsome, clean-shaven and sun-tanned with gleamingly sleeked hair. He had the look of an athlete, even in his firmly starched shirt and dazzling white tie; a severely cut tail-coat enhancing his slim figure. He did not seem the arrogant cliché of the Germanic military man that had been joked about over last night's dinner. He exuded instead an air of vast wealth and effortless poise. He must have been at least forty but his surprisingly youthful face was full of boyish smiles.

"Charmed, I am sure," he intoned, taking their hands in turn, bending a kiss over Maisie's wrist and clicking his heels. "Of course," he continued in a too-perfect English that could not entirely banish a sinister tone, "it is usual for guests to be presented to *me*."

"Yes, yes," Philippa hurried on, "but this is special company, Freddie; a quite extraordinary meeting. It blows away your silly protocol. This is my ex-husband and his new wife. They both had a hand in the building of this very ship, you know."

As might have been expected, the Baron was utterly correct. He seemed not at all flustered, as if uneasy encounters between divorced spouses and their new partners were routine. It crossed Maisie's mind that perhaps, in his circles, such meetings *were* routine. He smiled and showed polite interest while Philippa continued to talk.

"We might all have met properly last night…" her voice was of a woman chatting to friends, refusing to acknowledge the uncomfortable drama of this meeting. Jon found the effect uncanny; Maisie regarded every word with frowning suspicion. "…but that wretched train from London was late. I was dog-tired, couldn't face dressing up and coming down to dinner. I had something in my cabin, took a look around the deck and went to bed. Now I'm as fresh as a daisy."

"A daisy!" von Telschau beamed handsomely. "What a charming image of English freshness."

"Yes, isn't it? But freshness isn't quite what it was." Philippa turned brazenly to Jon. "There was a time when—perhaps after a meeting like this—you might have sent a bottle of Champagne to my table with a tag saying 'thanks for the memories'. Don't tell me I'm becoming more of a romantic than you are…though I suppose you couldn't do such a thing in front of your new wife. But I want you to know I would have accepted the gift and drunk it with affection."

"I do not believe you."

She turned a softening expression upon Maisie.

"He's proud and hurt. I hurt him, I know, but he keeps hurting himself. You look after him. He needs looking after."

"Good night, Philippa," declared Jon stiffly. "Good night, Herr Baron. We must go our separate ways."

"Oh no," said Philippa across the gap widening between them, "we should make up and stay friends on this voyage. There's a lot of ocean still to cross."

"We'll cross it our way," said Jon with determination, "you cross it yours. Good night."

"She seems different," whispered Maisie as they walked on a little shakily. "D'you think she's genuine? You know, about being friends? Not that I want to be."

"No. She is a mine of insincerity."

They went in to dinner, Philippa and von Telschau to a corner table, Jon and Maisie to join the Brysons and their chattering companions. They were scarcely aware of the food that passed before them. With difficulty they told the story of their visit to the stokehold and Engine Room. What should have been a vivid account of a special experience seemed lifeless and tiresome. They did not take coffee in the lounge and went early to their cabin.

"Well, that was bloody awful," said Jon. "I'm sorry."

"It's not your fault she's travelling on the same ship. It's just bad luck."

"It's devilish Fate. We just can't get away from her."

"We can get away from her." Maisie began to undress. "We already have."

"So Germans actually do that—click their heels. For God's sake come to bed. I need you. She was right when she said that."

They lay still for a while, feeling the ship rise and fall and roll, return to a solid heaviness, then repeat the motion through seemingly endless seas. Jon looked at the ceiling while Maisie snuggled into his neck. At last she spoke.

"Do you still find her attractive?"

"No."

"Liar."

"I'm not lying." He felt sad and sour. "How could I find anyone attractive who brings discord between us? This is the very last thing I ever wanted to happen: exchanging sharp words and awkward feelings and being accused of lying by the person I love most in all the world. I wanted us to marry, enjoy this honeymoon, and never see her again."

"All right. I'm sorry. But she is attractive, Jon. The men buzz round her. So, is the German buzzing round her or is she after him?"

"Bit of both, I imagine. If he has money and influence, she'll be after it. If he wants to add her to his list of conquests, he's welcome to her."

"We shouldn't have to talk like this," she sighed. "It's horrible."

"Yes, it is horrible, but we must get over it and be ourselves again. I wanted this trip to be a real joy."

"It will be," she whimpered. "I know she's spoilt it, but she can't spoil *us*. Trust me." They cuddled together, Jon rather stolidly. "Come on," said Maisie with a chuckle, "it's like cuddling an ironing-board."

Jon laughed faintly; she cuddled him more tightly. She would warm him up and make them both really comfortable. It was happening already. She felt there was something pure and magical in being aboard this great ship as it sped through an empty ocean, especially when it was the ship they had both worked on. She imagined being suspended in the dark sky above and behind *Mauretania*, riding the stormy air like an angel and looking down at the beautiful ship they had made, admiring her lines and blessing every part of her from bow to stern, especially the parts she had drawn herself. The childish, happy fantasy of this image banished the malignant embarrassment of Philippa being aboard. She told herself it really didn't matter where Philippa was, she was beyond them and outside their love. They were warm together now…but slept only fitfully.

* * *

Jakob Schramml sat in the Second Class Dining-Room with a slight headache. Perhaps he was going to be seasick; the pitching had certainly worsened, and there was now a roll to the ship's motion. People were saying it was becoming very windy on deck. Perhaps he wouldn't be sick; he may just have over-indulged. It would be easy to do so with this splendid food in such beautiful surroundings. He guessed the finely panelled and decorated room would be only slightly less magnificent than whatever lay upstairs in First Class, and that whatever was being eaten on the higher deck would scarcely be better than this, although he smiled to think that the privilege of eating it would be costing those diners twice as much. He understood that his roast turkey with cranberry sauce was what they liked in America. So, he would get used to it! Plum Pudding with a sweet custard sauce followed. Other people were choosing American ice-cream and fresh fruit. Fine! This was a long way from the Hamburg soup-kitchens. As for Third Class, he suspected stews and bread far below. Even that would be healthy enough, but he would be pleased to be where he was. He would enjoy it all while he could, and quoted himself the old saying that a rich man eats when he likes, a poor man when he can. When he had finished his coffee and returned to his bunk, he found the rocking was exaggerated by his lying down. Well, he wasn't going to stand up all night. He would take whatever the ocean threw at him. He wouldn't care if he was seasick all the way over and all the way back on the different ship he had been told to take. He would do what he had been ordered to do. He tried to relax his body while his mind went over his instructions again and again: 'left, right, left, right…left, right, left, right.'

CHAPTER
TWENTY-EIGHT
The Storm

If *Mauretania's* passengers slept through the worsening weather, they awoke restlessly to a severe storm. The great ship's massive hull rose and fell between monstrous waves, taking the ocean's punishment stoutly enough, but when mountainous seas broke over her bows and thrashed against her superstructure, alarming damage became evident. As yet, her funnels remained secure, but even as high as the bridge, some rails were twisted. A lifeboat's cover was torn away and windows on the Promenade Deck were smashed. Rivulets of water began to appear inside the ship, increasing the anxiety of passengers.

Jon and Maisie prepared to go down for breakfast. Grey light and lashing seas foamed beyond the windows, the floors heaved and the bulkheads tilted. They told each other how lucky they were not to be seasick, although Jon had developed a headache. He did not relish the prospect of breakfast but knew it would be better to eat something. Maisie seemed unaffected by the ship's motion.

"And I've never been to sea before," she smiled.

"It's all that practice you had on the Shields ferry," answered Jon as jovially as he could.

"Just think," she went on, adjusting her dress, "if I'd

kept going over the river to that job in South Shields, we'd never have met."

Jon hugged her warmly.

"I can't tell you how pleased I am you got the drawing-loft job." He placed a kiss on her forehead. "It all started there."

"Are you all right?" She looked into his eyes and stroked his hair. They were surviving this storm so far; in a way, it was part of the excitement of their honeymoon, but it was alarming and uncomfortable and getting worse. Even amid the luxury of their beautiful ship, she felt trapped in a situation that was dangerous and strangely unclean. She longed to be free of it, warmed by sunshine and rinsed in the blue light that had blessed her outside Thockrington Church, high on the moors of her homeland. They would return one day; at present there were other concerns—like Jon's strained expression.

"A bit queasy," he confessed, "but I shouldn't be sick. My mind's running on other things."

"You mean Philippa?"

"Yes, and the plans."

"Oh, they'll be safe enough in their little cupboard. Nobody will be bothering to nose around in this weather. And d'you know what?" She placed her arms round Jon's waist. "I've quite got over Philippa being on the same ship. It doesn't matter. She can't hurt us. She's got her German baron to keep her amused."

"Yes. I wonder how long she'll keep *him* amused. I fancy his eye will wander."

"That's not our problem," said Maisie briskly. "Come on, let's go into the Lounge and watch the sea from there."

On the heaving staircase they met Mrs. van Hoof.

"Oh my, oh my! There's sea-water coming into our cabin. I'm going to get help but I can't find our steward. I didn't know such a big ship could be thrown around like this. I don't feel entirely safe, even in First Class."

"Think what it must be like in Third," said Maisie.

"Now now, Mrs. van Hoof," Jon gave her a smile. "I promise you we are completely safe. We have some nasty weather but it's nothing this ship can't take. My wife and I know how strongly she was built; you'll be all right."

"Well, if you say so—and you're lucky not to be seasick. I left my husband feeling sick. I've had to deal with everything myself this morning"

"There you are—you're tougher than you thought. If I were you I'd ask the steward for some water and dry biscuits and go back to your husband. You'll be fine when this blows over and you'll have some stories to tell when you get home."

"I surely will." She gave a weak smile and staggered away.

"You're good with the old ladies," said Maisie with a chuckle.

In Philippa's cabin, Friedrich von Telschau dressed as steadily as he could. He had had his way with her and found her most stimulating, but now the wretched Englishwoman was seasick. Her face was grey, her body was damp and sweaty, and unlovely smells issued from her mouth. How quickly a little bad weather could turn a woman from a naked goddess into a glumly nightgowned animal. He was pleased to be out of her bed. She had spent the last sleepless hours tossing about, making sharp movements unbecoming to the accomplished seductress he knew she imagined herself to be, prodding him with knees and elbows as she sought respite from the intolerable motion. It was difficult enough to stand up and button a waistcoat, but at least he could counteract the regular rolling of the ship and keep straight; lying down would be much worse. He had told her that more than once and would not do so again—but he decided to show compassion.

"How are you feeling, my darling girl?"

"Don't call me that, Freddie. You make me sound like some Cockney's tart."

She was surprised to see this man of the world look genuinely hurt.

"I should like it if someone called me darling." His faint grimace showed a sunburst of tiny lines around the handsomely tanned skin of his face. "It would tell me I was loved."

"Oh, for God's sake, Freddie, don't go soft on me, especially when I'm feeling rotten." He was being little-boyish; all men had something of this in them. Did he have more because of his German sentimentality? Her tired mind wandered. Did Oliver Gaine have this in him? Oliver Gaine: the best of all her men. They'd only had a couple of times together, and she hadn't even taken him to bed. He had rescued her with the noblest intentions. This one wouldn't rescue her if she was falling overboard. Bloody Fate, bloody seasickness, bloody men! "If you must know, Freddie, you *are* loved. The world loves you for being so handsome."

"That was not what I meant."

"I know it wasn't. Now *you* be a darling and leave me alone with this bloody seasickness. I'm too horrible when I'm ill."

"Quite. 'Wiedersehen."

He had marked her down, correctly, as an adventuress—but their adventure would have to be brought to an end. He had other business aboard this ship.

When he left her cabin the storm intensified. The howl of wind from a blackening sky could be heard throughout *Mauretania* as she beat her way into ever-increasing waves. Tons of water crashing down on to her foredeck at last broke loose the spare anchor. It became a destructive monster, sliding and bashing into metalwork and fittings. Its drastic progress had to be arrested before more significant damage was done. The engines were rung down to Slow Ahead and the ship's bow was turned away from the wind while valiant crewmen struggled to secure the gigantic battering ram that the sea could toss around like a walking-stick.

If no panic was shown in First Class, alarm was increased as the ship fell prey to deepening troughs of grey water. Without significant forward drive, she wallowed badly. Some passengers tried to settle with unsteady drinks in the Lounge or Smoking Room; most kept to their cabins. Baron von Telschau decided there could be no better time to execute his secret orders: orders he had carried dutifully on to this ship, orders he had diligently concealed throughout all his conversations with passengers, orders that excited him to the very core of his being…but suddenly he encountered Philippa's ex-husband and the new wife. Did these two ever go anywhere without linking arms or holding hands? The man greeted him cheerfully.

"Braving a walk, Herr Baron? What's the storm doing on deck?"

"I have not been out yet, but from what I have seen, the Americans are panicking and the English are putting on brave faces."

"Oh, the situation's normal then; nothing to worry about."

"I am not worried," von Telschau replied without humour. "Where are you going?"

"We were going to the Lounge."

"Myself also. Let us have strong coffee if a steward will bring it."

The coffee was brought. Without Philippa's company, von Telschau had the air of a club bore and insisted on talking politics.

"The Kaiser was most annoyed when your government built Dreadnought battleships before he did—but we are catching up in the matter of battleships."

"Do you have turbine engines," asked Jon blandly, "like ours in this ship?"

"I think we should not discuss technical details at this stage, Herr Ferris."

Jon smiled knowingly.

"I can see why you wouldn't want to, in front of a competitor."

Maisie looked von Telschau fiercely in the face.

"But you *are* going to know they are my husband's engines," she stated firmly. "He helped to build them."

"Congratulations. They are driving us steadily to America, even through this filthy weather. But to return to this matter of international competition: you should tell your King to abandon his frivolous French friends and throw in his lot with Germany…"

Jon listened with growing distaste, but also a wry enjoyment. The man's arrogance would be a good match for Philippa's.

"…or approach your government. Kings must listen to governments these days, especially English kings."

"I'm afraid we don't move in such exalted circles."

"I could introduce you. Only a few weeks ago I had dinner with the Kaiser himself." Jon and Maisie saw the admission fill the Baron with pride. He seemed to grow taller, replacing the nonchalance of his youthful face with a look of grave seriousness. It was almost funny, but also annoying. Jon could not resist a stab.

"Well, my ex-wife always manages to get to know the right people. She has a knack for sniffing out influential society."

The Baron was more interested in his own importance than Philippa's, and his conceit had loosened his tongue.

"His Imperial Majesty expressed a great interest in recent technological developments. Indeed he charged me with a most important duty." He stopped himself with a smile at Jon and Maisie. "Please accept I am not permitted to disclose its details. Let me say it is to safeguard and advance the industrial interests of our country, also the security of our important persons." He looked at Jon like a schoolboy seeking a friend, like a man offering privileges. "You English could be our allies in this, you know, in defence of the ruling classes."

"Not so long ago, I was talking to some Russian friends who wanted us as allies *against* the ruling classes."

"Pah! Communist swine!" von Telschau became vehement. "Let them burn themselves out in the wastelands of Russia. They will never destroy the ruling families of Europe."

"They seem to think otherwise," stated Jon calmly.

"Don't tell me you sympathise!"

"Not especially. We have no particular interest in getting worked up about foreign politics."

"Of course, the splendid isolation of the British." von Telschau was plainly contemptuous, but his good manners reduced a potential harangue to a veiled warning. It was given with as benign a smile as he could manage. "Well, you are on honeymoon, and that I suppose is the most splendid isolation of all. Enjoy it before the world presses in on you. Foreign politics has a habit of doing that, you know."

"We hope to avoid that sort of pressure in America."

"Ah yes, the so-called land of the free. It will be amusing to see how long it is before America has to take a stand against Communism. But I am boring you, my friends, or frightening you." He stood up and gave them a little bow. "I do wish you a happy honeymoon and good luck in America. It is said to be a good country for business."

"Yes. I hope to start an engineering business over there."

"Indeed!" The Baron's face lit up with boyish enthusiasm once more. "We may truly find ourselves as competitors. My engineering companies intend to exploit the American market also. That is one reason why I am on this ship and suffering this most tedious storm to get there. But do not worry. I grant you first look at American opportunities. I must return quickly to Europe; there will be more urgent business in Germany."

"Hang on tightly if you're going outside." Jon bid him farewell with a faint smile.

"I am going for a short walk around the ship. There are places I have not yet seen. Be assured I shall take great care of my own safety—and perhaps meet you at lunch."

"Perhaps not," whispered Maisie when the Baron was out of earshot. "He might get swept overboard—and he wouldn't be missed, would he? He's too full of himself for my liking."

"Oh, we don't want rid of the rather annoying Baron just yet, Darling. We need him to keep a certain lady occupied."

"So we can get her off our minds and make the most of this." Maisie nuzzled a kiss into Jon's neck. "I say let the ocean do what it likes. Our big ship's all right, she's looking after us. Let's have something to eat and go back for a cuddle."

It was in this same alarming hiatus of the voyage, with the ship's public spaces eerily deserted, that Jakob Schramml decided to execute his orders. He had been advised to wait until *Mauretania* was docked in New York, but then the ship would be crowded with bustling passengers and he would risk being seen. Today, everyone was preoccupied with the storm and Schramml left his cabin without being noticed. Trespassing into First Class would be trickier, but he knew his route, his passage was unhindered, and in moments he found himself before the Grand Staircase. The spectacle of this vast space and the temptation of the splendid public rooms beyond it made him hesitate. The ship was truly beautiful, but he told himself he was not here to admire beauty. He was here to steal.

"Left, right, left right." Nobody heard the muttered repetition of his mantra. Nobody saw him approach the magnificent carvings at the foot of the stairs. His fingers shivered a little as he found the bunch of grapes and pressed the polished wood. His heart leapt when the panel opened silently with its miraculous revelation. It took only a few seconds to remove the briefcase, close the panel, and walk away…not too quickly. He must stroll out of this part of the ship, not look at or hold the briefcase as if it contained dynamite, and not be seen descending into Second Class once more. The rich carpets heaved beneath his feet, the panelled walls creaked, the few passengers he encountered were intent on keeping their balance or gazing with horror at violent seas making their billowed assaults on the windows. In moments he was back at his own cabin door, opening it, closing it thankfully behind him, putting the briefcase on his bunk, and relaxing the muscles of his arms and neck as he felt his heartbeat quieten. Really, it had been ridiculously easy. He would be able to celebrate with a better dinner tonight, perhaps allow himself more wine. The ship groaned and roared around him, covering his deed with convenient distractions. He didn't feel seasick at all.

The Baron von Telschau strolled down the Grand Staircase with an affected air of nonchalance. Behind it, his body was tense and his mind alert with excitement—but he told himself to approach this dangerous moment not with fear but with relish. There was nothing he could not train himself to do; nothing he could not achieve. He had only to follow his instructions and his own strictly imposed rules of caution. It was necessary only to ensure that nobody was watching and to remind himself of the code: 'left, right, left, right.'

The loose anchor was at last secured and the ship's bow turned once more to her course. She gained some speed and the wallowing abated. There was a general feeling of relief. It was not shared by von Telschau. He strode furiously towards his own cabin. This was a desperate frustration, but he told himself to overcome it and regain his calmness and dignity. He had instructions about what to do in such circumstances; he would simply carry them out. He returned to his cabin, covering his fashionable suit with a dull grey coat and a tweed scarf. These clothes, brought especially for the purpose, would lend him the nondescript appearance he judged necessary for a descent into Second Class. The ship's still-deserted corridors would minimise the risk of his trespass, but he would have to be careful.

Huddled into his coat and scarf, von Telschau made his way down to Second Class. He found it surprisingly comfortable. The public rooms lacked the glittering elegance of First, but were still monuments of grandeur. The passengers—most of whom appeared to be English—seemed jollier than their exalted fellows on the upper decks. They were taking the storm with better humour and praising the brave crewmen whose desperate struggle with the loose anchor had become the talking-point of the Lounge. The long, white-painted corridors exaggerated the ship's uncomfortable pitching, but the cabins into which von Telschau peered looked scarcely less luxurious than his own.

He was annoyed to be noticed by a steward who insisted on offering help.

"You look rather lost, sir. May I be of assistance?"

The Baron was tempted to knock the servant out of the way, but knew that it would be better to be English about this.

"Actually, you can, yes. I am looking for a particular cabin."

A few moments later, a rapping on Jakob Schramml's door brought every tension back into his body and a flash of fear into his mind. With hasty alarm he hid the briefcase in the locker under his washbasin. The knocking was repeated.

"Mister Schramml?" He recognised the voice of the steward. "You have a visitor." Nothing would be achieved by hiding; he would have to face this maddening stroke of the unexpected. He opened the door. "Ah, good afternoon, sir. I trust the heavy weather isn't upsetting you too much. A distinguished German gentleman for you, sir. Will you be requiring coffee in the lounge?"

"No thank you," von Telschau took charge of the situation, smiling broadly. "I am certain everything we need is this charming cabin."

"Then I'll be leaving you gentleman to your little chat. Good day."

The door was closed.

"How helpful the English can be," smirked von Telschau. "And now, Herr Schramml, we have business to discuss."

"Who are you?" Immediate fear had infected Schramml's voice. "What are you doing, coming to my cabin and bothering me with this nonsense?"

"What nonsense would that be? I am the Baron von Telschau, and I have orders to intercept you."

"What do you mean 'intercept me'? What orders? By whose authority?"

"By authority of the Kaiser."

It took only one jab of the Baron's fist to double Schramml over his arm, only one blow to the man's grey temple to knock him whimpering on to the bunk.

"Have I hurt you, Herr Schramml? Good," von Telschau settled himself in the only chair, "I am in the mood to hurt someone. You stay there while I ask you questions; but first let me explain why I have hurt *you*. It is to demonstrate a great truth of life: that I am a winner and you are a loser. It is also to make you think that if I would do that to you apparently for nothing, what might I do to you if you fail to answer my questions? Is your head hurting? Do you still have a brain to think with? Good. So, where are the papers you have stolen?"

"I have stolen nothing," grunted Schramml. "I have nothing you could possibly want. Now get out of my cabin."

"I disagree, and I will not get out of your cabin until you give me the papers."

Nothing came from Schramml's bunk but the sound of his laboured breathing.

"You are not only a liar, but also a fool. Give me the

papers now, and you will have the deep satisfaction of knowing you have served the Fatherland. All you will suffer is the anger of your masters who paid you and whom you have failed. Delay, and you will suffer much more."

"I have nothing to say to you. Get out!"

The Baron made himself more comfortable in the chair and put a smile in his voice.

"You know, you and I, we do share a certain opportunism which in other circumstances might be admirable. I considered the storm was the best time to thwart your ambitions at the secret door. I concede that you thwarted mine by having the same idea and getting there first: very clever. But now I have caught up with you and you will do as I command."

"I don't know what you are talking about."

"I wondered how long it would be before you made that overworked response. To lie is useless. I know who you are, what you have done, and who paid you to do it. Unfortunately for you, I have been ordered by a higher command to deny you the papers and take them back to Germany myself. They will not now be sold to the highest bidder to raise money for a Russian revolution. They will be used to further the power and security of my country."

Schramml gave another grunt.

"Different words but the same vanities," he moaned. "I have heard them from every oppressor in Europe."

"It is your tragedy that you remain unconvinced by *my* version." The Baron felt for something in the pocket of his coat and drew it out. "Do you see this, Herr Schramml? It was a present to me from my father. It is a coachman's knife; all kinds of ingenious blades fold out of it, including this one. I believe it is for taking stones out of horses' hooves. Ha! Such an antique! When would I be on a horse these days? I have a perfectly efficient Daimler-Benz at home—which, I may add, I shall be very pleased to ride in once I get back across this most uncomfortable Atlantic. Do you insist on my making it even more uncomfortable for you?"

* * *

The storm continued into the night, but *Mauretania* was brought up to speed again and pushed her way Westwards into less towering waves. Dawn brought persistent wind and rain; it was not yet possible to feel relaxed.

Jon and Maisie cuddled as best they could against their heaving pillows. At least they had not been seasick, thought Jon, and now the storm was abating slightly it looked as if they would avoid that horror and be able to call themselves good sailors in the tales they would tell of this memorable honeymoon. There would certainly be amazing stories to write when they eventually sent letters back to England. He looked at Maisie, now comfortably asleep against his shoulder, the creamy skin of her neck a delight to him. He debated with himself how and when to give her the secret present he had brought. It was meant specially for this voyage, but there had as yet been no good opportunity to give it in the romantic way he intended, and it would still have to wait. Perhaps the last night at sea would be the most appropriate time. Until then, he would best keep it a secret.

In Philippa's cabin, Friedrich von Telschau greeted

the grey dawn with a puff of smoke.

"These American cigarettes are good. They are the coming thing, you know. Would you like one? It may calm your nerves."

"Not now," mumbled Philippa, sitting up on her bed. "It would make me feel sick again and I think I've just found my sea-legs."

"Your Lord Nelson never found his, you know: an English weakness."

"Spare me your arrogant Teutonic version of history, Freddie."

"That's all right; I no longer need to bore you with the past. I believe I have just made some *new* history. It was not quite as easy as I had hoped, but now I have done it with efficiency." He beamed a smile at her. "I have struck a blow for Germany, for the future!"

"Everyone else is still feeling fragile and you're feeling efficient. How deeply German of you—but if you're going to crow about something, do pour me a drink of that cold water. Then when you've got whatever it is off your chest, you simply must let me go and have something English to eat."

"Don't be so cruel to me," chuckled von Telschau. "You'll like this story. Then we can both go and celebrate with breakfast. I think we have both worked up an appetite this morning."

"Go on then…and I will have one of those cigarettes."

He told her what he had been told in Berlin: that an

English engineer had drawn up plans and specifications for a revolutionary new engine which could have extraordinary military potential. Befriended by Russian carpenters agitating for a Communist revolution, the engineer had been persuaded to deposit the plans in a secret compartment which the Russians themselves had built into the panelling at the foot of *Mauretania's* Grand Staircase. This was supposed to safeguard the plans during the Englishman's voyage to America, but in fact the Russians were betraying him. They would have the plans stolen and sold to German military engineers; the money would be used to further the revolution and any use Germany might make of the invention would accellerate the coming war which the Communists regarded as useful to their cause. A Jew called Jakob Schramml had been paid to travel in Second Class, told how to open the compartment, ordered to return to Germany with the plans, then to sell them as instructed. The plot had been discovered by the German High Command and von Telschau chosen to foil it. And he had foiled it, only moments ago. A potential new weapon was now in German hands, the Communists had lost their deposit and wouldn't get another penny out of their shabby deal. The Kaiser himself was likely to reward him. One of his own companies, he added with an even wider grin of satisfaction, might actually build the engine. Wouldn't that be a neat and profitable end to all this and something else to celebrate at breakfast?

Philippa stubbed out her cigarette.

"Am I expected to take this seriously?"

"Of course," von Telschau's tone was humourless, "and here is proof of it." He reached under the bed, produced the briefcase, opened it, and drew out the plans. "They look complicated, don't they? In fact the principle is easy to understand. I believe the invention is perfectly feasible and will revolutionize motive power." He thrust the papers back into the case and tossed it on to the chair.

Philippa took a drink.

"I still have difficulty believing all this," she said, eyeing him harshly. "It's as believable as a penny novelette."

"It is interesting that people are always reluctant to accept the truth," von Telschau replied coldly. "Jakob Schramml was reluctant to accept it. He is now missing two fingernails."

"What?"

"Curious, I know. A man usually talks after only one."

Philippa dropped off the bed on to her feet and faced the Baron with grim fury.

"You tortured that man for those pieces of paper?"

"For the concept; the concept is far greater than the paper. It was necessary. I am amazed you should show sympathy for the little rat. He is nothing but a paid thief."

"And what are you?"

"I am in nobody's pay. I seized those papers on the direct orders of the Kaiser for the glory and security of the Fatherland."

"Oh, stuff the piffle, Freddie! I should have seen through it before; seen through it to the real Baron von Telschau. I thought I'd fallen in with some evil men in England, but they were pussycats compared to you. You're a brute; a cruel, ruthless, heartless brute!"

He gave her a wry smile.

"Now who sounds like a penny novelette?"

"Get out of my cabin!"

"I think I shall. I've had that said to me too many times on this ship." He replaced his bland confidence with the manner of someone making a stern declaration. "Before I go, you should understand that briefcase contains plans for something soon to be the glory of Germany's industrial and military future. It is interesting to realise it was conceived by an English engineer connected with this very ship." He slowed his delivery, savouring the moment he knew was to come. "By a delicious quirk of Fate, I think you once knew this man—somewhere in your long career with men."

"Really?"

"Yes. He is your ex-husband."

"Right!" Something white and hot and terrible shot through Philippa; her mind and body were fused by it. At the same time she felt herself being sparked into action. There was a decision to make and she made it immediately. In an instant that seemed like an age, she had thrown the glass of water into von Telschau's face; half shocked, half amused, he was staggering backwards, blinking the water out of his eyes; she was snatching up the briefcase, tearing open the door, and rushing out of the cabin.

CHAPTER TWENTY-NINE
Gifts of Love

Philippa's shoes thumped into the carpet, the pitching and rolling of the ship speeding or slowing her as she ran. She knew she had to escape this labyrinth of corridors and companionways before von Telschau caught her; already she imagined she could hear him beating his way angrily out of the cabin and catching her up at a furious pace. Then she would have to keep to the public rooms; the Baron would not dare attack or assault her in full view of the passengers.

She found herself opposite one of the electric lifts. She hit the button frantically. To her enormous relief the door opened at once and she sprang inside, clutching the briefcase against her body.

"The Lounge!" she panted at the bemused attendant. The gate closed and the lift hummed her to safety.

Jon and Maisie had finished their breakfast and settled in the Lounge, watching the sea. It was still heaving fierce waves against the ship, but the sky was brightening. They and the few other passengers taking morning coffee were suddenly distracted by a commotion at the doors.

Philippa hurried in, the heavy and masculine briefcase at odds with her slender figure and fashionable clothes. She recognized Jon and Maisie at the same instant they recognized the briefcase. They drew shocked breaths and sprang to their feet. Philippa scurried between the tables and chairs to meet them. A moment later she was followed by von Telschau. He, too, appeared to have been running, but he composed himself rapidly and offered a smile as he approached a gathering he must never have wished to address. Before he could speak, Jon pointed sharply at Philippa.

"How in God's name did you get that?"

"God had nothing to do with it. I know it's yours and I've brought it back to you."

"Yes, yes, but how did you get it?"

"Our friend the Baron will tell you that," continued Philppa, "if he has the gall to face you."

It was obvious that von Telschau was struggling to keep the urbane demeanour which had served him well through a lifetime of difficult situations. He could be seen working muscles in his face and clenching his fists; but he had assessed the risks of losing his temper or resorting to violence and retained the forced smile on his flushed cheeks.

"So," he found his breath, "I thought you might all be here." He looked at Philippa. "You rushed away without your breakfast…Darling. Shall we order coffee?" He turned to Jon and Maisie, brushing dampness off his shirt front. "She has quite recovered from her seasickness and this morning I find her spilling water and running about the ship like a madwoman."

Jon stood tall while Maisie took his arm.

"Never mind all that," he said to von Telschau. "How have you come to know about this briefcase?"

"I made it my business to know."

He was back to the infuriating composure and the dangerous smile.

"It was none of your business," Maisie told him fiercely.

"Oh but it was, and should remain so. And speaking of business, I think we may be able do a deal. Allow me to use that crass American expression since we are now approaching the continent of crass expressions."

"Enough of your wordmongering," said Philippa coldly. She turned to Jon. "Before anybody says anything else, this is yours and you're getting it back. There."

She placed the briefcase firmly in Jon's arms. He swung it down into his left hand and held it tightly, Maisie's hand over his.

"How did you get it?" persisted Jon. "I have to know."

"You will, but it's a long story."

"Coffee!" von Telschau interrupted loudly. "It really is what we all need. Philippa my dear, people are watching you. You are making a scene."

"I'll make a bigger one yet and you won't like it!"

"Steward," ordered von Telschau loudly, "bring Coffee for us—at once, d'you hear?" When the steward had gone he addressed them all. "And now it will be better I think if we sit down."

He was first into a chair and the others followed.

Maisie wanted to scream. She wanted action, wanted to snatch the briefcase before anyone else took it from Jon again, wanted to hurry back to their cabin, to kiss him madly, to make love with him in the dizzy relief of getting the plans back from these thieves. Philippa and the German could explain later if they had to, if Jon insisted, but for now she just wanted to be out of this Lounge with him, holding the briefcase and holding him…but here they were all were, sitting around a table looking like civilised First Class passengers making sophisticated chatter in a gilded ship. Surely no-one seeing them could guess at the drama and torment that was going on. Again, Maisie wanted to scream…but knew she must not. She clung desperately to Jon's arm that held the briefcase.

"Well?" Jon was addressing Philippa, not von Telschau. "You have something to tell me."

Maisie detected a glint of excitement in Philippa's eyes as she began to speak.

"You thought your plans were safely hidden in that secret compartment, but your Russian friends betrayed you to the Germans…"

"Oh come now," von Telschau interrupted airily, "it's not quite as simple as that." Maisie became aware of the scent of cologne rising from his skin and clothes. Even in the middle of her anxiety and alarm, she had to admit he was amazingly handsome. She told herself this was not the time to admire him, but to despise him. "Why don't we all enjoy our coffee?" he continued as the steward arrived with a laden tray. "Leave it and go," he ordered, turning a smile on Philippa. "What do the English say? You can be mother?"

"Mother my arse! Pour your own bloody coffee."

"We are still waiting to hear the truth of all this," said

Jon with quiet determination.

"And you shall." Philippa turned an expressionless face to von Telschau. "Tell them what you told me. If you don't, I'll report your theft and violence to the Captain and you'll be locked up."

They saw the Baron wriggle with discomfort, anxiety, perhaps even fear. His bluff had been called and he knew he had to speak.

"Very well," he said calmly, "there is no harm in your knowing the truth of this situation—in fact you deserve to know it. When you do know it you may actually be thankful to throw in your lot with me…"

"No tricks, Freddie." Philippa scowled at him. "Just tell them, or your nasty little career will come to the nasty end it deserves."

"She is right when she says the Russians betrayed you," continued von Telschau, ignoring Philippa. "Their intention when creating the secret compartment was not to protect your precious plans but to provide a convenient place from which they could be stolen—by a man called Jakob Schramml who is travelling on this ship in Second Class. The Russians saw the potential of your invention and sold the idea of it to the German military and industrial establishment—for money to help finance a Communist revolution. That German establishment put Schramml aboard and told him how to open the door, but you should be thankful that I represent a higher German authority. I was ordered by the Kaiser himself to intercept Schramml and ensure that your invention is put to proper use in Germany."

"Then he tortured that poor man to get the briefcase," Philippa interrupted hotly. "If he hadn't boasted about it to me, you might never have got it back. But I was disgusted and amazed by what I heard and I couldn't bear to see you lose your own creation to someone so…so…horrible. That's the only word for him. My relationship with him is at an end and I'm not sorry."

Jon looked at von Telschau with disdain.

"And you're proud of this behaviour, are you?"

"Most certainly. I obeyed my orders and succeeded. What I cannot understand," he turned a still-debonair face to Philippa, "is why you did something to make me fail."

"Perhaps because it's the first time I have been able to do something truly worthwhile." She looked almost tenderly at Jon and Maisie, then back to von Telschau with a bitter expression. "Well, Baron, as may have been predicted in your youth, women have been your downfall. You use us for your pleasure then trumpet your dishonourable achievements, never thinking we have honour of our own and might use what you tell us to right a terrible wrong. And I am the last woman on Earth you thought would do this, am I not? I know that's what my ex-husband and his innocent little new wife are thinking."

"So," the Baron dismissed her speech with a gesture, crossed his legs and spoke to Jon with a smile, "your resourceful ex-wife has stolen the plans from me and given them back to you. She is a clever woman, but cleverness can be tiresome. Your accomplishments are far more interesting. You are a talented engineer and you will find I value talent. You should sell the plans back to *me*, Mister Ferris. By the way, I detect some sympathy for the unfortunate Herr Schramml, but I advise you to forget him. I can tell you that although he calls himself a German he is in fact a Jew. He wants only his money; of course he won't get it now. He will have no idea that the plans have been so unexpectedly returned to you. He will believe they remain with me, and will certainly not wish to face me again. No doubt he will stay in New York rather than risk the wrath of his masters back in Europe when they discover his mission has failed. He will lose himself in some poor quarter of the city. Do not concern yourself with his fate; his type should be despicable to men such as ourselves. I and my fellow officers, the German élite, hold a very different view of our Fatherland and its future and your plans should come to us."

Jon gave a short laugh.

"This wasn't intended to be a political meeting, you know."

"But circumstances have made it one. A great war is coming. Germany should win it easily enough—unless interfering English fellows like yourself sell ingenious inventions to Jews and Americans. Sell them to us! A swift German victory will be better for everyone; and you English are our natural allies against Jews, Slavs, Poles, Negroes and all the other scum of the world. You will find America is full of such creatures. Why soil your spirit with them? Join us. You would not be a slave in the factories, you know, but an honourable Engineer-Director."

"This is all pompous and offensive tosh, Freddie," said Philippa sharply. "You might have killed that poor man."

"Indeed I might, but that was not necessary." The Baron had regained his urbane good-humour. "Killing is a business fraught with difficulties: how to dispose of the evidence and of the body itself. It was simpler to leave Schramml alive. Of course I might consider killing Mister Ferris here. Now I think about it, that would be quite simple: a tragic accident at sea, a foolish Englishman swept to his death in the manner of foolish Englishmen who must take their fresh air and exercise whatever the weather. In fact the conditions are quite favourable right now…" He turned to Jon with a grin. "…but we don't wish to kill you, Mister Ferris, we wish to employ you, in the German factories, for your own benefit, for everyone's benefit. You remain alive, you and your new wife prosper, Germany gains your inventiveness, nobody here loses."

Jon shuffled in his seat and pushed his coffee cup away.

"This is preposterous. I have never been threatened face-to-face with murder before…by some smiling, scheming lunatic."

"I have," said Philippa, "and I can tell you it always seems preposterous, and the scheming lunatics always smile. It was in an English country house, as a guest of supposedly civilised people. That's one of the reasons I'm here. We both have to get away from such monsters." She settled back in her chair, scowling again at the Baron. "And I don't much like your tone, Freddie. You sound like a bully, and we don't tolerate bullies in England. We try to accept people for what they are, not jackboot them into submission."

If von Telschau was baited, he scarcely showed it.

"Why are the English so inept in argument? Always ready to defend your little island with liberal principles—although I must say, dear lady, I did not expect you, of all people, to be burdened with them." He turned again to Jon. "Liberal principles do not win wars, Mister Ferris. And you are not taking the broader view. Our vision extends far beyond the German factories, where, I tell you again, your work would be valued. We openly embrace what has long been proposed by the greatest thinkers: that an Aryan master-race exists in Europe. By good fortune, you and I and your charming ex-wife are members of this race; I must add your charming new wife, also. Why be so shy and English about this? Why not admit what is so obvious? Join us. Germany will rise through the natural order of things, accellerated in this new century by inventions such as your own and by the work of intelligent men. But first there must be war, and the fortitude of good soldiers to cleanse Europe of its filth; and—although it might seem impolite to remind you—as far as the wider world is concerned, your British Empire may have to face the sunset it has never expected. There will certainly be a new German Empire."

Philippa was infuriated. She sprang to her feet and spoke loudly.

"If that's your vision of the future, you'll find plenty of decent people ready to fight you for a better one."

"Decent people? Are you classing yourself with such pathetic *bourgeoisie*?"

"Yes. I have decided to stand up for decency. It's been the last thing on my mind for years, but now it's time I did stand up for it—and for these good people. Apart from that, have you any idea how ridiculous you sound? There are cartoons in the English newspapers poking fun at Germans, but I never knew you were really as bad as this."

"You think we are funny? When the war begins you will not laugh so long." He was angry now, rose to his feet and flashed a severe look at Jon. "You agree with her?"

"I have to."

"Deal with your despicable Jew then, or your decadent Americans! We can eliminate them and steal the plans anyway. Even if we don't, German engineers can create an air-engine better than yours, and make it an effective weapon of war."

"You're on!" Jon gave him a jaunty smile. It seemed the only way to deal with this. "Just remember who thought of it first. If this war does come, I look forward to giving your lot a bloody nose with *my* version of the engine."

"Stupid child! You are thinking this is a cricket match. I tell you, German armies will march all over your precious playing fields of Eton!"

Philippa gave him a wry look.

"I don't think they'd let you in at Eton, Baron. Goodbye."

"Pah! You are ridiculous!" He turned to go. "But you will all be destroyed!"

He stalked out of the Lounge ignoring the stares from every table.

"Well," said Philippa with obvious relief, "that seems to be that. Don't worry, you'll be safe from him. I know what he's like. He'll sulk in his cabin for the rest of the voyage, then he'll plot some more wickedness, but he hasn't got away with this piece of wickedness. You've upset the Hun, Jon, and I must say I thoroughly enjoyed hearing you do it—even on an empty stomach. You've given me back my sea-legs." She smiled at Maisie. "Your husband is what the Americans call a cool customer and I'm very proud of him. You should be, too."

"I love him," stated Maisie simply.

"Will you be safe now?" Jon looked into Philippa's eyes and saw no fear.

"Oh yes, he won't bother me. He's lost, and he's a bad loser, but he won't risk anything else by harming me. I'm invulnerable anyway, tough as old boots."

"We're rather glad you are," said Jon.

She laughed.

"There speaks my old romantic. We need a brandy after all this. Will you order them, Jon?"

"Of course."

"Not for me," said Maisie. As Jon crossed the room to find a steward she turned to face Philippa. "I never liked you, but now I suppose I have to thank you."

"Yes, you jolly well do…and I accept your thanks…and your dislike. I understand it perfectly. I called you names and meant it when I did. That was when I was hot with jealousy and annoyance, but I've learned to be different. Not so long ago I glimpsed real evil, saw it being done to me and to other women more vulnerable than myself. Doing the right thing may be less fashionable these days, but really it's the only way to any peace of mind. I'm glad to see you carried on in spite of me and made something of yourself. You'll become a good wife to a good man. Jon really is good, but not good for me. His goodness slipped a little and he cheated on me with you, but he is not evil, not a bad person. I think he will be very good for you. I've just discovered that's what I really wanted to say. I should have said it a long time ago, on the day this ship was launched. You honestly have nothing to fear from me. Be happy. I won't and can't be. I am an artist…but we've been through that before, haven't we? I'll be boring you."

"Whatever you are," quipped Maisie, "you're not boring."

"Neither are you. I like that in you."

Jon returned.

"The brandy's on its way. What did you mean, Philippa, about this being the first time you could do something truly worthwhile?"

"You mean apart from marrying you?" She was laughing, vivacious, beautiful; now, in her triumph, she was almost impossible to resist. But he must and would resist her. Finally, it would take no effort at all. She had done him this great service but he would want nothing more from her, now or ever. "Marrying Jon was worthwhile," she was rattling on to Maisie, "until we went wrong. We did have some fun together, you know. He's a good husband with the right woman. Now I need to find the right man. As you see, Freddie and I have fallen out completely—thank God. I do fall out with most of them eventually."

Maisie admired Philippa's bravado but could not resist a smirk.

"No luck with the men, eh?"

"The story of my life—on occasions. On others I have been quite lucky. I reckon Jon was one of my better conquests. Don't blush, and don't be angry. I'm serious. He loved me. He did once, anyway. He brought me fame, fortune, sales of my paintings and fulfilment in my work. What more could an artist ask for?"

"Some decency?"

"Decency has nothing to do with Art, or artists, but you'll be surprised to learn I've developed a taste for it. I'll admit it now, I had a terrible fright back home by allowing myself to fall in with people who were anything but decent, evil dangerous people, people I swore I would never have anything more to do with—and then I found myself on this ship with another one."

Irritated by the long speech, Maisie looked from Philippa to Jon and back again.

"Yes, but what are we going to do about that poor man he attacked? What did he do to him?"

"You don't want to know," said Philippa grimly, "but he won't suffer any more. The Baron will lie low if we don't provoke him any further. We'd better not stir this up with the Captain or the authorities, it's all too dangerous, you must realise that, Jon, even from your dealings with those Russians. Just let's leave the secret compartment as one of the great mysteries of the sea, eh? Someone will discover it one day and wonder what was inside."

"Actually, there are two secret compartments," said Jon in a low voice. "The other one's in the children's playroom."

"You don't say? Well, it'll make a good story. For now, all you have to do is keep quiet, keep hold of that briefcase, and get it off the ship in New York."

"What will *you* do?" asked Maisie, suddenly proud to know this woman she had hated—and suddenly sorry for her.

Philippa looked at the lumpy seascape beyond the

elegant windows of the Lounge.

"I'm not entirely sure, but I know there comes a time in a woman's life—especially in a life like mine—when she decides to say no to pleasures of the flesh, or at least not to feel sour when they are denied her. The Baron will punish me by withdrawing his bedroom favours, of which, as I'm sure you appreciate, he is extravagantly proud. But I don't want them any more. I find I wish to spend time with people who have a certain…what shall we call it? The French say *douceur*. Such people may be bores but they have a common decency I have lacked for many years. You've just seen me take it up again."

"We are very glad you did," said Jon.

"Getting the plans back for you was worthwhile. That's what I meant." She returned her steady gaze to their faces. "Will you shake hands, Jon?"

"Yes."

"And you?" She held her hand out to Maisie.

"All right then."

"You're a lucky girl—Mrs. Ferris."

She drained her glass of brandy, set it down quietly on the table, and walked away. Jon and Maisie stood for a while, found they were holding hands, and felt a great tiredness settle into their minds and bodies. They went to their cabin. Jon examined the contents of his briefcase.

"Thank God it's all here. Wait until my father hears about this. He'll be talking about it for years to come."

Maisie sank on to the bed.

"I've had enough talk for today: enough of the clever talk, enough of the frightening talk. Just hold me, Jon."

She brought him down on to the bed and cuddled him. He relaxed. They slept. Hours later they woke, talked again about all that had happened, changed for dinner, and went down once more to the magnificent Dining-Room, taking the briefcase with them, not caring how odd it might look in these opulent surroundings. They talked politely to Chester Bryson and his friends, and were thankful that nobody mentioned the events of the morning. Then they returned to the cabin and held each other tightly and slept.

* * *

Mauretania's last full day at sea was blessed by better weather. Many passengers, Jon and Maisie among them, took pleasure in regaining the open decks and felt renewed by fresh air and sunshine. From the smooth, round, enchanting horizon came a marvellous sense of glass-blue days, of insouciant travel through a world of crystal dreams, of absolutes, of clarity, all to be enjoyed from dry decks and clean white rails. At last, after terrors and alarms, it felt good to be at sea on a magnificent ship, to have dropped below the edge of the life they knew, to find the muddles had been left on either shore and that emptiness mattered. Into this emptiness slid a new, late peace: soon to be ended by an inevitable landfall, but here to be enjoyed under blue skies and the merrily hissing funnels.

Jon and Maisie made a relaxed day of it, taking the

precious plans with them wherever they wandered on the great ship. At times the briefcase was a reminder of betrayal, violence, and a close brush with failure; at others a symbol of their achievements and hopes for the future. If they spoke of these things it was with a new lightness, as if their approach to America was signalling a secure escape from past difficulties and promising a fresh start. They took a scanty lunch, knowing that Chester Bryson had promised a huge farewell dinner. They walked the decks again, marvelled at *Mauretania's* speed through the blue water, braved the afternoon chill of the Verandah Café, then returned to their warm cabin to prepare for their final evening aboard. Jon knew the time was right for his special gift to Maisie.

They were kissing, nose to nose.

"I have something for you," Jon told her quietly, "but first I have to take off all your clothes."

She giggled as he began to undress her; stood silently, kissing him lightly when his face was close enough, felt shivers of excitement as he slowly stripped the clothes from her tingling body. At last she stood, pale and naked in the warm light of the cabin. She twirled on her toes like an animated statue.

"What is it?" she laughed. "What is it?"

"It's a dress, a special dress for your last night on our ship."

He produced a flat box from its hiding-place in his wardrobe and opened the lid. From folds of tissue paper he drew out a dress Maisie had never imagined. She saw, with a gasp of delight, that it was made entirely of shimmering silver satin. She watched it slide through his hands like a waterfall; now he was draping it across her breasts and arms, swirling its loose skirt around her legs, drawing her to him for another kiss with the dress across her back, then placing it as his gift of love across her outstretched arms.

"Especially for this last night," he repeated. "Especially for you, Darling."

"It's the most beautiful thing I've ever seen," she whispered, in awe of this moment and of the dress itself. "It's like something from a fairytale."

"And you are the fairytale princess to wear it," Jon brightened the mood, "although I must say I rather like you without it."

She laughed again and spread the cool satin under her throat and between her breasts.

"Is it another present from Fenwick's?"

"No, I had this made for you. I knew your measurements from your other dresses."

"Crafty, eh? It's so lovely I'll wear it with nothing else, nothing underneath, just the dress." In a moment she had stepped into it and Jon was fastening the satin over the delicious ripple of her spine. "I know the short sleeves are made for evening gloves, but I won't put them on. I'll have to wear shoes I suppose, or I won't be allowed into the Dining-Room...but just your dress, it's lovely over me."

"And you are lovely under it. You're so lovely I hardly know what to say."

"I know what my Mam would say," she turned to him with a flashing smile. "Put your knickers on, Maisie!"

"Don't you dare do that," said Jon with a laugh. "Find the best shoes to wear with it and go down just as you are."

They laughed and admired the dress in her wardrobe mirror. It clung to her body, exposed fresh skin on her neck and shoulders, and fell to her ankles with a loose elegance.

"Funny thing is," she observed as Jon stood behind her with his hands round her waist, "wearing it is like being naked—beautiful and naked."

"I know. That's how I'll always see you."

They went down to dinner. Chester Bryson was first to admire Maisie's dress and said if she wore it in town tomorrow night she would be the Belle of New York.

"What'll I be tonight?" she laughed.

"Tonight you're a magical mermaid, popped out of the sea to amaze us all in silver satin."

"Somebody else called me a mermaid, a long time ago." She smiled at Jon, then back at Bryson. "Anyway, that's how I feel: as if I belong here in the middle of the ocean."

"You belong in his arms, my dear. Will you two dance after dinner? That sure is a dress for dancing."

"I think it might be, Mister Bryson. You'll just have to wait and see."

"And what d'you keep in that bag, huh?" Bryson pointed his cigar at Jon.

"Secrets, Mister Bryson, secrets!"

"Don't you want both hands for your girl?"

"Now you mention it, I do, actually."

They saw Philippa, glamorous in a pale grey dress sashed with lilac and with jewels in her hair, seated with two other couples at a table next to Bryson's. She was unescorted.

"We can't ignore her," said Maisie quietly, "though I want to. You'll have to go over. I'll keep the briefcase at our place here."

Jon went to Philippa and was greeted with her whimsical smile.

"As we expected," she drawled, "the Baron is not dining tonight."

"He is missing a splendid occasion then," replied Jon evenly.

"But we are not missing him." She seemed in high spirits, glittering in the frothy conversation of her table. "I am well entertained by these fine people from, let me see now…Baltimore, have I remembered right?"

"That's right," the Americans confirmed with merry chuckles. "And Miss. Wellington is entertaining us with stories of her work as an artist—in Paris!"

"Miss. Wellington, eh?" Jon could not resist a huge grin. Was he drunk on relief and happiness? Did he care? "It's a while since I chatted to Miss. Wellington."

"Isn't it just! But that's who I'm known as now. I thought I'd never want to use the name again, but it's quite convenient—after my divorce. Are you surprised?"

"Nothing I hear from you could ever surprise me again."

"I should think not, not after all we've been through. I hope hearing from 'Miss. Wellington' again won't spoil your dinner."

"Nothing I hear from you will ever spoil anything of mine again."

"Good. You've grown up at last."

"I don't know about growing up," replied Jon quietly, "but like you I've grown away from bad things…" he looked over at Maisie, "…to better things."

"Quite. I'm so pleased for you. Go to her."

"Before I go I want to say thank you again for what you did."

"When I say it was a pleasure, I truly mean that."

"I know you do. So, thank you again."

Back at the table, Maisie quizzed him.

"You didn't feel you had to invite her to join us over here?"

"No."

"That would have been too awkward, eh?"

"I suppose it would, yes, but you know, after everything that's happened, I hardly feel awkward at all. I feel safe and secure."

"Me too."

The magnificent dinner began with Champagne and oysters and progressed with stately splendour through its nine courses. Jon and Maisie drank claret with their roast American turkey and returned to the Champagne with their sumptuous pudding, feeling light and happy and sweetly drunk—not only on the wines but on a new sense of freedom. Throughout the meal toasts were made to the ship and her Captain, there were shouts of "Tomorrow, America!" and whispers of speed and distance records being broken. All the time, from the depth of *Mauretania's* Engine Room, came the distant but thrilling pulse and throb of her turbines brought up to Full Ahead. At last, across calm seas, her power and her glory had been unleashed. She raced Westwards into the night, the expectancy of dawn behind her creaming wake and America before her slicing bows.

When the ice-cream and sweetmeats were finished they processed arm-in-arm into the Lounge, Maisie once again feeling the sensuous slither of her dress as she walked. She did not want to walk; she wanted to dance, and saw the pianist behind the lacquered curves of his enormous Steinway.

"D'you think he would play me something?"

"I'm sure he would. Go and ask."

There were whispers and smiles at the piano, then the first notes of the *Gymnopedie*, Maisie's shoes plucked off and thrust into Jon's hands, her bare toes on the carpet, her arms flung up, her eyes to the gilded dome, the chatter silenced, only the steady pulse of the music. She remembered her dance in the drawing-loft, splashing her feet and legs in and out of the moonlight; here there was rich carpet beneath her heels, warm electric light, rich brown woodwork, and a glittering audience. She was dancing again in front of Jon and he would love to see it, the other people would be shocked and she wouldn't care, but she was really dancing for herself—truly for herself, as she felt the great liner that was her own ship speeding through the Atlantic night. The dress was wonderful: it shimmered like moonlit rain. The music the pianist had offered was right: a modern, dreamy roll of music, curving like the bow wave, rolling and melting like the wide wake, pulsing with the beat of life and the push of her feet on the floor and the throb of desire through her body. It was like a long-promised love-making, suddenly made hot and sweet and blessed by golden light. She could feel the fast yet gentle stirring of the ship beneath her; at the same time she felt becalmed upon some diamond-sparkled sea. To steadily place her naked feet on this carpet was a perfection of feeling; paddling mercurial above the sumptuous carpet, like an impetuous silver swan with a water-sprite's laugh, washed in a golden sacrament of light, rich yet renewed in innocence, she had become the music and the memory and the dream—and because this was her ship and she'd dance where she liked in it, she didn't care what they were saying in the First Class Lounge.

"Who is that girl?"

"Don't know, but she dances prettily."

"What is that music? I call it very modern."

"It's by a Frenchman called Satie; written years ago."

"Improper, without shoes and stockings."

"I wish I could dance without *my* shoes and stockings."

"Should we know who she is?"

"Is she a famous dancer or just drunk?"

"Whoever she is, she's lovely."

"D'you notice she has no jewellery?"

"Just a wedding ring and that enormous sapphire."

"Married but outrageous. I don't think she's wearing anything under that dress."

"I don't think she cares."

"She doesn't need to."

"Barefoot: it's vulgar."

"No, it's free and sensual, very modern."

"Bravo I say, to she and her husband. Bravo to both of them. Bravo!"

From far away below many decks, she could still feel the hum of the turbines and the thrash of the screws, the delicious rise and fall of the hull, now relieved from the terrible storm and floating freely, just as she was free of the great storms she had suffered. The ship was pushing strongly through the black water, just as she was pushing her toes across the carpet, waiting for a fresh dawn to come up behind her with the delights of blue sky and sunshine and a new continent.

The new dress was perfect, just loose enough to allow her movements, but it would be a greater perfection to fling it from her body at the climax of this dance to music that had no climax, only a steady pulse down a mysterious route that was an enigma in itself. Then she would have nothing against her skin but the golden electric light and the sparkling reflections from the jewels of the onlookers. She wanted her own nakedness in this dance through the perfumed air of the Lounge…but she wouldn't tear the dress, she would wear it through this magical night, treasure it, keep it for ever. She would simply put one foot down to the music, then the other, twirl her arms, smile up at the dome…there was a final, sweet note, silence, the feel of the carpet, applause. Then there was the hug of Jon's arms, his kiss, more applause, a scamper on hot toes to give a kiss to the pianist, and Chester Bryson presenting a new bottle of Champagne.

Philippa had remained in the Lounge and had witnessed Maisie's dance, attaching herself to the group of Americans who stood around Bryson's chair. They had all clapped enthusiastically, Bryson waving his cigar above the applause to summon Maisie to the Champagne. A further encounter with Philippa was inevitable, but Maisie felt strong and happy and no longer intimidated by the copper-haired beauty who had once been Jon's wife. She had found her own beauty and her own life with Jon.

"The dress is extraordinary," said Philippa. "You wear it beautifully and you danced magically. I know it was a happy dance because I know it was a dance of love. The French say there is only one true happiness in life: to love and be loved. The French are right. And while we're on the subject of happiness, since I can't seem to keep any for myself, I thought I should secure some for you. That's one of the reasons I took the briefcase from the Baron. Oh, I know plans for an air-engine, whatever that is, don't equate to loving and being loved, but if you'd known Jon had lost those plans you might not have felt like dancing and your love might not be so secure. Call me a hard-nosed businesswoman—somebody will."

"I've hated you," declared Maisie, "but now I think

you're wonderful."

"Oh, I wouldn't go thinking that if I were you, not now you're married to Jon. Well," she looked across the room to towards Chester Bryson, "I can't stay here chatting all night. I have a millionaire to seduce."

"He's married," hissed Maisie. "You won't get him."

Philippa turned an elegant hand towards Jon.

"*He* was married and you got *him*." Maisie made no answer. Philippa stood tall in her grey and lilac dress, crowned with her bright hair. They were all conscious of something ending, yet never leaving their lives. "Well, as Shakespeare put it, 'lovers, to bed.' We may not see one another again and before we all go ashore, so let me shake your hand again…and the hand of my decent chap."

"You are terrible," said Jon when all their hands were parted, "but you are magnificent."

"Don't let your new wife hear you say *that* too often."

Maisie gave her a harsh look.

"Whatever he says, I know he loves me more than he ever loved you!"

"It must be nice to believe that. Goodbye."

They did not see Philippa's triumphant smile as she walked away.

CHAPTER THIRTY
A New World

Jon and Maisie went to their cabin just after midnight. They were numbed by a combination of shock, tiredness and elation—all experienced at the same time. But as they settled in the cabin, Maisie preparing to climb into their bed and Jon stowing the briefcase on the other, a new sensation overtook them. It was relief. At last they felt safe; able to talk about the future, knowing their present was secure.

"I wonder what America will look like," said Maisie, snuggling into her pillow. "What'll it smell like?"

"We'll find out in the morning." Jon was looking wistfully round their cabin. "Our last night in here. We've made it a proper little home, haven't we? Seems calm enough," he added, looking out at the benighted sea. "We shouldn't be thrown around any more."

"The storm was exciting for five minutes, then it was just frightening and horrible." Maisie peered over the sheet at Jon. "And we've been thrown around by worse than the weather. I could never have imagined all that business with the plans and Philippa and the German, but you know, already it's like a dream. It's all over. We're into something new. Come to bed. Like you said, it's our last night in here and we haven't had much sleep recently so let's make it a cuddly comfy one. If we do get another storm, just hang on to me."

"I'll hang on to you anyway, Darling. You were right about the Russians betraying us to the Germans for money, when I didn't see it, didn't think it would really happen, didn't think *any* of that would happen. It's been amazing, and you've been right about everything. I can't imagine how I could carry on through life without you."

"You won't have to. I'll be right here."

They hugged each other, grew comfortable, exchanged drowsy kisses, and fell asleep quickly…but elsewhere, further extraordinary revelations were to be made. In the same early hours of that morning, calculations done on the bridge revealed that *Mauretania* had travelled a record six-hundred and twenty-four miles the previous day.

Hours later, they awoke to an unfamiliar and disturbing sensation. The ship was rock-steady. No pitch or roll heaved beneath the mattress. Was she aground? No wind or seawash made their noises beyond the curtained porthole; only the faint hum of distant machinery told them the ship was still 'alive'.

"What's the matter?" Maisie stirred at Jon's shoulder. "What's happening? Have we stopped?"

"We can't have. We should be just off Sandy Hook."

They became aware that an odd gleam had replaced the usual sea-light penetrating the curtains.

"Fog," declared Jon, clambering out of bed and opening the curtains to a blank whiteness. "Of course, fog! Plenty of that off this coast, and we're right in it." He opened the porthole and looked down. "I think we're barely moving; might as well stay in bed," he smiled back at Maisie, now sitting up from her pillows. "You won't get your first view of America for some time. It's solid white out there." He returned to Maisie and they snuggled under the covers once more. "She'll have to drop anchor at Quarantine. It could take hours at this speed, and we probably won't see the Statue of Liberty. I was looking forward to that."

"Give us another cuddle then."

* * *

The cosy atmosphere to be enjoyed in Jon and Maisie's cabin did not extend to other parts of the ship on this morning of fogbound frustration. She proceeded with dead-slow caution into New York Harbour and anchored at Quarantine. Jon and Maisie went to a late breakfast and found an atmosphere of tortured excitement as the spectacular conclusion of a hazardous maiden voyage was delayed and stifled by this infuriating fog. By the middle of the day there was almost a riot on the bridge as irate passengers, some brandishing fists and others wads of money, sought to intimidate or bribe Captain Pritchard into putting them ashore. It was all to no avail. The Captain remained immovable, determined to protect his ship and his passengers and delay any movement until the lifting fog allowed safe passage up to Cunard's pier. By that time an early dusk had fallen across the huge, noisy, compelling city lying just ahead of *Mauretania*. Her needle-sharp nose seemed to point excitedly into the suddenly visible straight streets, long boulevards and towering buildings so tantalizingly close to the docks themselves. Excitement erupted all over the ship as disembarkation began, but Maisie and Jon were careful to remember his experienced father's advice and not hurry on to the pier before the most hectic crowds had dispersed. They returned to their cabin and tried to relax, lying on the bunk.

"What's the first thing we do when we get ashore?" asked Maisie.

"Well, straight to the hotel I think, before we do any sightseeing. We're booked in for a week; after that we'll have to find somewhere to stay, find a flat, rent an apartment. That's what they say in New York: 'rent an apartment'. Of course before we get off the pier we have to go through Customs. The Customs Hall is famously chaotic. The inspectors may want to see some of our luggage, but we should be all right. The plans just go through as the personal documents of a travelling businessman. That's what you married, Darling, a travelling businessman; soon to become a travelling salesman. Anyway, I think we look fairly respectable and I don't think we have anything unusual to declare."

"I wouldn't be so sure of that."

"Oh? What d'you mean?"

Maisie gave him a sly smile.

"Can't you guess?

Jon looked blank.

"D'you not have any idea at all?" she continued teasingly. "I've thought I've been carrying something special for a while. Now I'm sure." Her smile widened as she stroked her body, lying provocatively on top of the bunk.

"What," Jon began to giggle, "you don't mean—you're pregnant?"

"I do. I'm almost certain." She saw Jon lying against the pillow as if stunned. "That's right," she smiled. "We're going to be one passport short. Haway man," she laughed aloud, "you can cuddle us. I won't break, you know."

He rushed her into his arms.

"This is marvellous! Marvellous!"

"I was wondering how to tell you." She gave him a penetrating look. "You're not upset, are you?"

"No, no. How could I be? I'm delighted. I'm thrilled! This is the best thing that could ever have happened."

"You're not frightened? I suppose most men are frightened."

"Of what? Of being a father?"

"Yes. I'll bet you are."

He kissed her lips, neck and throat and looked into her eyes where tears of emotion were beginning to form.

"Neither of us have anything to fear about this," he declared passionately. "Don't you see it's the best possible news? It's wonderful! It's the start of our new family, here in America. Our whole new life together...and a child! What could be more perfect?"

"I know, I know," she breathed into his neck, relaxing from pert humour into confession of her truth. "Oh, I'm so glad you're happy. I can't tell you how glad I am."

"You'll have to take it easy from now on," said Jon as they slid into a softer embrace. "You'll need to see a doctor."

"Plenty of time for that. We'll get settled in New York first."

"No. First thing we do is get you to a doctor."

"I'm not ill, you know. It's perfectly natural. I'll be fine."

"That's my girl. You'll be fine, but I won't be until you've seen a doctor."

"All right."

They snuggled into the pillows again.

"A child," breathed Jon. "A child for us, carried across the ocean in our special ship and born in America. It's a fairytale come true, don't you see?"

He felt Maisie bury her face in his shoulder and give a quiet sob of happiness.

"Yes, I see. It's romantic, isn't it?" She sniffed, and held him more tightly.

"It is, Darling. It most certainly is."

* * *

Manhattan and the rest of the great city before them was enveloped in darkness before Jon and Maisie disembarked, but there were bright lights everywhere. The row of piers that *Mauretania* had joined was busy with shipping and ablaze with floodlights, the huge buildings stretching from the shore into the heart of the city glittered with yellow lamps, the dramatically straight streets were canyons of illumination. Yet even the glamorous lights of New York could not entirely dim the many stars that twinkled above them in a clear sky of midnight blue. The wintry air of a late November night seemed to have lost the tang of the sea and held instead a mint-cool freshness, as if a foretaste of the vast plains, distant mountains and fragrant forests of the new continent. To Jon, it felt like the Night before Christmas, as if jolly old Saint Nicholas might swoop down with his reindeer on to the snowy roofs of the old Dutch houses that still stood somewhere beyond these modern buildings, and he imagined the Dutch sailors who had landed here so long ago and called it New Amsterdam. Maisie thought not of times past but of the exciting present surging all around her. It was cold here. She was glad of her thick coat and the expensive fur hat Jon had bought at their first Christmas, but she was warm inside, with her baby warm too. She felt quite safe carrying her child, even as she stood on the brink of a new land and a new life.

They stood for long moments on the pier, looking back at *Mauretania*. The immensity of the magnificent ocean liner was tethered by hawsers, yet she seemed ready to slip them as a greyhound might slip a leash. For all the battering she had taken in the storm and the strenuous efforts of her maiden voyage, she looked capable of turning round this very night and steaming swiftly back to Liverpool, determined to start a long and famous career without too much fuss.

"She'll take the Blue Riband on the way back," said Jon proudly. "I know she will. She looks so strong, so beautiful. With a wind behind her and better weather, she'll beat the record and take it home."

"This is home for the moment," said Maisie, taking Jon's hand. "We'll start our new lives here. We'll have our child here. But I do know what you mean about the ship. She's lovely isn't she?" The lights winked up on *Mauretania* and the stars winked down. How glamorous the new ship looked, caught in this glittering night. "You helped build her engines,

Jon, back there in that different part of our lives. Now someone will build your air-engine over here, in this new part of our lives. You've got every reason to be proud, and I am proud of you."

Mauretania stood at her elegant ease, looking haughty but homely. Her massively riveted hull, her gleaming rails and her towering funnels in Cunard red-and-black spoke of the old world, of British industry and commerce, invention, progress and tradition: known, trustworthy, reliable. The glittering lights of Manhattan, spread so enticingly before them, spoke of all that was exciting but uncertain in the new world.

"I'm proud of *you*, Darling. And I'll be proud of our child, growing up in this new country."

As he spoke they became aware of music: the sound of a piano floating from the open windows of the liner's great public rooms.

"Hear that," said Maisie. "Somebody's taking the time to play us a tune in all this mad rushing about—and leaving the windows open on a freezing night."

"It'll be the chap who played for you last night, for your wonderful dance," breathed Jon, enraptured. "It's a piece by Debussy: *Claire de Lune*. He obviously likes French composers."

"Not the new sound of America then, whatever that's going to be."

"No, but you must listen, it's quite wonderful. Let's just listen for a moment. It reminds me of…I'm not sure what. You dancing last night of course, then of myself, being alone, wanting things…"

"You've got them now."

She was right, he thought, he had struggled for the things he had wanted and won many of them—but not all. There was still a new life to establish, and the whole business of selling and developing the air-engine, and now their child to care for. He looked up at the great ship whose creation and growth had been, at least to him, like that of a child. He remembered his father telling him about the job at Parsons', he remembered Philippa excitedly showing him her startling painting of the imagined ship and his equally startling view of the hull as its bow swung to face him after the launch, and here he was now with the lovelier woman who was his wife and a lovelier vision of the ship: completed, whole, and in service. He looked up at the lighted windows of the bridge soaring so high above this pier and remembered their cosy seat at Pumphrey's, watching gilded weathercocks flying the cold air above the Cathedral in Newcastle. He looked at the majestic four-stack silhouette against this luminous sky and remembered the air surging out behind the turbine on that day of its test and the night in the Boardroom with Vladimir Druginin and the joy and the terror of falling in love with this girl and how her chance comment about the tram had led to the amazing spectacle of driving motor-cars driving through the funnels when they lay on their sides at the yard. The memories came like a gush of laughter or a flooding of tears, but both Jon and Maisie remained composed and silent listening to the delicious rise and fall of the music. She looked at the razor-sharp bow and remembered the carpet-slippered men rolling out the plans on that first day in the drawing-loft, being there with her father and meeting Jon and showing him her drawings so shyly. She looked at the towering funnels and remembered the rain that cleared for her launch-day picnic before the sound of all the hooters and sirens on the Tyne. She looked at the open windows from which the music was drifting and remembered making love with Jon on the plans in the moonlit drawing-loft and laughing about the linen-store and dancing barefoot again in the real ship only a few hours ago. She looked at the rows of port-holes and remembered her happiness in the little house at Tynemouth that would forever be cherished as their first home.

The music flowed on. And now they could not know what their new home would be, nor the shape of their lives in it. They could not know the future of Jon's air-engine, nor imagine how it would be developed and built by other minds and hands to accelerate both war and peace and revolutionize long-distance travel through the sky. They could not know their child would grow up in a dramatically altered world and return one day to an England at war. They only knew they were at peace for the present at the beginning of their most exciting adventure, and that the great bulk of the ocean liner which had carried them here was somehow transformed into the sleek little ship of a perfect dream, smiling down at them until Maisie's voice broke in upon Jon's thoughts.

"What d'you think America will *really* be like?"

"I'm not sure yet, but I know one thing: it feels a long way from Newcastle. Come along, Darling—we'd better get you to that doctor."

"I'm all right," giggled Maisie, "really I am."

"Have you thought about names?" asked Jon.

"No, to be honest."

"I have. What about Mary, after yourself?"

"Not very original." Maisie looked doubtful. "And two Marys in the same house?"

"Yes," Jon conceded, "but you'll always be Maisie.

She would be named after the ship as well. The workers at the yard used to call *Mauretania* 'the Mary'. Yes, Mary. Lovely idea—if you like it."

They kissed and took each other's hands. They walked again, steadily along the pier towards the Customs Hall, carrying their small bags, the piano music fading behind, the noises of crowds and luggage and trundling wheels ahead. New York and a new life were before them—but suddenly, Maisie stopped them in their tracks.

"Hold on." She looked Jon in the eye. "What if it's a boy?"

The End of 'Maiden Voyage'

POSTSCRIPT

On her maiden homeward voyage, *Mauretania* broke the transatlantic speed record at an average 23.69 knots, thus capturing the Blue Riband for an Eastbound crossing. In 1908 she took the Westbound record at 24.86 knots, only to lose it to her sister liner *Lusitania*. In September 1909, with a new set of screws, she broke that record at 26.06 knots. Overall, she held the Blue Riband for twenty-two years: a record in itself. She saw successful service as a troopship and hospital ship during the Great War, after which, refitted as a liner based at Southampton rather than Liverpool, she resumed her transatlantic voyages. In the early 1920s her interiors were refurbished and her coal-fired boilers converted to burn oil. This increased her speed but did not prevent the German liner *Bremen* from beating her record in 1929. *Mauretania*, however, remained a much-loved ship on the Atlantic and for Caribbean and Mediterranean cruises. Her final Atlantic crossing was made in 1934; the following year she was sold to the breakers at Rosyth. On this last voyage, flying the Blue Riband, she stopped at the mouth of the Tyne to salute the river of her birth and receive many tributes of affection from local dignitaries and sightseers in a large flotilla of boats. *Auld Lang Syne* was sung with pride and sadness as the old liner stood away to the North.

The concept of the jet engine might have been suggested by Charles Parsons' 1884 patent application for the steam turbine. This simply noted that it could be run in reverse, which would have created a gas turbine. The early Twentieth Century saw many experiments with gas turbines leading to the construction in 1910 by a Rumanian inventor of what is regarded as the first jet engine. This was demonstrated in Paris, but it was not until 1930 that English RAF engineer officer Frank Whittle presented a complete jet engine design to the Air Ministry. Whittle struggled against officialdom and many setbacks to get his engine into production and was overtaken by the Germans, whose Heinkel He178 of 1939 became the world's first jet-powered aircraft. In 1944 the Messerschmitt Me262 entered service just prior to the Gloster Meteor, the first RAF fighter powered by Whittle's engine. The speed and agility of these aircraft made it clear that jet propulsion was the future of military and commercial aviation, and it was Whittle's version of the turbojet that became the prototype of modern jet engines.

ABOUT THE AUTHOR

Poet, novelist and scriptwriter Roger Harvey was born in 1953 and lives in Newcastle. He took a degree in Law and became a teacher of English, History and Drama before establishing his career as a writer. His published works include the novels *Percy the Pigeon*, *The Silver Spitfire* and *A Woman Who Lives by the Sea*. He has written many works for radio and is one of Britain's most published poets. Among his poetry collections are *Raising the Titanic*, *Divided Attention* and the award-winning audio production *Northman's Prayer*. His published plays include *Asra! Asra!*, revealing the secret love-life of Samuel Taylor Coleridge, the black farce *Money! Money! Money!* and the pantomines *Up the Pole* and *Donkey Skin*; after its stage tour his play *Guinevere-Jennifer* was made into a film. *Poet on the Road* is the intimate travelogue of Roger's reading-tour across the U.S.A. and *The Writing Business* a miscellany of essays on the literary life. Recent releases include the children's adventure *Albatross Bay*, the romantic comedy *River of Dreams* and the short-story collection *The Green Dress and Other Stories*. His latest works are the novel *Room for Love* and its sequels *Room for Me* and *Room for Us*. He is married to Sheila Young, an expert on Royal jewellery whose book *The Queen's Jewellery* became the definitive work on the subject. His other interests include music, photography and classic cars. For more information about Roger and his work please visit www.roger-harvey.co.uk.